PENGUIN BOOKS

LIES *like* LOVE

Praise for Louisa Reid:

'Some books stay with you long after you've finished them and Reid's debut is one of them . . . A moving, gripping story' *Sun*

'Emotive, sometimes shocking story' *Sunday Times*

'Absolutely wonderful' *Guardian*

'Stunning, shocking, sad and incredibly touching' *LoveReading*

'We read this in one sitting . . . ★★★★' *Teen Now*

'Louisa Reid creates vivid characters that drag you into their world by both hands, desperate to tell their stories. Both heart-breaking and full of bittersweet yearning, *Lies Like Love* demands to be read all at once, but will stay with you long after. Highly recommended!' Teri Terry, author of the Slated trilogy

Louisa Reid is married with two young daughters and currently teaches English in a girls' school in Cambridge. She is originally from Hale in Cheshire, studied English at Hertford, Oxford, and has lived in London and Zurich. *Lies Like Love* is her second novel, following critically acclaimed *Black Heart Blue*. Find her on Twitter: @Louisareid.

Books by Louisa Reid

BLACK HEART BLUE

LIES
like
LOVE

Louisa Reid

PENGUIN BOOKS

PENGUIN BOOKS

Published by the Penguin Group
Penguin Books Ltd, 80 Strand, London WC2R ORL, England
Penguin Group (USA) Inc., 375 Hudson Street, New York, New York 10014, USA
Penguin Group (Canada), 90 Eglinton Avenue East, Suite 700, Toronto, Ontario, Canada M4P 2Y3
(a division of Pearson Penguin Canada Inc.)
Penguin Ireland, 25 St Stephen's Green, Dublin 2, Ireland (a division of Penguin Books Ltd)
Penguin Group (Australia), 707 Collins Street, Melbourne, Victoria 3008, Australia
(a division of Pearson Australia Group Pty Ltd)
Penguin Books India Pvt Ltd, 11 Community Centre, Panchsheel Park, New Delhi – 110 017, India
Penguin Group (NZ), 67 Apollo Drive, Rosedale, Auckland 0632, New Zealand
(a division of Pearson New Zealand Ltd)
Penguin Books (South Africa) (Pty) Ltd, Block D, Rosebank Office Park,
181 Jan Smuts Avenue, Parktown North, Gauteng 2193, South Africa

Penguin Books Ltd, Registered Offices: 80 Strand, London WC2R ORL, England

www.penguin.com

First published 2014
001

Text copyright © Louisa Reid, 2014
'Medusa' taken from *Ariel* copyright © the Estate of Sylvia Plath and
reprinted by permission of Faber and Faber Ltd
All rights reserved

The moral right of the author has been asserted

Set in 12.5/14.75 pt Garamond MT Std
Typeset by Jouve (UK), Milton Keynes
Printed in Great Britain by Clays Ltd, St Ives plc

British Library Cataloguing in Publication Data
A CIP catalogue record for this book is available from the British Library

ISBN: 978-0-141-34319-8

www.greenpenguin.co.uk

For my parents, David and Gillian Barry, with all my love

Did I escape, I wonder?
My mind winds to you
Old barnacled umbilicus, Atlantic cable,
Keeping itself, it seems, in a state of miraculous
     repair.

Sylvia Plath, 'Medusa'

PART ONE

THE PAIN PLACES: ME AND MY DEPRESSION
BY AUDREY MORGAN, AGED SIXTEEN AND TWO MONTHS

I died three times before I was five years old. I can't see it, can't picture the scene, but my lungs still scream when I run and in winter it feels as if someone's scoring my chest with hard bright nails. Mum says when I was small I only had to see water to throw myself in, no hanging about, like I was born to be a mermaid not a girl: scales for skin, eyes the colour of seaweed and a cry like a scream. But now I won't go near pools or ponds or sea and in all my nightmares I'm turning and tumbling in filthy dark depths, weeds around my wheeling feet, water in my eyes and mouth and I'm swallowing tons of it, gasping, shrieking, falling deep. In my dreams I can't find the light and my head is heavy, held under.

It's because of Mum I'm still alive. Because each time I dived into that danger she's the one who pulled me free like a fish on a line, she's the one who pumped my chest and put her mouth on mine to give me air. She's the one who called the ambulance later, took me to hospital, got me checked over and sat beside me the whole night through as I coughed up the silt and the sludge. Not that I can remember, but you can read about it if you're interested: our local paper ran a story the last time – Hero Mum Saves Tiny Daughter! – with a picture of her holding me up like some sort of trophy. Mum kept a copy.

3

Stored it with her special things in a box I'm not meant to look in. But sometimes I take out the yellowing page, smooth it flat and read about how I died. It doesn't mention my dad though, no matter how many times I look.

I'm writing this so you'll know all about me and my mum and what it's like to be a teenager and poorly like this. Depressed. Not many people understand. Please leave us messages to help us get through!

Thanks and bye for now!
Audrey

September

Audrey

It was getting late when we pulled off the country lane and on to the drive, and the first thing I saw was the water. It circled the house, the Grange, our new home, and as we drove over the little bridge I grabbed the door handle – holding tight. Mum didn't notice. Peter was still crying and I reached into the back with my other hand.

'We're here, Pete. It's OK,' I said, wiping away fresh tears. He'd been sick twice in the last hour when the roads had got so windy, and wet his pants ages ago, on the great stretch of motorway that had brought us here. I'd done what I could with the last of the wipes and an old towel that Mum kept in the boot of the car, but my brother needed a bath and cleaning up. That's what I was thinking: that and how we'd driven off the last road to nowhere, and how instead of being glad we were here, I wished we were back at our old house, even though it was small and grotty and all burnt out. The Grange was a monster, waiting to swallow us up.

Mum pulled over and I jumped out of the car, running back down the drive just to see, to check and make sure – I had to be wrong. But no. From the bridge I stared down into the water that ran like a moat the whole way round the house and I knew it was bad.

'What d'you reckon, Aud?' Mum stood beside me, her

hand on my back, and I looked at our reflections, broken and shifting in the murk, and wondered what was hiding down there.

'Pretty nice, isn't it?' she said. We stood on the edge. Teetered. I felt the slide of mud and the pull of the water and wanted to run. Instead I turned and stared up at the house.

It was such a big place. So tall, towering nearly as high as the trees, twisted over with vines and crawling with moss. A moat belongs with a castle. But this wasn't a castle at all. It was a 1960s rectangle – a prison or a hospital, not a home. I don't know what I'd been expecting. But I'd thought it might be something beautiful, perhaps – an old country house where Peter and I could play at being Old Fashioned. But the hard angles and the empty windows made me think of boxes closed and taped tight, life packed away, dusty and dying. At least the garden was lovely, September green and gold. And the sky was blue, stretching forever. Peter tumbled out of the car on to the gravel and I ran back and scooped him up and on to his feet. He'd turned five in the summer, but five is little, if you ask me; five is still a baby.

'We're going to live here?' I asked Mum. She nodded and stretched her arms wide, yawning.

'Yes, what d'you think? Great, isn't it? I never thought we'd make it though – did you, Aud? God, the traffic. Bloody terrible. But worth it, don't you reckon?'

Mum was tired, gasping for a cuppa, she said, and Peter needed cleaning up, so Mum grabbed a bag from the boot and forged ahead. I helped Peter scoop his toys – his soft old rabbit and collection of stones – back into his bag and we followed her, scurrying to keep up. Thick grey walls, blank windows, flat roof. I smiled at my brother, tried to look excited and he looked back at me, his face hopeful, scared. *No one in their right mind would live here*, I thought, as Mum swept us towards the door of the house, and it opened before she even turned the key, like a yawning mouth, toothless, greedy. I listened, waiting in the hall, staring up into the dark stairwell, and then straight ahead into long corridors. Was it here? Lurking? The Thing we'd run from? But the only sound was the thud of Mum's shoes as she climbed the stairs, speeding up as she ran the last bit, turning corners too fast, then skidding and fumbling with the keys for our flat. I pulled my T-shirt over my nose. The hallway stank of mice and mould. Gross. Mum had said the Grange was posh, renovated, all new, and she'd been excited the whole drive down – holding the wheel so tight her knuckles almost glowed, singing along to the songs on Radio 2, golden oldies, she called them – but posh wasn't the word I'd use. No.

I found the bathroom, leant down and put in the plug and ran the bath. Water sputtered and then gushed, but at least it was warm.

'Come on, mate. Let's clean you up,' I said to Peter, pulling off his shirt and his socks and shoes, damp trousers, stained vest.

'Sorry I was sick, Aud,' he said as I plopped him into the water and splashed it over him.

'Don't be daft – you're OK now, aren't you? Good as new.' But I wished we had bubble bath, rubber ducks, fluffy warm towels. Instead I sang a silly song, something from a children's programme on the telly about scrubbing and washing and getting nice and clean, and Peter joined in and laughed.

Rummaging in Mum's bags, I found her shampoo and washed Peter's hair, careful not to let the suds run in his eyes, and when he was all done we found his pyjamas and made up his bed with sheets and a blanket.

'We'll get some new stuff, Pete, don't worry – a nice cosy duvet and some pillows. We'll get it all set up for you, OK?' Peter nodded and started to rearrange his stones. They were pebbles he'd found in a service station en route, picked out of a tub of flowers. Now they had names. Mr Briggs and Rupert. Bad Hat and Jim. Jim had been his friend back home, the boy next door, with a jam-smeared chin and freckles like patches of gold. Sometimes Jim let Peter share his bike. The others, I didn't know.

'It's not nice here though, is it, Aud?' Peter began to make a tower with the stones then scattered them with his hand, but I shook my head and retrieved them.

'It *is* nice. It's lovely, and you and me we can paint your room and decorate everything how you want it. And get you some new toys.'

'What about my old room?' he said, and I squeezed him tight and said maybe we'd go back one day, even though that was a lie.

I walked over to the window, rubbed the glass clean with my sleeve and rested my forehead there. The ring of dark water was calling. It was singing and waiting as if it had always known a girl like me would arrive here one day.

The best thing to do was not to look. I walked down to the living room and pasted on a smile.

'All right, love?' Mum asked.

'Yeah, I'm OK.'

I didn't tell Mum that I still felt sick. She'd given me pills for the journey but they hadn't worked, had made it worse, and I was always queasy, anyway, my stomach churning fear. The easy part was hiding it from Peter. The hard part was hiding it from Mum. She always knew.

'Well, I'm going to get dinner. You tidy up a bit here, Aud.' She looked at the room, but didn't say anything about the tatty furniture, the bare plaster walls, the carpet that already looked old, and I wondered what I was supposed to do about it.

'Fish and chips? All right?'

'Great. Thanks,' I said, but when she came back an hour later with fat parcels of greasy, lukewarm food I couldn't force any down and Mum finished it all, even the scraps.

Later that night I crept out. Peter was in bed, fast asleep already, but Mum sat staring at her phone, waiting. I hoped her friends, the people she said she knew here, would ring soon; that we'd all have friends soon. We'd always been so impermanent, spindly and frail, ready to topple in the slightest gust of wind, but Peter needed roots; we both did. I left the flat and walked downstairs, letting the heavy front door slam behind me, then trod towards the water – stepping lightly so as not to feel the pain of sharp stones underfoot. There's a way, if you think really hard, to make it stop hurting. Anything. But I shouldn't be afraid, Dad always said that — *no worries*, whistling and swinging my arm when he walked me to school all those years ago, and I looked up at him and he was a hero, the safest thing. *No worries, be happy, Aud*, he'd said, and I was warm for a moment, remembering.

Leo

'So.' Graham looked at Leo. 'How've you been?'

Leo rubbed his hands through his hair then grinned. He picked up his glass of water and drank it down in a long gulp. Graham watched, waiting.

'I'm OK, I think. No, actually, better than that. I'm fine,' Leo said, clearing his throat and nodding as if to assert the truth of his words. Graham sat forward, pleased. He liked this lad.

'Yeah? Good, that's what we want to hear. You're sleeping all right?'

'Yes. Fine. It's all the running.' Graham laughed and Leo smiled, a small grudging smile. You had to when Graham guffawed like that; the noise was so large it demanded acknowledgement.

'Ah, yes, the power of fresh air and exercise. It's underestimated, you know, Leo. You'll be joining me, then, for the marathon, this year?'

'No. I'm not a fanatic, unlike some.' Leo met Graham's eye. His therapist had a rosy face, blunt nose and a wide laughing mouth. He could say anything to him.

'All right, well, we'll see. You'll be a convert yet.'

Leo shrugged.

'What about friends? Found any of them yet?' Leo wasn't really interested in any of the kids round here or their lives. But Graham said that wasn't a healthy attitude, that he needed to interact and make an effort. It was a theme.

'Yeah, sure, I have friends.'

'I don't mean kids you pass the time of day with, Leo.' Graham leant forward again. 'I mean people you talk to, open up to.'

'I know what you mean. And I have you for that, don't I?'

'No. Not all the time.'

Leo thought about it. Since he'd come to live in the sticks, he had his aunt, and Graham, and that was about it. The guys at school were all right; he'd been out to a few parties and so on and there were plenty of invitations and some girls who'd been friendly too. Too friendly, some of them. Like Lizzy Carr. But mostly he had lost touch with his past and that meant there wasn't really anybody to text or call, or just sit and talk about nothing with for a while.

'All right,' he told Graham, 'point taken. I will make an effort.' He saluted, made a serious and determined face and Graham nodded and the consultation time was up. Leo wandered out to find his aunt, who'd been browsing in the small art gallery in town while he'd had his therapy. The word made him feel ridiculous, but Graham didn't; Leo always came out feeling just a little bit more certain that the days were going to get brighter and better and the past was just that. Past.

They drove home to the farm through the rich, thick brightness of the afternoon, the sun shining on turning leaves that tunnelled the lanes back into the country. The feeling that summer wasn't quite done with, not yet, that he could snatch a bit of that time back, hold the green for a while longer, made Leo itch to get home and out into the last of the day. He'd spent July and August outside, in the woods, the fields; cycled the miles to the sea, throwing himself into the rising waves, hot and tired after the ride. And now, in mid September, he was thinking of what lay ahead, not behind.

He thought about school. Friends. It was an easy way out, to say you didn't like something therefore you didn't need to bother. Leo decided he would have to try.

Audrey

The day after we moved in, Mum let me and Peter loose in the supermarket. We could have whatever we wanted for our rooms: new covers for the beds and sheets, lamp-shades, rugs, toys for Peter. Mum filled up the trolley, piling it with mugs and throws, a toaster, saucepans, doormats, curtains. I grabbed essentials: toothbrushes, soap, towels. And then there was my school uniform and brightly col-oured files and felt-tip pens and paper. She even got me a Parker pen, like I'd always wanted, not to mention tons of other stuff we definitely didn't need — a coffee machine, electronic scales, a huge print of Marilyn Monroe in a thick black frame, which I guessed would never get hung. The till bleeped and Mum packed, the numbers flickered and I winced. It was too much, but Mum handed over the credit card like it didn't matter. She caught me staring.

'Don't worry, love. We got the insurance money, remember?'

I smiled back and nodded, following her out and into the car park; the trolley rattled over the concrete.

'We'll do the place up nice, won't we, Aud?' Mum yelled over the racket.

'Yup.' I walked quicker to keep up, the bags were heavy and cutting into my fingers. Mum's strides were long, determined.

'And we'll be happy here. I'm going to look up some old friends.'

'OK.'

'You'll do well, won't you, you and Peter?' she decided, and my brother jumped ahead in excitement, waving his new box of Lego like it was maracas and this was carnival season.

'Good. Right, let's get to the doctor.'

The surgery was quiet, ticking over, warm and snug. Mum smiled at the receptionist, who smiled back. Her name badge read Elizabeth. She set us up appointments, sorted it all.

Peter and I waited while she and Mum chatted. I didn't want to hear what Mum was saying and looked at my brother and took his hand. Peter was my best friend; it sounds stupid to say that – he's a little boy. But he was the one who was always there, looking up to me, following where I led. Listening. I loved him: his butter-yellow hair, his eyes two trusting brown beads, his high, sweet voice. Now his face was anxious, frowning, thumb dangling from his mouth. I had to make all this all right for him. It was what I did.

'Don't worry, Pete.' I squeezed his fingers gently and pulled him on to my knee. He was getting a bit big for that and squirmed away, looking down at the carpet, kicking at the leg of the chair. 'Are you OK now, Aud?' he said.

'Yeah, course I am. You know that, don't you? You know we'll be fine.'

His eyes were big and round, and the stones in his pocket rattled as he turned them over. He looked up for a minute and gazed at me, then sat closer and I held his hand that was still so soft and small that it reminded me what a baby he was and I whispered that we'd be OK.

'I promise, mate. I swear.'

Later Mum stood in the door of my room, her eyes bright in the dark.

'What do you think, then? Happy?'

I nodded slowly.

'Good. And you'll like the school; it's small. You know I wouldn't send you anywhere I didn't think was right for you. And, like I said, I have a good feeling about this place. Like we're home here.'

Home here. What did that mean? My home was miles away in the future. I didn't think I'd been there yet, I was still searching. Wherever it was, my dad would have to be there too.

'I'll do my best, Mum,' I said. And I meant it; it was a chance. I needed those.

I lay back on the pillow and closed my eyes.

'Audrey, are you all right?' Mum stepped into the room and picked up a bag I'd not bothered to unpack. It was only teddies, hospital souvenirs every one, somehow saved and now here, reminding me. She began to arrange them on the shelf.

'Aud?' she asked again, turning to look at me when I didn't answer.

'Yeah. Bit of a headache.' It was nothing new, just something to say.

'I'll get you something for that,' she said. 'But, you

know what? We can't go on like this. I'd like you to see someone here about your depression.' Mum sat on the bed and I shuffled up, leaving a space. 'You want to get better, don't you?'

'Yes,' I whispered, screwing my eyes tighter.

'That's the main thing, then. So let me help you, please? We'll do it together?'

'OK.'

'Anyway, we've got the appointment with the GP next week. We'll get a referral. Get you sorted, love.'

'OK, Mum. All right.'

'Right, then, good.' She placed my hand back on the covers and patted my cheek. 'You know I'm here, don't you, whatever you need? So don't worry. Have a sleep now. You'll feel better in the morning. It's the weekend so you can lie in. And I'll grab you those pills; they'll help with the head. Poor sausage.'

She closed the door softly behind her and I lay in the glowing dark, listening to the house breathing around me. It wheezed and groaned and I listened closer, listened through the walls, beyond the bricks, to the world outside and how it grew and shifted, the grass creeping higher, squeaking and whistling as it pushed its way through the soil, the trees shuffling towards us, their heavy tread shaking the earth, the very air expanding and shrinking, pulsing like blood.

The next morning Mum went out early and Peter and I raced out of the flat, down the stairs and out towards the woods.

My brother pelted ahead, and I followed, branches cracking underfoot, wood pigeons calling on the breeze. Here and there the trees opened out into clearings and under a towering larch we paused.

'Let's make a den,' said Peter, 'with a camp and a fort and everything. Can we, Aud?'

'Course,' I said, and, handing my brother branches, we began to build. Sharp ends were jammed into soft soil and he ran to find more wood, good tall pieces.

'Here, Aud, this'll be a good one, won't it?' Peter dragged a heavy branch, still covered in dark green leaves, towards us. I took it, slotted it in, patting the wood with the palm of my hand, enjoying how dry and strong it felt.

'From here we'll see all the birds, won't we?' he said.

I nodded. 'Yup. And maybe if we're really still and really quiet, we could see rabbits or badgers. Mice. I don't know. There could be all kinds of animals around.'

I ought to know more – Peter was looking at me in wonder and then gazing everywhere, his cheeks rosier than they'd been in a long time, his whole face sparkling.

'What else?'

'Shrews,' I said in desperation, casting about for something more exciting, 'maybe deer or a hare.' I wouldn't say that if he looked really carefully, he'd see hearts beating inside the trees, hear their inhalations, the steady rumble of life. All was calm today though, nothing jumping out of time: the woods were sleeping.

Our fort was a messy bunch of spindly twigs tangled

with the odd sturdy branch and somehow remaining upright – not too bad for a pair of city kids.

'What do you think?' I asked.

'Awesome.' Peter dropped to his knees and crawled inside. 'It's really cool in here, Aud, come in with me.' He patted the ground. We sat, snug, quiet, taking care not to touch the sides and send the whole thing toppling. It might last the afternoon if we were lucky.

'You're right. This isn't bad, Pete.'

'Shhh. If you talk, the animals won't come. We're supposed to be quiet.' He set out his stones in a row and talked to them for a bit, but after a while his head drooped against my side and we waited, Peter with a short stick clutched in one hand, grass stains on his knees and elbows. Leaves in his hair. He sighed and shifted, wriggled, kicked out a leg and I held his foot, reminded him to be careful.

'Sorry, Aud,' he whispered.

'It's OK, mate,' I said, squeezing him tighter. 'You're doing well, being really patient.'

'Really?'

'Yeah. Like a proper woodsman.'

'Knight you mean.' I smiled.

'Can we come here every day and do this?'

'Well, maybe. At the weekends or after school.'

'Shh,' Peter told me and we stared together at the deep thickness of trees, watched for the faintest stirring, for a miracle or magic. And then as the sun broke through the thick canopy of leaves and caught a patch of earth, lighting it like fire, a tiny rabbit hopped into the circle of light – its ears pricked, its nose twitching – and we froze, our breath held, skin prickling.

'Can I catch it?' my brother whispered. 'Keep it for a pet?' He shifted, tensed, aching to hurl himself out towards the bunny, but the creature darted away and Peter charged after it too late.

'Come back,' he yelled into the undergrowth. 'I won't hurt you, come back.'

'It's gone, Pete,' I said, following, reaching for him. 'But don't worry, there'll be others. Hundreds of rabbits and mice and birds. We'll come back tomorrow, check our den, but now let's go. Time for tea.'

'But I want that bunny! Did you see it, Aud? It could be our pet. I want a pet. I want Nibbles.' I didn't want to remember. The fire. Nibbles trapped inside. Peter had cried himself to sleep thinking about it and I didn't want to start that again. I squeezed his hand. He was still looking at me, hopeful.

'I'll train it and look after it. I promise I'll clean out its hutch and everything, give it its food. In the wild it'll probably die.'

'It won't. It's gone back to its burrow to its mum.' I swallowed and smiled. 'So she'll look after it. Won't she?'

'Do you promise?'

'Yeah. I promise.'

We walked back slowly and, when we neared home, I saw Mum's car was back; she was busy with more bags of shopping and we ran to help her unload, and the idea came to me that maybe she was right. I was thinking again about high hopes and fresh starts. Mum hadn't lied when she'd told us about this place and here we were at last, with all this air and sky and trees to climb and fields to run in. We could be new. We could be well. My heart relaxed, unclenched, and I grabbed Peter's hand and we ran to meet her.

Leo

The new kids from the Grange moved in a line across the horizon. Leo had watched them take the path out of the woods and followed at a distance. They hadn't seen him, were unaware of anything else, just focused on walking their own line, treading it like tightrope walkers. It was the girl that caught his eye though, holding her little brother's hand and tugging him along so he didn't fall too far behind. She was different-looking: all sharp angles. Her T-shirt stuck to her body, her long hair scorching out behind her, a pale flame. Every now and then it looked as though she might take off, as if the wind would pick her up and throw her into the sky. And then Leo caught the jut of her chin, something defiant in it, saw the strength of the arm and the hand that held on to her brother, and thought no, she was definitely earthbound.

He could have caught up with them then and introduced himself but Sue had plans for that later. There weren't any other families at the Grange – no one local would live there, not with the stories that came out after the place had shut down – and Sue thought they must be lonely, moving in and discovering the building deserted. His aunt was making them a casserole; he could smell it from out in the yard.

'Leo, where've you been?' Her face was rosy with the

heat from the oven. Sue still had her wellies on and Mary was sniffing round the floor, looking for a treat. 'I thought you'd got lost.'

'No. Just out for a wander.'

'Good. That's what weekends are for. Doing nothing. Kids these days don't do enough of it.'

Leo threw his coat off and narrowly avoided being thrashed by Mary's tail as he sank into the sofa to pull off his boots.

'Don't get comfy. We're going to the Grange. That new family I told you about? They're in.'

'I know. I just saw the kids.'

'And?'

'And what?'

'Verdict?'

'Looked nice, I guess. I mean, I don't know. It was from a distance.'

'So why the blush?' His aunt was looking at him with a big grin on her face and Leo laughed.

'Suc, you're ridiculous. Quit it. I don't need a girlfriend.'

'Who said anything about girlfriend?' she teased. 'I just thought you might be lucky, find a kindred spirit. I didn't even know there was a girl involved, how could I?'

'Yeah, yeah. Come on, let's go. And stop stirring.'

'Never.' She handed him the basket and they set off over the fields towards the Grange, which loomed darker than ever, Leo thought; only one small light in one small window promised a welcome.

Audrey

The quiet in the flat that evening was thick, sort of humming and spooky, and even though Mum kept the radio on as she cleared up after tea, filling the cupboards and whistling along, I sat on the sofa with my hands over my ears and nearly didn't hear the banging that sent Peter charging to open the door.

By the time I caught up with him, a woman was standing in the hallway and smiling at my brother. She was tanned, like she spent her whole life in the sun. Her skin was a bit like leather, all wrinkles round her eyes. She looked comfy. Soft round the middle, her arms strong.

'Hello,' she said, spotting me, raising an eyebrow. 'Sorry to drop by unannounced; we're your neighbours. I live across the field. I heard on the grapevine there was a new family in the Grange so I wanted to come over and give you this. Housewarming.' She proffered a basket.

'Thanks.' I took it and my arm dropped with the weight and a delicious smell drifted into the flat. Mum appeared then, touching her hair, straightening her top, and I passed it to her.

'Hello,' the woman said again, looking at Mum this time. 'Sue Bright. I'm your nearest neighbour, I was just explaining to your daughter here.'

'Oh. Hello. Yes, I'm Lorraine,' Mum said. 'And this is Audrey.'

And then another figure appeared and I turned fire red, my cheeks blaring like the sirens on the top of police cars that used to race round our old estate.

'This is Leo,' the Sue woman said, 'my nephew.' They didn't look a bit alike. For a start, this woman wasn't Chinese or even half Chinese. And Leo definitcly was. And he was slouching outside my door. And I was in my horrible jeans and ratty T-shirt and Mum had ketchup on her chin and Peter was pulling on my arm and Sue was pulling Leo inside.

'My brother's son. He's living with me for a while; we're at the farm, just over the fields,' Sue explained again. She rooted in her bag, producing a pack of Smarties and holding them out to Peter.

'Oh, lovely,' Mum said, and I knew she was being polite. She's big on manners; not so much on neighbours.

'So, if there's anything you need, just ask.' Sue was still smiling but it was getting awkward now.

'Do you want to come in?' I said in a rush because I couldn't help it. These people looked nice, like they weren't afraid of anything. The more people in the flat, the better it would be.

'Oh, well, if you're not busy, just for a minute.' She took a step forward, and started admiring the décor, commenting on everything, exclaiming at the renovations.

'You know this place was half falling down,' I heard her say as they headed down the hallway. Leo followed and I

27

didn't look, kept my eyes trained straight ahead, on Sue's back. Mum was giving her a potted history.

'We've moved down here from up north. I got a job at Pond Street. You know, the kids' hospice? I'm a nurse, Sue, so it's not too hard to find work, and back home, well, there were other reasons, family reasons, for us to make a fresh start.' There was a long gap and Sue didn't ask and for once Mum didn't elaborate. She'd be saving it up for the next time, building up the tension. My mum knows how to tell a good story.

They drifted off into the kitchen. Water splashed and ran, the kettle began to boil. Peter sidled round the back of the sofa with his Smarties, shy again.

The boy, Leo or whatever his name was, had to have noticed I looked rank. No make-up. Greasy hair. And he was in a duffle coat and dark green wellington boots, like he'd stepped straight out of one of those horsey magazines there were piles of at the GP surgery here. Plus he wasn't actually a boy at all. He was practically a grown-up and he didn't belong in this flat, with its dark smell and horrible bare walls and all Mum's stuff scattered about. I sat on the sofa and that left him the chair – nasty grey velour and saggy in the middle. I should have offered to take his coat. Got him a drink. But I didn't want to get up now so I put a cushion on my knee and hid behind it, remembering my arms too late – he'd already seen.

'So,' he said, his eyes moving quickly up to my face before he cleared his throat and directed his next question at Peter: 'What's this you've been doing?'

He looked at our notebook open on the floor, the

brand-new coloured pens scattered around it. Peter peeped at him, thumb back in his mouth.

'Aud says it's for keeping track,' Peter mumbled, and Leo turned to me as if I should explain. I leant down, picked up the book and closed it tight. My drawing of the bunny was useless. Plus it wasn't his business.

'It's just a journal,' I said, 'like a nature diary or something. Peter likes nature.'

'Yeah? Me too.' Leo's smile was kind. He didn't sigh or roll his eyes or drum his fingers on the arm of the chair; he leant forward, forearms on his knees and spoke softly to my brother.

'I saw a badger the other day. It was huge. This big.' He opened his arms wide. 'Tell you the truth, I was pretty scared. Massive teeth.' He pulled a face.

'I never saw one,' Peter said, then paused. 'Do you have pets?' he asked, and I smiled at my brother. He'd emerged and sidled over to stand beside Leo. 'I had a hamster but it's dead now.'

'Oh. That's a shame. Yes, well, Sue has a dog. And a pony, but she's rather old and slow, I'm afraid. In fact they both are. What I'd really like,' he said, holding Peter's gaze, 'is a snake, but I don't think Sue's too keen.'

'A snake?' I laughed a little behind my hands. Peter's face was a picture.

'Yes. I wouldn't be surprised if you spot one in the woods out there. But don't worry – they're not poisonous. At least, I don't think so.' Listen to him. It was like chatting with a prince. Not that I knew how princes talked. But he sounded like he'd been brought up dining on peacock, sipping water from crystal glasses, hobnobbing with Lord and Lady Posh Pants. I remembered to shut my mouth again.

Peter turned to me.

'Can we get a snake too, Aud?'

'No, Pete. I doubt it. But we'll watch for one. OK? And do a picture.'

Leo grinned at me and I smiled back, careful. It was all right if he talked to Peter, but I didn't want him talking to me. I pulled the cushion tighter against me.

'So, how are you settling in?' he asked.

'It's OK, I guess.' That was code for badly. For all the nature I was still trapped. Trapped by the house and the past and the water. The water was everywhere. He seemed to get it; his eyes were sympathetic.

'It's hard, coming to a new place. Will you be starting at the college?'

'Yup.'

'I'm in Year Thirteen – last year, thank God.'

'Oh.' Why was he still talking to me? It made me feel complicated, like I ought to be someone I wasn't.

'What about you?' he said, so I had to answer.

'Year Eleven. But I've missed loads of school. I have to catch up.'

'Well, good luck with that.' He had a kind, serious face, very fine, and a straight nose, amber-brown eyes, ever so clear. And he filled the space up, his body strong, his shoulders broad. His mouth moved and he smiled, waiting, as if he expected a response, but I hadn't been listening, too busy looking, which I hadn't meant to do. I was only trying to suss him out.

'What?' I gazed at him. Gormless, Mum would say, and I shut my mouth on the word.

'I said, I hope it goes OK. I'd be happy to show you around a bit.' Leo shifted in his chair. 'If you want.'

'Oh.' I tucked myself smaller, legs almost in a knot. He was having a laugh, just being polite. I looked away but he kept watching and when I glanced up I suppose our eyes locked, just for a second, not that I'm a good judge of that sort of thing. Well, whatever happened, it made me get hot and red in the face and I looked away again. Because a boy like Leo would never be interested in a girl like me. I'm the sort of girl who disappears in a crowd, who you can forget you ever knew five minutes after meeting. I reckon I'd make a good thief: flitting like a cloud into a room, then drifting away with something precious – quiet as air. Leo would forget me fast, forget this conversation. Well. Never mind. I remembered my manners.

'Thank you,' I said, to the floor. 'That'd be great, if you don't mind.' And then that was it, nothing left to say. Except: 'But you don't have to. I mean, you don't have to pretend to want to. It's OK. We're all right. Aren't we, Pete? We like being on our own.'

Peter nodded and came and picked up the notebook from my lap. He settled himself on the carpet at my feet and grabbed the brown felt-tip and started scratching away at the picture, colouring it in with short stabbing strokes.

Leo flushed. I'd never seen a boy blush like that before. And I hadn't meant to be rude. I chewed at my lip but there would be no clever stories. Flirty chat. Intellectual banter. Leo would soon find that out.

'Well, the offer's still there,' Leo said to the wall before picking up his coat, and now suddenly I wished I'd said something different and tried a bit harder, but I wasn't good at making friends. I got hot again. Embarrassed. It was one of those moments that you want to last forever and you want to end straight away. Agony either way.

Mum appeared in the doorway with his aunt and Leo jumped to his feet. He couldn't wait to get out. That was my fault, but I hadn't meant it.

'See you,' I called, wanting to make it better, but he'd gone so fast I'm not sure I heard him answer.

Leo

'That wasn't so bad, was it?'

Leo thought about a discreet eye-roll but you couldn't get much past Sue. He might, if pressed, describe the encounter as excruciating.

'The kids are sweet. Nice family,' his aunt continued, and he felt what was coming next and didn't want it. For a woman who'd lived on her own for years, she was the opposite of hermit. Which was a shame.

'Just tell me we don't have to go over there again. It was pretty obvious they didn't want us intruding, Sue. Plus the place gives me the creeps.'

'Don't be so daft. And you know I like to be friendly. So, no harm done. And you offered to show them around a bit, didn't you?'

'Yes, so now will you get off my back?'

'I will.' Leo knew his aunt meant well, that she wanted him to have a social life, but this business about friends was a pain. Well, he'd reached out, as Graham would put it, and made himself look like an idiot. He groaned and rubbed his face with his hands. Sue looked at him, grinning.

'What was her name again?' Leo asked Sue, thinking of the girl and her long pale hair straggling down her back, the heavy fringe disguising eyes that blinked behind her glasses, like she had some sort of tic. Not that it bothered him. He'd met plenty of people like that in the past couple of years. She had long fingers, he remembered now, delicate hands, graceful. And she was tall. He'd noticed that first, her long neck, legs, arms. Her arms. He wiped the memory, crossing the image out.

'Audrey. Funny name, old-fashioned these days,' Sue said, breaking his line of thought.

'Mmm.' If he was honest with himself, he liked the look of her. Leo laughed, remembering how almost rude she'd been and then how shocked, as if she wasn't used to saying what she thought. It had been his fault; he hadn't exactly sounded enthusiastic and she must have sensed it. Maybe he gave off vibes. *Piss off, I'm not interested* vibes.

Sue drove towards the farm and Leo smudged his finger into the mist on the window, leant his head back and thought. There was something tough about that girl; something that said, *Don't touch, don't you dare. Don't hurt me or my brother or you'll pay.* He hadn't meant to make her feel like that. He had to be kind. Lose the negativity; that was what Graham would recommend. Graham was right about a lot of stuff, but then that was his job. Making fucked-up teenagers better.

'Shall I invite them over for supper?' Sue looked straight ahead but he could see the smirk at the corners of her lips. Playing Pandarus, or something.

'You just can't stop yourself, can you?' he teased, and his aunt laughed; she never took offence.

'Nope. And you be sensible, all right?'

'I'm always sensible.' And it would be good to be nice

to Audrey, to show her around, make her smile. He could do with a challenge.

'Good boy.' They pulled up in the drive; he jumped out to shut the gate, swung on it as it closed. It was good here, all this space, all this air. No one getting inside his head and fussing. Leo grabbed his aunt and gave her a kiss. She'd sort of saved his life when she'd agreed he could come and live here, and if that meant he owed her, then he'd pay up.

Audrey

Mum walked fast through the corridors, all busy and businesslike in her work uniform, and I slipped back into the crowds of kids so I could pretend I didn't know her. Monday meant starting school and I'd told her not to come, but she'd said that would give the wrong impression. People might think she didn't care. And didn't I need her? She didn't see me shaking my head, just marched up the drive anyway. Some of the other kids were staring at her, but she had her lipstick on and her smile and didn't care.

'Audrey.' She stopped, turning back to hunt for me, shouting my name again, actually bellowing it. 'Come on, love – get a move on.' I saw the girls I'd been following gawp, then giggle, look at me, put two and two together, and my plan to pretend I wasn't different was over before it had even begun. She shunted me into the form room and the group of kids clustered round the tables in the far corner turned and stared.

'Mum. Just go. I'm fine.' I sounded like I'd been sucking helium.

'No. I'll wait until your form tutor gets here. Make sure everything's OK.' She put out her hand, smoothed my hair, fussed with my jacket. The uniform she'd picked up looked bad; it hung off me as if I were made of sticks or straw. As if you might blow me down or set me alight with a match.

'It will be, I promise. Just go,' I hissed back, staring at the floor.

'Audrey –' she looked hurt and I hated that – 'don't you want me here?'

'No.' I shut my eyes tight, then opened them and looked at her hard. 'Please, Mum, just go. You're making me look like a total dick.'

'Aud,' she warned, frowning, looking round to check no one had heard.

'Mum. Please.'

The bell rang and the room filled with girls who looked like bunches of flowers. Bright and glossy, newly picked, still wearing their arrogant bloom. As if they were untouchable, as if they never even thought about what time, what the future, what words like that really meant, and believed that it was all going to last. That no one would or even could take their sunshine away.

Mum marched up to the form tutor, stuck out her hand, not bothered that the teacher's arms were full of books and papers.

'I'm Audrey Morgan's mother. She's new?'

'Oh, yes, it's nice to meet you. And Audrey, of course.' She looked over at me and I smiled back, shifted my bag, then looked out of the window.

'Well, here she is. I'm going to be late for work if I don't get a move on, but I thought I'd better come and say hello.'

The teacher kept smiling and staring like she had no

idea what to say and was just pretending this was normal. I cringed again.

Mum cleared her throat. 'I'd appreciate it if you'd update me at the end of the day. I need to know how things go for her and I won't get a word out of her at home.'

'Of course. I'll call you, I expect we have your number on file.'

'Yes. If I don't hear from you, then I'll telephone in. Audrey's been a very poorly girl for a long time, Miss –'

'Miss Jones.'

'Right, that's it, Miss Jones. She's missed a lot of work. Of course she'll do her best to catch up, but she's not the brightest button – no offence, love.' She looked at me quickly and reached out, wiping some imaginary stain from my chin. I tossed my head, trying to get her off me. The room was watching, agog, and I knew I was the colour of ketchup. 'It runs in the family – I was useless at school myself. Came into my own later. So, we'd both appreciate it if you'd take that into account. And I hope that the moment she's not feeling well, you'll let her go to the nurse, or call me.'

Miss Jones looked at me, hesitating, her smile strained.

'It's lovely to have you in our form, Audrey. Everyone's welcome in our school community and we'll do our best to help you any way we can.'

'That's wonderful. There's a warmth to this place; you can feel it.' Mum smiled, turned round and looked at the class as if she actually expected them all to think she was totally normal. They stared back, their faces stupid with smirks no one was bothering to hide

'I'll let you get on. Have a good day, Audrey, love.' And then Mum hugged me, as if she hadn't made me look enough of a fool, and I sloped off to an empty desk; trying hard to disappear.

First we had French. I'm rubbish at French, but the girl next to me nudged my arm.

'Don't make eye contact,' she said. I stared at her, confused.

'With Madame Partridge, she's a bit of a bitch,' she whispered, 'and if you look up, then she'll keep on asking you all the hard questions about the past perfect. So, eyes down. Right?'

My neighbour had dark hair, dark eyes, rosy cheeks and wore bright yellow boots, Dr Martens. She saw me looking and stretched out her legs.

'Cool, aren't they?'

'Yeah, really.'

'I'm not supposed to wear them, but I get away with it. If you smile, you can get away with a lot.' She grinned, showed train-tracked teeth. I smiled back.

'I'm Jen. You're Audrey. I heard your mum say.'

'Oh. Yeah, well, she was a bit full on. Embarrassing.'

'My mum's the same. They all are.'

'Really?'

Jen nodded. When Madame Partridge asked me my name and I replied, '*Je m'appelle Audrey*,' Madame cringed and let loose a torrent of words.

'She says your accent's a nightmare,' Jen muttered. 'But if you ask me, so's hers.' And then she laughed and I laughed too. It didn't last. I couldn't follow a thing, even with Jen's help, and fifteen minutes in I stuck up my hand.

'Can I go to the loo?' I said.

'Pardon?'

'I need the toilet,' I repeated and someone behind me laughed.

Madame said something in French and I stared at her until she threw her hands up and waved me out and I pretty much ran from the class and down the corridor, no idea where I was heading until I found the toilets. The smell of disinfectant scored my throat, but I locked the door of a cubicle, sat on the closed lid of a seat and clenched my fingers tight, balled them into fists so I wouldn't scratch or scrape at my skin, and waited for the bell.

At lunchtime I retraced my steps to the front office. No one was watching and I slid out of the doors and down the drive, shrugging into my coat.

The primary school was across the road; Mum and I had dropped Peter there earlier and I needed to find him now.

Staring through the netting into the playground, I searched for my brother among the screaming, racing throng. The longer I couldn't see him, the more my heart thumped, sick and sinking in my chest.

'Where are you?' I muttered, scanning the edges until I saw him, on his own, leaning against a wall. Behind him towered a huge painted sunflower; his head only just touched the first leaf.

'Pete,' I yelled, cupping my hands round my mouth,

pushing my face against the wire. 'Pete!' I waved and called, walking my way round the perimeter, trying to get a little closer. The third time I called he heard and his head jerked up, eyes scanning and then fixing in my direction.

'Audrey!' I saw him say and he ran, little legs scissoring towards me. Peter grabbed my hand through the chain-link fence. I crouched down and kissed his fist.

'You all right?'

'I'm OK,' he said. 'Are you OK, Aud?'

'Course I am, mate. What are you doing?'

'Just playing,' he said, and shrugged. I smiled.

'There might be some nice children, Pete. You should join in, maybe play tag or with the boys playing ball.'

'They said you can't play if you're new.' He shrugged again and I bit my lip.

'Tomorrow, then,' I told him. 'You won't be new tomorrow, will you?'

'I don't know, Aud. I might be.' His eyes widened and I saw him counting the days in his head, trying to work out how long different lasted.

Leo

Leo was late for Biology again. Tuesday's double lesson was something he was finding it difficult to get excited about. He strode down one of the many corridors, thinking how the school was like a long-tentacled creature and how maybe he'd go diving in the summer, see how things looked underwater, when he came face to face with Audrey.

'Hey,' he said, and she stared at him and blinked as if he were the last person she'd ever expected to see again. He couldn't help smiling – she looked as if she needed smiles. Sue was right; friendly was good.

'Are you lost?' Leo watched her, wondering.

'No. I was just looking for the nurse's office,' she said, and then blushed like before.

'Oh, well, it's down there.' He pointed back the way he'd come.

'Thanks.' Audrey began to move again. Leo found himself following.

'Are you ill? Do you need anything?' It was only polite to ask. He couldn't have her wandering off and then passing out somewhere.

'No. I'm all right.' She pulled her sleeves down over her hands as she spoke, chewed a fistful of cardigan and then stopped, looked at him, and walked on in the direction he'd indicated. Leo fell into step, forgetting Biology, and

Audrey glanced at him out of the corner of her eye and her mouth twitched, just a tiny bit, the hint of a smile. *Gotcha*, he wanted to say, but that would be annoying and he was sure he could think of something else instead, but all he knew was that her hair was the colour of moonlight and that she didn't so much walk as glide. Obviously those observations were not appropriate, conversationally speaking. Obviously she did not want to talk or be escorted or anything.

'So, yes, well, it's just up there,' Leo said eventually, as they reached another corridor and it snaked before them, long and white and empty.

'I got it. Thanks.'

'No worries,' he said, and stood and watched her float away.

Audrey

The next day at break I asked Jen about Leo. He'd appeared the day before, in the afternoon when I'd been dodging Science, and now he was walking past the lockers where we were standing. He raised his hand, a brief wave, mouthed hello, then strode on. I just wanted to know if she knew him, that was all, but another girl butted in.

'Leo? In Year Thirteen? That Leo?' She gestured with her thumb down the corridor where he'd gone. I tried to smile at her and nodded.

'Yeah. I think so.'

'He's taken,' this other girl said. Jen grabbed her books and slammed her locker shut. She didn't look at the girl.

'What do you mean?' I couldn't help asking.

'I mean taken, like, you know. Taken.' She leant back against the wall and folded her arms, so I smiled quickly, not meaning it, and looked away.

'Thanks for your help, Lizzy,' Jen said, rolling her eyes and pulling me with her.

'So, what do you want to know for, anyway?' The girl, Lizzy, followed us, moving herself into my line of sight. Her eyes picked at me, searching for something to hate.

'No reason. Forget it.' I shrugged and smiled at her again. Leo was nothing to me; I didn't even know him.

'You should stay away,' Lizzy called after me, but I

ignored her and followed Jen into the classroom, taking our seats and arranging our books.

'What did I do to her?' I said. 'I don't get it.'

'She just gets off on being a bitch. Strange species of human being, I admit. Plus she has a major crush on you know who,' Jen whispered as the teacher called the register. 'I think maybe they had a thing.'

'I'm not bothered.'

'Well, just ignore her anyway, OK? I'm afraid it's a case of the green-eyed monster.' She looked over at Lizzy. Lizzy looked back and stuck up her middle finger. Jen just raised an eyebrow and looked away.

I wondered if I could follow Jen everywhere, make her my friend just by virtue of my presence as her shadow. It wasn't necessary.

'Come on,' she said at lunch. 'I'll show you the cafeteria. It's pretty grim, mind you. I hope you brought lunch from home. Lesson one: don't trust the natives. Lesson two: don't eat their food.'

Jen pulled out a magazine, stuck it between us and munched her way through a plastic tub of pasta and pesto. She didn't talk much and I picked at my own food, glancing at the pictures of bands I'd never heard of and looking up now and then to scan the big echoing hall. Lizzy and her mates, whose names I didn't know, spotted me and strode over.

'Where's your boyfriend, then?' Lizzy said, her breath too near. I could smell cheese and onion. Jen looked up, then back down at her magazine. I did as she'd suggested and smiled. These girls weren't really a threat.

Last year there'd been dog shit in my school bag; coins stinging my skin, flicked by boys from the back row; bile in my mouth and Aidy Parker standing, his crotch in my face, grabbing my head and pulling it against the rough scratch of his trousers, his fists in my hair. Laughter bouncing off the ceilings and walls. Lizzy was nothing, compared.

I grabbed my bag, stood up and pushed into the little throng.

'So, come on,' said Lizzy. 'You should go look in the sixth-form common room; maybe he'll be in there. We'll take you. Then we'll see, won't we?' They closed in. No. If she touched me, I would freak. No one is allowed to touch me, no one except Peter and my mum.

'No, it's OK, thanks. I'm busy.' My voice sounded smudged, wrong. Not as sure as it should. Help. Now.

Jen stood up, slung her arm round my shoulders. That felt OK.

'Actually, we're on our way somewhere, Liz, so you know, sod off,' she said, towing me out of there, past them. She looked at me when we were well away, considering.

'You know what, Audrey, I reckon she's got it in for you.'

Mum's voice drifted through the walls, from wherever she was – I saw her standing, legs akimbo, finger wagging: *You're a victim, Aud*, she was saying, *a born bloody victim*, and underneath her concern I knew she thought I brought trouble on myself. But this school was supposed to be different. I was different here. I wasn't going to take it.

'It's OK,' I told Jen, 'I can handle it.'

'Good. Don't let her think you're weak. She's like a cat chasing mice. You need to show her who's boss. Right?'

'Right.' I nodded and followed Jen back inside. She strode, head high, her boots flashing like sunflowers, and I caught up, walked beside her, my insides turning over when she shoved her arm through mine, linked me like I belonged.

Leo

Chucking his apple high in the air, Leo caught it in one hand and made as if to bowl it over the fields, then stuffed it back into his pocket. It was sunny and it was lunchtime, at last, and the air smelled clean outside. He sat down on a bench, throwing his head back and shutting his eyes, basking, he thought, like a lizard. But when he opened them again, there she was, appearing out of the autumn mist like something from Arthurian legend. He jumped a bit. That was weird. A girl just standing there, staring at you; a bit intense.

'Oh, hello.' Leo smiled at her. It was his default position. No one could say he wasn't trying.

'Hi.'

He'd not seen her for a week and had almost forgotten to wonder how she might be doing, but now he grinned.

'You gave me a shock. I thought you were, I don't know . . .'

'What?' She stepped closer.

'Well, a ghost, a fairy, maybe.'

'Ha.' Audrey pulled a face that bore no resemblance to anything ethereal whatsoever and Leo grinned.

'Here,' he said, unpacking his lunch, 'have a sandwich. I've got heaps.'

'No, thanks,' she said, but he could practically see the

48

saliva pooling in her mouth when she saw what he had.
Sue's home-made bread. Loads of cheese and salad,
pickle. They'd made it together, with fruit grown in Sue's
garden – it had gooseberries in it, of all things. He pointed
them out. Audrey smiled. Her eyes were gooseberry green
today. Her cheeks apple pink all of a sudden. He couldn't
say that though. This self-censorship was exhausting. But
at least she sat down, gingerly, on the end of the bench.

'Go on, I don't need it all,' Leo said. Maybe she was just
too polite. Maybe she had an eating thing. That would
explain how thin she was. He knew plenty of girls like that
too. But he didn't ask and usually they didn't tell.

'No, really. I've got loads of allergies and stuff. It's why
I look like I look.' Her eyes challenged him to contradict
her, so he didn't. Maybe it explained things. Like the skin
on her arms and hands, cracked, sore-looking, partly
bandaged. He'd noticed it that first day at the Grange
before she'd hidden behind that cushion. But he was
pretty sure he hadn't been looking at a rash. Hadn't her
mum said she was a nurse? Not that it was his business,
and he wanted to look away, stop giving a damn. But it
seemed as if he'd turned into a good Samaritan. More like
a busybody, sticking his nose where it wasn't wanted. He
felt in his pocket.

'Here, have my apple, then,' Leo said. Audrey hesitated
a moment, and he nearly chucked it at her, to force her to
catch it, but in the end she took it, her face splitting open
with a smile as she took the first bite. They didn't talk. She
ate like it was a serious business, requiring attention. Her
eyes half closed.

'So, are you feeling better?' He remembered she'd been looking for the nurse last week. But, reaching out like this, it was like putting his hand into a bowl of ice-cold water.

'I'm OK,' she said eventually and moved away, just a fraction, sensing his scrutiny, and he kicked himself. This wasn't how it had been before. Well. Actually it was.

'It must be hard for you, coming here, after you lost everything,' Leo said.

'What?' She looked up at him.

'The fire, you know. Your mum mentioned it to Sue. They had coffee last week? I'd be gutted if I lost all my stuff.'

Audrey looked down at the ground.

'Yeah, that.' Her voice was flat, her expression dead. Leo shifted on the bench.

'Look, meet me later,' he said. 'Really, I'll show you and Peter the shortcut home, like I said. And I'm not just being nice. I'm bored; I could do with the company, OK? We'll find Peter a badger. Or a snake, even. How is he, anyway? Does he like his new school?'

'He's all right. Not that good.'

He hated the sadness that he saw in her eyes; it hurt.

'Well, come on – we need to cheer him up, right?'

'Yeah, all right, then.'

'It's a date,' he said, and then winced at his expression, but Audrey didn't seem to have heard and let him walk her back into school.

Audrey

At the end of the day Peter and I stood waiting for Leo, getting drenched in rain that cut past the sun, sparkling and fierce.

I looked at my watch again when Leo approached and he laughed.

'God, I'm really sorry – I had to stay behind in English. My teacher, Mr Bruce – do you have him? No? Lucky you. Well, he didn't like my essay, so we had a bit of a row. And all the time I was thinking, *Damn, Audrey's waiting.* And here you are. And Peter. God, I feel bad.' He reached out and ruffled Peter's hair. Peter squirmed away and Leo grinned.

'Are you OK?' he asked. 'Not too wet?'

'No. We're fine.'

We fell into step and Peter held my hand.

'How was it today, mate?' I said.

He hopped over a puddle, then said, 'I played with Jim and Bad Hat and then a big boy stole them and threw them in the bushes.'

'What?'

'Yes, but I crawled in and got them. But I did get dirty.' He showed me his palms, his face anxious.

'It doesn't matter. I can wash your stuff. And you.'

'Who're Jim and Bad Hat?' asked Leo, and I wished he hadn't.

'My friends,' said Peter.

I thought of things to say to change the subject and blurted something about the stew his aunt had given us, if she wanted her basket back, before I bit my lip. Boring.

'So, I'll show you my favourite route,' Leo suggested. 'It's a good shortcut home for days when you don't want to take the bus, days like this, when you should be outside.'

'You should never be outside in the rain. Rain's for ducks, not people,' I said. For a second I saw my dad again: this vague outline, really tall and thin, in a white T-shirt, pale jeans. I almost smelled the sweet bag of white bread, felt it claggy in my fingers. *False memories*, Mum said. *Get over it; he left us. His choice.*

Leo pointed at the sky. 'Look – it's stopping.'

We stood and stared for a bit and he was right. The last drops came in a sporadic patter and in the distance the sky was clearer. I didn't really care whether there was thunder or lightning, snow or storm, a blinding apocalyptic sun. It felt free. It felt right, like I should have been doing this for years. Like Mum said, it was better here. I could wipe the past away for a while now, clean it up, breathe in a future with all this fresh air.

'I run this way, most evenings,' Leo told me, turning to look at me.

'It's nice,' I said. 'Peaceful.' I looked right back into his face and he grinned, then put out his arm, touching me gently on the shoulder, to pull me to a halt.

'Hang on, look up there,' he said, and we all stopped and turned our faces to the sky.

'It's a dragon,' Peter called, grabbing my hand, pulling me. 'Is it a dragon, Aud?'

'I think it's just a bird, Pete.' I laughed.

'Yup, a kestrel,' said Leo.

'It's still amazing,' I whispered, holding Peter's hand, crouching down to stare from his level, see his eyes widen and glow as Leo explained how it was seeking out prey and would feed on mice or voles hiding in the fields around us.

'Let's catch it,' said Peter, his hands grabbing towards the sky, and Leo laughed.

'I'd say it's fairly unlikely you will ever catch that bird, Pete. It's wild. And it's hungry. Nature,' he told him, 'red in tooth and claw. Not a pet.'

'But I still want it,' Peter insisted, and I imagined it swooping down, grabbing us by the collar before wheeling and screeching back up into the sky, carrying Peter and me off to its lair. It would feed us in little pieces to its young. My skin would easily tear. A shiver like spiders crawled over my skin, up my neck into my hair.

'So, how's it all going?' Leo asked as we walked on.

'Oh, all right, I guess.'

'I don't envy you the Grange. You know it used to be a sort of institution. For people with problems.'

'What sort of problems?'

'There's loads of stories. It got closed down in the end.'

'What like?' My stomach lurched. I didn't want him to be talking about me. Spouting off about mental girls who needed locking up for their own good.

'Not sure. Don't worry, I'm sure all the ghosts are long

gone.' Leo was laughing and then stopped when he saw my face.

'It's all right. I'm joking.'

'Yeah, well, it just creeps me out, that's all.' It was a dead house. All that water. And the Thing would like the Grange, I knew it would.

'I don't blame you. I'd be freaked out too. It's way too haunted-house, that place. And you're missing home. Right?'

'Not really.' I did miss the idea of it, although I couldn't explain that. It was like my life was a puzzle with a huge piece missing. If my dad were around, maybe that would solve it, help things make sense. Leo was staring at me like he wasn't sure he understood. I gave him a quick smile, shoved my hair out of my eyes and stuffed my glasses in my pocket. Sometimes it was easier to see without them.

'You're lucky, then. I miss my parents. They're abroad. Hong Kong.'

'Hong Kong!'

'Yup.'

'So why aren't you with them?'

'I like it here, plus my mum and dad are busy. They're go-getters. High-flyers. Over-achievers.' His voice was a little bitter and he stopped for a minute, looking out at the horizon. 'Still, it's easier for me here. My aunt's pretty cool. I don't have to pretend to be something I'm not. I was at a boarding school for a while – lasted five years actually – but I hated it. So I came here.'

He didn't need to explain. Leo looked at me as if he wanted to be understood, so I looked away.

We started to walk again and that was easier.

'Careful,' he said, as the ground turned boggy under-foot near a stile that led over a hedge and into a field. He reached out to take my elbow to steer me through the mud. That was twice he'd touched me.

Sue was in the barn grooming a pony, who Peter instantly went over to pet. It was nice to see him like that, racing forward, not checking behind. Sue's face radiated welcome; my shoulders dropped and I breathed.

'Ah, home at last,' she said, 'Good. Leo, I'm going in for a cup of tea – bring Audrey and Peter.'

'We should go,' I said, edging backwards, not wanting to intrude.

'Why?' Peter interrupted. 'I'm hungry. You made me walk miles and miles.'

'Come in for just a minute?' asked Leo. 'We have cake. Anything you like.' And, looking at my brother's face, I couldn't refuse.

The minute grew into thirty, and then an hour. It was so warm in Sue's kitchen that it was easy just to sink into the sofa and watch Leo filling the kettle, making tea, feed-ing the dog, singing along to the radio. Time washed over us and I looked down, my mug wrapped in my hands, tak-ing tiny sips, making it last. This cup of tea was the nicest thing ever.

Leo

The fact that he'd asked her to come inside, drink tea, eat cake, didn't actually mean he liked her any more than he liked anyone else. Leo walked back from seeing them home to the Grange, ready for Sue's teasing; he knew exactly what she was going to say. That he'd never brought a girl home before, that he'd fussed over her like she was a delicate flower. Leo stopped, turned, looked behind him. That place. The smell of it came to him again: damp, cold. Like something had recently died there. They must have got the rent cheap, that'd be what it was.

He would walk home with her. That would be fine. If he had to have a friend, well, why not her? And the fact that he liked watching her face and her eyes shift and change. He couldn't help that, could he?

His mum called when he got in and Sue passed the phone, turning back to her crossword.

'Hey, Mum, how's it going?' Leo rested his legs on the table and Sue batted them with her paper.

'Leo. We're well. And you?'

'Fine, all good here.' He winked at Sue and she sighed: she'd berate him later, looking over the top of her half-moon specs, for being offhand. Then instantly forget it.

'Excellent. I was thinking about you today – we went to

a wonderful concert and it made me miss you. Miss your playing.'

'Oh.' And then she was off on one about the piano concerto, one he'd played when he was thirteen and what a talent he had and how sad she was that it was going unused. All the money that had been spent on lessons, the hours of practice, blah blah blah. Leo could see it now. In his dinner jacket, bum fluff on his upper lip, his Adam's apple bobbing, stiff as a board, taking his applause; Mum in her black evening dress, elegant in the front row. Thank God he was out of it. Maybe he could interrupt, tell her about Audrey. See what she thought. But he stopped himself. He knew what she'd say. No. She could dismiss another human being in just one damning syllable, easy as that. *Not our sort of people.*

'So, I'll be back at half-term. And you'll come up to London. All right, darling?'

'Yeah, looking forward to it, Mum.'

'Yes, not *yeah*.' She spoke with a cut-glass accent. Used to swipe him one when he copied the children in the park near their London flat.

Leo liked voices, sounds, the weirder the better and Audrey's voice was rustling leaves. It scratched at something in him, made him feel like sitting down to listen, although she'd said almost nothing this afternoon, her eyes full stops.

'Yes, Mother,' Leo countered with a dramatic sigh.

'Good,' she said. 'Lots of love then, darling.'

'Love you too, Mum.' Why would you say that, aged seventeen? Leo did though, always.

'You too, darling. Now go and do something extremely useful. Right?'

'Sure.' Whatever, he thought when he put the phone down. His mum clearly hadn't been listening when Graham said no pressure.

Sue didn't have a piano and she didn't give a damn about his exams either; she seemed to forget he had his mocks coming up in January. The word homework didn't even belong in her vocabulary. No doubt his mother would make up for that when he saw her next month. He'd have to take ear plugs.

Maybe tomorrow he'd tell Audrey about the fair and see if she was up for it. And if not that, then something else. Graham was right – he did need friends.

Audrey

The next day after school I didn't wait for Leo but pulled Peter off to the bus. The evening before had been too much. We couldn't expect to go round there all the time, making a nuisance of ourselves. But when we got back to the Grange the flat was dark and I heard a hiss, something scurrying into the kitchen. I slammed the front door shut and leant against it, not ready to go inside.

'Hide-and-seek?' I said. Peter chucked down his bag and was off – running down two flights of stairs, dashing along the corridors.

'Stop,' I shouted. 'Not down there.' And I pulled my brother back and up to the top of the house. The fire escape – I'd seen it from the outside and now we'd found it. *Good job*, I thought.

We were on top of the world. From here Peter's kestrel might really be close enough to touch if it came swinging by.

'Awesome,' Peter agreed, reaching up into the late evening sky that seemed so near we could climb the clouds, the long white bands unfurling like sails. Suddenly the house was a pirate ship and I was the captain, Peter the first mate.

'Ahoy there,' I called, taking up position at the wheel. He climbed the rigging, jogging up and down the first flight of steps, making them rattle and clatter like snapping castanets – and we were in Spain, I told him, drawing into port, dropping off our cargo of ivory, apes and peacocks, sandalwood and cedarwood and sweet white wine. Peter paused, looked up at me, bored of me reciting poems at him. Wanting some facts.

'What's it really like in Spain?'

'Hot,' I said, looking into the distance. The whole sea was in the sky, rose-pink clouds morphing into a cutlass, a flag, intrepid divers with spears chasing fish and whales, mermaids combing their long flowing hair, flicking their tails.

'Can we go there for a holiday?' Peter asked. 'Luke from my last class went to Spain every year.'

'We're right there now, Pete,' I told him. 'Look.'

We stared together, sitting on the top step.

'See, we're in the market – look there, the piles of slimy octopus, shrimp, fat red tomatoes.'

'Yuck.'

'No, it's good, different – breathe in – the air's full of spice, hot and delicious. You smell it? Your skin's all warm, golden with the sun; you smell yummy too, of sun-tan lotion, the seaside. Fresh air.'

He pulled a face, so then I told him about the beaches: golden sand, clear blue sea, waves to ride. All of us – even me, not afraid – splashing, laughing, getting hot and sipping ice-cold drinks, licking ice cream.

'Let's ask Mum if we can go,' he said, his face full of the thought.

'It would be nice if we could. Tell you what, when I've

left school and got a job – next year maybe, or the year after – I'll save up and take you. OK?'

'OK.' He nodded, edged closer, thumb back in his mouth. He was really too old for that now. I put my arm round him.

'We should go in, it's getting chilly.'

Before I pulled him inside I took one last look at the horizon, the long blue sunset, spreading its arms round the edges of the planet. Then something caught my eye, something real: a flash of white dipping in and out of the trees, getting closer. Peter was pulling at me.

'Hang on.'

We watched together as the figure approached. Tall. Fast. Still too far away to see me if I waved, which I wouldn't. What made me blush, I don't know; perhaps the thought of calling out. Saying his name like I had a right to.

'Is it Leo?' Peter leant on tiptoes over the railing, arms waving. I pulled him back.

'Come on. Let's get something to eat. Mum's been shopping. She's made her spag bol. Fancy it?' I didn't want Leo to spot me. What if he banged on the door and stepped inside and started asking questions again? He was all right, maybe, but Peter and I were OK on our own. We didn't need other people. And Leo was too different. We couldn't really be friends.

I stared down. Leo was nearer. Fast. Something told me I had to trust someone, some time. But how could you be sure? How did you know who?

October

Leo

The first Saturday evening in October, they gathered at the table. Sue had made roast lamb. 'No, not one of ours,' she said, laughing in response to a question from Peter.

Lorraine and Sue laughed some more. Leo wasn't sure when this soirée had been organized but he wished Sue had consulted him. He got the feeling he was being set up. Or that Sue was lonely, and both thoughts made him worry.

Audrey wasn't looking at him though – she was busy chopping up Peter's dinner into bite-sized chunks. Leo cleared his throat.

'So,' he said when she'd eventually finished and had begun to eat her own food. 'How's it going?' She had started vanishing, just as he'd started to look out for her, so they hadn't spoken in a while.

'Yeah, I'm all right; just the same.' Her voice: soft, gruff, like smoke. It was at odds with everything else about her. The sharp bones of her face, the long sweeping line of her neck.

'Good.' Leo poured water into their glasses. 'I'm glad.'

'You don't have to keep asking me, you know,' she said, and then turned away to help Peter with his drink and stop him feeding his dinner to Mary. Leo hunted for another topic, rolling his eyes when he was sure she wouldn't see.

'So, what about school? Are your teachers all right?'

'Mostly.' Audrey brushed her fringe out of the way and looked at him properly. 'I like English. This book, about Jane Eyre; that's good.'

'It is, isn't it?'

'You've read it?' She sounded surprised.

'Yes.' He'd studied the Brontës at his old school; it felt like forever ago.

'I like how when that cousin beats her up she doesn't take it; she fights him,' Audrey said, her face serious but with something gleeful dancing in her eyes. Leo wanted to laugh again, but he coughed instead and concentrated on his dinner for a second.

'That's right,' he said. 'I forgot about him. He comes to a sorry end.'

Audrey shot him a look. 'Don't flipping tell me what happens.'

'Sorry.' Leo sucked in his cheeks and raised his eyebrows while she stared at him as if he were an idiot. Were all their conversations going to be this weird?

After they'd cleared the table, Leo helped Sue carry in bowls of apple crumble and ice cream. He went to put one down before Audrey. Her eyes flicked towards her mother.

'It's all right, Leo, Aud's allergic. I'll take that,' said Lorraine, reaching out and helping herself to Audrey's portion as well as her own.

'Oh. OK, well, I'll get you something else, then – fruit, Audrey, all right?' he said. She looked again at Lorraine and then nodded.

They finished the meal and Leo beckoned Audrey into the living room, leading her to a wall of shelves crammed with books.

'When you've finished with Jane you might like this.'

He found *Wuthering Heights* and put it into her hands.

'Have you read all these books?' She examined the cover, then ran her eyes up and down and along the titles.

'No.' He laughed again. 'Maybe a quarter, if that.'

'Why not? If they were my books, I'd have read them all,' she said, her voice outraged, and he sat down, giving up. The television was on for Peter, and Leo pretended to watch with him as Audrey settled herself into an armchair, legs tucked against her chest, burrowing into the novel.

Voices drifted from the kitchen; Sue and Lorraine were taking their time over coffee and Leo wondered what they had in common. A few things, he supposed. He listened more carefully, trying to hear what was being said, didn't much like the sound of it and cleared his throat. He wanted to talk to Audrey. That would definitely be more fun.

'So you like reading?'

'Yeah, I had some books, poetry books mostly. But not any more.'

'What happened to them?'

'I dunno. I lost them.'

That was odd, but he didn't ask and Audrey didn't elaborate. *Blood, stone*, he thought, shaking his head, then he caught her watching him before her eyes darted away, back to the page.

Audrey

Not much happened in the sticks. We went to Sue's for dinner – well, they called it supper, which sounded silly to me – and then after that every day was the same. I didn't mind though; there was enough to do with just getting Peter ready in the mornings and getting to school on time and remembering where everything was, the names of other kids and teachers and making sure there was something for our tea. I had the book from Leo and homework, and Mum was working all the time. The book went everywhere with me, in case it disappeared, and because maybe I wanted to be like that Catherine Earnshaw, half savage and hardy and free, and, well, just because. Mum came home with flowers one day, windswept and bright-eyed.

'Look at these, Aud.' Her cheeks were flushed with pleasure and I buried my face in the bouquet of roses and breathed in. They smelled of nothing, but I didn't say so.

'Who gave you them? They're lovely, Mum.'

'Oh, one of my patients. A lovely bloke. I've been caring for his son. Poor little lad. But, hey, we do our best. And it's nice to be appreciated,' she said, then frowned. 'I don't know why your dad couldn't have shown a bit of bloody appreciation, Aud, then we wouldn't be in this mess, would we?' I didn't know what that meant and didn't ask. But I knew how much Mum's patients loved her.

They were lucky to have her and they knew it too; she fussed over them worse even than she fussed over me. Sometimes they wrote her notes, gave her flowers – like these ones – or chocolates. Mum kept the thank-you letters sealed up in a special folder, said it kept her going when she felt low.

'Well,' she said, 'put them in water for me, Aud, arrange them. And then do us a cuppa, would you, while I watch a bit of telly? I'm knackered.'

I nodded and arranged the flowers, placing them in the living room where she could see them. She nodded absent-mindedly, checking her face in her compact mirror, tweezering her eyebrows, then turning back to the television and flicking through the channels before checking her mobile phone.

Time passed. Our fourth week in the Grange Mum was working nights so I had to get Peter up for school on time. So far October had been nothing but rain and the mornings were colder and darker. On Thursday we overslept.

'Pete, come on.' I pulled him gently out of his dreams. 'We'll be late if we don't hurry.'

He snuggled deeper under the covers, so I tickled and cajoled until he pulled himself up and crammed down some breakfast. It was almost half eight already. The pills from the new GP knocked me out and it was hard to really wake up. I made myself coffee. Swigged it back, poured another.

'Come on, mate,' I said. 'Piggyback.'

I hitched my brother on to my back and set out across

the field towards the route Leo had shown us. It was definitely the quickest way, but we were still going to be late.

Peter clung to my shoulders.

'Hold on,' I said. 'Wrap your legs round, I'm going to
try and run.'

It was more of a hobble: he was heavy and I was slow
and the ground was so muddy that I slithered and slipped,
but I set my shoulders forward, ploughed on as if I meant
to turn up the soil, plant a story of our own whatever the
cost. Peter liked it, laughing and cheering me on.

'Go faster, Aud! Come on!'

I couldn't. When we got to the embankment he slid off
my back while I bent over to catch my breath. It wasn't
just that; it was my ankle too. It always got like this when
the weather was bad. Mum said I might need another op
on it some time, but I couldn't face the thought of that.

'I want another piggyback,' Peter said when I stood up,
so I hauled him up again, shifting him higher, and plod-
ded along. He kicked and waggled his legs like I was a
horse he could persuade to go faster and I laughed, losing
more breath, almost losing my footing. It was pointless. I
stopped and tried to gather myself.

'Maybe you should walk, Peter,'

'No way. This is better.'

'Yeah, for you maybe. But you're getting heavy, mate.'

'But there's someone coming. Look. Race them.'

I swung round. Of course. Leo: pelting along like he
was in the Olympics in a dark-blue hoody and mud-stained
trainers. His cheeks were pink. His eyes bright and amused.

'What are you two up to?' he said, looking at Peter first,

then at me. 'I saw you in the distance, thought I'd catch up.' He grabbed a breath. 'You all right?'

'Yeah, I was just trying to get Peter to school on time. But he's heavy.'

'No, you're not, are you?' Leo said, grabbing Peter and swinging him up on to his shoulders like he weighed nothing. Peter squealed, half in fear, half in delight.

'Come on, then,' Leo said, and off we went again. I just about kept pace, jogging all the way to town, my heart punching against my ribs.

We dropped Peter off, just in time. For once he didn't look round or check over his shoulder to stare at me with wide woebegone eyes. For once he ran along without a murmur and I was glad. Leo checked his watch.

'We're the ones who'll be late at this rate,' he said.

'I know.'

'So, come on.'

When we got to the road Leo moved to walk beside me, his body between mine and the cars.

'It's busy,' he said, 'the traffic's ridiculous at this time of day.' And I understood that he meant to shield me as a gentleman might his lady and a great hot blush began in my chest and ran its fingers up my neck and face and scalp. Taken, Lizzy had said. I wondered if he walked with her like this.

'I'm OK,' I said, but he stayed right next to me and slowed his stride to match my steps. Our arms brushed when the pavement narrowed and I jumped away like he'd got me with a cattle prod. He pretended not to notice, and I pretended I hadn't done it. Staring straight ahead, I walked. Never looking at Leo. Well, not that much – once, maybe twice.

'Thanks for the rescue,' I said, thinking about how he'd carried my brother all that way and with a smile on his face and everything. Not a lot of people would do that.

'No problem. Although for it to be a proper rescue mission, there ought to have been a white horse with a flowing mane and I should have been in armour. I think that's how it goes, at least.'

'Oh, I don't mean like that.' He made me feel silly. I wasn't a damsel in distress.

'No?'

'No, well, I don't know.' I looked at him, no idea what to say. Was he flirting with me or something? I stared at the floor and tried to rearrange my face to make it bland and neutral. Blank. But I was blushing like an idiot. If I actually wanted him to flirt with me, that was worse. Especially if he wasn't. Oh, I just didn't know.

Leo

'So.' He hunted for another topic, something easier. 'You coming to the fair?' It was at the weekend and now he knew he really wanted her to come. With him. Even if she only wanted to talk about the books he hadn't read.

'I dunno.'

'Well, it should be good.' He nudged her, very gently.

'Oh.' Audrey blushed, her cheeks flaring a hotter pink. Leo was confused again; damn – this was all over the place. He forged on, determined to save the conversation even if he ended up making an idiot of himself. *Try and make her laugh*, he thought. *Employ wit, irony, anything. Break the ice all over again.*

'You don't have to – it's not a required extra-curricular activity.'

'What?' Audrey was the one wearing armour. Leo shifted, trying to stand so she'd see him, alarmed at his inability to flirt. Had he always been this bad?

'Nothing. Joke, not funny.' She giggled then. She had a great smile. Really goofy, it took up half of her face. There, mission accomplished. She was still glowing from their run. But her glasses needed cleaning, he noticed, her shoes too – she was covered in mud but she hadn't complained.

'You will come though?' His mouth had a mind of its

own. Straight away he wished he hadn't said it. Desperate, or what.

'All right, well, if I can. I'll have to bring Peter.'

'That's cool. You should meet more people. Have fun. Otherwise it'll get rather dull, won't it, stuck in the Grange the whole time. All work, no play. And so on.' He sounded like Graham now, doling out life lessons and clichés, and cringed. Maybe he should go into social work. Maybe he should back off.

'Maybe. Just, well, I don't know; I'd better go,' Audrey said, moving away, shaking her hair back, her chin jutting up with that defiant pride. She started to walk away, but Leo followed; he couldn't stop himself. Now he noticed that she was limping a bit, trying to hide it.

'Audrey.' The bell was summoning them inside; Leo pretended not to hear it and when she paused and looked at him with her big solemn eyes he spoke without thinking.

'Is everything OK? Are you all right, Audrey?'

'Course. I'm fine. Totally fine.' Her expression changed, he felt a glare, and he knew he'd said the wrong thing again.

'Yeah? Good. Well . . .'

What was it he was going to say? Her face was a distraction, her eyes full of shadows, blue and grey and green. They were like water. The bottom of the sea. He wanted to take the glasses off, look properly. Stare for the rest of the day and work her out. A tricky equation. More like a sonnet. *My mistress' eyes are nothing like the sun*. He realized she was staring at him. They were staring at each other.

'Just, come if you can, yeah?'

'Sure.' And she smiled so sweetly; it was a pure sort of smile, no side to it. No flirty, sugary *let me hook you up and reel you in and get you dancing to my tune* kind of thing. And that had been worth the whole horrendous conversation.

Audrey

Everyone was talking about it. Jen shrugged, said it was something to do. Better than watching paint dry. I didn't tell her Leo had asked me. I wasn't sure if I'd said yes or not. But Lizzy hung over my desk, annoying me.

'You going tomorrow?'

I shrugged.

'We'll look out for you, if you do. See you in the haunted house. Whooooo!' she wailed in my face, then grinned, like that was funny. I didn't trust her smile or her shiny hair. She wasn't a flower; she was a weed. A foxglove.

'Whatever,' I said. 'I'm going with Leo, actually.' I don't know what made me say that. Her mouth fell open.

'God, you're a bitch, aren't you?' Lizzy said, and for a second I felt really mean until her mouth puckered into that tight little O! of disgust I'd learned to watch out for. Not bothered, it didn't matter, I talked back.

'I guess I must be, if you say so, since apparently you know everything.'

Jen linked my little finger with her own, shook. This was congratulations. I got back to my chapter – Heathcliff was shouting at Cathy again – hoping Lizzy hadn't seen my hands shaking as I turned the page, and she walked off with her gang, looking over their shoulders, not ready to give up yet.

The next afternoon when we got back to the flat there was a note pinned to the door. My name was on the envelope, written in black ink, in flowing writing. I snatched it, tore it. Gobbled the words: *Just in case you forgot. Fair tonight. I'll be the one in the armour. Love Leo.*

Love Leo. Boys did not write messages to me like that. That was the kind of thing that happened in one of Mum's soppy magazines, not real life. Nobody had ever asked me, me in particular, to go somewhere or be somewhere, as if I were important. As if my presence would make a difference. I hadn't known I was waiting to be chosen. And the fact that it was Leo who'd seen something he wanted. I swallowed and looked at Peter, who squinted his eyes.

'You look like you're going to be sick, Aud,' he said. 'Are you?'

'No,' I shouted, squealing and chasing him inside. 'No, I'm not.'

Peter darted ahead of me and we made for the kitchen.

'How about the fair, Pete? Shall we go?' I called, rummaging in the fridge for something to eat. I gave him a piece of cheese, then found some crackers in the cupboard. Peter's eyes widened as he nodded and chewed and I picked up my medication. Mum had left it out on the worktop, with a big note saying, DON'T FORGET!

'Really? Can we?' he said, pulling at my sleeve.

'Yup.' I popped the pill out of the foil. Held it in my hand. 'I'm going to have to try and find some money though. Help me look.'

Peter ran off and I stuffed the pill into the bin, grabbed

a glass, filled it with water and sipped a little, left it by the note, just in case.

We went through the pockets in Mum's old jacket, searched the bottom of her bag. Scraped together almost seven pounds. Peter emptied his money box and that gave us another fifty pence in coppers.

'Great. We'll get a hot dog each, maybe candy-floss too, and go on some rides and meet Leo. OK?' It came out in a big rush. We danced about a bit, holding hands. I swung him up and off his feet.

'Come on, then,' Peter said when I put him down, dragging me out, pulling me along, and even though I knew we shouldn't do it we left the Grange behind and jumped back into the world.

The field beyond the school flashed with noise. In the dark faces blinked neon, Halloween pumpkins, their skin too bright, back-lit. I didn't recognize anyone from school – no sign of Lizzy and her gang – or Jen either, but I held Peter's hand tight as we wound our way through the crowds of candy-floss, cherry-red sugar dummies, cheap teddies, yellow floating ducks. It would be easy to lose him here. The thought made my stomach drop and I squeezed harder.

'Ow,' Peter said, wriggling away. For a second I let go, too busy scanning the rides for Leo. He wouldn't come. He'd been taking the piss.

'C'mon, Aud,' called Peter, dragging at my arm. 'C'mon, I want to go on the waltzers. With you.'

Peter towed me into the crowd and we weaved through the swarm of kids and grown-ups, then clambered on to the ride, the metal steps ringing.

'Hey!' A shout. I startled, nearly jumped off again when Leo climbed in beside me.

'Found you.' He paid for the ride and I stuffed my money back in my purse as the seat juddered, then began to move. I held tight and a boy, face silly with freckles, hair frothing on his upper lip, grabbed our carriage, swung it round and we were spinning faster, out of control, into the swirling darkness, the techno beat pounding, pushing, pulsing in time with screams. Mine too. I screamed for the future, for the hopes that I didn't dare let out. I screamed because there was no one to stop me, no one watching, no one who cared.

Leo slid along the seat, crushing against me. 'Sorry,' he gasped, and I laughed, sandwiched between him and Peter, who was almost crazy with excitement, shouting at someone he recognized from school, waving, hands free.

'Hold on!' I yelled, screwing my eyes shut. We spun again: wild, jerking. When I opened my eyes the world was upside down.

Stop, I wanted to shout, although what I meant was, *Don't stop ever*, as we turned in faster circles, drilling into the sky, up and away, in a spin that was scary and loose, slipping because there was nothing to hold on to any more, flying stars in another Milky Way.

The ride groaned to an end and we tumbled back to solid ground. Leo held me up, dizzy, still spinning. My legs jelly. All this touching. In one night.

The things I said to Leo, like, 'I think I'm going to puke.' Which was not the thing to say to a boy like him.

And him not minding, holding my hair away from my face.

'Take deep breaths. It'll be all right.'

I took in lungfuls of air that smelled of grease and sugar but mostly excitement, and we stood not saying anything much when Peter disappeared into the crowds, and then we were weaving behind, holding hands somehow; how did that happen? I didn't know.

'Look,' Leo said, pulling me to the left, towards a stall. 'I love this. Bows and arrows. Let's win something.'

'All right.'

Half an eye on Peter queuing for the helter-skelter, I took the plastic bow and handed over my money. Lining up the arrow, I took aim. Leo was ready.

'After three,' he said, and counted us down. We released our shots. Mine hit home.

'Yes! I won,' I cried, stupidly excited, not caring. 'Look, see – it hit the bullseye. Yes!'

'I expected nothing less.' Leo was laughing too. 'Choose your prize. I'm having another go.'

I picked out a teddy bear, saggy, without enough stuffing, nothing like the plump and fluffy things that lined the shelves in my room. I used to love those bears. Then I started hating them and I didn't know why. This one looked sad, but sort of winsome with its forlorn, grey expression.

'Here.' I handed it to Leo, not thinking, just wanting to give him something, even if it was only this. 'You can have it.'

'What? No, you won it – it's yours. You shoot a mean arrow.'

'Don't you want it? Look, it's cute. And sad now you

don't want him.' The bear waved at him and wiped away an imaginary tear.

'Well, yeah, all right. Thanks.' He took it, smiling, inspecting the silly toy. 'I guess I'll have to think of something to call him.'

'Sad Sack,' I said, pulling a face. Leo chucked it in the air, caught it.

'He's not sad now, not now we've rescued him from the fair.'

'True.' There was a pause. I put my hands in my pockets. 'Where's Peter?'

Leo pointed; he was whizzing down the helter-skelter and we wandered over and grabbed him at the end.

'Can I go again? Can I, Aud?'

His hair was all over the place, his cheeks pink. I pulled him close, kissed his face, but he struggled free, wiping at his skin; he was desperate to be off. I held on to him as he wriggled and grumbled.

'It's all right – I'll take him,' said Leo, handing over another pound coin and chasing Peter up the metal steps.

I don't know how they balanced on the little hessian mat. Leo was way too big, but somehow he managed it, Peter safe on his knee, and they came whizzing down, whooping together. Peter stared up at Leo with a look I'd not seen in his eyes before. *Awe*, I thought, *hero worship*. Mum had a photo of me looking up at my dad with just the same expression. I swallowed down the lump in my throat.

'That was a laugh. What now?' Leo said, coming over and slinging his arm round me, perfectly casual, so casual that I didn't freeze. Well, not exactly. I must have been squeezing Peter's hand though.

'What's the matter, Aud?' Peter said, peering at me and pulling away.

'Nothing,' I whispered, still hiding behind my hair, 'nothing.'

'Ghost train?' Leo said, saving me.

'Yeah.' Peter jumped up and down, dropping my hand to hold Leo's and I let myself be dragged on to the ride.

Lizzy was a couple of places behind us in the queue. I pretended not to notice her when she hollered, 'Hey, Leo!' So loud he had to turn and look at her, but he just nodded and then we clambered into a car and were off, jolting into the dark. Peter jumped against me as a skeleton dropped into our path and I squeezed him closer.

'Pete, it's pretend. It's fine.' I could hear Lizzy screaming too and that made me grin. She should try living in the Grange if she wanted to know about scary. Leo took my hand again and we held Peter between us.

'That was fun,' I said. 'Thanks.' We climbed off, still laughing, jelly legs.

'More?'

'No, we should go.'

'Seriously, it's early,' Leo said, scanning the field. 'I'll buy you more candy-floss?'

'No, we really should go,' I said, not wanting to, wondering if he'd take us back to the farm if I asked. The flat would be dark and cold. No way was I going to sleep on my own in my room. Peter wouldn't mind if I crawled in with him. We stood for a bit. I looked at Leo again. He was tall and broad and looked warm and clean, his cheeks bright from the cold, his hair a bit tousled. He suited messy. The thing about Leo was, he made you feel safe. He made you feel OK about things. Peter felt it too.

'Sorry,' I said to Leo. 'Mum'll be worried.' He opened his mouth to answer, but I gabbled on, like someone had flicked a switch and all the words I'd never meant to say were fighting with one another to be heard: 'But, well, this was good, you know, so thanks for inviting us and everything. It's been fun. Really.'

'Good. I'm glad you came,' Leo said.

'Yeah, well, I was going to ask you –'

'What?'

'Well, I have this essay; it's about that Jane Eyre book. And, I kind of didn't go to school that much last year, not really, because I wasn't that well, and now I want to do the essay but I got stuck. I did try, and then I thought, would you help me? Give me a couple of pointers?' Hot coals in my cheeks, my eyes thick and stupid, I toed the earth with my shoe, grinding a hole which I hoped might swallow me up if he said no. I hadn't planned on saying any of it, but I really did want to do well. And I wanted to see him again. Soon. He jumped on my words, speaking fast too.

'No, seriously, that'd be fine, cool. Tomorrow? I'll come over?'

I nodded and grabbed Peter's hand and ran, excited now for the next day, for what would happen and for the night I'd had and how I had another friend and everything was getting better at last.

Leo

Audrey disappeared too fast for him to stop her, and then he didn't want to follow in case she thought he was some sort of stalker. He'd thought she'd stay out longer; it was only nine, and things were only just revving up. Then again, he'd see her tomorrow, he thought, as he wandered around for a while on his own, carrying the teddy by its arm, wondering if he should dump it. In the end he couldn't do it. A group of kids from school huddled in a group by the ghost train and called out to him to join them, but it wasn't fun any more. Especially not when Lizzy caught up with him.

'Saw you before,' she said.

'Yeah?' Leo walked on.

'With Mental.' Lizzy opened her mouth round the candy-floss, twirled her tongue into the sugar.

'What?'

'You with that new girl. What are you doing hanging around with her?' She waited, and when he didn't respond, taunted again, 'She's mental. Didn't you hear what she did in Maths? She passed out, just like flat out on the desk and no one could wake her up. There was dribble all over. It was disgusting. She's rank. Really manky.'

'Oh, whatever, Lizzy. Just forget it, right?' There'd been one party, last summer – Leo remembered now – and

Lizzy had been drunk. So had he. She'd sat on his knee, her hands worming on his thighs. He should have pushed her away. Big mistake.

Lizzy was grinning, her eyes small and hard, and although Leo had never sworn at a girl he felt like it then.

'You know what,' Lizzy shouted after him as Leo strode away, 'I'll find out the full story for you. Then you'll thank me.'

He walked faster, didn't look back, didn't listen, left the field and went to meet Sue, who'd been visiting a friend in town and would give him a ride back.

'Good night?' she said, starting the car. He fiddled with the radio, tuning out of Radio 4, looking for something loud to stop him thinking.

'Leo?'

'Yeah, I guess so. Audrey didn't hang around long. I got bored after that.' Got harassed after that. Lizzy, what a cow. What a mean-hearted, cruel creature. She was so spiteful. Why did girls get like that? It was so pointless and boring.

'Well, I suppose if she had her brother with her she had to get him home. He's only little.'

'True. Yeah.' It was a good point. It could explain why she'd dashed away. He should have walked them home.

'I shouldn't worry if I were you.'

'OK. I won't worry.' He glanced up at his aunt and half smiled.

'It's sweet though.' She squeezed his hand, just once, quickly, and winked.

'Stop it. We're just friends. I'm going over there

tomorrow, to help Aud with some homework, OK?' He'd
sensed something wild in Audrey tonight, a spirit she
kept tamped down, and Leo wanted more of that. His old
life had shown him enough straight and boring to last
him forever: a book full of straight ruled lines covered in
uniform script, the answers perfectly performed, gram-
matically correct. But then, without warning, pages and
pages of scribble. Black and hard and gouging through it
all. Until this: like a poem, the words had begun to shine.
Leo rubbed his forehead, squeezed his eyes shut, then
opened them again and stared straight ahead, impatient to
be home, impatient to be asleep so tomorrow could start.

'Sure. Good,' Sue said. 'She's a nice girl. Pretty too.
Lovely, actually, although I agree – not your usual type.
Not like those glamorous creatures I've seen in your pho-
tos on Facebook.' Sue raised her eyebrows. Glamour
wasn't her scene.

'Who says they're my type? They're just girls, Sue. Old
friends. Who I don't even keep in touch with any more.'

'Just suggesting. Anyway, Audrey seems very sweet-
natured. If anything, she'll be a good friend.'

Leo nodded. It was true, he liked her. A lot.

'I think she's . . .' He searched for a word he could use
with Sue, settled on something objective, that didn't make
him sound too serious, too involved. 'She's kind of
enigmatic.'

Sue chuckled. 'Aha. Enigmatic.'

'What?' Leo shrugged his shoulders, his arms wide,
empty. 'You know, you could read a subtext into anything,

Sue.' He put his hands in his hair, then rubbed them furiously over his face.

'Leo, calm down. You know I'm just teasing. I'm glad you've found someone you like. I was beginning to worry.'

He nodded. Sue was deep, deeper than their banter suggested. And discreet. She'd had her own problems – life events, she called them now, which didn't do justice to her story at all. He liked how she could be so pragmatic though, and took a deep breath, fixed his thoughts on the morning, wiping out the bits of the night Lizzy had spoiled.

Audrey

'Where've you been?' Mum said. Her breath came in short sharp bursts as she stood in the hall, illuminated, the lights burning so bright they hurt my eyes. I squinted up at her.

'Just out, sorry – it's OK, we're here now.' I tried to hustle Peter past her and up to his room. It was way past his bedtime and I knew he'd be tired in the morning. 'Sorry,' I said again.

'You don't just go out, Aud. You know better than that.' Mum grabbed my jacket, reeling me in.

'Well, you weren't here to ask, were you?' I bit my lip. That had come out wrong. Peter went ahead and I gestured that he should go and clean his teeth.

'Because I was at work earning money, which you've just been out throwing down the drain. Who've you been with?'

'No one. We went to the fair. I'm sorry, all right?'

'No, Audrey, it isn't. I've been going spare. What if something had happened?'

'What do you want me to say?' I asked, turning back to look at her. Mum stepped forward and gripped my wrist with her left hand and poured whatever she'd been holding in her right into my palm.

'What's this?' she said.

It was my pills. She'd found the ones in the bin, the

ones down the side of the sofa. The ones under my mattress. I swallowed and didn't dare look at her. I should have chucked them somewhere else, somewhere she'd never have found them. Into the moat, that would have been better. Under the water.

'Audrey —' she was shaking her head — 'do you realize what you're doing? Do you realize how stupid you're being?' Her voice got panicky, tighter and tighter. 'If you don't take your pills, you'll get very poorly, Aud.'

'I won't. I have been taking them. I have. Just . . . just not all of them, Mum,' I said, trying not to cry, a throb beginning to beat between my ears, like your heart underwater, swollen and heavy. 'They make me feel worse.'

Mum pulled me to her and held me so tight I almost couldn't breathe. The pounding grew louder, pulsing in my brain, until, with my hands over my ears it was all I could hear.

Leo

The next morning Lorraine answered the door, a bright smile on her face. He stepped inside. The flat smelled better than before. She'd been hanging pictures, had a hammer in her hand, nails. A gust of air blew past and he heard a door slam somewhere.

'Oh, hello, it's Leo, isn't it?' Lorraine said, and Leo smiled back, shifting from one foot to another, then standing up straight, shoulders back.

'Yeah, hi. I'm here to see Audrey. Homework?' He gestured at his books. He'd brought them all, as if that proved it was his only motivation.

'Oh. Oh, I'm sorry.' Lorraine pulled a face, sympathetic, a bit sad. 'Audrey's not well this morning. Stupid girl's not been taking her meds and got herself in a state. She gets bad sometimes, you know. So, she was up all night and so was I, sitting with her. I'll have to take her to the doctor later, I reckon – she won't be up for homework, Leo. Not today.'

It was a lot of information all at once. Audrey had seemed fine to him at the fair though. Better than fine: lovely, like Sue said. He felt his heart, pierced a little with last night and now the disappointment of not seeing her. Leo followed Lorraine, trying to catch everything. She bustled into the kitchen, put down the tools and grabbed the kettle.

'Do you want a drink? Something to eat? Peter's watching a DVD. You can sit with him if you like, or stay and chat to me.' She looked at him, slowly, waiting, her hands stuffed into the tight pockets in her jeans. When he didn't answer she gabbled on: 'I'll understand if you're busy. I've had to take the day off work myself to stay home and look after Aud.'

Lorraine offered him a chocolate biscuit. He took one. It seemed best to be polite.

'Can I see her?'

'Better not, love, not till she's feeling brighter. She won't want you seeing her in the state she's in.' She pulled another strange face, as if she had a series of masks, he thought, and this one made her neck tighten, the veins standing out like ropes. Under her make-up her face was pale; there were bags under her eyes.

'Is she really unwell?'

Lorraine nodded slowly, but he didn't want to pry.

'I'd better go, then. But will you tell her I called? Say, when she's ready, if she still wants me to help . . .'

'Sure. And give my love to Sue, won't you? Tell her I'm still on for Wednesday. Looking forward to it.'

Leo walked away from the Grange and paused as he crossed the moat. The water levels had crept higher and a rank smell rose from the surface, which was clouded with weeds and leaves. Something was rotting down there, he thought, and even the vaguest reflection was obscured by the thick black sludge. Glancing back at the house, he stared at the window he thought might be Audrey's, but the curtains were closed and the window was shut. Even if he called, she wouldn't hear. He hoped Lorraine would give her his message.

Audrey

Mum sent him away; she thought I didn't hear. This was the start of it. I was a fly in a bottle, a rabbit trapped in wire, and the shine of the fair was dying like a cheap glow stick run dull. I should never have said anything to Leo about coming over, that was the problem. That and the Thing. I paced the room, three steps forward, three steps back, touched the walls with cold fingers, feeling the slick damp slime of water on my skin.

It had been waiting for me last night. Mum had put me to bed, my head still pounding, and then it had started. The thud in the back of my neck, the rumble in my brain, like a train, like a lorry, out of control, veering off edges, ploughing from high bridges and sailing into deep water. The sink and pull of the beat, metronomic, impossible, forced me out of bed and I marched to its tune, rubbing my arms, twisting my fingers, and tried not to hear the stories that bubbled in my brain. Stories of girls who would come up from the water, of how they were pushed, and how they died down there and how I would too: choking and strangled by weeds and the will of invisible hands.

'Why did you have to spoil it?' I whispered. 'Why?'

The Thing had gone, but my head was hungover with those dreams. I watched Leo walk away. We were supposed to have changed; Mum said this was home. But I was frightened and alone again and everything was as it always had been.

I shut my mouth and lay back down and listened to the water. It lurched and churned and everything I'd nearly had was sinking deep and under.

Leo

Audrey came back to school the following Wednesday. Leo had been looking out for her and when he saw her in the corridor she seemed different. He almost hadn't spotted her, if he was honest. The fire had gone; in its place a pale shadow, dark circles under her eyes.

'Hey.' He walked over and stopped her with a gentle hand on her arm. She flinched and stepped back as if to skirt round him, then seemed to reconsider.

'Are you OK?' Leo said, because this time he really did want to know. She didn't look quite right; Lorraine had been telling the truth after all. He'd wondered if maybe she'd been putting him off.

'Are you better? I'm sorry you weren't well. I came over – did your mum tell you?' he said.

She nodded and sort of smiled, her eyes blinking too fast, checking over her shoulder. Her shoelaces were untied, he noticed, her jumper on inside out. But her hair was neat and tidy, the long blonde wave tamed into two schoolgirl plaits.

'I can come again, if you like. Help with the essay?'

'No. That's OK. I've done it.'

'Oh, fine. Good, well, shall I wait for you after school? I was going to go to the talk, you know, this archaeology thing? Do you fancy it?' He was determined not to lose the thread, sure he could get through if he kept trying, pull closer; mend this.

'I have to get Pete.' Her face was so hard to read today, opaque. Leo shifted his bag on to the other shoulder, the bell signalling the end of break telling him to get a move on. Right, so try something else.

'Oh, yeah, I forgot. Shame. Well, do you want to get together tomorrow, then?' This was starting to look like desperation. No more, Leo. This was her last chance.

'No. Thanks though,' she said, and walked away, hurrying into her classroom.

Audrey disappeared for the rest of the week. As the next few days drifted past, blurring into the weekend, he began to wonder if the way he thought she'd looked at him had been real. Well, he was busy with his work, with the farm, helping Sue and with his running, a bit of drawing, reading. He had enough to do. But still, when he thought of Audrey now, he didn't quite believe that he'd ever held her hand or that she'd smiled and screamed like she was on fire.

Audrey

Most days were OK. Never better than that though, and I tried to forget that there could be more. OK would have to do.

At least I had school, a safe place to go, so long as Lizzy wasn't bothering me. She didn't tend to when I was with Jen. Jen was solid, a proper girl, and I liked sitting with her and having what I had decided to call a friend.

'You know what?' Jen said to me the week after the fair, looking up and staring across the cafeteria, chewing her sandwich slowly.

'No, what?'

'Leo Bright is permanently staring at you, Aud.'

My head swam, different dizzy, and I looked for my stomach, which had dived to the floor. I was trying not to think about Leo; it was dangerous to even look his way. I had put the night of the fair away, shut it up safe, and I couldn't let myself go there or feel like that again. But it was all I wanted, really. That wild, free feeling and Leo's arm round me. I remembered the scratch of his thick duffle coat on my cheek and how his hand was bigger than mine.

'He isn't,' I muttered, not following the line of Jen's gaze in case I caught his eye and he came over. Jen turned to me and grinned.

'If I were you, I'd be well chuffed. He's cool. And sweet, really nice. One of the few guys in the sixth form who'll even acknowledge us pathetic Year Elevens exist. You should capitalize on this, Audrey.' There were a lot of things Jen thought I ought to do: go round to her house, meet her older mates who didn't go to college, go to gigs with her, exhibitions in town, even stay the night. She kept inviting; I kept saying no. Soon she'd get it, and then what?

'Yeah, he is nice,' I had to say, because I owed it to Leo. He was better than nice, but I couldn't find the words for it, for how he made me feel. 'He lives near us. So I know him a bit.'

'And?'

'And nothing.' I laughed and shrugged, trying to get the message across. 'Anyway, I've got to go.'

Mum was waiting outside school in the car. She drove fast to the surgery.

'So,' said Mum, 'you're getting on all right, then?' She took my hand, examined my fingernails and tutted.

I nodded. I was all right. Mainly because of Jen.

'But Pete's lonely, I think, Mum. I'm worried about him.' I took my hand back and folded my arms.

'Oh, he'll settle in. It's an upheaval. Kids at that age are adaptable, so don't fuss, Aud. You've got yourself to be thinking of.'

'Yeah, well, I don't want him to be sad, do I?'

'And I do?'

'I didn't say that.'

I stared at the clock. I was missing English now. Then French. And I'd learned my vocab.

'It should be Dr Caldwell again,' said Mum. I nodded.

'So, you tell her everything, right?'

'Yeah, OK.'

We were in and out in five minutes. Mum dropped me back at school and drove off to work. Dr Caldwell had looked at me, listened to Mum, printed the prescription and off we'd gone. Mum had picked up the pills, then ripped open the packaging and handed me one in the car.

'There. You'll feel better now. And don't forget to pick your brother up. I'm working late.'

'OK, Mum. All right.' I swallowed it and kissed her cheek. She tasted chalky and hot. Too much powder.

'See you, Mum,' I called as she drove away, the horn tooting just once.

Jen and I often went to the art block at lunchtime. She could really draw – her pictures were up all over school, of cows and horses and sheep. She gave them personality; I hadn't thought a sheep could have a personality. My chin in my hand, I watched her, admiring the speed of her pencils, how she knew where to shade, light and dark. She looked up and grinned at me, then pulled a new piece of paper in front of her.

'Right. Stay there,' she said.

'What?'

'Just keep still.'

I realized what she was up to and opened my mouth to protest.

'No, be quiet. Don't ruin it. I don't usually do people. But I reckon I'll give you a try, Audrey.'

'Do you have to?' I muttered.

'Course. Just sit there and be still for ten minutes. All right?'

So she had me. And when Leo walked in I couldn't move or even look in the other direction, but I saw Jen's mouth twitch when he walked over, although her hand never paused.

'Hey, Jen. Audrey,' Leo said, looking at Jen mostly. Only once at me. It made my eyes hot. His thick dark hair was its usual mess. His mouth was still smiling, but it wasn't the same. Something inside began to sink.

'That's good,' he said, looking at Jen's half-finished sketch.

'You think?'

'Yeah. I do. Very –' He paused. I waited to hear what he was going to say. What word he would choose. But he didn't finish the sentence, just shrugged, and that hurt too. It wasn't supposed to hurt, I was supposed to have forgotten about the fair and how kind he was and how much I liked him. Because Leo was a good person. I felt that, like I felt sure that the sky was forever and that Peter was precious and that everyone deserved a chance.

'Look –' Jen suddenly stood up – 'I'll be back in a tick. Just need to ask Mrs Moore something, OK.'

And she abandoned me there, and I was alone with Leo, for the first time in ages. He shoved his hands deeper into his pockets, then folded himself into Jen's chair, leaning forward across the desk.

'You OK?'

I nodded.

'Sure?'

'Yeah.' God, what did he think?

'Good. So, you know, I've been meaning to say . . . Your mum told you about our annual bonfire party?'

'What bonfire party?' It was the first I'd heard of it.

'Oh, well, it's in half-term, Saturday evening. Sue says she's invited you all, but I just wanted to mention it and say, well, I'm looking forward to it. To seeing you there. That is if you're coming?'

'I dunno. Mum doesn't like going out much.'

'Really? But she and Sue are quite pally, aren't they? So, hopefully she'll have remembered. Do come, if you can.'

'OK.'

'I mean it, I'd like it. Like to see you, I mean. At school, well, you can't ever really talk at school.'

'No. I guess so.' The bell rang and I stood up. He had his hand on the picture Jen had been drawing. I couldn't very well snatch it out from under his palm.

'I'd better go,' I said, 'registration.' He nodded, still smiling at me with his whole face, making me hot again and bothered again, and I knew how I felt wasn't going to go away, no matter what I did.

'See you, then, Audrey,' Leo said, still standing there, still watching me, and I somehow unfixed myself from the spot and walked away.

Leo

Lizzy was waiting for him again. Ever since the fair she'd started appearing in the corridor just outside whichever room he happened to be vacating, falling into step beside him and making small talk. Small being the operative word. What did he think about the latest crap TV show she'd been watching, did he want to maybe listen to her new boy-band album, why hadn't he found her on Facebook, why didn't he come out with them on Friday night?

'Hey,' she said, falling into step with him again, just before lunchtime. Leo was on his way to the art block. Finding Audrey there yesterday had been a bonus and he thought he might be lucky again.

'Hi.' Leo's plan was to keep looking straight ahead. To walk fast, like he had a purpose. Which he did.

'So, you want to know what I heard?' Lizzy took a run of little steps to catch him, tugged the sleeve of his jacket.

'Um, I don't know. Do I?' He hazarded a quick glance her way, didn't like the look in her eyes and focused again on the main doors. In under a minute he'd be out of here. If he ran it would be just seconds.

'I think you might be interested,' Lizzy teased.

'Well, what's it about?' Her hand on his sleeve was a drag.

'That girl, the new girl.'

'You mean Audrey.' He couldn't help it; he looked at

Lizzy. There was a sly cast to her expression, a twist to her smile. 'I'm not interested in rumours, Lizzy, or in bitchiness. OK?'

'No, this isn't that. It's worse.'

'What? What are you talking about?'

'Just that, well, you know how she's weird, right? Well, I heard from my mum that's she's definitely mental. So my mum knows her mum and she says she's been in homes. Like properly locked up and stuff. Apparently she's really violent. I don't think they should let people like that in schools though, do you? Not with us normal kids. I mean, you don't know what she might do.' Lizzy's eyes goggled at him. She licked her lips, her tongue darting, excited.

Leo tensed. He stopped walking and took Lizzy's arm, pulled her to one side, looking at her hard. She took a step back.

'Lizzy, you know what? I think these rumours you're spreading are horrible.'

'They're not rumours. They're true.' Her eyes beat out at him, hot with outrage.

'Well, I don't care. I don't want to hear it. The only person who looks bad here is you, you see, because Audrey's my friend. I actually like her. So, please, just leave it, all right? Stop talking shit. And grow up.'

She stared, her face heating to a beetroot glow, the blush spreading up her ears into her scalp. Leo let go of her arm and tried to smile once, just very briefly.

'OK,' he said.

'OK,' she answered, quieter, and he turned round and walked away.

Audrey

I'd nearly managed a whole half-term in school. That was something, I thought, as I went to the nurse's office at lunchtime and took my pill, like Mum had arranged. There were only two days left until the holidays and that was a relief, because I was sleeping too much and then feeling sick, dizzy, almost upside down. Mum said it was a side effect, worth it if I got better and could be brave and strong like other girls. I wanted to be like Jen – Jen would never be scared of the Thing – so I swallowed my pills and tried to smile at the school nurse, calling a cheery goodbye. On my way to registration, I pushed through the heavy doors into the next corridor, thinking about how I might take Peter to our den after school; it was brightening up outside. We'd filled half of the notebook with drawings and I wanted to collect leaves to stick in, acorns, maybe look for animal markings in the damp rich earth. Peter could copy and label them and start to keep a record. But first I had to sit through afternoon lessons. More French. More Science. *Stay awake now, Aud, try your best.* But I took a wrong turn, bewildered by the meandering corridors, not certain where I was or where I ought to go. So I didn't see Lizzy until it was too late. She stopped me and barred the door.

'So, you seeing him, then?' I didn't like her hand on my

shoulder. I shifted and tried to shake it off; I had to act hard.

'Seeing who?'

'The Chinaman.' Her mates laughed. One of them popped bubblegum near my ear. I turned and tried to dodge past them.

'What?'

'You know who I mean. Leo.' She drew the word out, her mouth twisting as if she were going to be sick.

'Mind your own business,' I said. Where was Jen? I needed her at my side, a silent back-up.

Lizzy took a step forward.

'He wouldn't want to get with a little skank like you, anyway. Who would? Who knows what you've got?'

'Oh, shut up.' I edged away, trying to make my way without touching any of them, but a hand on my back sent me sprawling, my glasses flying. The shock jarred my arms as I landed, but I didn't make a sound, reached for my specs and shoved them in my pocket. If I waited on the floor, didn't move, didn't cry, it'd be fine. They'd go away and leave me alone. But Lizzy had a better idea.

'Get up, come on.' A pair of hands grabbed me, pulling me to my feet.

'You know what you are, don't you?' Lizzy said, smiling, straightening my jumper, her fingers like little pincers. She didn't expect an answer. I zipped my mouth shut.

'You're a schizo bitch, aren't you?'

I still didn't answer. Better not to. Better to pretend they weren't real, just ghosts flitting in and out of my mind. They would die soon; we'd all die soon. They just didn't know it yet.

'We all know. That you're sick in the head. That you cut yourself up like a dirty, skanky bitch.' She grabbed my arm and wrenched back my sleeve, then held the evidence in front of the others. Her fingers manacled my wrist and the scars glowed. 'Tried to top yourself, once, didn't you? What went wrong? You screw up, Mental?'

Her spit hit my face. I closed my eyes. I felt sick. How did she know? I pretended I was deaf and dumb. Played stupid, the fool.

'We don't want you here,' Lizzy said. 'You should fuck off. Tell you what, we'll help you.'

And then she was dragging me towards the girls' loos and there were arms round my neck, round my shoulders and waist and I couldn't escape them, not by pulling or twisting or screaming or fighting back. Lizzy's hand covered my mouth and I tried to bite her. She squeezed my face, tightening her grip.

They slammed the door. Someone stood against it. I yelled out for them to stop.

'Let's make her shut up, yeah?' Lizzy said, and they dragged me into a cubicle and shoved me to my knees, pushing my head into the filthy toilet bowl. My stomach heaved as water flooded my mouth and eyes and nose and ears. Twisting and writhing, like a thrashing animal hooked and caught, I lurched and pulled. But they held me there; someone flushed and flooded my face and I saw the blackness of the moat, felt the panic of drowning, the horror of knowing I couldn't save myself, the thud of it coming.

When they let go I slumped to the floor. Gasping, I lay there, a puddle of victim.

'Hey,' Lizzy said, and I raised my eyes. She had her phone and was filming.

'Say hi,' she said, grabbing my hair and pulling back my head. 'Say hello to the camera.'

I had to stop her. I had no choice: she was hurting me and it was cruel and I didn't want to be the one they laughed at any more. I lunged forward, with my fists, my feet, my teeth and caught a little of her, knocking the phone out of her hands and into the toilet bowl. She screamed and I fought her, scraping my nails down one cheek, snagging her shin with my shoe as I got to my feet, kicking and pushing and punching my way out of there. I heard myself scream, *I hate you, I hate you*, and then I fled, my hair hanging down my back in a heavy filthy mess. *It doesn't matter*, I muttered, under my breath, *it doesn't matter*. But something burned and I felt the heat and scratch of it in my throat and coughed out the first sob, swiped at the tear. No one saw me when I left the school, slipping out through the gap in the fence at the edge of the field. I didn't feel the chill in the air, or the wind on my shoulders through my soaking shirt. I didn't notice the long walk towards the Grange, I just concentrated on moving, on putting one foot before another and getting away. My head thumped, the drumbeat, the sign. The Thing whispered that I was useless. The Thing told me not to hope. That there would be nothing good for me ever, that I deserved what I got. Lizzy was right, it said. I was nothing. But I didn't know what I had done wrong.

I wished I could go home. Every ten paces I stopped, dizzy, and I made my way as if walking up and down see-saws, balancing on the shifting planes of the earth. If my head would just clear, if my thoughts would untangle, if I could just see myself as others did. Make my life make some sort of sense.

I made it to the woods. The smell of the dank soil rose up like a mist and I walked into it, breathing the rich sour odour of decay. The sun caught a cobweb, set it alight, birds rattled the branches overhead. My breathing slowed, I was safe here in the clearing at least. Our den was still there, just, Peter's and mine, ragged now, almost entirely collapsed, but I crawled inside what was left of the shelter, imagined the leaves folding over me, the soil opening, accepting, digesting, and that it was warm in the belly of the earth.

Leo

The rumour spread along the corridors fast. In and out of classrooms it skittered: Lizzy Carr had been attacked. Lizzy Carr was with the nurse, rushed to hospital, might lose an eye. And Audrey was to blame. She'd gone nuts, they said, spazzed out; attacked Lizzy and smashed up her phone and run off somewhere, no one knew where. Leo closed his ears to the words, bandied about, careless. He decided they were more lies, but when Audrey didn't appear on the last day before the half-term holiday he wondered if she really had been excluded. He heard the kids say 'schizo' again, 'nutter', 'mental', and his stomach turned. Whatever might have gone on, he was sure it couldn't all be her fault.

It was Saturday night and he was supposed to be going to Joel Blake's Halloween thing, but he wanted to go for a run, nevertheless, before he left to catch the bus. Late October and the evenings getting shorter and shorter; there was just enough time before the night dipped into darkness. Graham was right: it was addictive. His breath made big clouds as he paused, hands on hips, and stood and stared up at the Grange. He ran his eyes over the walls, the blank windows, vacant yet glaring. NO TRES-PASSERS read a new sign that had been hurriedly rammed into the ground near the gates. He ignored it and ran up

109

the drive, refusing to be afraid of mere bricks and mortar. And then there was a movement at the window he'd decided was Audrey's. Just a shadow, a flitting, fleeting thing, butterfly light. It was worth a try. He could get the full story, try and help maybe.

'Hey,' he yelled, cupping his hands round his mouth. 'Audrey,' his voice boomed, and carried, bouncing off the walls and the water in an echo that chased itself round and round. *Audrey, Audrey, Audrey*, he heard, the voices singing back at him as if they laughed, and for a second it looked like nothing was going to happen. But then the movement was back and this time it was clearer; the shadow took shape. A figure was standing at the window, struggling with the latch, wrenching open the casing.

'Hi,' she called back, her voice dipping on the wind. 'What are you doing?'

'Out for a run. I thought I saw you, so I called. You OK?'

'Yeah. Not doing much.'

'Can you come out?' he shouted. 'Or shall I come up?'

But she didn't answer; she'd disappeared already and the next moment she was charging out of the front door, running towards him, gravel flying under her bare feet, her hair streaming pale and long behind her.

'What's up?'

'Nothing.' The way she'd run, like there'd been something chasing her, Leo wanted to put out his arms and steady her. Be something solid and strong for Audrey to hold on to.

'What are they saying?' she said, and Leo didn't know

how to answer. Her eyes blinked behind her glasses and her cheeks burst red; she held her arms across her chest, defending herself. There was no way he could make this worse and tell her the truth, so he smiled, pretending he didn't know what she meant. It felt like smiles were all he had to give Audrey and that made him angry.

'Look, why don't you come out with me tonight? There's a party.'

'I can't. I have to babysit. Mum's at work.'

'OK. Do you want me to stay with you?'

She took a step back, her face closing.

'Right, well, never mind. But listen, Audrey, don't worry. It doesn't matter, this thing with Lizzy; people will forget about it. Everyone knows what she's like. Just don't get down, OK?' God, he was useless. This wasn't what he wanted to say at all. He wanted to invite himself inside, sit down and really talk to her, find out what the hell was going on and who she really was. Right now he didn't have a clue.

'I'm OK. You enjoy yourself, anyway. Have a good one,' Audrey said, and he nodded and waited until she was inside before he ran down the drive and across the fields to the farm.

The party sucked and Leo wasn't in the mood. Some idiot had thought it was funny to come dressed in a white coat spattered with fake blood, axe in hand, long blond wig, glasses, eyes wide and staring and, just in case the ever-so-subtle message hadn't hit home, the words MAD AUDREY painted in red on the back of his lab coat. Leo curled his lip. His fists clenched. He walked in the other direction and there was Lizzy laughing her ass off, barely a scratch on her. She saw him and shifted in her seat to stare at him full on before she grinned and raised her eyebrows – an invitation. *My God*, he thought, *Lizzy is actually deluded*. He spun round on his heel, walked back to the guy who thought he was funny and shoved him hard.

'Hey!' The lad turned round. Leo recognized Mark Brooks from his tutor group. They'd never spoken.

'Don't you think this is pretty pathetic?' Leo gestured at Mark's costume. Thought about tearing off his wig. Landing a hard punch in his face. 'Taking the piss out of a girl who's not here to defend herself?'

'It's only a laugh. What do you care?' Mark said, holding up his hands as if to say calm down, and Leo could tell he really didn't get it.

'Well. You're not funny. Think about it, right?'

Leo walked into the kitchen. Grabbed a beer and drank, his lip still curling. Jen came over.

'All right?' she said, and he shrugged.

'I'm pretty knackered actually. I might just bail.'

'Sure, sorry about Mark and that stupid costume.'

'Not your fault.'

'Is it true though?' Jen asked him. 'Is Audrey . . . well, is she a bit, you know . . .'

She didn't know how to say it, especially not to him. Leo had thought Jen was better than that, he thought she was Audrey's friend, and he gritted his teeth.

'I don't know, Jen. If you mean has Audrey got mental-health problems, well, I haven't a clue. We barely know each other. But what I do know, I like. I know where she's coming from. I've been there.'

'Yeah?' Jen sat up on the kitchen worktop, kicked her legs back and forth, picking at her black nail varnish. She was dressed up as a vampire – Dracula's bride – and pulled out her fake teeth, so she could talk. 'The thing is, Lizzy's totally got it in for Audrey. And you know Lizzy. She's such a nightmare.'

'Well, maybe someone should have a word.' *Like me*, Leo thought. *I could go up to her now, tell her to shut her evil mouth. Make her actually hear it this time. That would really finish this party off.* Jen jumped down, held his sleeve.

'That would make her worse, I reckon – you know she does it for attention. She'd be accusing you of all sorts if you did that. You'd have her mum round yours, like she came down the school, mouthing off.'

'I guess so.'

'Well, maybe Lizzy'll leave Aud alone now she knows she'll get it back.'

'I hope so. It's really shit, Jen. She was trying to fit in, trying to have a fresh start.'

'I know. But it's not always as easy as that, is it?'

Audrey

I sat up waiting for Mum to get in from work, thinking about Leo at the party and how I could have gone too. It might have been fun. Jen would have been there. It would have been a chance to try again with the kids at school, to show that I was all right and knew how to have a laugh. I wanted to talk about it, but Mum was tired again; she banged into the kitchen, slammed the door and I knew it was my fault. There was no point trying to talk to her when she was like this, and I went in the opposite direction, up the little flight of stairs to my room. Mum was angry at the school, after the thing with Lizzy. And then this morning she'd said, 'What I don't get is why it's always you, Aud. Why can't you just keep yourself out of trouble? Have you been messing about with your medicine again?'

And then she stood over me as I swallowed my pills, checking and counting and making me feel like a criminal. Mum was right, when I didn't take the pills then the Thing came, worse than ever.

I sat cross-legged on my bed, my skin prickling. It had to be my fault somehow, my fault that they always chose me to pick on. My fault that I was odd and different. But how did I change? Shivering, I lay down and pulled the covers up and over me but the pillow was wet and clammy under my cheek and I reached for a jumper to bunch under my head. Downstairs Mum was still crashing around; the smell of her cigarette leaked into the room, lighting it with the burning stub of her anger. And she wasn't the only one who was mad. My brain began to ache. The Thing was here. Throbbing, beating, gathering speed, pulsing into the walls and the window, making them rattle and the room shake. I pulled the sheets tighter round my chin and curled smaller.

'Go away,' I whispered, putting my hands over my ears, trying to stop the rumbling threat. 'Leave me alone,' I told it. 'You can't get me – I've been taking my pills. You don't exist, so just go away.' Muttering, I lay in bed, my body beginning to shudder. It didn't matter what I said; it could do whatever it liked. It had been at it for years, visiting me and hurting me, and even when I tried to recreate the Thing as a girl like me and push it away its face ripped and peeled, shedding skin like a snake, crumbling to dust in my fingers.

Leo, I wrote, once, twice, three times, with a fingertip on my skin. Leo liked me. I scratched a pattern of flowers around his name before I gritted my teeth and tried to steady myself.

Night gathered. I listened, alert, on guard.

The floor creaked, the sheets shivered. It was coming, coming now. My heartbeat quickened, in time to its march. You couldn't resist the Thing. I tried and held on to the bed. *No, please, no*, whispered someone, very far away.

It led me. Out of the house, down the stairs and into the freezing night we went, my hair flying and winding away from my head, the cold breathing ice into my bones. I let it pull me forward, forward towards water that sung and summoned, and the Thing opened my skin, scoring with a blade, put its lips to my flesh and sucked up the blood.

November

Audrey

Mum was standing over me when I woke up. She grabbed my arm and pulled up the sleeve before I could stop her.

'What's this, Audrey?'

'I didn't do it,' I whispered, staring and cradling my arm against my chest. Crusts of blood. Pain stabbed at my eyes, my stomach, my thighs.

'So explain it to me, then.'

'I don't know, Mum, I don't know what happened.'

'Come off it. You think I'm going to buy that after what I found in the bathroom, Audrey? Where did you get the blades?'

'I didn't do it,' I told her. I knew where this was leading.

'Rubbish,' Mum said. Peter appeared in the door, pale, still wearing his pyjamas. He was watching us, so I tried to keep my voice calm and swung my legs out of bed.

'Come on, Pete. Come on – let's go and put the TV on or something.'

He nodded and let me lead him away and I heard Mum pick up the phone, asking for an emergency appointment. 'Pinch, punch, first day of the month,' I whispered, so no one would hear, especially my skin.

Why did the days have to get so dark? The doctor's surgery. Mum at my side, staring at a magazine without turning the pages. She'd been reading the same article about some woman's gastric band for forty minutes.

'I don't know why these bloody doctors don't work weekends,' she muttered. 'We should have gone to A and E, Aud, yesterday. But I thought it was better if we saw Dr Caldwell. Don't you think?'

I plucked at the wool on my jumper, twisting the threads into a tight knot. When my name was called, Mum stood first and led the way and I trailed in her wake, a little tug boat, bobbing on a line.

'Hello, doctor,' Mum said, sitting forward on her chair, legs folded, voice all pretend business-like. 'Us again.' The doctor smiled like she didn't mind and nodded. 'As I explained when we saw you before, Aud's not doing well. She's been battling depression since she was about thirteen; that's three years now. God. Three years.' Mum's eyes were wide, like she couldn't believe it. 'Anyway, last year she began self-harming. We worked on it and she stopped, or at least I thought she had, but now it's happening again. That's why we're here, doctor.'

The doctor looked at me. Her expression interested, intelligent.

'Anything else you can tell me, Audrey? How do you feel generally at the moment? How are you sleeping?'

I yawned.

'I'm not,' I said, and stared out of the window. Bit at the insides of my cheeks. Mum chimed in, filling in the gaps.

'That's been a pretty constant thing. I mean, going back years, this insomnia. I don't know, doctor, I'm no expert, but it's obvious the treatment isn't working.'

'Yes?' The doctor looked at me again. She took my hand. Very kind. Gentle. And my heart stopped for a moment as I looked at her and wondered. Mum was still talking.

'Audrey started school very introverted, very shy. Never made friends, fell behind. There were times when she was off for months at a time. Lots of chest infections, breathing problems. I did my best to make things as normal as I could, but she got too used to being on her own, I think. And now we've got this depression, as if she's internalized all her problems. Well, I'm no psychiatrist, like I said. That's my interpretation. And the bullying at school doesn't help. But now she's lashing out, violent. She was in trouble at school last week and now she won't go back.'

Mum looked at the doctor for confirmation, biting her lip. Dr Caldwell indicated with a little nod that she should go on.

'I wonder if maybe Aud gets like this because she's not like other girls. Not as bright. Maybe the cutting and the anger, maybe it's her way of asking for help? I don't know – I'm just looking for answers really. You're the experts. But I think this is serious; I think she's verging on psychosis, doctor.'

'OK, thank you, Mrs Morgan.' Dr Caldwell turned to me again. 'Audrey, how do you feel about all this? Would you agree with the way your mum's described how you're feeling? Or is there something else, anything else you'd like to tell me?'

Mum looked at me; they both did. The air in the room was very still. I could hear them breathing, hear my own heartbeat, the scream on my skin.

'I'm fine.' And there was my voice. So pathetic. So small. I wasn't a mouse. I tried again.

'I just want to be left alone. I'll be all right if everyone leaves me alone.' And now tears welling. That wouldn't help. I wrapped my arms round my knees, folding myself into the chair and stared at the floor. I didn't want to hear Mum's tears.

'As I said, she's difficult. I try and get her help and she won't cooperate. Messes about with her medication.'

The doctor held out her hands, her voice gentle.

'Your mum says you've been self-harming, Audrey. Can I see?'

'Look at the state of her – I mean –' Mum threw her arms up in despair.

I let the doctor touch me, pull up my sleeves and inspect the wounds. I didn't want this. Didn't want anyone to see. It was my body and it was ruined. Hurting. The pain was private, not Mum's to give to the rest of the world.

'Yes, these are deep. Quite nasty. I'll clean and dress them. Although by the looks of things someone else has done a good job.' She glanced up at Mum.

'That was me. I'm a nurse.' Mum smiled. 'It's the least I can do for her. I just want to help Audrey; I'm desperate for her to be happy. To have the things other girls her age have. Friends, some fun.'

Mum, I cried in my head. *Mum, please. Don't you see that I want that too?* Mum didn't see. She was wiping her eyes on her sleeve.

'Of course,' Dr Caldwell murmured. Calm. Serene. How could she be like that? Didn't she get it, that my life was a sheet of black ice, that I was slithering, sliding, out of control?

The doctor worked quickly. I watched her light-brown glossy hair catching the sun, wished I smelled of summer and had soft clear skin like hers, sharp clever eyes. Her touch was light. She smiled at me as she dealt with the mess on my arms and chatted about nothing much.

'So you don't like school, Audrey?'

'Not really,' I said, and Mum sighed but I ignored her. I wasn't speaking to her now, or for the rest of the day. Forever.

'And why's that?' the doctor pressed on.

There was no point moaning about Lizzy.

'She's being bullied. I've had the teachers on the phone already,' Mum said. The doctor murmured something about talking to the school, sorting out my medication, referring me to some AMHT.

'And how about friends? Is there anyone else you can lean on for support, Mrs Morgan? Is Dad around?'

'Oh, no.' Mum coughed out an angry laugh. 'He opted out pretty sharpish. Aud was, what, six, seven? I have a son too to worry about. God knows the impact all this is having on him. I just feel so guilty, like I'm letting everyone down. Audrey included.'

'You mustn't feel like that. From where I'm sitting, it looks like you're doing a pretty incredible job. But we're here to help. Both of you. As I said, anything I can do, let me know.'

The doctor started printing off prescriptions. She talked over the sound of the printer.

'You should hear from the hospital soon, I'll try and ensure things happen sooner rather than later.'

'Thank you. You've been absolutely wonderful, Dr Caldwell.'

'As I said, anytime. Pop back if you need me. I'm writing a paper on adolescent mental health, so I'm glad to be here for you. I'll take an interest in Audrey's progress. We'll get on top of things – it may take a little time, but we'll get there.'

I turned back to look at Dr Caldwell as we left the surgery with the new prescription, but her back was turned, her fingers busy on the keyboard typing up the notes. I wondered what she was writing, wished I could see, put it right.

Everything slipped over half-term. We didn't really get up; if we did, then we didn't get dressed. I was glad there was no school so I didn't have to face Lizzy, but I missed Leo and Jen. Peter stared at the TV in the gloomy living room, his hand diving in and out of the sweet bag, eyes fixed, red-rimmed. Mum sat there too. The mould smell was back. When I pulled the curtains open, she told me to shut them, saying she had a bad head.

Mum bought a new nail-varnish set. It arrived in the post on Wednesday. She sat in front of me, her fingers in bowls of water, softening her cuticles. She liked playing beauty parlour and it had been a while.

I filed her nails, and Peter's cartoons squealed in the background. Mum closed her eyes; a small smile lifted her face when I rubbed in the hand cream. I stared over her shoulder and out of the window, but couldn't see much from here. Just sky. And clouds that looked like nothing today.

'Audrey –' Mum's voice snapped me back; she shook a wrist – 'come on.'

I paid more attention. Dried off her skin with paper towels. Started with the base coat. Mum had all the paraphernalia. She'd want to do the pedicure next, I thought, and my hands felt tired.

I thought about Leo, wondered what he was doing, if we should go over to the farm.

Peter jumped up, wired on sugar.

'I'm bored. I want to go somewhere.'

'Off you go, then,' Mum said. 'Bugger off.' She laughed, winked at me.

'Where? Can we go somewhere, Mum?' Peter asked, climbing on to the arm of the sofa before jumping off, then clambering up to do it all over again.

'No. Get down. I'm busy.' She nodded at her hands. I was just beginning to apply the first coat of the bold red she'd chosen.

'I'm sick of watching TV.' Peter aimed a kick at the wall.

'Go outside, play with your football,' she told him.

'You said you'd get me a bike.' Peter was really fed up. Like he needed to punch something.

'Yes, well. There's no money for a bike right now. Wait for your birthday, like I said, and go and do something else for now.'

The door slammed behind him.

'How are you getting on?' Mum said.

'Nearly done.'

She sat up, spread out her fingers. Nodded.

'Nice job, that, love. You could go into this sort of thing, Aud – there's a lot of money in it.'

'I think I want to do something outdoors,' I told her, staring out again. 'Like, archaeology or something.' She pulled a face. 'Maybe explore the world. Go to loads of hot places, find really interesting stuff. Or maybe study different people, cultures – anthropology that's called.'

'You what?'

'It'd be fun.'

'Forget it. I can't think of anything worse. You'd be filthy all the time. Forever off and on planes, picking up God knows what. And think of all those awful men, foreigners, waiting to trap girls like you. I've read about them.' She gestured at an old newspaper on the floor.

'I don't think it's that bad.'

'It is. And with your problems, well, it's too risky. You stay at home, love, with me. I don't want you disappearing off halfway round the world. What'd I do without you?'

'You'd be OK.' I started packing away, trying not to hear her.

'You should be glad I care.' She looked hard at me. 'My mother didn't give a toss what I did, the old bag.'

I tried to remember Grandma, but my memory was like a page ripped from a paperback book, folded and then torn in random places, all the important words missing. Open the paper and the holes made no shape at all. Words started and stopped. Jagged rips gaped. I'd tried to find the missing letters, lying in bed at night and scratching at my memories like a nail at a scab. But I couldn't decide what fitted where.

I stared at Mum. Thought about it a bit more. Of course I'd met my grandparents, but it had been way before I broke my ankle; Peter hadn't even been born and Dad still lived with us. Mum's family seemed to seep out of the walls, although their faces were blanks, masks wearing bright lipstick, just like Mum's, and dull smiles. It was Christmas or someone's birthday, not mine. My head reached Mum's waist and I held her hand, trying to listen to the conversation and work it out, watching Mum, seeing her fingers twisting in her necklace, then scratching, probing at something on her neck, squeezing, worrying. When she opened her mouth to speak I don't think anyone heard, because they didn't laugh when she did and her face fell like she'd dropped something, lost it forever.

We were watching TV and I was squeezed between Mum and my grandma, whose hands were cold and clammy when she took mine and stared at the chipped nail polish Mum had put on the week before. Grandma tutted, examined her own hands, heavy with rings and freckled with age.

My grandpa didn't notice us at all. He pushed his glasses up his nose and turned up the volume – the programme was something noisy and fast. He smoked cigarettes, one after another, and drank coffee. His breath smelled when he said goodbye later, peering at me as if only just noticing I was there.

I kept waiting for us to go, but Mum fell asleep beside

me. Snoring, loud, through her mouth. Grandpa kept looking at her in this way that made me want to cover her up. Hide.

No one really noticed when Dad finally arrived to take us home; no one stood on the step and waved goodbye or even came to usher us out. I remembered sitting in the back and the car was so quiet it felt like no one was even breathing or would ever breathe again.

I finished the top coat and said, 'Right, I'm done.'

Mum held her fingers high, wiggled them. I turned on the heat lamp, stood and stretched.

'I'm going to find Peter, OK?'

'Yeah, get me a tea first though; I'm parched. And pass me the remote, would you?'

I got her set up with everything she could possibly need for the next hour or so – tea, her cigarettes, a half-eaten pack of sweets, her bag in case she needed her phone – and dashed away. My stomach twisted as I went, but I ignored it and her voice, calling. It echoed down the stairs, following me, like a beating angry heart, but I couldn't hear. I wouldn't.

My mother was the moon. Waxing and waning. Sometimes bursting, glowing and full. And then so thin and mean, needle sharp. And I could only move as she permitted, my body like the tide, tied still to her strings. I broke away now, but soon I'd go back to her; she'd call me, as only she could.

Leo

Half-term. He'd looked forward to this, to meeting his mother and to catching up. So when he saw her he hugged her, way too tight, and she laughed, before sweeping him towards the taxis, striding on soft leather pumps that matched her handbag and her camel coat. They faced each other and he could see her making a real effort not to mention school. Leo had made a bet with himself, reckoned that the longest she'd last was fifteen minutes. But he'd overestimated her again. She managed a full ten. And then: the inquisition.

'Well, how's everything?' she began. Full-beam headlight attention. Her eyes bright. Focused. He didn't want to talk about that. He wanted to ask her other things, talk about what was real. He supposed he never would; it wasn't the way they worked.

'Good, thanks.'

'Good? What does that mean, Leo?'

'I think it means fine.' She raised her eyebrows – they were impressive: perfect, almost architectural. Leo elaborated on his theme: 'No problems, all well. No need to start getting stressed out. That's what good means.'

'It's hardly a specific form of measurement though, is it, darling?' She was keeping it light, pretending to banter.

Mum's banter was pretty dangerous. Almost as dangerous as Mum's lectures. She brought new meaning to the word polemic. Should have gone into politics.

'Not really. But then again, what is?'

'Well. A percentage, for example. You might like to tell me what percentage you achieved in your last Biology test. We haven't had a report from the school, although I've emailed several times. I can't say I'm surprised. The place is clearly designed to babysit inbred farm hands.'

'Mother. Stop it.'

She pursed her lips and put her hand out and held Leo's. She had really delicate hands, small and soft. Audrey's felt a bit dry and sort of colder too, and her fingers were longer and very gentle.

'Sorry, darling. You know it's because I care. And because I miss you and want you to do well, that's all. Despite everything, it's still incredibly important that you leave school with a decent set of qualifications.'

'So, leave me alone, then. OK? I thought we'd been through all this.' He didn't want to remember the hideousness of it. Not getting out of bed. His housemaster calling the doctor. The doctor calling an ambulance and then weeks of silence, medicine, his mother green and sick with guilt. It looked like she'd managed to forget though. Forget what had driven him to the edge. Leo tried to forget it too. Most kids did their GCSEs no bother, but he'd buckled. *Thirteen GCSEs*, Graham silently reminded him, *not to mention your Music A Level, when you were only fifteen. Hell of a lot of pressure, Leo.*

'Yes, you're right. We did. And I will try to be less

interested in my only son's life and education. After all, a good mother lets her son go to the dogs, right?'

'Right.' He'd rather go to the dogs, his own way, than end up back on antidepressants, hers. He was prepared to spell that out in words of no more than one syllable if need be.

'Did you think about what you might like to do this week? I've got meetings back to back Monday to Wednesday, but on Thursday we could take some time,' she said.

This wasn't a surprise. Leo had already looked up events in that week's *Time Out*. He was going to catch a couple of films they hadn't shown in town, browse the big bookshops, go to the theatre. *Lear* was playing and he wanted to see how they did Gloucester's eyes. If he told his mother that, she'd be straight on the phone to Graham. Unhealthy obsession with violence.

His mum was on her BlackBerry. She hadn't even considered that he might be gutted that her week was taken up, that he'd been granted a measly seventh of her time. Perhaps he should present her with that fraction, see if it made more sense.

'Dad says hi, by the way. He misses you.'

'Sure. I miss him too.'

'Oh, Leo.' She looked up, took his hand again. 'Don't sound so sad. I can't stand it.'

'I'm not sad, Mum.' The taxi swung past Buckingham Palace. Leo yawned and picked up his phone. He checked his messages, email. Plugged in his headphones and searched for the right song.

'You're very distracted, darling.' The implicit criticism was there.

He put his phone away. Didn't sigh or shrug. Remembered his manners. His damn manners.

'Sorry. It's wonderful to see you.'

She reached out and smoothed his hair neat, like he was a little boy, then tsked and said he needed a good cut and that she'd book him in with her stylist. Leo was about to say that he liked his hair the way it was, but shut his mouth as his mother looked away. What was the point?

'Here's the hotel. Let's get settled, have tea before my conference call at six. Over dinner I want to hear all your plans.'

'Plans?'

'Yes, university plans. You have made your application, haven't you?' He shrugged, but she was insistent. 'There's a lot to prepare for, interviews and so on. We'll talk about it. Don't worry. We'll do lots of practice.'

He followed his mother inside. She walked fast, talked fast, thought fast and Leo was already looking forward to getting back to the farm.

Audrey

Mum was working nights, then on Thursday she was back at six in the morning.

'Audrey,' she yelled, waking me. I'd only just got to sleep.

'Hi.' I stood on the landing, bleary-eyed.

'I'm knackered,' she said, heading straight up to bed, so I took her tea and biscuits before going back down to get Peter's breakfast and to make plans.

'Baking? A cake?'

Peter nodded. He stood on a chair and helped measure out the ingredients, laughing when he got flour in my hair.

'You look like an old lady, Aud,' he said, and I tried to smile.

The cake didn't rise but it smelled good and we covered it with strawberry jam. We sat and ate it all and my belly ached.

Eventually, on Friday, Mum got up.

'I need a bath, Audrey – run the bath.'

It took six lots of boiling water to turn the lukewarm bath hot. I ran back and forth with the spitting kettles.

'That's better,' she said at last, taking off her nightie, lowering herself in. I looked away.

'Pass the soap.'

I handed it to her and made to leave.

'Hang on, love – you have to scrub my back, remember?'

Kneeling by the bath, I picked up the flannel, soaked it, scrubbed her skin.

'That's good, love. That feels better.' I dropped the flannel, stood up again.

'No, hang on, I need help with my hair.'

She lay down, immersing herself; I sat on the loo and waited. After a while Mum pointed at her belly; I hated looking.

'See that, Aud? My scar.' It was long and ridged. Red, still, after sixteen years, which seemed wrong to me.

'Yeah, I know.'

'Funny to think you came out of there, isn't it? They had to cut you out, otherwise I could have died. I wanted a nice natural birth, you know. But it was an emergency; you could have died too. Both of us. But the doctor, he was amazing. He saved our lives.'

'Yeah? Good.' I hated this conversation. It cropped up every couple of months. The whole giving-birth thing was basically revolting and I didn't want to be reminded.

'Thank God. I think about him a lot, that doctor,' She looked at me from under her lids.

'You thinking about that lad again, Aud?'

'No.'

'Come off it, I know you are.' She took the flannel, started to wash her stomach, breasts, under her arms, then held it out to for me to take over. 'I know you fancy him, Audrey.'

'I don't.'

'It's normal, at least, to have a crush. You shouldn't be ashamed of it. But you know you can't do anything, don't you? You'd better not, anyway.'

I dropped the wet cloth and stood up.

'I'm going to go and iron Peter's school stuff now, Mum. OK?' And I walked away before she could say anything else.

I was sick that night. Puked in the toilet while Mum held my hair back from my face and stroked my skin, wiping it with the flannel that was still damp from her bath and beginning to smell. I heaved again.

On Saturday evening, the night of Leo's bonfire party, I sat staring at the telly with Peter, trying to keep still, calm, not let my legs judder and jump, not check the clock or stare at Mum with a hopeful smile. I kept my mouth shut and my fingers crossed and then –

'Here,' Mum said, around seven, 'we're going out.'

I jumped up; she handed me her old black fake fur and I pulled it on, and felt instantly different. Like a kid playing dress up. Like a girl who could be someone else. Because I couldn't go on like this, sitting in the Grange, just waiting.

'Really, can I wear it?'

'Well, I don't want it. So you might as well.' She had a smart new black overcoat and warm boots.

'You look nice, Mum,' I said, catching her eye with a small smile, and she nodded as if she knew.

Mum didn't catch me twirling though, admiring in the mirror. I couldn't jinx this. I had plans. If I saw Leo tonight, I would do something, say something. Change things. Even if he told me to get lost. It didn't matter; at least I'd have tried. I'd tested out the words: *Leo, I like you, Leo, can we – Leo, will you – Leo Leo Leo –* and wondered how I'd fill in the gaps. Inside my heavy coat I was trembling already and I hugged myself still.

'What's the matter with you, Aud?' Mum said. 'You look hot and bothered. Have you got a temperature?' I shrugged out from under her hand and cooled my cheeks with my palms. Our car smelled of spices, cinnamon and apples: Mum had spent the afternoon baking and was taking wine and a packet of sparklers too. I tried not to fidget and stared at the night ahead. Dusk had fallen in great pink and purple ribbons, the sky undulating, sweet and seductive. Now it was pitch black. I bit my bottom lip, distracting myself from the flurry in my belly, like a shoal of tiny fish were swimming, flitting and fluttering, tumbling inside.

'Nice of Sue to invite us,' said Mum as she parked up outside the farm gates. 'You do me proud and mind your manners. Careful round the fire, Peter, and wear your gloves.' She wrestled with the top button of his coat, gave up. 'Let's find Sue.'

The farm was lit up like fairy land. Twinkling lights glittered around the door of the barn, around the house. Lanterns swung from trees, huge glowing candles dripped in glass bowls, lining the driveway. And somewhere in all this was Leo. This was another world. Anything could happen here.

'All right, Aud?' Mum looked at me. 'You're quiet. What's up? You feel all right?'

'I'm fine. This is good. Thanks for bringing us.' I smiled at her but she didn't see; she was peering into the darkness.

'Recognize anyone?'

'No. Not really.' There were lots of faces, mostly adults, some littler kids writing their names in the sky. No Lizzy. I let out my breath. Peter stuck close to my side, his hand in mine. I kept scanning for Leo.

'Lorraine!' Sue appeared out of the darkness, kissed Mum on both cheeks. 'I'm so glad you came, and Peter – wonderful. Come on – let me introduce you to some of the other guests.'

Mum handed over her bag of goodies.

'Oh, that's lovely – really you shouldn't have,' Sue exclaimed and swept her away. I jammed my hand in my pocket, stared down to the lower field, where the bonfire already crackled.

'Right,' I said to Peter. 'Come on.'

We wandered down towards the light. Closer, I saw Leo in the field wearing his duffle coat and wellies, navy-blue bobble hat on his head. He was messing with the fireworks, setting up a rocket. It burst into the sky, one long stream of fire, then exploded, making Peter jump.

'Leo,' I shouted, waving, 'Leo, hi.'

He jogged over.

'Hey.' Just that word lifted me, I felt taller.

'Hi. We came.' Stating the obvious, like an idiot. But he didn't say anything, just kept grinning, smiling too much for it to be normal. It made me nervous, like there was some joke here I didn't know about. Perhaps it was all a trick. Maybe Lizzy and her pals would jump out from behind the bonfire, Halloween masks on, bundle us on to the pyre.

'Brilliant. Here, let me get you something to drink, something to eat.'

'OK.'

We followed him back up to the house, then stood together outside, watching everything from a distance. There were loads of people I didn't recognize, milling everywhere, more arriving all the time, and I scanned the crowds, searching for school kids I'd need to avoid.

'Who's here?'

'The world and his wife.'

'Did you invite anyone else from school?'

'No. I don't think so. Sue might have done; there's bound to be the odd one lurking around. But, you know, we're not so friendly with the school lot.' He pulled his hat lower, peering over his shoulder, making me smile.

'Hah. Yeah. Well, let me know if you spot one. We can do a runner.'

'I like the sound of that. Where'd you want to go?'

I pointed at the sky.

'Hitch a ride on one of your rockets. Up there looks good. Peter made this incredible spaceship,' I said, and my brother looked hopeful. 'We should have brought that.'

'Fantastic – Mars, then?' I nodded. 'Great,' he said, 'it's a plan.'

We stood quiet for a bit. I shifted, tried to look as if this was easy, wondered what other stupid stuff there was to say. Anything was better than silence, standing there like two idiots, our tongues tied in knots. I felt hot and glad of the darkness so he wouldn't see. Leo spoke first.

'I like this one. What about you? Favourite firework? And you only get to choose one,' he said.

'Same. The pretty ones. Like flowers on fire.'

We were standing close. Peter wrote his name in the air with a sparkler. The smell of gunpowder, hot and smoky and sort of magic, misted the air, and when I looked at Leo he wasn't staring at the sky any more; he was looking at me. And for a second my stomach dropped. I didn't blink, just looked back at him, eyes wide, and the world was really clear for the first time in forever, lit up by the blazing bonfire in the distance. I hadn't imagined it: he liked me.

We finished our food and walked back down to the field. When he put his hand out and steadied me I tried not to jump like a frightened rabbit. *You're such a dickhead*, I told myself. *Aud, get your shit together*. And I swear I was trying, but it was hard. Because I knew this was my chance, maybe the only one.

He was standing close. His arm – I felt it, through all the layers of clothes, as if our skin were touching. My cheeks prickled. Bits of my body I hadn't wanted to know existed were sharp and alive. On the back of my neck, on my cheeks, on my scalp, inside my jumper, up and down my legs. Like if you licked me, your tongue would fizz. He didn't lick, but he did say my name and that meant he had more to say, that we hadn't run out of stupid things to talk about. The words were invisible wires, running between us, spinning a web that linked us. It turned us from strangers into friends. From friends into something else.

'Look,' he said, 'we can't talk here.' He took my hand and led me away from the fire.

'What d'you want to talk about?' I said. It was dark and still in the barn, smelt of fresh hay and the pony. Leo didn't have a chance to answer: I talked more.

'I bet Mum's told you, hasn't she?' Leo didn't bother pretending he didn't know what I meant. 'So what do you think? Now you know that I'm *mental*, like Lizzy says.' I made little quotation marks with my fingers around the word. It was better to face it.

'I don't care.' He was smiling.

'You mean that?'

'I do.'

'I get depressed,' I told him. 'Like, properly. And I cut myself sometimes.' I shrugged. 'Does that make me mad?'

'I don't think I'm the one to say, Aud,' Leo said quietly. 'I think you're lovely. That's all. And everyone has their pain. You don't need to be ashamed of it. And if you're ill you can get better. That's the thing.'

I thought about that and closed my eyes. Get better. Yes. When I looked at Leo again his eyes were on my face. It was a serious type of looking, the type that made my insides churn. I blinked, took off my glasses, rubbed my eyes, trying not to believe too hard. But Leo was fabulous. That was the only word. He reached out and took my hand.

'Wait,' he said, touching my face. He leant a bit closer.

'Audrey, what d'you –'

I didn't let him finish. Enough talk. Nothing to lose, I kissed him, suddenly brave and hopeful and stupid and sure all at once. It started off quick; then, when he didn't pull back, when it looked like he wanted to too, it was proper: a real grown-up kiss that I didn't know I knew how to do. My head exploded. My skin burned. When he held me close to him I kissed harder. Fast, hurry, steal this, all of it; there might not be another chance, not ever, and I put my arms round his neck and my heart into his hands.

And then there was my name being shouted, echoing all over the night.

'Audrey, Audrey – where are you?' Mum. 'Auuu-drey,' she hollered.

Leo

Audrey ran. She kissed him and she ran, and Leo caught a glimpse of her face, full of joy and fear and horror, before she shot away and he got up to follow, still a little dizzy and shocked. He could hear Lorraine from twenty paces, her voice twanging like a guitar string, out of tune.

'What've you been doing? Where've you been? I've been looking all over,' Lorraine was complaining when Leo caught up with them, standing right outside the barn. She might have seen them. Well, so what? He wasn't ashamed. But Audrey's expression was hidden in the dark and Lorraine stood between them; of course, he could just push past her, grab Aud's hand and drag her away. Kiss her like that again. All night. Apparently he had missed kissing. Not that he hadn't had the chance, but it wasn't something he took lightly. There had been Jecca, of course, but her mind had floated off, far away. Like he'd not been doing it quite right. And he preferred not to count Lizzy. With Audrey something had locked into place.

'Nowhere; I was just around,' Audrey said, and he saw Lorraine give her a look, before she turned and eyed Leo, staring him down. What was this?

'Your brother missed you,' Lorraine said, still watching Leo, and Audrey swung round to search.

'Sorry; where is he?' They scanned the drive and Leo spotted Peter with Sue, waving another sparkler.

'He's OK,' Leo said. 'Look, over there.' Lorraine followed the line of his finger. She grabbed Audrey's shoulder and gave her a little push.

'Right, well, he needs the loo, Aud – go and take him.'

Audrey ran off and Leo was about to follow when he felt Lorraine's hand on his arm. He stepped away without meaning to.

'Leo,' Lorraine said, but his eyes followed Audrey. 'Leo?' she repeated, saying his name like they were close, leaning in like she wanted him to look at her full in the face. Her eyes found his but he looked away again, searching for something to say.

'Can I get you a drink?'

'Yes,' Lorraine said, sticking by him as they walked towards the makeshift bar, chattering, asking questions about his parents, about his past. No matter how hard he tried, he couldn't sidestep Lorraine's attention. And Audrey had disappeared.

'Come on, Leo,' Lorraine said. 'Let's go down the field, warm up by the fire. It's a good one. You built it, didn't you, you and Sue? She says you're a good lad.' Lorraine was smiling at him. 'I could do with someone to help me, Leo, a bloke around. But I've no luck with men. My husband was a waste of space; he dumped us years ago. He couldn't cope with Aud being sick all the time. And what with Aud's problems, well, I don't have time for a life of my own.'

Leo didn't like the fact that Lorraine linked her arm through his or that she stumbled against him as they walked. When Lorraine laughed her breath was on his face, in his face, intruding.

'You're a good-looking lad, Leo,' she said, examining him too close, and he gave a short laugh, surprised.

'Thanks.' There wasn't much else he could say to that.

'No wonder my Audrey fancies you,' she confided.

Leo had no answer now. No idea what he was supposed to say under these circumstances.

'But she's a little girl, Leo; she's not ready for boys. I mean, if she even started her periods, that'd be a nightmare for her.' Her tone was low and confiding, as if inviting him to commiserate, comfort, share. No.

He released himself. Lorraine's breathing was heavy, too close, like the lurch of her body. The oily sheen on her forehead and nose. Lipstick like a second skin, thick; her tongue running over it, fast, sticky. Leo didn't like this, not any of it.

'Don't take this the wrong way or anything,' Lorraine continued, 'but, well, I think you should go for someone more mature.' Leo coughed. This couldn't be weirder. Maybe someone had spiked his drink and he was taking a crazy trip. He looked everywhere, at the sky, the night, the other faces. Not at Audrey's mother. Her *mother*.

'Well?' she said. Clearly she expected an answer.

'Sorry? What?'

'How about we go for a drink, the two of us? Talk about things. About Audrey. Whatever you like. There's a nice bar I know. I get lonely, Leo. I need to get out. Have a bit of fun. I moved for the kids, to give them a better life. But sometimes you have to think about yourself too. I mean, they're not going to be happy if I'm miserable, are they?'

He shook his head. This was the weirdest conversation he'd ever had. If he understood right, then Audrey's mother was coming on to him. Which was revolting. Which was, in fact, beyond foul. But she also wanted his pity, like she was trying to guilt-trip him into agreeing to this date. He plunged his hands into his pockets. Cleared his throat.

Lorraine was still waiting for an answer. He couldn't look at her. A rocket boomed and split the sky.

'I'm going to help with the fireworks,' he said, and turned and raced away.

Audrey

Mum was waiting outside when I came out with Peter. We'd spent a while in the house with Mary, who was hiding from the fireworks. Peter liked to pet her and I was trying to get my head round what I'd done. I'd kissed him. What now?

'Don't disappear again. Right?' Mum said. She was hot-cheeked, her breath sweet but acid. She put her arm round me, but I pulled back.

'Yeah.' I wriggled away. 'All right.'

'It's getting late.'

'Do we have to go?'

'I'll give you another half hour. This is a good do, isn't it?' she said, as Sue joined us and they clinked glasses. 'We had bonfire parties, didn't we, Aud?'

'Did we?' I said, searching my memory for when. My brain was like a sieve – that was the medication, Mum said, and she must have been right.

'So. What's going on, then?' Mum whispered, a little later, and I nudged her.

'Shhh. He'll hear you.' Leo was chatting to a group of Sue's friends. His cheeks were pink, his eyes like coals.

'So what? He's a bit of a dish, isn't he, Aud?'

'Mum!'

'Oh, come on. Just tell me. You know what, I reckon I

146

wouldn't mind. He's like that Harry Styles, only posher and a bit more foreign-looking. My type, I reckon.'

'Mum, don't be disgusting. He's nice. A friend. That's it.'

'I'm sure.' She slurped at her glass, drained it. 'I wasn't born yesterday, Aud. I know what girls are like. And boys. At your age it's all you think of.'

Another firework launched. Crackled and sang. Red. Amber. Green. Mum clapped, we oohed and ahhed. I looked around for Leo but he'd gone, and I wondered if it had really happened, that I'd kissed him and he hadn't minded. He'd kissed me back. My face flashed like the sky.

In the morning Mum shouted that her head was banging. *She shouldn't have got so pissed, should she?* I thought, but I took her plenty of water and a couple of paracetamol, tea and toast.

'I'm sorry, love,' she said, looking up, her face sore, smeary with the make-up she hadn't cleaned off. 'I'd had a bad week. Then too much to drink, trying to take the edge off. It never ends well.' She groaned, then sat up and took the mug, sipped and winced.

'Never mind, Mum. Doesn't matter.'

'You looked like you were having fun though.' She put her mug down and took a bite of toast, crumbs flying.

'Yeah. Course.'

Mum looked at me and I thought she saw something good, because she smiled, before speaking through a mouthful of bread, her voice just as thick and stodgy. 'Well, just make sure you watch yourself. I like Sue; she's a nice woman. But that nephew. I don't know.' She was watching me, chewing. Her eyes were red, piggy.

'Why?'

'I've just got this bad feeling about him. He's up himself. Thinks he knows it all.'

'He isn't.'

Once Mum turned against someone, that was it – they'd had it. 'He's a snob,' she said. 'I saw how he was looking at me. How you were both looking at me.'

I turned from her, wanting to get away.

'Come here; come and sit with me.' Mum patted the bedcovers and I sat beside her. As she sipped her tea she changed the subject, back to her shifts the week before. The little girl she'd been looking after. She was only eight.

'Remember when you were eight, Aud? You were in hospital all that summer. And then you got that infection. What a mess that was. And last night I just couldn't get it out of my head, how bad it had been, and how it had felt when you'd been the one lying there, so sick. So that's why I reckon I overdid things last night. Silly, I know.'

I tried to believe her. I tried to feel sorry.

'She's such a pretty little thing. Annabel, she's called. Lovely name. Looks a bit like you.' Mum's fingers ran through my hair, twisting strands, tying knots. I jerked my head away and flattened my hair with my hand.

'Don't think about it, Mum. Try not to dwell on it. I'm fine now. Maybe Annabel will be fine.'

'But you're not fine, are you? And nor's she, and no amount of wishing things were otherwise helps. It's a nightmare. That poor mother.' She sat closer, making me hot. 'I went over and I just held her. She was crying like it'd break your heart. Almost broke mine. I'm not cut out for this job any more, Aud. Can't take it. I suppose that's why I got a bit tiddly.'

'It doesn't matter; forget it.'

Mum kissed the top of my head, then reached for the remote. 'I'm going to watch some TV. You go and sort out the washing for me, Aud. Clean up a bit. And no more holding hands with boys. You didn't think I didn't see, did you?' She winked. Took a bite of her sandwich, attention drifting to the programme.

'Whatever,' I said, wondering if I should go over to see Leo and explain.

I went downstairs and lined up my pills on the worktop. The one to stop me feeling depressed. The one to stop me feeling sick. The one to stop me sleeping all day. The one to stop me cutting rivers in my arms and legs and thighs. There was a pill for everything. Everything except a pill to be free.

Leo

Audrey's kiss had been a shock. Leo hadn't been sure that she really liked him that much at all. He'd thought that if any moves were going to be made, then he'd be the one to make them, and the fact that Audrey had beaten him to it made him laugh. He'd call her later, he thought, and say something. About how he was glad. About how it felt, how *he* felt. He screwed up his face, thinking, and stared at the phone. Damn. He didn't have her number. It didn't matter; they were back to school the next day and he'd see her then, but in the meantime he could maybe run past the Grange, just to see if she was there.

'What's made you so sprightly?' Sue said as they cleared up the debris of the night before.

'Nothing.'

'You enjoyed yourself last night, then?'

'Sure.'

Sue smirked.

'What?' Leo laughed, facing her with wide, innocent eyes. 'What?'

'Oh, nothing. Nothing at all,' she answered, leaving him to it, whistling as she walked back into the house.

But later when he passed the Grange all was quiet, eerily still. He paused, his breath clouding in the chill November air. From now on he was going to do more to help, Leo decided. And if Lizzy Carr started up anything else he'd be straight in there. It was a mission. He jogged away, throwing glances back over his shoulder, but nothing stirred.

Audrey

Leo found me at break on Monday when he strode into the classroom and grabbed my hand. Someone whistled and I saw Lizzy's face out of the corner of my eye before he pulled me out into the corridor. At first we just grinned at each other.

'Leo –'

'Audrey –'

Our voices overlapped and I blushed and looked down at the floor, then back up into his eyes. I could just kiss him again; that had worked before. But this was school. And I couldn't make a habit of it, of kissing people the second they showed me the slightest bit of attention.

'I missed you,' he said, and that made me shout out a laugh.

'I only saw you on Saturday,' I said.

'Ages ago. And I don't have your number. Why don't I have your number?'

I shrugged, still smiling. He frowned, tangled both hands in mine.

'So, after school? Come over?'

'I'll try,' I said, and he nodded and held my hand for a second before the bell made us both jump and he let go and walked away.

At the end of the day Mum was waiting in the car

outside the gates and I didn't even get the chance to tell
Leo that our plans would have to wait.

'Come on,' she yelled. 'I'm over here, Aud.' The kids
milling around outside the school turned and stared. Peter
was already in the back, tapping the edge of his stone
against the window. Mum reached in and snatched it out
of his hand.

'What's going on? What's happened?'

'No panic. Just your appointment,' she said. 'Don't tell
me you forgot?'

'Oh.' I started to breathe again. 'I thought that was next
week.'

'I brought it forward. Lucky I phoned; they had a space.
I managed to persuade the secretary.'

'Mum.' It came out in that whiny voice little kids use.

'What's the problem? You don't have somewhere else
you need to be, do you?' She raised what was left of her
eyebrows. She'd picked them red raw.

'No. Obviously not. Because I don't get to have a life,
do I?'

'Watch your mouth, young lady.'

The rest of the drive she didn't speak. The air in the car
grew thick and hot and I wound down the window to lean
away from the smell.

At the hospital we waited ages; you always do. Then we
went in, leaving Peter in the waiting room, sitting there
playing with the box of toys meant for much littler kids.

'You'll watch him for me, won't you?' Mum said to the
woman on reception, who nodded and smiled.

'Audrey. Mrs Morgan?' The bloke was in a pinstripe

suit. Clean shaven. He didn't look like any of the other shrinks I'd seen.

'Yes, that's us,' Mum said, holding her bag in front of her like a shield, her eyes narrow and assessing.

'I'm Harry Wakeman. Take a seat.'

Mum sat, raised an eyebrow, looked at him – her dead-eye stare. It made no impression. Harry Wakeman just smiled and rubbed his hands together before placing them flat on his thighs and leaning in.

'So, Doctor Caldwell has referred Audrey to me. She suggests that Audrey's dealing with a number of issues. I'd like to talk a little about them, if that's all right; try and work out where we are as things stand today.'

'I can tell you straight off,' Mum began. He held up his hand.

'Bear with me, Mrs Morgan, I'll come to you in a moment. Audrey – how are you doing?' He had this matey voice, like we could be pals. I hated this sort. I didn't need a friend; I needed a life.

'Fine.' I folded my arms, crossed my legs.

'Fine, Aud?' said Mum, huffing, rearranging herself on the chair.

I nodded. She sighed.

'I'm afraid, that's not the case. I wish it were.' She began to tick off my problems on her fingers: 'Depression. Self-harm. She's not sleeping, paranoid, refuses to go in her bedroom – says there's something in there, for God's sake, something that's going to get her.' That meant Mum had read my diary. She wouldn't know that otherwise. I stared at her, wanted to slap her. Hard. 'So I've got her sleeping on the sofa, taking up the living room every night. Her moods are up and down: one minute she's delightful, the next minute moody and unpleasant and out of my control. And I'm not talking about your normal teen angst, here. I need help. And now.'

'OK. Mrs Morgan. If you could take a minute to calm down. Let's try and deal with things one step at a time.'

But Mum was seriously going for it, sitting up ramrod straight, shoulders tant.

'Plus there's sex. There's this lad; she's mad about him and I'm worried where this could lead.'

'How do you mean?'

'I mean, she's clearly vulnerable. And this boy's older and could be out to take advantage. I'm on the verge of saying I'm not able to cope. I'm on the verge of saying I can't have her at home any more.'

'How does that make you feel, Audrey?'

I shrugged, kicked my feet on the floor, making the tiles squeal.

'It must make you feel something, to hear your mother so evidently concerned. So upset.'

'She won't talk to you,' Mum told him, and I zoned her out, began to hum quietly, then louder. Mum's mouth was still moving but at least now I couldn't hear, and I watched as she pulled up her sleeve, bared her arm to Harry, showing her bruises.

Harry said something to me. I didn't hear what, so I just nodded again. Like those stupid dogs you see sitting on the back shelf in cars, heads bobbing up and down, fixed inane grin.

It went on like that for another twenty minutes. Mum saying things about me. Me not speaking. The therapist trying to get me to open up, as he put it. But there was no point telling him the truth. I wasn't shy or a mean girl or insane. Not any of those things. Blocking them out, I wrapped my arms round my legs, dropped my head on my knees, humming then rocking. Backwards and forward; forward and back, a cradle for a baby. Whatever it took to get out of there, to shut them up.

When we got back in the car I couldn't help a huge sigh. It was so much work, so hard not to feel. Not to care. Mum patted my knee, singing along to the radio as she drove.

'Don't worry, Aud,' she said, turning to me for a second. 'I'm here. You stay home with me tomorrow, love. Nice and safe.'

The next morning Mum dropped Peter off at school, then came back home to be with me. She sat talking for ages on the phone.

'Your form tutor's very understanding, Aud,' she said when she finally hung up. 'Nice lady. She says they'll get some work home for you, that she'll notify your teachers so you won't fall behind.'

'I reckon I'll just go in.' It was stupid to sit here when there was nothing wrong with me. And I actually wanted to go. Lizzy was nothing. I had Leo.

'Don't worry, love. I think you need the rest. Just take a day – you've been overdoing it; you look tired.' Mum gave me a hug, passed me a glass of juice. 'What can I get you? What d'you need?'

'Nothing.' I walked to the window and looked out.

Mum sat at the computer, reading her favourite websites, her horoscope, then mine, tutting, laughing, reading out little snippets about her favourite celebs and the royal family. I didn't listen. I thought about Leo. Itched to get out of the house and find him, just to talk more. My head was full of him. Carrying Peter on his shoulders, holding my hand at the fair, finding me at school, his face pleased to see me, and how he always knew what to say. I thought about kissing him again.

'I've been thinking of ways to keep you busy, Audrey, take your mind off your problems,' Mum said, chewing on a bit of toast, gesturing towards me with the crust.

I didn't answer that. She'd once tried to teach me to knit; apparently that would help me deal with things. I'd been useless, all fingers and thumbs. The same with cross stitch – I turned the silk thread into a tight ball of knots within minutes.

'I thought you could set up a page.' She typed 'blogging' into Google. 'Look at all this. It's all here, all the advice, how to get started. I was thinking you could do your own little page or something, just to keep yourself busy while you're sitting at home.'

'What would I blog about?'

'You know, how you're feeling and things. We could call it something like "A Prayer For Audrey". What d'you think? There'd be a lot of people interested, you know; there's a lot of kids out there like you.'

'I dunno.' I hated it. Really hated it. I didn't want random people knowing about me. Staring at pictures. It was like holding me up, saying, *Look, come and laugh at the weirdo*. Imagine Lizzy, if she found it. Imagine what she'd say.

'Look,' she said, loading a page. 'Look at this girl here.'

I read through it. The page was all about a little kid's battle with cancer; she was only thirteen, there were pictures of her in hospital and a long bucket list of things she wanted to do before she died.

'Mum, I'm not terminally ill.'

'Well, you are sick though. Very poorly. Audrey, mental illness is a serious condition. Sometimes I think you don't realize.' For a second I wondered if she'd rather I had cancer. Then at least she could make people feel sorry for me, for her. I would be a much better patient then.

'I think it might be a bit OTT, Mum, that's all. I just want to get better. Get back to normal. Things were going all right before.'

'They weren't, Aud. That's just it. You've started cutting again; you're not sleeping. You can't pretend that you're all right; you've got to face up to things and work a bit harder to get better. And if these doctors can't sort you we'll find some who will.'

I slumped into the chair.

'Well, tell you what, let's get it set up anyway. Then see how you feel.'

So Mum spent the morning doing that. I had to sit next to her and watch. Admire. Agree. Mum chose a colour scheme, designed it all pink and yellow, found some pictures of me that she said she'd scan in at work. They were old ones from when I was a baby.

'Here you are, just out of hospital,' she said staring.

'Look, you're so cute. Tiny though. My God, I thought I'd break you, just picking you up.'

'All right, Mum.' When she got like this it was hard to stop her. She'd be crying in a minute and I hated it when she cried. It made me itch, want to walk away and scratch my face to ribbons.

'You were so precious. Just this little scrap of a thing. Your dad fell in love with you the second he saw you. He was always a right soppy bugger.'

'My dad?'

'Yeah.' She never usually mentioned him. Never let me ask questions.

'Do you know where he is now?'

'No. Why would I?'

Why did he leave us? I wanted to say. *Where did he go? Can we find him? I want to know him, Mum, please.*

She checked her watch.

'And it's time to get Peter. You go, Aud. Fetch something for tea too. I'm knackered with all this. Need a bit of lie down.'

She took a pill, one of the sleeping tablets a doctor back home had prescribed me, and took herself off to bed. Those pills worked. Like horse tranquillizers or something. She wouldn't be up for hours now, which meant after I'd met Peter I could see if Leo was around after all.

Leo

Leo was thinking about Audrey a lot; when he should have been doing other things, mostly. Like taking notes in English, or listening to the teacher at least. He rested his head on his hand and remembered her, lit up. Her eyes staring at him wide and dark, a shifting smudge of grey, green. And her mouth. Soft. Ridiculously soft. All half-term he'd imagined her with him and that they were hopping on and off London buses together, peering into cases holding ancient artefacts, staring at dinosaurs, skulls, sarcophagi. He could feel how excited she'd be about everything. As if it were all brand new. And now she wasn't at school.

'Anyone tell me what a paradox is? Hmm?' The teacher prowled past his desk. Turned on his heel; prowled back the other way.

No one answered his question. Of course. Leo looked round the room; by all accounts they were mostly asleep.

It was a mistake to have raised his head. Mr Bruce pounced.

'So, Leo. Perhaps you can enlighten us. You seem to be a mine of technical information.' For some reason his prior knowledge of this subject irritated Mr Bruce. He was pretty sure he'd heard him sneering about posh kids waltzing around with their silver spoons dangling from their mouths. Leo could have set him straight but he had stored up the story for Sue and they'd laughed about it instead.

'Sure, I know.'

'Would you like to share your interpretation with the class?'

'If you really want.'

'I do. Go ahead.'

'A paradox is a strange contradiction,' he said, staring out of the window, 'like the fact that we're supposedly free to leave here –' he looked back at the teacher for a second, then gestured at the classroom – 'any time we choose, but in reality if we did, then the shit would hit the fan. So we are both free and not free at the same time. That's a paradox. Something that's true and false. At the same time.'

The teacher smiled. That was a first. At least he'd made one person happy today.

'An interesting definition, Leo, thank you. I'll remind you of what Jean-Jacques Rousseau said, perhaps only a little more eloquently than you: "Man is born free, but everywhere is in chains." You'd agree, I suppose?'

'Yeah, maybe. But Rousseau was a bastard. Dumped his kids. Apparently philosophy was more important than fatherhood. So I wouldn't necessarily agree with anything he said.'

Leo switched off again after that. He'd studied *Macbeth* too many times to care about equivocation and the supernatural and paradoxes.

The bell rang and he walked fast, forgetting to dawdle,

after spending a week with his mother. They'd charged in and out of museums like there was someone chasing them. It seemed the faster you went, the more you'd know, or something like that. And Mum rabbiting on and on about his future, the bloody UCAS form he still hadn't completed nagging at his conscience. Leo was considering running away. Building a boat and sailing round the world. Maybe Audrey would come.

He was some way out to sea when he heard his name being shouted.

'Leo, Leo!' Voices in unison. Thudding feet behind him. He spun round. Peter barrelled into him, Audrey was a bit behind, but hurrying, her hair streaming out behind her like the girl in the painting in the Tate he'd stared at last week, thinking he recognized her. Not realizing, until now, how that could be.

'Can we come with you?' Peter said, charging past as Leo paused. 'I want to play football.'

'You're on.'

Leo grabbed Audrey's hand, didn't listen to her squealing, 'Stop,' but he caught her laughter like a bird in his heart and dragged her along the path; he could have sworn right then there was a chance they might fly.

Audrey

At Sue's we stuffed ourselves, raiding the cupboards for snacks, then lay on the worn rugs in the living room as the light began to fade. Leo crouched beside a record player and began flicking through a pile of albums. Peter and I knew what albums were because once we'd had a huge collection spanning decades: they'd belonged to my dad, Mum said, but he'd left them behind when he'd buggered off. The Beatles, the Velvet Underground, Lou Reed, mixed up with my mum's Elton John, Tom Jones and Cher. Dad's prized possessions were the Rolling Stones LPs, first editions which he'd trawled auctions to find. Mum had flogged them at a car boot before we moved. She'd said it was about time; I hadn't been able to watch and had walked off with Peter and left her to it. Now I sat beside Leo and looked with him.

'Oh, my God. We had these.' I turned over the copy of *Loaded*, the names of the songs smiling at me like old friends.

'Yeah?'

'Yeah.' I remembered dancing. Swinging high off my feet, then staggering, dizzy, hands clutching fistfuls of carpet as I sank to the floor, Dad lifting me up, laughing. A kiss on the top of my head.

Leo laughed. 'Pick a record. Anything.' He sat back and let me get on with it.

It was a hard choice; I could have spent all day just rummaging.

'OK. I'll take this.' I handed over *Please Please Me*. 'I feel like dancing,' I said, then bit my lip. *Seriously, Aud. Seriously? You're going to dance? In the middle of the day? In front of Leo?*

'Cool.' He unsheathed the black disc, holding it at the edges, balanced between fingertips. 'These records belonged to Sue's husband. She lets me play them. Thinks maybe he'll hear, wherever he is.'

'Why? What happened to him?'

'He disappeared; just walked out over the fields one day and never came back. Sue reckons he stepped in the sinking sand, you know, a few miles down, along the embankment. It was early; no one would have been around or seen it happen, heard him call.'

'Sinking sand? You're kidding?' I shivered. Imagine it: trying to save yourself, grabbing at handfuls of dissolving earth, mud filling your mouth, your eyes, swallowing you up. My breath quickened; my blood thumped.

'Yes, sorry. Not a very jolly tale.' Leo bit his lip; he looked guilty for some reason.

'No.' I shook myself. 'It's my worst nightmare, that's all. Drowning, like that. Like anything. Getting buried alive.' I rubbed my ankle; it was hurting again after the walk, but I stood up, pushing the pain away. 'Let's not talk about it.'

He dropped the record on the turntable, pressed a

button, the speakers crackled and the music began. 'Love Me Do'. Shit, that was embarrassing.

'Pete,' I called, 'Peter, come and dance.'

Peter ran in, stuffing in the last of his jam sandwich, Mary chasing behind. I took Peter's hands, like Dad had once taken mine, and spun him until he was squealing and I was dizzy. When I let go we stumbled into a heap. The next song was slow. Leo picked up the needle and dropped it on the last track.

'"Twist and Shout". You'll have to get up again now, Audrey. No excuses.'

'All right. Bet I can twist better than you.'

'We'll see.'

Jumping up, John Lennon's raucous voice egging me on, we stamped and twisted and shouted and roared, competing for who could hold the top notes longest, who could scream hardest. Peter put his hands over his ears and I was laughing and singing at the same time, Leo too. Leo could move. He wasn't embarrassed; he didn't care, so nor did I. The dog jumped and barked, up on hind legs now and then; that made me laugh too. When the record ended, the room faded into silence and we stood there, staring at each other, out of breath, still smiling.

'It's a long time since I did that,' Leo said. 'Why did I forget?'

'Me too. I think we should do it every day.'

'For sure.'

'Not me,' said Peter, running off again. 'I'm going outside.'

He belted off, Mary at his side.

'My choice now.'

Leo picked up the Velvet Underground record I'd been looking at and as the music played more memories flooded back: a little sitting room, Dad lying on a sofa, feet up, smoking a roll-up, flicking through a magazine, the windows open, curtains flying in the breeze, and me, dancing my dolly round the furniture. Leo held out a hand, I took it; he pulled me close and began to waltz. I followed where he led.

'What is it? Glockenspiel?' I listened, head on his shoulder.

'No, celesta; similar sound though,' he murmured.

'Wow. I never heard of that before,' I said, as Lou Reed breathed out the words to 'Sunday Morning', Nico singing all weird behind him. 'How do you know that?'

'Audrey, I have to warn you – I know a lot of pointless and random information. I apologize in advance.'

We glided across the rug; he tipped me back and pulled me straight, my hair streaming like a sail.

'It's not pointless. It's good.'

Leo shrugged and spun me.

'Can you play?' I asked.

Pulling me in, closer, he ignored the question.

'Course he can, Audrey. He just won't.' I jumped; there was Sue, popping her head round the door and smiling. How much had she heard? And seen?

'Thank you, aunt.' Leo waved her away.

'Pleasure, dear,' she said, disappearing again.

'Why don't you play?' I asked Leo when he pulled me back. His chin rested on my head.

'Because my mother forced me to play the piano for years when I was a kid. I hated it. I hate it still. It was a form of torture, actually.' He waggled the fingers of one hand. 'Surprised I have any hands left. There was hours of it.'

'My mum never made me do anything like that. I would have liked lessons though; maybe piano. Or the trumpet.' It must be weird to have a mother who thought you could do stuff – no, believed you could. Expected it.

'Piano was just the start. The Mandarin Chinese and all the tennis and the fucking violin.' Bitterness dripped off him. It was the first time his mouth had looked ugly. But it was because it hurt; I got that. The track ended and Leo let me go. He stretched. Then he smiled, walking over to the bookshelves, pacing back. I threw myself on to the sofa, curling up to listen.

'Sorry, saw her last week. She was just the same.'

'The same how?' I caught his eye.

'She's spent her life wanting me to be something I'm not. Some hideous little genius kid.' He laughed, embarrassed. 'I'm afraid I'm a bit of a disappointment.'

'No way.'

'Oh, yes. But don't worry. I'm perfectly happy with that.'

'So, is that why you don't live with them? Because you don't get on with your mum?'

'Not exactly. Don't get on –' he mulled over the words – 'that isn't it really.' He scanned the room, stared out of the window for a minute, then looked back at me. 'This sounds awful. Don't get me wrong, Mum's actually

great – clever and sharp and funny. You'd like her, I think.'
I nodded because I knew how this felt and Leo's face was
anxious, he was trying to find the words, and rubbed his
face with his palms. 'But, I don't know, when I'm with her
it's like we're playing this hideous game of ping-pong;
she just keeps hitting those little balls as hard and fast as
she can and every time I return one she whacks it back,
double the speed. Eventually she catches me out. Every
time.' He gave a short laugh. 'But Sue doesn't care about
exams, or extra-curricular or anything; she just wants me
to be happy. It was my dad's idea for me to live here. After
I had this breakdown. I suspect he was embarrassed.'

'Yeah?' I pressed my chin into my knees. Leo had had a
breakdown. I'd never have thought it; I'd never have
guessed. I blinked slowly, letting it sink in before I looked
at him. I tried to make my face show what I felt. That it
didn't matter and that I got it. I got him. He sat down next
to me.

'It was a couple of years ago now, Aud. I freaked out, I
guess; too much pressure. I couldn't take it. But, hey –' he
touched my hand briefly – 'don't look like that. I'm
fine now. Totally sorted.' I thought he was sad, but then he
grinned. I had to smile back. And I felt like telling some
secrets of my own.

'Mum told this new therapist that she can't cope with
me any more and that she wants to send me away, but I
don't believe her.'

'Why would she say it, then?'

'I dunno. Maybe she thinks she'll scare me into being
good.' I shrugged again, and tried to look like it didn't

matter, but it hurt. Mum saying she didn't want me. I'd hurt her, not helped myself, and she'd had enough.

'Are you bad?'

I laughed again. It was stupid to laugh.

'I have no idea. I don't try to be. I'm just me. Maybe that's the problem; she just doesn't like me.' Coughing up bits of truth here, like pebbles, shiny and hard, spitting them at Leo's feet like the bottom of the sea was in my lungs. All those secrets. The doors in my mind creaked and swung. I slammed each one shut, dropped my head for a moment, dizzy. I could never tell him everything; he'd hate me if he knew.

'I don't know how that could be.' His voice was soft and sorry and my blood rose, staining my face. I put my palms to my cheeks, hiding.

Leo reached out and put his arm round me.

'Don't worry.'

'I'm not. I'm sorry; I'm fine.' I looked up. 'It's just sometimes, you know, sometimes I hate her.'

'What?'

'Sometimes I hate my mum.' I swallowed. Even saying it hurt. And it wasn't true, really, was it? I screwed my fists tight. Leo was about to say something but I stopped him, putting my finger on his lips.

Leo

Make a move, Leo. Come on, this is pathetic, he thought. But it had all got too intense, like some impromptu therapy session. Not that he didn't want to help Audrey and be there for her, of course he did. What she was going through was horrible. But she didn't need to hear his mess too; he hadn't invited her back for that. There had been other reasons. Very different reasons. The problem was she was too easy to talk to – so still and gentle and intent; like every word he said sank deep, like she really gave a damn.

Audrey dropped her finger from his lips, jumped up and headed for the door, grabbing her stuff, saying something about Peter and getting their dinner.

'No, hang on.' Leo chased after her, crossing the room before she could disappear. He held her arm, gently though.

'Don't go yet, Aud.'

'I have to,' she said, turning and smiling.

'No, wait.' His arms were round her. It was that easy. He pushed the door shut with his foot. The room dimmed, twilight was creeping in, and in the shadows her eyes looked darker and deeper than ever, like he could drown there. Her hair glowed, moonlight.

'You can't go. Not yet,' Leo said.

'I can.' She laughed, twisting a little. He held her, not so tight, nearly letting go.

'Well, all right, you can. If you want. But I wanted to say –'

'Yeah?' she appeared to be teasing him. He caught her eye and produced his best serious look.

'I really missed you. At half-term. I kept thinking about how I wanted to talk to you. I wanted to call.' He took a deep breath. For God's sake, they'd kissed. Now this? It was ridiculous. He should just go for it. 'Will you give me your number?'

'Course. Well, the home number. I don't have a mobile.'

'Bugger.'

'Why bugger?'

'I wanted to text you. All night. Drive you crazy with evidence of my devotion.'

Devotion. That was a big word. That word meant things. *So what, Leo*, he thought, *you mean it, don't you? You wouldn't say it if you didn't mean it.*

'Sure. You'll have to send a pigeon though,' Audrey said.

'Right. It's a plan.'

'Cool. So, can I go now?' She put her head on one side, half smiling. Leo was never sure.

'No. One more thing.'

The room fell quiet. Their bodies touched, close again, she pulled back, then moved forward, near, her fingers tangling with his. If this were the rest of his life, he'd be happy, he thought. Leo kissed her. That definitely wasn't enough. He kissed Audrey again, for longer this time, and she kissed back, her hands round his neck, her body very close. He put his hands in her hair and closed his eyes. *Eternity was in our lips and eyes*, he thought, *bliss in our brows bent.*

'Heeeelp! Audrey, Aud, heeelp.' The hollers broke the spell and Audrey pulled away from him.

'It's Pete,' she said, and Leo followed her out of the house and into the garden, where Peter was waiting, high up in a tree, pretending not to be stuck now they were near. Leo climbed up, swift and sure, helped him to find his footing and climb back down and to pick out a splinter. Then he touched Audrey's arm one last time before she set out for home.

'Here, take my jacket,' he said, 'you'll freeze otherwise.' She nodded and smiled like that was sealing a pact, and off they went: one tall, one small, their figures melting into the dusk. Leo hoped she could hear him calling goodbye and he watched them until they disappeared.

Audrey

'Where've you been?'

Mum was supposed to have been asleep, but the flat was full of choking cigarette smoke and I opened the windows, walking straight past her.

'Where've you been, Aud?' She followed me, lifted my hair, sniffed at my neck, my skin. I shrugged her off and pulled away. It was Leo I wanted. My mouth felt swollen. I closed my lips tight.

'At Leo's,' Peter piped up. 'We could have stayed too. But Aud said you'd be doing the tea. I wanted to stay.'

Mum stared at me, her mouth hanging open.

'What do you think you're playing at, Aud? I thought I said no more going round there, didn't I?' She was so rough, like sandpaper, scratching my skin with her words.

'What do you mean?'

'I mean, you and Leo. Forget it.' She had her hands on her hips. Mrs Bossy Boots.

'Yeah, all right, whatever.' No way.

I unpacked the shopping and started heating soup. Peter hovered close, like he always did when Mum and I rowed, checking my face, then Mum's. Mum was just standing there watching us, and I moved stiffly under her stares.

She lit another cigarette – she must have got through a

whole pack this afternoon – and then said, all casual, as she took a drag, 'I know what you're up to, Aud, and I'm just saying, I wouldn't make a fool out of myself if I were you. I'm not being funny, but no lad's going to want to touch you, believe me.'

I pushed my hair out of my face and tried to smile when Peter looked at me, his face all in a worry. My brother tugged my sleeve, and I crouched lower to hear him.

'I think you're pretty, Aud,' he said, and I dropped a kiss on his head.

'Look at the state of you,' Mum continued. 'He'll be sorry for you, that's all. And you don't want sympathy like that.'

Mum's words were little daggers that scored and stabbed. But Leo had touched me. He'd kissed me. He liked me. The soup began to bubble; I turned down the heat and stuck some bread in the toaster, smiling at Peter and pretending I couldn't hear her.

'Are you mad with me,' Peter whispered, 'for telling?'

'No, no. You're fine. Don't worry, mate. Here. You stir. Carefully, so it doesn't slop over and splash you; it's hot, all right?'

He nodded and took the wooden spoon, standing on tiptoe and biting his lip with concentration, stirring round and round and round, and we pretended Mum wasn't there.

The next morning Peter and I got up early to cook pancakes. I'd told him he could be head chef after he'd done such a good job with our tea the night before, and I watched him mixing, like I'd taught him, then going too fast and slopping the batter over the sides of the bowl. Mum watched with me and we exchanged a glance, smiling. There was no point in my staying mad at her. For Peter's sake I had to forget it. Tell her what she wanted to hear, then do my own thing. When Peter was born I was almost eleven and she said I could be his mummy too. What I wanted most was to push the pram, and Mum let me put him in the buggy and push him around as if he were my toy. I was careful though. I fastened the straps round him, made our perambulations slow and gentle. He never fell out, not when I was pushing, not when I was in charge. Peter never had a dad. At least I'd had mine for a little while.

'Ready!' called Peter, as I helped him flip the first pancake and catch it before it fell. We clapped and cheered and he put it before Mum as if he were presenting her with the Crown jewels. Slathering it with syrup, she ate slowly, savouring each mouthful, and my own mouth filled with saliva; I wanted to take a bite, just a little, to please Peter and because it smelled so good. She saw me reaching out, raised an eyebrow.

'Can I, Mum? Just a mouthful?'

'Audrey.' There was a warning note in her voice.

'I'm fine though, Mum. I'm sure it'll be all right. I could try.'

'Allergies don't just disappear, love. The reason you're fine is because you've been steering clear. I know it's hard, but we can't be too careful.' She pointed at me with her right hand, another forkful coming to her mouth with her left. 'And do you really want to end up like me? Bursting out of your clothes? That's not going to do your health any good, is it?'

I looked back down at the table, at my fingers spread there, long and thin and empty, but when she'd gone to get a shower Peter passed me a bit of his pancake that he'd saved.

'Eat it,' he whispered. 'Quick – it tastes of sunshine.' And I crammed the lot in, all at once, chewed it slowly and helped him with the washing up.

Mum checked the mail on our way out of the Grange. I knew what she was looking for – the next appointment card. It had arrived two days ago and I'd found it first, taken it to the moat and stood there and shredded it into tiny pieces, impossible ever to reassemble. It wouldn't give me much time, but maybe a little more.

'Nothing. Again.' Mum riffled through the envelopes she'd snatched from the letter box. The front door was still broken, swinging on its hinges and I shuffled leaves underfoot and waited. It was all junk. Mostly.

'I mean, where are we, mid-November now? They usually send the cards out straight away. I'll give them a ring,' she said, then: 'What's this?'

Something fluttered out of her fingers and she snatched it up, staring.

'Give it here.' I held out my hand. The paper was a little crushed, but you could still see what it was. A flower. Five petals. Someone had folded paper, old and yellowing, and I made out the words: tiny print, disappearing into the petals, the stem. There were few words left whole: *I, and, love, sure, bird, my, at last.* Unless I unfolded the paper, smoothed it out flat, I wouldn't know what they said. The mystery was better.

'Can I keep it?'

She shrugged and I took it, put it in my pocket, planned to plant it later in my room, like a magic talisman to chase away a bit of the dark.

On Friday evening after school Mum and I worked on the blog again. I kept looking out towards the farm, wondering what was happening there, which record Leo was listening to, which book he was reading, what he and Sue were talking about. So I was watching for him as he ran past. Every night this week he'd stopped in exactly the same spot and waited, ten seconds, then lifted his hand before running on.

'Come on, Aud – what are you doing?' Mum said, dragging my eyes back to her laptop.

'What shall I put?' I rested my head on my hand, yawning. Leo had brought a picnic to school. We'd sat at our bench. I couldn't remember what we'd talked about. I just remembered our ankles, tangled under the table, and his cool strong hand, holding mine, swinging my arm when we walked back inside. Our eyes, locking, as he walked backwards down the corridor because he said he didn't want to look away, and how all afternoon not a single word a teacher had said had made any sense.

'Describe what you're feeling like. Like you do in your diary,' Mum said. She was close at my shoulder, her breath in my ear.

'Mum.' I ground my teeth, crushing the words I wanted to shout. She ignored me.

'Write about the meds, the therapy with Harry. You can write about me if you like, how I'm your support network. Write about why you cut yourself, why you're not doing so well at school. How it feels, your depression.' She leant forward, her elbows on the table. 'Anything really. It'll be therapeutic.'

Mum had taken some pictures and I let her load one. If I was supposed to look like shit, then she'd done a good job. The girl in the photo was pale and sickly looking, all skinny long legs and greasy hair. At least my face was a bit blurred.

I started to type.

> I've been a bit ill, things have got a bit crazy – excuse the crap pun. I can't really explain it – the whole story is way too long – but thanks to my mum I'm doing all right, oh, yeah, and Harry, my therapist. Yeah, I have a therapist now, which I suppose means I truly am INSANE. NUTS. MENTAL. PSYCHO. That's what they say about people like me, that's what the kids say at school anyway. Like all I am is a madness, a hideous, frightening thing. But I'm real. I'm a girl and I'm trying to get by, even though I'm scared too. Deep breath. Well, Harry seems all right. Maybe he'll help.

If I really tried, I could imagine her. This girl, aged sixteen, really screwed up. I imagined her feeling so shit that she wanted to get away from everything, could see no other way to be happy other than by slicing into her skin and setting it alight with blood. I saw the dark stain of that girl in my bedroom window, saw her screaming and bleeding. Her mother rushing her to the doctor. I wrote the story for her. Put her pain into words.

Usually I cut myself to get away, I typed.

Because, and I know this sounds weird, sometimes I feel dead and the pain brings me back to life. Sometimes I think I'm so bad that I need to hurt myself – to dig as hard as I can into my skin, teach it a lesson. But now I'm feeling better. And I hope it lasts. So long as I take my medication, so long as I'm good, maybe I'll be OK.

It was like the stories they used to make us write in English lessons. Imagine you are Miss Havisham. Write a diary entry explaining what it feels like to set yourself on fire. Until it turned into an essay factory about more things I didn't understand. The real me? Well, I was saving her for other things.

Mum read through what I'd written.

'Is that it?'

'Yeah. What's the matter?'

'Well, it's not really very interesting, is it, Aud? Plus you hardly mention me at all.'

'Mum, I don't think you get it. I don't want to do it. This is all I could come up with.' My finger hovered over the delete button. She held my wrist, pushed me aside.

'Right, well, give me a go,' she said, and I got up and left her to it.

Leo

Nearly two weeks later and Lorraine was downstairs in the kitchen again. She'd become a bit of a regular fixture since the bonfire party, but when she came over Leo tried not to be around. Often there was crying. It got heavy. Sometimes it was about Aud's dad, who'd left her way before she had Peter. Other times it was about her job and the sick kids she looked after. And today: Audrey. Thoughts of Audrey made him restless. He couldn't sit still, couldn't finish a meal, couldn't read a line without forgetting its beginning, but when he heard Lorraine start, his stomach turned.

'Audrey's not good, Sue,' he heard. 'Really; she's seeing things, talking to people who aren't there. I thought this new medication she's on would help, and the therapy with Harry. But she never makes progress. We just go round in circles. What if she never gets the help she needs, what if she never gets better? What's the future for her, Sue?'

His aunt murmured something, Leo couldn't hear what, but he knew he shouldn't be listening at doors like a spy. He stepped away, ran back up to his room, then the front door slammed and it was safe to venture out and go for a run. Sue called him into the kitchen, hearing him crashing about. It stank of fags; there were three butts stubbed out in an old pottery ashtray that maybe Sue had made thirty years ago when she was at school. Whisking it away, binning the contents, opening windows, she told him to sit down.

'Right. So we need to have a chat.'

They didn't usually have premeditated conversations like this. This was more his mum's style. Leo swung back on his chair, looking at the ceiling.

'Lorraine's pretty worried,' Sue said. Leo righted himself, sitting up straight.

'Audrey's OK, isn't she?' He knew she was. He saw her every day at school.

'It depends how you define OK. You know she self-harms.'

'Yeah, and?'

'It's not our business. It's up to Lorraine to deal with this. Audrey's a pretty fragile girl. Lorraine thinks her friendship with you, lovely as it is, might not be helping.'

'Why?'

'Well, she's still hearing these voices, seeing things. Lorraine says maybe psychosis. She's not happy with the diagnosis. That it's depression. Audrey's very anxious and unstable.'

'Meaning?'

'Meaning no boyfriends, I'm afraid.'

'Sue, for the thousandth time. I am not Audrey's boyfriend. I have not upset her. I am not going to make her cut herself.' He hoped all of those things, apart from the first, were true. Felt pretty certain.

'All right, all right, I'm not suggesting you are. It's just that Lorraine hasn't been that explicit and of course you can't ask for the grisly details. I don't want to upset her. And I think talking about it is hard for her. I get that. The upshot of it is: Lorraine doesn't want Audrey getting attached to you. She doesn't think it'll help, in the long run. Either of you.'

'Everyone needs friends, Sue.' Leo returned his aunt's words to her and folded his arms. No way was this happening.

'Agreed. But if you can give her some space.'

'Sure.' He shrugged, pretended this was cool. 'Why wouldn't I? She can have all the space she needs.' He gestured at the world beyond the kitchen. 'Just look out there. There's miles of space.'

Sue gave him one of her looks. 'You know what I mean, so no need to get all clever, clever.'

'Yeah, I know.'

'Just a guess, but I thought you were getting keen.'

Leo stood up. He couldn't help but grin at the understatement.

'Is that it? Lecture over?'

His aunt nodded. 'That's it.'

Leo pulled on his trainers. It was getting dark and it was cold, but he needed out. Their conversation played in his head, over and over, a really bad record he couldn't switch off. He wanted to take it and smash it to pieces. It was bullshit. First Sue asked him to make friends, and then when he found someone he liked, someone he could actually talk to, next thing he was being warned off. What the hell? No way would Audrey want her mother interfering with things between them, and he wasn't going to listen to any of it either. The shock of the night took his breath and, gulping for air, he ran as fast as he could towards the Grange. His daily pilgrimage, whether she was there or not. Just to check, make sure.

Audrey

November got darker but school got better. It was like I had bodyguards: Jen on one side, and then every break, every lunch, Leo. He would be waiting outside the classroom, like my timetable was tattooed on his brain or something, and then he'd sling his arm round my shoulders and we'd slope off. The last Monday of the month we wandered along like that, tied up in each other, a cat's-cradle. I put both arms round his waist and he rested the side of his head against mine as we walked and I felt his brain whirring even through his blue bobble hat. He was always thinking, thinking, thinking.

'You should be some sort of professor,' I told him.

'No, thanks.'

'What, then? What are you going to do next year?'

'Next year? I prefer not to think about it. I'm a *carpe diem* sort of guy.'

I butted his shoulder with my head. 'Don't be flipping daft.'

'Daft?' He raised his eyebrows in outrage, then spun me into his arms.

'I'll show you daft,' he said, and we stood there in the playground among the footballs and the yelling and the bored kids chewing gum, stood amid the piles of autumn leaves, our foreheads touching, then our cheeks and chins and I wrapped my arms round him, inside his coat, and he pulled me close like that, keeping warm.

It was the rain that woke me up the next morning, tapping and pattering on the window. I ran to the kitchen; Peter had already gone to school. I had a History test and couldn't be late.

'Why didn't you call me?' I said, hunting for my shoes. 'Look at the time, Mum.'

Mum was sitting watching telly and knitting. She was making Sue a jumper for Christmas, to thank her for being such a good friend.

'I thought you needed the rest. You were pacing again, Audrey, all night.'

'I wasn't.'

'Yes, you were, and I heard you talking. I've been on the phone to the unit. I'm trying to get hold of Harry'

'Mum, I don't want to see Harry.'

'Tough.'

I pulled on a pair of old plimsolls and ran out of the flat down to the lobby, checking the letter box on the way. Today there was a tiny bird. Not a real bird, but another paper creation twisted out of poetry, its wings spread wide, even its tiny feet perfectly fashioned. I made out the words – *I*, *heaven*, *light*, *dreams* – and I whispered them over and over, trying to decipher the code.

'What are you doing?' Mum said, appearing in the doorway behind me, her uniform on.

'Nothing.'

I hid the bird behind me. It fluttered in my hand.

'Well,' she said, 'get a move on. And get Peter after school – don't forget.'

'Course I won't.'

'Good. And I'll get that appointment sorted, right?' she challenged, her eyes popping at me as if daring me to complain.

'OK,' I said, and raced away to school.

That afternoon I stood waiting for Peter at the primary-school gate, wrapping my scarf high round my face so no one would talk to me. I stared across to the college. I'd not seen Leo all day; I'd done extra work at lunchtime with Jen on our English project and Leo had had a meeting with his tutor at break.

Peter emerged and I bent down to hug him.

'This is my friend,' he said, pulling me over to meet a little boy in a red anorak, then hiding behind my legs.

'Hello,' I said. The mum smiled briefly at me.

'Pete, hey, why don't you introduce us?' I said, prising him out from behind me.

'This is my sister. She's called Audrey,' he said to the little boy, who grinned at me, and then they started chasing.

'Nicky, come back,' the woman yelled, abandoning her buggy and dashing off after them. But Nicky was fast and he and Peter flew in circles. All I could do was laugh.

'We'll be late now,' the woman said to Nicky when she caught him, pulling him along by his sleeve, and they hustled off without saying goodbye.

'Right, Pete, I guess we should go too.'

'Can we invite Nicky to play round our house?'

'Maybe. Let's ask Mum, OK?'

'She'll say no,' he said, jamming his thumb in his mouth, and I grabbed his hand.

'Let's sing the going-home song,' I said, but he stuck out his bottom lip, dragging his feet as I started to walk him out of the playground.

Where was Leo? I would have missed him by now, the last stragglers were just leaving college and Leo always got out first. He'd be halfway home along the embankment, I reckoned.

'I've got a good idea,' I said, 'let's go to the farm.'

'I'm tired. My feet hurt.'

'I'll carry you?'

Peter stared at me, a big *no* in his face, so we stood at the bus stop instead and it began to rain.

Leo

'Pull over, there's Aud and Peter.'

Sue nodded and stopped. Leo wound down the window and leant out.

'Lift?' he said, thanking the gods, or whoever was in charge of life's little tricks of fate for this. Usually Lorraine picked them up from school.

Audrey helped Peter up first and then squashed in beside him. Leo reached for her hand without thinking and held it.

Sue cleared her throat. She touched the indicator and pulled back out into the traffic.

'Well,' she said, 'good job we found you, or you'd have been drenched by the time that bus came.'

'Thanks, Sue,' said Audrey. Leo squeezed her fingers and leant across Peter to whisper in her ear.

'Where've you been?' he murmured. His mouth was very near her neck. Her skin smelled of the cold, and roses, deep-red winter roses. He let his lips touch her ear and she jumped.

'We'd better drop you off at home,' said Sue. 'We're on our way to visit friends.'

'Oh, thanks; thanks for that.'

'It's no problem,' Sue said. 'Get those sweets out of my handbag, Leo – share them out.'

When they got to the Grange Leo got out of the Land Rover too. He walked them up to the front door.

'Right,' he said, 'I have to see you – so, when? School's not enough. Lunchtimes are too short. And cold.'

'Soon,' Aud promised. 'Friday. Mum always works Friday nights. Can you come?'

'Yeah.' He looked back at Sue, who was pretending not to be watching. Peter was kicking at the front door.

'Aud,' Peter said. 'Come on, Aud.'

'You'd better go.'

'Yes,' Audrey said, still standing there.

'Bye, then.'

'Bye.'

Then they stumbled into one another, very fast, and there was the smudge of a kiss, but it burned his mouth and she fumbled with her keys and that was all.

Leo

At some point his mother had to find out about Audrey. Sue claimed she hadn't mentioned her, or if she had she certainly hadn't meant to. But his mum just knew. Leo wondered when he'd stop being an open book to her, how thousands of miles away she could still read him. It was after they'd got home to the farm, after the dull supper at some WI mate of Sue's, that she called.

'So. A new girlfriend?'

'Pardon?'

'Leo, I can guess, just by the look in your eyes.'

He dodged out of view and she shouted at him from the computer screen, half laughing.

'Well, I hope she's a nice girl, bright and gives you a bit of challenge. And I hope she appreciates how lucky she is. Jecca only emailed the other day, said she wondered if you two might hook up in the Christmas break. But I suppose you're staying in the sticks?'

'That depends. If you want me to come to London, I will. You'll be coming over, right?'

'Sorry, darling, I'm not.' Her voice was tinged with regret, then she justified herself: 'Work's hectic. You could always come out to us, you know. Either way, Jecca would love to see you if you make it to town. And take the girl-friend. What's her name?'

'Audrey. She's not really my girlfriend.' He scratched his nail on the wood of the table, caught a splinter in the soft skin of his thumb. He didn't know why he'd lied.

'Good.'

'Mother,' Leo warned, and his mum smoothed her hair back, regarded him with a cool, appraising stare.

'And how's school? I hope this Audrey isn't getting in the way of your work.'

'As if, Mum. You know I live and breathe my work.'

'Don't be sarcastic. Lowest form of wit, darling.'

He'd been surprised: she left it at that and their conversation had finished soon after. Like she said, she was busy. And he ought to have been busy on his latest essay for Mr Bruce. They'd moved on to Renaissance poetry: John Donne. He had to admit he rather liked John Donne.

On Friday, instead of grappling with metaphysical longings, Leo called round for Audrey, as they'd planned. When he knocked on the door of the flat she answered, pink-cheeked and smelling of sugar.

'Pete and I made biscuits. Here –' she held out the plate – 'they're good. A success for once. Despite the crap oven.'

He crammed the warm biscuit into his mouth, grinning while chewing. There was no sign of Lorraine, and Leo let the tension out of his shoulders. They had the place to themselves and it smelled better; that musty, mouldering odour had all but gone. Leo spied a bottle of bleach in the kitchen bin, rubber gloves on the worktop and guessed Audrey had been cleaning. Up close she smelled of swimming pools. He didn't mind.

'Pete's going to bed soon.' She cast him a swift look, brushed her hair out of her face and smiled.

Audrey was still tidying up and Leo watched her wiping the counters, bustling about, and that made him smile too. It was good to be here and see that she was OK. He didn't know what Lorraine had been talking about; the Audrey she described was never the one he saw. 'I'll read Pete a story if you like,' he said, 'and then we could watch a film. I brought a DVD.'

Leo could hear Audrey humming downstairs as he read the bedtime story. She wasn't exactly tuneful, but he liked the cheerful sound. Peter had his thumb in his mouth and snuggled under the covers.

'I love you, Leo,' he said when Leo closed the book and stood up.

'Thanks, Pete,' he told him, surprised, not sure what to say, really. 'You're a good chap,' he added, which he knew was the kind of thing his own father would have said to him on receipt of such a declaration of affection. Regretting it, he bent down, tucked the covers over Peter and kissed his forehead.

'Love you too, pal.' He felt Peter's smile against his cheek and smiled himself.

It was the first time he'd spent the evening at the Grange and Leo wondered if his imagination had tricked him. He'd been sure there'd be something to be scared, or at least wary, of. They ate biscuits, drank flat coke and watched the film, sitting close on the sofa. It was cold, but Audrey pulled a throw over them and they huddled up.

'It's snowing,' he said later, looking out of the window.

'You'll be all right walking back?'

'Sure. It's not far.' He had his arm round Audrey and hadn't actually been thinking about leaving at all.

'What shall we do?'

'I don't know. Do you want to explore?' Something in him wanted to see the place for himself. Check she was safe here.

'Sure,' she said, 'get your coat. I know where to go.'

Audrey

We climbed the two floors up to the top of the Grange and I pulled Leo out on to the fire escape.

Snowflakes fell softly, melting flowers on to our faces.

'I've seen you up here,' he said, as I stuck out my tongue to catch the icy flakes.

'Yeah. I've seen you too. Not that I've been watching or anything.'

'Haven't you?' he said, and I raised an eyebrow, took off my glasses and wiped them.

'Well. Maybe. I watch you and I wonder.' His face was a little blurred now, and I stared into a muddle of brown and gold, soft and sharp. His collar was up, his scarf wrapped loosely.

'What do you wonder?'

'What you're running from.' I shoved my glasses back on, still all smeared. What a stupid thing to say. He was jogging. Taking exercise; people did that sort of thing – that's all it was. But Leo laughed and brushed the snowflakes from my hair.

'Running from? Nothing. Running to, Aud, running to. That's the question you need to ask yourself.'

'Oh.' I sat down on the top step and he joined me, fitting in exactly. 'Well, there's a lot I don't know about you,' I said, staring out at the white winter sky.

'Yeah? What like?'

'Well, when's your birthday for a start?'

'August, annoyingly.'

I clapped my hands. Perfect.

'You really are a lion, then!'

'Oh, well, I suppose so.' Leo looked at me, a bit puzzled.

'Mum's into horoscopes and all that. Leos are brave, I think.'

'And proud and pretentious. It's all the hair,' he said, shaking his head. I nudged him with my elbow.

Leo went on, considering, 'Anyway, I don't think you can tell if someone's brave or good or whatever because of their name, or when they were born. It doesn't work like that.'

'It helps.'

'No, I think it's different. Being brave's about being strong. And being strong, well, strong comes from being loved, don't you think? If you know you're loved, then that's all it takes. Love gives you legs of steel.'

I thought about Peter and how I was his armour and saw that Leo was right.

'I still have your coat,' I told him, 'as you can see.' I wore it all the time.

'That's OK.' He grinned. 'I'll grab it back some other time.'

'And I found this.' I reached into the pocket and clasped my fingers round the tiny paper figure I'd found hiding there. 'Did you make the others? The bird, the flower, the arrows?' I held the figure on my palm, and it seemed to quiver as if it had a life of its own.

'I think it was that pigeon you mentioned,' Leo said, making me laugh.

'It's beautiful,' I said. 'Can I keep it?'

'Of course, it was for you anyway. I don't know if you can tell, but it's supposed to be you, superhero-style. Because I reckon you're brave too, Aud.'

I flushed. That was one of the nicest things anyone had ever said to me and I wanted it to be true.

Leo

It was easy to make Audrey happy, to make her smile. And easy to kiss her then, with no one to spy or shout or interrupt, the easiest thing he'd ever done and it lasted a long time. Much longer than before. If Lorraine was working every Friday, then Leo would be here every Friday.

'Shit,' Aud said when they stopped. Her glasses had misted over and she pulled them off and wiped them clean with the tip of a finger before shoving them back on her face.

'What?'

'Nothing. Just. Oh my God, and stuff.'

Leo laughed, he couldn't help it. She was acting like this was a surprise or something.

'Audrey, you're hilarious.' He kissed her again. 'And lovely –' she laughed, made a scathing noise – 'and totally weird.'

'That's better,' she said. 'I like weird.'

They didn't explore the rest of the Grange, didn't waste time searching for secret hidden horror. Instead, they wasted all their time kissing, in secret, totally hidden from everything and everyone, high above the world, snow-blind and sure.

Audrey

I was glad Leo hadn't come up to my room. I hadn't had time to deal with it and didn't want him to see the mess. After he left I sat on the bed, slowly taking off my clothes. My mouth was hot and swollen, and I couldn't stop smiling.

I took off my pants and stood up, naked, my body turning to goosebumps in the cold. My scars ran up my arms, my legs, up my thighs. Running a fingertip over the bright white ridges, I searched for words, a picture, maybe a map. Like ancient hieroglyphics, I tried to read the messages.

'So,' I whispered, waiting for the Thing, looking round, searching. 'Here I am. And?'

I listened for the hammer in my head, the drumbeat in my veins. But there was no answer. Not now I was so brave.

'I'm fine, you see,' I said. 'I'm growing up. Grown up. I don't need to be afraid of you now. You're not going to stop me doing stuff; you're not going to make me ill, get me thinking I'm mad again. I'm not going to die out here,' I said. 'I won't drown.'

Since I'd been seeing Harry, my arms had healed and I held them out in front of me.

'See? I'm better. It won't happen again. I can promise you that. You won't get me again.'

I pulled on my nightie, got into bed and covered my ears. It wouldn't wake me; it wouldn't dare disturb my dreams. Not tonight.

December

Leo

Suddenly there were only a few days of term left and Leo wondered where all the time had gone. Christmas party invitations were delivered and class nights out were planned, but Leo wasn't bothered unless Aud could come with him.

'I can't. You know what my mum's like,' she said, staring at the floor.

'Overprotective?' he hazarded, which was the least offensive thing he could think to say about Lorraine.

'Yes.' Audrey stared up at him and he couldn't look away. 'You go without me.'

'No, I'll give it a miss.' They lingered in the corridor, ignoring the bell. Leo considered. 'We should just take the afternoon off. There's nothing happening here, just DVDs and quizzes. It's a waste of time. Come on – let's go.'

'Are you serious?'

'I am. Never more so. I want to be with you, Aud. Just us again, OK?'

She looked up at him and brushed her fringe out of her eyes.

'Just us,' she said, an echo, a spell.

They couldn't stop laughing, lurching through the slush and the mud, trying to run down the embankment away from school and back to the farm. Audrey gripped Leo's hand and threw herself at the wind. He pulled her back to him and for a while they waltzed and he hummed 'Twist and Shout' as he turned and danced them home.

When they got back Leo made tea, passed Audrey a mug, and then carved big doorstep sandwiches from a fresh loaf and presented her with a plateful.

'Last of the gooseberry chutney,' he said, 'just for you, Aud.'

'Thanks.' She nibbled a corner. Leo crouched in front of the fire, which had already been laid with kindling and logs and coal. It burst into flame when he touched it with a match.

'Good,' he said, grabbing his own plate and sitting opposite across the pine table. 'Come on – eat up.'

She nibbled again as Leo tore through his.

'Aren't you hungry?'

'Not really; sorry.' Audrey pushed her plate away.

'But we didn't have any lunch. And we've been walking. I can make you something else?'

'No, it's all right. I just feel a bit sick, that's all. The tea's helping.'

'Why d'you feel sick?'

'I don't know. Maybe my meds.' Aud wouldn't look at him. He hated that.

'I thought you'd stopped taking them?'

'Not exactly.'

'Why?'

'I just can't.' Her voice rose, frustrated, and Leo leant back in his chair and raked his hands through his hair. Audrey reached forward and touched his cheek.

'Don't worry, OK?'

'You can talk to me,' Leo said.

'It's nothing. Just leave it,' she told him, and he pushed his own plate away and took her hand, pulling her up and over to the fire.

Audrey

There was no way I could tell Leo the way things were. That if I didn't take the meds and talk to Harry and go to Caldwell, then the Thing would come worse than ever. Who'd want a girlfriend who said stuff like that? I just had to keep things even and calm, in fine precarious balance. Mum happy, Peter. Even Leo. Give everyone the version of me they needed.

'Audrey,' he whispered when I started to kiss him, like he still wanted to talk. But I didn't. I wanted to be close to him, so close you wouldn't even fit a blade of grass between us. I wanted to kiss him for longer than thirty seconds for a change, to forget everything here and now, in his arms.

'Shh,' I said, pulling closer, kissing harder and he moved towards me. I undid his buttons, pushed off his shirt, his jeans too, kissed the muscles in his shoulders, in his arms. And he took off my clothes, gently, his eyes full of questions.

But there was no question. This was just now, and the afternoon dipped and swung like the comfiest bed, and everything was right. That's how it felt. I forgot to hide when it was Leo's eyes looking; I forgot to be frightened of feeling, forgot to be ashamed. If he said I was all right, then that was the truth, because Leo didn't lie. He was mine. And I understood the point of everything, right then and there. That happiness was being loved for who you were without reservation or hesitation, without stepping backwards and checking your phone or seeing what someone else thought. It was trust; it was faith; it was knowing that the love you gave was safe in someone else's heart.

Leo sighed and breathed and stopped. He kissed my hair and my eyelids and the tiny mole on the right-hand side of my jaw like I was precious.

Leo

Someone had to be the sensible one and Leo guessed it would have to be him, although his brain was burning like the coals in the fire, glowing with heat; his whole body too.

'Aud,' he said. He had his shirt off. So did she. And her body was beautiful. He leant and kissed her breast and she shivered.

'We should stop,' he whispered, looking up at her. 'Sue'll be home soon.'

'OK,' she answered, not moving, looping her arms round his neck. Leo lay next to her again and ran his lips across the sharp line of her collarbone. She tasted of the winter day outside and of fire, of hot, dancing fire. Audrey's hands clutched at his shoulders; her mouth was everywhere and his body was ticking like a bomb.

Kissing her like this, and her holding him, pulling him tightly against her, it was impossible to stop. No one would. But it was all so fast: from a kiss, to this, to lying with her, naked, her long legs and arms, her hair wild and everywhere, and her heart thumping so hard against her ribs.

'Is this right?' she said as she touched him. He nodded, of course; how could he say no?

But he couldn't go on; he couldn't let it happen.

'OK,' he said, smiling. 'I'm getting dressed. And you

should too.' It was the hardest thing he'd ever done, he reckoned, to stand up and pull on his T-shirt and jumper and compose himself. He opened the back door and let in a gust of cold December air.

When he turned round Audrey was still sitting on the rug, her knees folded to her chest, her head resting there, her hair cascading down her back. She was a willow, a lily. She looked up at him, her eyes big without her glasses, and blinked, then said, 'Is it because of this?'

She held out her arms.

'No.' Leo shook his head and went to her. 'No. Don't think that.'

He held her and kissed her again until the moon passed the sun and the sky ached into evening.

School broke up and so there was no more skiving off to be had. In theory he should have been able to talk to Audrey all day: to make plans, plot and whisper. Because now Audrey was the only thing; he thought of her and his stomach swung, his eyes blurred and usually he had to sit down. Leo stood in the field; he was supposed to be bringing the pony up to the stable. The vet was coming later. Frost glittered on the fields in the morning light and he looked over the woods to the Grange, thinking how he should be revising maybe. A line of poetry came. *Thank you, Mr Donne*, he thought, whispering the words in the direction of the Grange: '*I wonder, by my troth, what thou and I did, till we loved?*' Perhaps he could smuggle Audrey into the farm. They'd hibernate for the winter, up in his room or out in the barn. His head swam at the thought. Sue kept looking at him, an exclamation mark in her eyes, and he guessed it was written all over him: love. That's what this was. It had happened in a hurry, in the end, and now it was the feeling of running incredibly fast, the feeling when his legs began to fly as if barely touching the ground, like you could conquer the world in a stride. He put his head against the pony's face and breathed in the sweetness, stroked her velvet nose. Love. Should he tell her? Not yet.

Leo racked his brains for something special to plan, maybe they'd go up to town and see the Christmas lights. Go Christmas shopping, hear a band, ice-skating, anything. He wanted plans, decisions, and so he rang the landline. And for once someone answered: Lorraine.

'Hi, it's Leo,' he said, worrying in that moment that this was a mistake and that he should have hung up. But he needed to hear Audrey's voice, at least, just for a minute or two.

'Who? Pardon?' Lorraine hadn't been over for the past two weeks and Sue had wondered if she was OK. He could confirm now that she was not.

'It's Leo,' he repeated, keeping his voice polite, formal. 'May I talk to Audrey, please?'

'No. She's not home. I've told you before; don't ring here. I don't want you pestering my daughter.' There was a tightness to her voice like she was holding something back, like she'd have preferred to swear at him, scream or shout. She hung up before he could answer.

'What happened?' Sue asked, staring at him.

'Nothing. Wrong number.'

'Oh, well, try again.'

'No, no it's OK. I'll call later.'

He walked up to his room – he should have been revising – and tried to read, but the sentences ran into one another and made no sense.

Audrey

'Mum! Was that Leo? Why did you speak to him like that?' I snatched at the receiver. She held it away from me.

'You what?' Her face reddened, eyes popping, staring at me as she put down the phone.

'What are you trying to do? Are you trying to ruin everything for me?'

Mum's voice was pretend calm. Patient. 'Audrey, you know fine rightly that your welfare is my only concern. And, that aside, I thought I told you. I don't want you seeing that boy.'

'There's no big deal. I just like him. He likes me. That's it. There's nothing horrible going on. Don't you want me to have friends?' Stupid question. Where were all my other friends? And hers? And Peter's? Our emails, letters, phone calls, texts? Even my dad hadn't bothered to keep us. I saw our lives and our future spinning and spiralling in smaller and smaller circles, then disappearing into the dust of time. Just Mum and me and Peter. And nothing.

'There's no need to be hysterical about this, Audrey. I don't want that lad interrupting our precious family time, end of. You're on another planet these days, racing off out of here every chance you get.' She threw up her hands, exasperated. 'I get little enough time with you and Pete. That is why I asked your boyfriend not to call.'

'You shouldn't have. I could have spoken to him and explained.' We stood there, not close, held apart; two magnets, poles repelling.

She rolled her eyes and sighed as if I were the unreasonable one. I got that Mum had taken time off again for the holidays and we were going to spend that time together, but Leo had only phoned; that wasn't a crime.

I looked at Peter – he had his coat on already and was waiting by the front door. Mum had said she might take us up to town Christmas shopping, or maybe to the cinema or the panto. He was dying to go to the panto and was practising shouting, 'He's behind you,' every time he caught one of us off guard. A minute ago Mum had been smiling, looking like she could be persuaded.

'I don't want to hear it,' she said, walking away, lighting her fag, pretending to watch the TV.

'What about the panto, Aud?' Peter said, looking from Mum to me and back to Mum. I nodded and whispered it'd be OK.

But when I spoke she turned up the volume.

'Mum, please, let me tell you, let me explain, please.'

She lifted the controller. The volume increased until the flat shook with the noise of the saleswoman's voice as she squawked about the range of kitchen utensils on special offer, and I saw Mum rummage in her handbag for her credit card, then scan the room searching for the phone.

I walked to the TV and positioned my hand, ready to turn it off.

'Don't you dare,' Mum said.

I pretended I couldn't hear. I'd stood up to Lizzy; I could stand up to Mum. I turned and pressed the button.

'How bloody dare you, Audrey!' Mum braced her arms on the side of the chair, ready to stand up.

'Because I want you to listen to me. You never listen. Leo's really nice. I swear. You should give him a chance; you're not being fair.' Mum pulled herself up, moved to the telly to switch it back on.

'I know what's best for you, Aud; you're my only daughter. You're not well. You're not mentally fit to be deciding to start a relationship with a lad who's older than you and more experienced. So you're staying here, at home with me, where you're safe. You may call that not fair. I call it for your own good.'

She was planted in front of me. Solid, immovable, like a slab of concrete. *Concrete heart*, I thought.

'I'm not going to stop seeing him. You can't make me.' I realized I was as tall as her, almost. Straightening up a little more, I looked her full in the face. She held my gaze and didn't flinch.

'Let me tell you a few things, shall I, Audrey? Let me tell you what this boy is after. What do you know about sex?'

'Enough,' I muttered, trying to press past her and leave the room. My face flared red. I remembered the day at the farm, how we'd come so close, and it had all been my idea, and how Leo had seen all of me and kissed all of me and now I couldn't think about anything else. Mum was watching me, her breath coming faster.

'What've you been up to, Audrey?' she said, stepping closer.

'Nothing.'

'I know what this is,' she said, moving sideways as I did. 'You're planning on some dirty little romance, you and this lad. Well, he won't be happy until he's got your knickers down and got you in trouble. And I'm not going to let that happen. So.'

'That's rubbish,' I said. 'You're being ridiculous.'

Her mouth hung open; her chest was heaving. 'I bet a doctor could tell me different,' she said, grabbing my arm and pulling me round to face her.

'What do you mean?' I said.

'I bet if I got a doctor to check you out he'd tell me what you'd been up to, no problem.'

'I don't understand what you're on about,' I said to her, even hotter, scared.

'It's pretty easy to tell if a girl's still a virgin, Audrey,' Mum said, and I put my hand over my mouth and swallowed down vomit.

'I am a virgin. Why don't you believe me?' I whispered.

'Because I wasn't born yesterday, that's why. You're a little slag, Aud, aren't you? I never thought I'd say it about a daughter of mine. But you're a dirty little slag. I can smell it on you; you stink of it.' She stormed away, slamming the kitchen door and I walked upstairs, very slowly, like an old woman, and the room dipped and fell as I rolled on the waves of her disgust.

On Christmas Eve I went down to the kitchen, which was cloudy with steam and hot like hell. The smells had been wafting up to my room for ages and if Mum was doing the cooking I reckoned I could help. Plus, I wanted to make it up. But Mum was cooking and stirring something which bubbled and boiled in a cast-iron pan and she didn't look up, so I watched her bashing and crashing around, her lips pressed tight, and when I spoke it was as if I wasn't even there.

'Mum,' I said. She ran water into the kettle, set it to boil, her face vicious with whatever she was thinking.

'Mum, will you listen to me?' I asked, but she kept her back to me. 'Mum, I wanted to tell you, about me and Leo, please.'

A lid clattered off a pan as the water boiled over and on to the stove, spitting and hissing. It was pointless trying, I should leave her, find Peter and make sure he was washed and dressed; we could maybe make up our own panto-mime or head to the woods for the day. I turned to go, but the Thing barred the door so I couldn't edge away, and in the heat a bead of sweat ran from my neck, between my shoulder blades and down my back. The Thing pushed me forward again, against the edge of the stove, and the water sloshed and spilled and bubbled and spat and burned and I screamed.

Later we sat in the back of the car. Peter whispered were we going to the panto after all, and I couldn't answer, cradling my arm.

The waiting room was packed. Little huddles of people on their phones, drunks shouting, babies crying. Mum went back and forth to the reception hatch asking, 'When?' and at last we were called into a cubicle. The doctor asked how it had happened as he gently inspected first the burn on my arm, then the one on my stomach. I began to hum, softly, then louder, as Mum explained. Her mouth moved. I refused to read the words. I wouldn't put them together, I couldn't. I looked up at him.

'It was an accident,' I said, 'but it hurts.' I wasn't sure which bit I meant. If it was my arm I was talking about at all. Perhaps that pain stole the one from inside me.

'We can give you something for that.' He smiled and carried on asking Mum about my treatment and who was I seeing and that he'd follow this up.

A nurse put on a dressing, Mum talked and held my hand and the nurse looked up at her and smiled.

It was late when we got home and I took another of the pills and walked up to bed without seeing anything.

Mum came upstairs, much, much later, carrying a glass of water and a bottle of medicine. She sat beside me and stroked my hair; she was ever so gentle and calm now. When she held the spoon to my lips, I swallowed like a good girl should.

'It's all right, love, you're all right now. See? See what I mean? You're in no fit state. Poor little girl.' And there was nothing left of me to argue. I listened to her go back downstairs, the rattle of her keys, the creak of the door as she left, and the rumble of the car as she took off into the night.

Leo

One of Sue's traditions was to spend Christmas Eve in the pub. There were usually carollers; the landlady put on a buffet. Everyone was cheerful, rosy with the roaring fire and mulled wine. The last person Leo had thought they'd see that evening was Lorraine; their exchange of the day before still lay under his skin like the fading ache of a wasp sting. She came in with a gust of wind, her lips painted their customary red, and he saw Sue lift her hand in welcome, but Lorraine looked the other way, pretending she hadn't noticed her.

Lorraine walked through the bar, into the snug and disappeared from view.

'That's a bit odd, isn't it?' Sue looked at Leo. 'Should I go and talk to her, find out what's up, do you think?'

Leo finished his drink. 'Leave her to it. If she wants to be rude, well, let her.'

'Maybe she didn't see us? I don't think she was being rude, Leo. I'll see her later.'

'OK. But she saw us all right.' If Lorraine was here, then Audrey was back at the Grange. He could nip over there, quickly; just say Happy Christmas in person. He picked up his coat.

'Where are you off to?' Sue raised an eyebrow. She knew full well.

'I'll be back soon. No worries.'

'Take the car. Quicker, then.'

'Sure.'

Leo drove fast in the dark, his headlights on full illuminating the road, startling a rabbit, then a deer into the hedgerows. The roads were clear, not icy; the day had been mild and bright and he sang a noisy carol, grinning at the thought of this surprise – and Audrey's face bright in the future.

Audrey

The banging seemed to go on forever. I turned, deep in sleep, trying to block it out, but the noise didn't stop. And then a voice calling, *Audrey, Audrey* – the sound came so kind and sweet that tears leaked again and I turned to follow it in the dark, wondering if it would lead to somewhere brighter. If I could leave my body behind and be lifted into the air.

'Aud.' It was Peter now. Shaking me. I was groggy, couldn't see well; my eyelids were too heavy to lift.

'Aud, wake up – there's someone here,' he whispered, and I reached out and pulled him close with arms like lead.

'Go to sleep, Pete,' I grumbled. 'They'll go away.'

There it was again, the banging. Peter jumped in my arms and huddled against me; this time I sat up, my head a weight on my shoulders.

'Audrey.' The call again, real. 'Audrey!' I recognized the voice at last. It was Leo.

'It's all right, Pete. Let me get up.'

Peter still wrapped round my waist, I opened the door.

'Hey,' he said. I was glad it was dark. I felt him staring, his hand on my cheek. He was cold and I shivered.

'Hi.' I put my hand up and held his.

'Can I come in?' he said, and I didn't know how to

answer because I knew I was a mess and I knew what would happen if Mum came home.

'Your mum's at the pub; I saw her there,' he said, reading my mind.

'What?' I thought she must have gone to work. What did I know?

'So, I thought you might be lonely.'

'I was asleep.' It still felt as if this were part of the dream, that any second I'd wake up and realize that my mind had tricked me again.

'You're OK, aren't you?'

'Yes, come in, quick.'

He did and he put his arms round me and I knew then that it was all right. That he was the safest thing in my life and that I wasn't disgusting or wrong and that Leo didn't mind anything. Not my greasy hair and pale scorched skin, my thin fingers, my crooked bottom teeth, my glasses. All the things I didn't know. None of it mattered to Leo. He was here, after all.

Leo

He'd been about to give up when Audrey opened the door, about to forget this madcap mission. And then there she was, standing before him like a ghost. Her face was confused in the dark as if she didn't recognize him.

'Can I come in?'

For a long time she didn't answer and then, when he stepped inside and put his arms round her and held her, he felt her come alive, his own cold hands warming on her sleep-heavy skin. He kissed her cheek. He felt her smile.

Peter turned on the lights and before Leo knew it Peter was dragging out a game, one he'd not played in years, and they assembled themselves round the plastic square, bright hippos snapping and grabbing at little rolling balls. Audrey fierce with competition but letting Peter win, shouting with pretend despair; Leo holding hands with her, just glad to be here for a little while because this couldn't last. That was something they all knew.

'What time is it?' Audrey asked.

'It's only ten.'

'Oh, really?' She walked and pulled back the curtain and looked out on to the drive.

'We'll hear her on the gravel,' Leo said, and Audrey nodded and rested her head against his chest.

'What are we going to play now?' said Peter. 'Hide-and-seek?'

'No. It's bedtime,' Audrey told him. 'Father Christmas will be here soon, Pete, and if you're not asleep, how's he going to leave your presents?'

'Where's Rudolph's carrot?' said Leo and they went to the kitchen and found a carrot and a biscuit and a glass of their mum's sweet wine, leaving it all by the window. He'd have to come by the window, Aud explained, since there was no chimney.

'You know, when I was little,' Leo said, as Audrey tucked Peter in, 'we always went away at Christmas, skiing or something like that. And do you know, Peter, one year we went to Lapland where the *real* Father Christmas lives.'

'Did you see him?' Peter sat up again. They both listened; Aud had a smile playing on her lips but her eyes glowed too.

Leo nodded, remembering quite vividly a frozen lake, huskies barking, his mother in a heavy fur coat, the stillness and beauty of winter.

'I did. And do you know what I asked him for?'

Pete's eyes widened. Flying saucers. Leo leant close.

'I asked him for a little brother,' he whispered, and then stood up and smiled and Peter smiled back.

Audrey led him back to the living room. 'I guess I should go,' he said. 'I hope Santa comes.'

Audrey crossed her fingers and held them up, the sleeve of her pyjamas falling back, the light from a lamp catching the fair hairs on her arms and something else: a dressing on her arm.

'What happened? What's this?'

She pulled away sharply and pulled down her sleeve.

'Nothing. An accident.'

'What sort of accident?'

'I was making tea. It was the kettle.' Her laugh was small. 'I'm always dropping stuff and making a mess.'

'Oh.' He could say that wasn't true, that he thought she spun straw into gold, but instead he whispered, holding her hand again, standing close, 'OK. Does it hurt?'

She shook her head against his chest.

'I'll be back. New Year's Eve. Make sure you can get out. OK?'

She nodded. He wasn't sure she'd heard.

'I'll be thinking about you, Aud, every minute. Right?'

Her eyes asked him, *Really?* So Leo kissed her, kissed her so she'd know just how much he missed her and wanted her and loved her. She kissed him right back. And everything he felt came bursting back at him. He loved that too.

'I'd better go.'

'Don't,' she said.

'I have to; I don't want to.' They kissed each other again and this time she was the one to pull away and then bundle him out of the door as if realizing what it meant if they were found, as if the reality suddenly made sense.

'Don't forget,' he shouted as he pounded down the stairwell. 'Don't forget. New Year's Eve. I'll be back.'

Audrey

The next morning Peter woke me up early and we opened our stockings, sitting on Mum's bed. The night before seemed a dream and I tried to see out through the window across the fields to the farm, but the glass was fogged with condensation. Turning back to the moment, I stared at the gifts. Mum had gone mad with the shopping, as usual, and she lay back against the pillows watching us, still half-asleep. She hadn't come back until one.

Mum's room was a bomb-site. It wasn't just the presents; there were piles of clothes and shoes and jewellery. Bags and boxes, unopened parcels full of things that I guessed she'd forgotten she'd even ordered. Maybe I'd tidy it for her some time, fix it up nicely. It would be something I could do, at least, to tell her I was sorry for us fighting, sorry that she was angry. Peter was working his way through the parcels, ripping through paper and assembling a pile.

I'd bought Peter a chef's hat and a set of kids' cooking utensils, plus a recipe book. It had been cheap, all I could afford, but he didn't care.

'Awesome, Aud, thanks,' he said, tearing open the box, handling the whisk and the wooden spoon. 'I'll make us breakfast in a minute,' he declared, all serious and important. I hugged him and Mum handed me her gift. It was a box, beautifully wrapped in shining gold paper. I almost didn't dare open it, couldn't imagine what it might be. Half of me thought about a typewriter, old-fashioned, elegant, but didn't dare even imagine it. Or perhaps a globe. Maybe a huge box of books. It wasn't heavy enough for any of those things and I swallowed down my expectations.

'Go on,' she said. 'The suspense is killing me.' The expression on her face told me I needed to love it, whatever it was.

I peeled back the paper. Stared. A Madison baby doll smiled up at me from behind her plastic casing.

'She's brilliant, isn't she?' said Mum, taking the box, releasing her from her manacles, careful not to rip the packaging. 'Look, you can pose her in different positions.' She started rearranging the thing's limbs, straightening her gingham romper suit and matching bow. 'She's adorable. I thought you could start your own collection, Audrey. She's good quality, Ashton Drake, like some of mine.' She gestured at the shelf behind the bed, the dolls arranged in perfect lines. I tried never to look at them, their faces freaked me out. 'She'll look good in your room.'

'Thanks, Mum. She's nice. It's really kind of you. Thanks.'

I leant across the wrapping-paper mountain. Kissed her on the cheek. Her face tasted of stale make-up. Breath sour. She grabbed me and hugged too hard. I squirmed away, putting the doll to one side.

'What? Don't you like her?'

'Yeah, but, you know, it's not really my thing.' I was trying to be honest. Not the best policy.

'Well, that's bloody charming that is, isn't it?' She sat back, folded her arms, refused to open anything else or to eat the breakfast Peter made.

After that, things went flat. Later Mum decided she couldn't be bothered with the turkey after all. We had jam sandwiches on our knees in front of the telly, pulled crackers. Laughed fake laughs at the jokes. Not even the *EastEnders* special or the Mr Bean film could lift our spirits.

Mum shifted on the couch, tapping her fingers on the arm of the chair, checking her phone and then casting looks my way. Then she started.

'You know, without me, without the doctors, you won't manage.'

'What?' I said, not looking at her. I leant over and helped Peter fit another piece into his new jigsaw.

'You think things are bad now?' Mum went on. 'Imagine what you'll be like when you can't get out of bed, can't eat, if you're hearing things, seeing things. You let your voices get any worse, Aud, and that's it – you'll be at breaking point. You can't cope alone.'

'Mum. Stop it.' I stood up, fetched a glass of water and stood watching her from the doorway.

Mum heaved herself up and came over. 'Let me see that arm,' she said, grabbing at me, wanting to check the burns.

'No, stop it. Leave it.' I pulled away.

'I'll do the dressing. It might be infected,' she said, snatching again at my arm. Her fingers grabbed right where it hurt.

'It isn't.'

Mum folded her arms. The way she looked at me, like Lizzy looked at me. Like I made her sick.

'You should go to bed, Audrey,' she said eventually – it must only have been half past five. 'It's time you went up. You're not well.'

'Mum, it's still early,' I complained. Plus I didn't want to go up there, especially not now it was dark. Mum got up and wandered into the kitchen, opened the fridge, rummaged inside. When she turned back, her hands full of cheese and a jar of pickle, she saw me still standing behind her and stepped forward.

'Early night for you. It'll do you good. And don't forget Madison.' She filled her plate and pulled Peter with her back into the living room, shutting the door behind them.

It was hours before she went to bed and too late to creep out. But I waited until I heard the sound of her snores before I sneaked downstairs, Madison's eyes following me, out of the flat and down to the letter box, just in case.

Inside was a chain of paper hearts, curled and coiled like a sleeping snake. I pulled them out. Each one carried words, as usual, precious words that I could treasure and try to understand: *dive, dreams, trust, heart, seas, fire*. It was perfect and I went back up to my room, smiling.

New Year's Eve

Audrey

Early on New Year's Eve I sat on my bed and attacked a skirt with a pair of scissors before pulling it on, with a black T-shirt of Mum's. It was too big but I found a belt and wrapped it tight round my waist. I almost had a little black dress. With a needle and thread I tried to hem the skirt, pricking my finger in the process and making it bleed. Next I attacked my hair, piling it up in a messy bun and spraying it with half a can of Mum's hair spray. I stared in the mirror in the bathroom. Still too thin. Still too pale. Circling Mum's blusher on to my cheeks, I wondered where Leo and I would go and what we would do. I wondered if he'd definitely come. Yes, he'd promised. A seed of excitement took root, began to grow. I couldn't remember my last party. The finished product stared out of the bathroom mirror. I looked a mess but at least I was me. A work-in-progress sort of me.

'What do you think?' I asked Peter.

He glanced up. 'About what?'

'My outfit?'

'You look weird, Aud,' he said, without looking up again. He was right. I stuck my tongue out at the mirror. Pulled a silly face, made myself laugh.

I changed the skirt for jeans, left the hair and added

lipstick. Mum's red was better than nothing. I had to stare in the mirror to do it. It was all right; I was all right.

'Where are you going?' Peter had come to watch. He sat kicking the side of the bath.

I thought about it. He'd have to come too.

'Do you want to go and see Leo?' I asked him.

He nodded, slowly.

'It'll be fun.' I smiled, tried to make it look like it wasn't a problem, that I couldn't care less. 'Mum won't find out.'

'OK,' he said. 'All right.'

And then there was a loud banging on the door. Even though I was expecting him, I jumped.

'Who is it?' Peter said. I raced out of the bathroom, down the stairs and flung myself at the front door and wrenched it wide.

For a second neither of us said a word. We just stared. Then I straightened the dodgy outfit, thought about my face, my mouth wearing such a grin. The stupid lipstick. I covered my mouth.

Leo read my mind. 'You look beautiful,' he said. 'Different. Good though.'

I wiped my lips with my hand. Smeared a dark stain on my skin.

'Come on.' Leo grabbed my hand. 'Get your coat.'

'Where are we going?'

'You'll see. Come on, Peter.'

'I'd better leave a note, hadn't I?'

'Yeah, sure.' He paused.

'Saying what?'

'That you'll be out for the night. Back tomorrow. That

you're safe and Peter's at Sue's – she won't mind babysitting, although I've not said where we're going. I think she might object to that bit of the plan. Anyway. Those are the only clues you're getting. Quick, let's go.'

I scrawled the message and left it propped on the worktop by the kettle and dashed after Leo and Peter, whooping out into the fresh air, racing my brother down on to the drive.

Parked on the gravel was Sue's Land Rover.

'What's happening?'

'We're going on a road trip,' Leo said. We faced each other. He wanted me to get in the car with him and drive away. My legs began to shake at the thought. I'd not travelled anywhere without Mum. I wasn't sure I could.

'You're kidding me.'

It wasn't a good idea. I almost turned and walked back up to the flat, but Leo put his arms round me. 'It's OK, Aud; you'll be with me.'

I put my cheek on his chest. I could hear his heart pounding too and I took a deep breath.

'A road trip?'

Leo waited for me to agree and I stared back at the Grange. It was watching us, silently reprimanding; the trees bent a grave, dark warning too. But the wind didn't shake Leo. He stepped towards the car, opened the passenger side, and swept a way forward with his arm.

'Come on, Aud. Get in. Buckle up. You too, Pete – let's go.'

'Mum's going to go mad,' I said, out of the side of my mouth to Leo, strapping Peter in.

'You left her the note – give her a call once we're en route, explain where we're going, where Peter is – Sue said she'd babysit – then at least she won't worry. What do you think?'

My legs were still wobbly; I sat next to my brother, tried to calm down, and took his hand. Peter was smiling and I wished he could come too. Leo started the engine and I watched his hands switching on the headlights, manoeuvring the gears.

'Don't worry, you know we'll be fine.' Leo was staring at me – his face demanding smiles with his own, and I felt the hope and excitement in the thud of my heartbeat, the speed of my breath. Leo kept looking as if he expected something and I tried to see how he felt, but couldn't read it all – such a mixture of things, though mostly it was light. Like Blackpool Illuminations, the whole wonderful happiness of it, impossibly hopeful. *Come with me*, his eyes said, *I'll take you away, take you somewhere where the only thing to fear is the brightness of stars and how incredible the world is when you see it from the sky.*

The gears crunched and we were off, down the driveway towards the gates. I expected to see them swing back before we could drive through, locking us inside, but we sailed past, probably too fast to be safe, but what did it matter? We were free.

'Where are we going?'

'Surprise. Wait and see.' He checked his watch and we drove along the narrow lanes to the farm, only Peter's chatter interrupting the quiet. Any second now something was going to explode. I hugged my brother tight when he climbed out, kissed him, but he pushed me away and wiped his face, then, just before he ran inside, he turned and blew me a kiss. I caught it, put it in my pocket and climbed back into the car, sitting so close to Leo our bodies may as well have been Velcroed together at the hips, shoulders, thighs. I didn't know if he could drive like this, but I wasn't going to move. He put his face in my hair, his mouth to my ear.

'I missed you,' he whispered, sounding sort of different – out of control, maybe.

I grabbed his hand and held it, crushed his fingers. How much I'd missed him was there in every bit of my body; I wondered if he could see everything beating, that I was burning. I swallowed and wound down the window for fresh air but the icy blast didn't cool anything.

The roads were busy but Leo handled the car like a pro, only stopping to fill the tank.

'What is this?' I asked him.

'Magical mystery tour,' he said again. 'I told you.'

'I'm scared.' I smiled as I said it, not meaning it any more, not really. Scared of all kinds of things, of me, and him, and being together. Of escaping.

'Don't be,' he said. 'I don't want you to be scared, not ever with me. I'll look after you, Aud, I swear, and this will be fun; it's meant to be exciting.'

'What about my mum?' I stared out at the traffic. It was a stupid thing to say. She didn't matter, not right now and how could she know where we were? She couldn't follow us. She couldn't stop us.

'Call her now.' Leo got out his phone and handed it over.

'She's going to be so angry, you know that. She'll spoil things.'

'OK, call her in the morning. Or we can text.' I held the phone, dangled it from my fingers, doing nothing. 'Go on, ring her. It'll be fine. I can explain if you like.'

I couldn't think about it. Mum wasn't welcome here, with us; she'd make me go back and I didn't want to now. I handed back his phone.

'Don't worry,' he said again as he started the car and pulled back out on to the motorway. Names of towns I'd never heard of tangled, confused, in my head, and as the miles passed I started to think about what we were doing, what it meant.

'Thanks for this, Leo,' I said. 'Whatever it is. Wherever we go. I like it. We could just drive forever. Not stop. What do you think?'

'Why not?' He squeezed my hand, pressed play on the CD. Started to sing. I grinned and sat back in my seat, watched the traffic and the fields pass, laughed at Leo getting the words wrong, joining in with the chorus.

'You sure you know where we're going?' I peered out of the window, trying to catch the names of towns, looking for clues.

'Yup. Memorized the route.' Leo looked so pleased with himself that it made me smile. I nudged him gently.

'Wow.'

'Yeah,' he said, grinning, 'I'm pretty amazing like that. Total hero.'

'You are amazing, Leo.'

'Well, thanks,' he said, not even bothering to disguise his blushes. 'Say it again; I like it.'

'No. Then you'll get all big-headed. Leos are arrogant too, you know. Well, they can be.'

Leo stared out of the windscreen, overtaking, then briefly caught my eye. The look made me blush. 'You know, it's a good job I think you're amazing too, isn't it?' he said.

'You do?'

'I do. And don't laugh.' He frowned. 'It's not funny. It's seriously affecting my ability to be a useful human being. Sue says I mope.'

'Mope?'

'Yes. I had to stop myself from storming the Grange paratrooper-style, stealing you out of there under cover of night. Or from hanging out outside your window like that idiot Romeo.'

'Romeo was an idiot?'

'Well, I always thought so. Until I started to experience some of his angst. Now I have more empathy.'

My cheeks ached from smiling. 'Really?'

'Yes. My least favourite of all the tragic heroes, because quite frankly he has no gravitas. Can't hold a candle to Othello. Even old Macbeth is more interesting, and you know how I feel about him. Look, nearly there. We need to turn off here. Let's hope the traffic doesn't get any worse.'

London. I'd never been to London, didn't know what to expect. As the evening turned truly dark we rumbled down another busy road.

'Leo?'

'Umm hmm.'

'Are we going where I think we're going?'

'That would be telling.'

Leo

He hadn't been sure if London was the best choice, but when he saw Audrey's face he knew he'd done the right thing. Pulling up outside his parents' place, he felt nervous again.

'Here we are. We can dump our stuff.' He led the way up marble steps to the imposing front door. The house was all lit up, even though no one was home.

'What is this?'

'Well, this is where my parents live sometimes, when they're over here, if they're not using a hotel. Which for some reason my mother often prefers. I think it's because then she doesn't have to do any cooking or any domestic duties whatsoever.' He locked the car and pulled Audrey towards the building. 'My mother, as you will see when we go inside, has transcended the domestic.'

'Oh. That's pretty weird.'

'Agreed. But find me someone who isn't.'

'It's cool though. I'd like to transcend the domestic, or whatever. Basically, stop doing all the flipping jobs is what I think you mean.'

'Exactly. When I'm a rich man, not just a rich man's son, I'll buy you a robot to do all your chores. Or maybe we'll just travel the world; no possessions, no ties. Just you, me and wherever we want to wander.'

Audrey kissed him on the cheek, fast. 'I'll be there,' she said. 'Don't go without me, OK?'

She held his face in her hands and he wondered if they both saw the same thing: an aeroplane, Audrey in a white dress and sunglasses. He'd be in jeans and a vintage leather jacket. He saw them holding hands above the clouds and the endless opportunity of their forever, and wondered if he could fix it for this summer; they should find a way to make something like that happen, some time soon. Anything was possible.

He led her into the hallway, downplaying it all the way. Audrey gawped: the baby grand, white carpets, glowing art. He knew it sang of money, style, luxury. But to him it wasn't really a home, not like Sue's place. As a kid he'd played quiet games, contained and controlled – moving his little cars sedately through the thick pile carpet – and later awoken from dreams of walls covered in thick scrawls of black crayon, sweating and shaking at the thought. He'd get up every time, pad to the living room, switch on the lights. Check the wallpaper remained pristine after all. Audrey wanted to linger, admire and inspect, but he told her they could only stop a minute, freshen up, then hit the town.

Audrey put down the figurine she'd been examining – a little bronze Cupid – and realigned it on the chest of drawers.

'First, though, you have to play me something.' Aud perched on the edge of the sofa, her long legs crossed at the ankles, her face expectant.

'What?'

'I want to hear you play. I never knew anyone before who could play the piano. My dad, he had this old banjo or something, like a little guitar it was, but he wasn't much good.'

'Seriously?' He lifted the lid to reveal the keys and felt a strange pull towards the instrument as he flexed his fingers, already thinking. What would he play? Something special. Something for her. And for him. Something for them. Leo rested his fingers on the keys. His heart stopped and restarted.

'All right,' he said, although he wasn't sure how this was going to feel. In his head the piano was still partly to blame. All the music that had run through him before he cracked up, his fingers dancing over imaginary keys, his dreams full of whirling storms of crotchets and semi-quavers, riotous arpeggios, taunting major chords marching like soldiers, the minor lament making him cry.

'Right. Here goes.' Leo thought for a while longer. Then it came to him and it was like he'd never stopped, every note was still there in his fingers, waiting like memory, like fingerprints, fossils. He forgot Audrey was there. Forgot about everything.

'Oh, my goodness,' she said when he finished, and he only just heard her; he was shaking a little, wanting to start again, play it all over from the beginning, better this time.

'Leo,' Audrey said, clapping her hands, 'you're like flipping Mozart or something.' Breaking the spell and making him smile. He turned round slowly to look at her.

'Yeah? How did you know?'

241

'What, you mean it was? Actually Mozart? You're kidding me. Will you teach me?'

'Sure, some day. But now we should go.' He pulled himself away from the piano, grabbed his jacket, handed Aud hers, ushering her back out on to the street.

'You know this is massively posh, this place, don't you?' she said, pausing to stare up at the white Georgian mansion as she zipped up her coat.

'I guess I do. Although there are posher places.'

'We're not going to them, are we?' The fear in her voice made him laugh again.

'No. Far better than that. OK?'

They caught the Tube down to Trafalgar Square. It was getting colder outside, but was hot and stuffy on the Tube. They had to stand, swinging from the overhead bars, grinning as they collided.

'What are you doing?' He stared and grabbed her arm. Audrey was pulling off her coat.

'I'm hot.' Audrey let go of the hand rail and chucked her jacket at Leo, then threw her arms out, insisting on space, forcing the other travellers to back away. People stared, then looked away as she began to twirl and swirl – singing the tune he'd played for her, or what she remembered of it at least, la-la-ing the rest. Her head was back, her hair flying. Leo watched her, part alarmed, part in awe.

'This is wicked,' she said. 'You know what? We're free,' she sang, spinning on the long vowels. She grabbed Leo, wrapped her arms round his waist, made him dance with her, their waltz, until they ricocheted into the side of the carriage, almost collapsing on top of one another. Someone tutted, but mostly people ignored them, probably thought they were drunk. Leo held her up, pulled her straight as the train shuddered to a halt.

'Come on – we get off here. You can be as excited as you like now, Aud,' Leo said, dragging her on to the platform and towards the escalators.

'I don't think London's big enough for how excited I am. Trafalgar Square? Is that where we're going?' She yelled and ran up the escalator, making him chase.

'Yes. Then the river. It'll blow your mind, Aud.'

'It's blown,' she said, 'long ago,' and bumped him with her hip, making him stumble a little. All night she'd be tripping him up, surprising him, making him fall again and again, head over heels.

'Thank you for this.' Audrey stood on tiptoe, kissed him and they walked into the crowds squeezed tight together, bodies attached from waist to shoulder, and he thought that this was what happy felt like. This was almost perfect.

Audrey

None of it frightened me. Not the crowds or the noise or the feeling of being cut loose, like a kite or a kid's balloon. I was with Leo and we walked through the throng of people like we floated, as if they didn't even exist. We didn't talk about anything real. But Leo made me believe in possibility as we pushed through the crowds with the stars above us and the night ahead, and I saw flashes of the future, one I'd never imagined, and realized how different the world was through his eyes. He believed we were only just beginning.

'Can we stay here forever?' I asked as the first firework exploded way in the distance, and Leo nodded.

'If you like. But it gets pretty gross. Pigeons and the pollution, bad combination.' I stared at the dancers on stage, swayed to the music.

'You could turn me into a statue. Then I wouldn't care about pigeon shit,' I shouted over the noise.

'Hmm. Like a reverse Pygmalion.'

'What?' He was too clever; there was some erudite comment for every occasion. And the way he played the piano. How he'd lifted something out of the keys, a magic that had made me giddy. What the hell had I been doing for the last sixteen years? There were a lot of gaps I needed to fill.

'It's a play. But also a myth. About a man falling in love with his statue, or with the girl he's created in the image he desires. Pretty sick.'

'Sounds it. But maybe worth it. Would you fall in love with me if I were a statue?' I kept my eyes away from his. Fishing for compliments, Mum would say. Flirting like a fool. But Leo didn't seem to mind.

'I don't know.' He smirked, pulling my eyes round to his with his voice, teasing. 'Maybe.'

'You're mean.' I stuck out my tongue.

'I know. But I like it when you frown. '

'What? That's doubly mean.'

'And when you laugh and when you yawn or sigh and smile. Everything becomes you. Except crying though, I don't think I'd like to see you cry.'

'I'll have to try not to, then.'

He hugged me and all of a sudden I was thinking of Peter and swallowing back tears as I stared at the iridescent beauty of the night, the glow of the city, a wild fairyland blazing neon mystery and light. My heart felt heavy and full all at once and I put my hand to my chest.

'It hurts,' I said.

'What?' Leo whispered. 'What hurts?'

'Everything.'

'Don't,' he said. 'Don't think about it. Just be here, be happy with me.' He held me tighter, like he could squeeze away my sadness.

'I am. I am happy with you.' His hair was soft, his cheeks softer. He was always good. Always kind. *People should be like that more*, I thought, *all people*.

'Have I ruined things?'

'No, course not,' Leo said, touching my cheek, holding my face in his hands.

'Good. Thanks.'

'What for?' He looked down into my eyes. My legs trembled, my hands, my heart.

'This, for everything. For being my best friend,' I said.

'Best friend?'

'Yeah. Aren't you?'

'Maybe; I thought something else,' Leo said, smiling.

He kissed me again and there was music and stars and laughter and happiness, all the things I hadn't known existed but which were ordinary in other people's worlds.

Counting down the time, we screamed ourselves hoarse and then there was more kissing, Leo and even strangers, and jumping up and down and singing without knowing any of the words, and arms were lifting me off my feet and I was whirling again, turning and spinning and the world was something utterly beautiful.

Leo

He could have watched her forever. She was beautiful and everyone knew it, everyone who smiled at her caught a little bit of the magic of Audrey. Leo held on to her for fear she'd float away, buoyed up on her own excitement, the power of her own happiness. He felt it coming off her like beams of light and it made him realize how sad she'd been, how the Grange had dulled her, not allowed her to glow.

'We should get something to eat,' he told her after they'd sung themselves hoarse. They wandered through the weaving crowds to Chinatown, ate dim sum holding hands, strolling and staring.

'I love it,' she said. 'I love everything.'

'I'm glad.' His face was aching from smiling and hope leapt like a stag in front of them, leading the way. 'Let's go home.'

Back in the flat Audrey announced she didn't want to go to bed.

'Maybe if we stay up, this'll last forever. As long as we don't sleep, the night has to stay night, right?'

'We could try. Film?'

'Yes.'

He put on *Badlands* because Aud had never seen it. She lolled against him as she watched; he held her and didn't think about the film at all.

'Tired yet?'

'No. Not at all.' She stretched. 'What time is it?'

'Four thirty.'

'Oh.'

Audrey lay back down, her head sinking into the cushion, hair fanning out behind her.

'This was the best day ever. Crazy killers on the run and all.' Leo laughed.

'Yeah?'

'Yeah. Thanks to you.' Audrey turned to look at him, reached out to trace his lips with the tip of her finger.

'Did you have fun?' she asked, scrunching up her face and examining his expression.

'Absolutely. Although I don't think that word does it justice. I think we should find a better one.'

'Fun is fun.' Audrey shrugged.

'Yes, but it's too small a word.' He pulled Audrey closer, wrapping both arms round her. 'Good time doesn't do it either. I don't think there's a word for it, Aud, about how I feel, right now, about you and all this. You'd have thought there would be; someone should have invented one.'

'You could write me a poem about it,' she teased, but her eyes were serious and he wished he could find the words.

Leo had thought about this. That they might go to bed. And about what would happen then. He'd tried not to think about it a lot, but it had cropped up more and more often. Not that he planned on doing anything about those thoughts, but if love was this deep hole in the centre of his chest, the one that opened up whenever she was far away and hurt like hell, well, then he loved her. It was almost impossible to feel this much, all at once, and impossible not to think about what having sex with Audrey would be like. He coughed, clearing his throat. She raised an eyebrow.

'What?'

'Nothing.' She crossed her eyes and stuck out her tongue and he grabbed her wrists, gently, and pushed her backwards on the sofa, so she was lying under him. He kissed her lips, her eyelids, her cheeks, her neck, lower. He could hear her breathing. It turned him on. Her skin was hot and soft. That turned him on too.

'I guess we should watch another film,' she said, pulling away. He grabbed one last kiss. Her cheeks were glowing, flushed, and so were his. Leo didn't want to watch a film.

'OK,' he said, not moving his mouth away. Speaking through the kisses.

'Or maybe, just go to bed?' Audrey said, lying back again and looking up at him with big eyes.

'Yeah?'

'In the same bed?'

He shrugged and made a good attempt at looking neutral at the thought. 'If you like.'

'Maybe. I dunno. My mum would freak out.' It was the first time she'd mentioned her mother for hours. Leo did not want Lorraine anywhere near this. He gathered Audrey's hair in his hands, twisted it on top of her head, then let it fall like water all around her face. She looked away, avoiding his eye.

'She thinks you want to get me pregnant, then run off and leave me with a screaming brat.'

'She said that?'

'Something like it.'

'Jesus.' Leo could have said a lot more.

Audrey bit her lip, staring at him. He tried to smile, to laugh it off.

'Sorry. I shouldn't have said it. You really didn't need to hear that.' She struggled upright, smoothed her hair flat and rearranged her clothes.

'It's up to you. We don't have to do anything that you don't want to,' Leo said. 'But I would love to sleep with you. In the same bed, I mean. Anything else, up to you.' He coughed and stood up.

'OK.'

Leo lent Audrey a T-shirt. She changed in the bathroom, then dived into the bed and under the thick downy covers. He didn't touch her; he couldn't. Lorraine. Leo thought he quite possibly loathed her, but of course he couldn't say that. Or maybe he could. He was about to speak when Audrey moved over and put her arms round him, holding him tight.

'Sorry for spoiling it all,' she said, whispering into his back. 'I'm sorry, Leo.'

'No, you didn't – don't worry.' He turned to her. They held on to one another now, tight, like earlier; like a promise it would be impossible to break.

Their legs tangled together, and their arms. Leo ran his hands over Audrey's back, her smooth soft skin, and felt her hands tracing the same paths on his own body. He touched her hair, and her neck and her shoulders and she touched his as if he were a mirror in which she found herself, and then she sat up and pulled off the T-shirt before she lay down next to him again: utterly, beautifully naked. She was smiling and pulling him closer again and this time Leo couldn't stop.

January

Audrey

You don't get a night like that without paying for it. That's
what I was thinking as we drove home, but I didn't say it
aloud; I didn't want Leo to worry. We'd slept late and I'd
woken up with my heart in a panic, grabbed my clothes
and insisted we leave at once. No breakfast, no nothing.
The spell was broken. And all I felt now was sore. In my
head, in my heart, in my arms and thighs and between my
legs. We shouldn't have done it. Mum would know, the
second she set eyes on me, she'd read it. I might as well
have it stitched into my skin, scarlet and bleeding: I am
not a virgin.

'You're quiet,' he said. Leo kept looking at me out of
the corner of his eye. I tried to smile at him.

'Mmm. Just a bit tired.' I took the hand he held out and
our fingers locked. It wasn't his fault; Leo hadn't hurt me,
of course not. I reddened, remembering, how I'd been
the one to say, *Yes, I want to*. How I'd closed my eyes and
then opened them and not been afraid; how I'd loved
being with him. Loved him. Even though it was awkward
at first. It wasn't like we were experts. I bit my knuckle, my
heart racing, remembering: skin hot, slippery with sweat.
The mess of the bedclothes, rumpled and ruined, Leo's
body with mine. His tongue in my mouth, on my skin. My
stomach rolled. Oh, my God. Mum would definitely

know. I shifted on the seat and cleared my throat. He blinked, looking at me again.

'Well, catch up on some sleep when you get home. Then let's meet up tonight.'

'No way will Mum be up for letting me out two nights in a row. In fact I think she's going to be really pissed off with me.' I swallowed. This was serious. I was in serious trouble and saw it coming, belting towards me, out of control.

'Look, it's ridiculous. Seriously, what's she got against us?'

'It's not you. Don't worry, I'll talk to her. All right?'

'You've got to think positive, Aud. The more we prove that we're serious, not mucking about, the more she'll see that there's no point being all Victorian about this.'

'I know, I know. But it would be the same with anyone. You could be Jesus and she'd still think you were out to give me STDs before running off with my best friend. I don't know the word for someone who hates men, but she's it.'

'Misandrist,' he said.

'Oh. Nice.'

'It's OK, Aud. I can take it.' Leo's smile almost broke my heart. It was brave and bold and I knew he meant it. That he'd stand up for me, whatever.

'Thanks, Leo,' I said, 'for everything.'

We were almost home. I stared out of the window and watched the fields rush past, dank and netted with the New Year mist.

Mum and Sue were waiting outside the Grange. They

weren't speaking, but Sue was wearing the snowflake jumper and a thick matching scarf. Mum had her arms round Peter, pressing him into her side. Leo grabbed my hand as we climbed out of the Land Rover and walked towards them.

'It'll be OK,' he said for the millionth time as he squeezed tight, but I dropped his hand, folded my arms and stared straight ahead into the first cold sun of the year as it broke through the clouds, so harsh it was knives in my eyes.

'Get in the house,' Mum said, that was all, and we trooped inside, no time to even say goodbye.

'See you soon, Lorraine,' Sue called, but Mum didn't turn back.

I thought about stopping on the steps. I could turn round and run, get back in the car and go to the farm with Leo. But Peter caught my eye and twisted his fingers into mine, so I followed Mum upstairs and the sound of her feet pounding the concrete, echoing like slaps, rang in my ears.

'All right, Pete?' I said. Of course he wasn't. There was no way this was normal.

'Audrey.' Mum pointed at the kitchen. I did as I was told.

'What?' I smiled at my brother, trying to pretend this was a game. He wasn't stupid. He was going to cry.

The table was set. Bowls of crisps, sausage rolls, sandwiches curling at the edges, a bottle of pop and little plastic jewel-coloured glasses. A trifle, dusted with hundreds and thousands and beginning to curdle, sat centre stage. A slab of cheese, surrounded by crackers and grapes, looked too soft, a little green; a thick foul smell rose and pulsed in the air. There were party poppers dotted among the food. Tatty Christmas crackers. A packet of sparklers.

'What's this?' I whispered.

'Where've you been, Audrey? I've been sat waiting here, waiting for you,' Mum said.

'Mum set it up,' Peter whispered. A trail of snot ran from his nose, I wiped it clean. 'It's a party,' he said.

'I'm sorry,' I told him. He looked smaller than ever, as if he'd shrunk overnight. I wanted to gather him up and hug it all better.

'You didn't come home,' Mum went on. She'd scraped her hair back and her forehead glared, white and high. 'You were out all night.'

I sat down opposite her. Mum's eyes followed a line from my forehead to my lips to my chest and my groin, where they rested, and my cheeks burned hot. She could see it; she could smell it. I should have showered and changed my clothes. Peter hovered beside her, his hand stroking Mum's sleeve, but she didn't move, as if she were made of marble.

'It's OK, Pete,' I whispered, crossing my legs tight, wrapping myself small, and he sidled over to me, standing close.

'I'm sorry, Mum,' I said, but that wasn't going to be enough.

She picked up a sandwich. A white triangle, curling at the edges. Put it on my plate.

'Eat it,' she said. I took a tiny bite. Dust.

'Here.' She began to pile my plate with crisps, a Scotch egg, a fat spoonful of leaking trifle.

'Eat it up. You too, Peter.'

Peter spooned up cream, gagged on the first mouthful and spat it out all over the plate.

'It's OK,' I soothed him. 'Don't worry.' I poured his drink and he gulped the fizzy liquid, rubbing his cheeks with his knuckles, his tears leaving grimy trails.

'Mum. I could make us some fresh,' I said, but she looked at me as if she hadn't heard, cramming a cigarette into her mouth.

'The note said I'd gone with Leo. That Peter was fine at Sue's, waiting for you. I'm really sorry, Mum. I know it was out of order; I know I shouldn't have.' Her silence was hell; I didn't understand it and I almost opened my mouth and told her everything, confessed then and there, just to get it over with, just to make her scream and shout, so this bomb could explode.

'Eat your food, Audrey.'

I picked up a sausage roll. The pastry crumbled, ashy in my fingers.

'I can't.'

'What?'

'It's not nice, Mum. It's old, gone off.'

'I made it for you,' she said. 'So you eat it.' I took a deep breath. I had to stop this.

'No. We can't eat this, Mum. Don't you get it?' She stared. I thought she would slap me and waited for the screaming, the shouting and swearing. For her to tell me I was grounded for life and could never see Leo again. But she just stared at me, stubbed out one cigarette and lit another, her mouth closing round it, puckering and thin.

'Are you going out tonight?' Peter asked later when I was sitting with him, holding his hand as he drifted off to sleep. He was wearing his pirate pyjamas; Mum had got them for Christmas. He loved them.

'No,' I said, 'not tonight. Some other night maybe. Tonight I'm going to stay in with you. I missed you last night, I kept thinking, *Oh, Peter'd like this*. But I'll take you next year maybe. There were all these crazy dancers in masks, lots of strange music – some of it really good. And we walked along the Thames, saw the most amazing fireworks. Then ate yummy Chinese food. You'll love Leo's place; it's amazing. His telly's the size of a football pitch, but it's all hidden behind some special doors which open when you press a button. But you have to take your shoes off when you go in; the carpets are all white, like snow. So thick your feet sink. Can you imagine?'

His eyes widened. 'I want to go. Can we go there?'

'Sure, some time soon. Leo would love to take you. I know he would.'

Back in my own room I didn't think I'd sleep, but it came on fast, sinking me deep. The pounding began in my ears; it throbbed at the back of my head, a nightmare remembered, a dream of drowning.

Lurching through the window, dripping with sludge dredged up from the bottom of the moat, the Thing was stronger than ever before. It placed its weight on mine, held me by the arms: pinned. *No*, I cried, my voice lost in the turn and tumble of sheets and mattress, swallowed by the thickening mire. We wrestled and I wrenched an arm free, pulled its hair, strands of it tangling round my fingers like wire. The Thing had grown so solid, and I bit into it, surprised at the sink of my teeth into flesh, gagging on blood as it wrenched and grappled, dragging me out of my bed, towards the window, holding me there.

See, it hissed, and I stared out. The moat glittered darkly, a warning. And, as the moon slunk behind a cloud, the water's surface blackened and dulled.

See, the Thing sang again, its fingers tightening on my wrists, squeezing and slicing with hard, bright nails. I stared at the blood dripping into the night, drops of it falling like rain. It was coming from me, I realized, and I screamed and howled for mercy as I saw my life gushing from me, the jagged edges of the broken mirror on the floor, the holes in the window where the Thing had punched through the glass.

Leo

'What on earth were you thinking, Leo?' He'd never seen Sue quite so angry. Even last year when she'd stood up in the planning meeting and shouted at their MP about the wind farms, she'd not been so cross. He really hadn't meant to make her mad.

'I'm sorry, it was stupid. We should have called.' Leo paced the kitchen, picking up mail and putting it down again, drumming his fingers on the worktop, avoiding Sue's gaze.

'Too right. You didn't even answer my texts. And you should have said from the outset that you were taking off for the night. For the entire night, Leo!'

'I know, I know.' There was no getting out of it; he'd screwed up and there was going to be a lot of grovelling to do. He started by bringing in more wood for the fire, taking Mary for a walk, tidying up his books and records from where they were scattered around the living room – Sue had been asking him for weeks. Then he helped in the kitchen too, wondering if he'd done enough yet, if it was ever going to be enough. Sue's back was still tense.

'So, what did Lorraine say to you when she came and picked up Peter?' Leo asked later, when they'd finished supper and Leo couldn't withhold the questions any longer. The fire was burning itself out; he stood up and added another log. Sue sipped her coffee.

'Not much. But she wasn't pleased, Leo. Why couldn't you have just phoned and told her your plans? That's her daughter you spirited away, her not-very-well daughter at that. She wanted to call the police. I had to talk her out of it.'

'Oh, bloody hell. I didn't think she'd be that bad.'

Sue eyed him and he blushed at the lie.

'I think Lorraine thought I was in on it. It made me look bad, Leo; you put me in an awkward spot too.' His aunt was still frowning.

'I guess so. I'm sorry. I cocked up. But we had a great night.' He grinned for a second, remembering. Audrey's face, alight, shining, her dancing on the tube, singing in the streets. He remembered later, in bed, her body, her skin and her smile. That had been wilder and brighter than any firework.

'It was worth upsetting Lorraine for, was it?'

He pushed the images out of his head.

'Oh, come on. She'll get over it,' Leo protested. But he wasn't so sure, and repeated the words as if that might make them true.

Sue tutted and cleaned her glasses, and they stared at the television for a while. Leo drummed his fingers on the arm of the chair.

'Maybe I should go over? Apologize?'

'A bit late for that. But yes, maybe tomorrow. Not tonight; it's too late now. They'll be in bed, I bet. Lorraine said she didn't sleep all night for the worry. I should think some serious grovelling is in order.'

'All right. In the morning.'

Leo wondered if he'd sleep. He sat up late, watching a film with Sue, a soppy rom com that they both laughed at but which made him worry about Aud. He pulled his jumper up around his nose, breathed in, smelled Audrey's skin and hair on his clothes and wished she was with him.

Audrey

Mum wouldn't stop talking. To me, the doctor, the nurses, to anyone who would listen.

'Can you help us?' Mum begged. 'This is an emergency,' she hollered. 'Help us, please.'

Her hand was stroking my face, her voice softening, like goo, like mushy peas. I wanted to be sick, felt it rise, fall from me, everywhere. If I could be sick enough, then there would be nothing left, I would be empty. Like an egg cracked in two, only sharp jagged edges remaining.

'Oh, God.' Mum held my hair, my face, holding me up. 'Someone, please.'

They whisked us into a little room; someone was cleaning my face, wiping, quick and deft. Mum was still talking.

'Audrey, love? Don't worry, we're at the hospital. Everything's all right.'

Her voice came from far away, like she was talking to me from another continent over a dodgy line. I opened my eyes long enough to see that this hospital looked just like all the others: white walls, curtains, people who glared and stared, antiseptic smells like the inside of Mum's cupboard. And doctors who never knew what to do. I wondered if I was still bleeding. About the trail of it, spots and smears on the walls of the flat, down the steps of the

Grange, dotting the gravel, all over the car. Would anyone see? Follow? Find me?

There were fingers pulling up my lids, a bright light in my eyes, hands holding my wrists too tightly round thick bandages.

'I got her here as soon as I found her.' Mum was holding me on the examination table. My body moved under her hands, as if she were settling one of her dolls, pulling its arms and legs into position.

'I'm a nurse,' Mum kept on, 'so I shouldn't have panicked. But when it's your daughter it's different. My God, I was terrified. Why would she do this?'

Why couldn't I go to sleep? Why couldn't I still be safe with Leo in that big double bed, lying on fresh cold white sheets smelling of blossom.

'She self-harms. I thought it wouldn't come to this. Never thought it was more than a cry for help. I don't keep anything sharp in the house, so she must have planned this. Been thinking about it. How she'd do it. We were supposed to see the doctor, I made the appointments, but she refused to come. I never dreamed something like this would happen. If we'd just been to that appointment –' Mum's voice broke. It sounded like she was swallowing a sob.

'She watched TV with me earlier and then she went up to bed. It was the first time she'd slept up there in weeks, so I thought it was a good sign. She says there's voices up there, ghosts. That she's hearing things. Next thing I know, I'm up for the loo, and there's Audrey on the floor, cut to pieces. I think it's this boy she's been seeing. I think that's what's done it; she ran off with him, over New Year. I think something must have happened. I can't bear to think about it.'

'OK.' The doctor sounded calm. 'Mrs Morgan, thank you. We'll get Audrey cleaned up. Try to keep calm; I think she'll be fine.'

'Do you? I don't know if this is what I'd call fine.' She lifted my arm, showed him my wrists.

'Perhaps you could get a cup of tea, talk to one of the nurses. Try and calm down; explain what's happened. We'll talk in a while.'

'I can't leave Audrey.' She clutched at me. I felt her hanging, clinging.

'She won't be alone. We'll monitor her. And of course get in touch with children's psychiatric services. They'll want to talk to you both. All right. Audrey? You're all right. Look, she's opening her eyes. Hello, Audrey.'

I held my hand out; I wanted to hold on to Mum and for the doctor to leave me alone. The lights were too bright and I screwed my eyes tight shut again. Mum picked up my hand, rubbed my skin; trying to make me warm, I thought.

When the doctor disappeared, pulling the curtains behind him with a quick swish, she sat beside me and held my hand, kissing my knuckles, breathing in.

'He's a kid, that one,' Mum whispered. I looked at her, saw how she rolled her eyes. 'I mean, fancy giving us a kid. It's a good job I'm here, Aud.'

She sighed, rested her head on our joined hands for a moment before standing and leaving me with another brief kiss on my forehead. My wrists were beginning to throb. The ache was unbearable. I heard her out in the corridor, asking someone what was happening; how long before they'd get me moved up to the ward, how long we'd have to wait for the psychiatrist. *If you don't ask, you don't get.* That was Mum's mantra.

And I couldn't remember doing it. Couldn't remember at all. Just the Thing coming for me, and the water and then the pain. And that was more frightening than anything.

'When can I go home?' I asked the nurse who said she'd be looking after me that day. This year was supposed to be my fresh start; I'd promised myself, made resolutions.

'I don't think it'll be yet, not for a little while, Audrey,' she said in her gentle voice. She treated me like a princess, this nurse, bringing me things, drinks and food and magazines, before rushing off to one of the others. The ward was loud and all I wanted to do was sleep, but I didn't dare. Not after last time.

'Where's my mum?'

'She's gone downstairs for a bit. To ring your brother.'

'Oh.'

I stared down at the bandages on my wrists. Thick. White. Under there somewhere was the blood. The thought of it made me sick again, and I lay back on the pillows clutching the cardboard bowl the nurse gave me, thinking about Peter and how I had to get home for him. He'd be needing breakfast, a bath. Something fun to do today.

'Are you all right, Audrey?' The nurse straightened my sheets and offered me a drink of water.

'Yes. I'm OK. I want to go though, I want to go home.'

Even as I said it I knew I didn't want to go back there, not to my room, never again. I couldn't go in there, where the Thing was waiting. It would finish me next time, once and for all. We'd have to move again; Mum would have to find a new place.

'Well, just rest for now, all right? The doctor will be here shortly and I'm sure Mum'll be back soon.'

I didn't watch her go, didn't look round; I didn't want to see the others, the ones in the beds next to me. Instead I stared out of the window at the sky. The heavy rain had stopped and the afternoon had lightened to a pale, fragile pink; the naked arms of trees reached and pointed to something far beyond this bed and I dreamed for a while into the dusk of pigeons and statues and a tiny Cupid, heavy in my hands.

Mum was back before the doctor came on his evening rounds. A strange violet light gathered behind her as she blocked my view of the last of the day.

'Where's Pete?' I asked as she leant over me, all smiles, holding balloons, a giant Pooh Bear, a box of sweets.

'He's all right; don't worry about him.' She bent and kissed my cheek, placed the teddy in my arms.

'But, Mum –'

She talked over me, kissing my fingers, the back of my palm. The sun was setting behind her and I strained to see the last glimpse of the sky as it streamed sails of purple and blue and gold. Mum dropped my hand and snapped the curtains closed and I knew that even if I could jump up and run out of here, run hard, that moment was lost forever. I couldn't catch the sun. And now it was dark.

'Right, then, where's that doctor? We've got a proper

psychiatrist at last, Aud.' Mum checked her lipstick in her little compact mirror. I watched from under my eyelashes. 'They're going to have to take this seriously now, love. I mean, look at the state of you.'

I didn't answer. The throbbing in my wrists was building, a drumbeat that pounded; shaking my head, I lifted my hands and covered my ears. My arms ached as I held them there and I think I moaned.

'Come on, Aud – that's right,' Mum whispered, and then the curtains were pulled back and the doctor was with us.

'So, you must be Audrey. Good afternoon. I'm Mr McGuiness, one of the doctors here. Will you open your eyes, please?' he said, gently taking one of my hands and lifting it from my ear.

'I'd like to talk to you, if that's all right.'

I didn't need a shrink. I turned away from his voice, screwing my eyes tighter, my whole face, until it ached.

'Well, you know the sooner you talk to me, the sooner we can help you. What happened is very serious. We want to help you get better, and we don't want this to happen again. Can we talk a little bit about the events leading up to last night?'

I didn't answer. There was no point. Mum grabbed her chance.

'She went off on New Year's Eve with this lad she's been seeing. He's a bad influence; Audrey wouldn't normally do something like that without telling me. And then when she got back she was in a terrible state. Wouldn't talk to me about it. Anyway, I was worried, but she went off to bed. The next thing I know she's cut her wrists to pieces.' Mum lost it then. I heard her smothering her sobs.

'OK.' The doctor's voice was still calm. I imagined his face: kind, a strong jaw, intelligent eyes. My dad had kind eyes, bright eyes. *No worries*, Aud, he said somewhere very far away, *no worries*. 'Audrey,' the doctor spoke again, insisting on an answer, 'did something happen? Did something trigger you cutting yourself?'

The air was very still. Everyone waited. I heard my own breathing, coming too fast. But there was no way I was mentioning the Thing. They'd throw away the key.

'I'd like her to be examined,' Mum said. 'Really as a matter of urgency. I think the police should be involved.'

'I'm sorry?' The doctor sounded confused. Mum lifted my left hand, uncurled the fingers, held it between both her own. When she spoke again her voice was very quiet. Utterly controlled.

'I think my daughter was raped. I think that's what's happened, why she's tried to kill herself, why she's not speaking now. She hasn't said a word to me; she's silent like this, just staring, crying. I want Audrey examined, checked, for bleeding, bruising. There will be physical evidence and we need to collect it fast.' I wrenched my hands free, sat up and looked at Mum. What had she just said? What were those words? She was staring at the doctor, her eyes fixed and sharp.

'Mrs Morgan, has Audrey said or done anything to suggest she was raped by her boyfriend?'

Raped? Raped by her boyfriend? What were they talking about?

'Only try and top herself, doctor,' my mother replied, staring him down, her voice deadly, booming in the back of my head, between my ears. 'As I said, she got back from her trip. She was in a state. Then this happens. For God's sake, doctor, this is my daughter and she needs help. I can't keep quiet about something like this. Sit back and wait for someone to help her. She's got no one else to fight for her, just me; I'm the only one who cares.'

'Audrey?' The doctor turned to me and I looked at him for the first time, but he didn't understand the fear in my face and read it as something quite other. Mum knew we'd had sex. And she thought Leo had forced me. No. Oh, God, no. This wasn't right. This couldn't be happening. She couldn't make this up about Leo. It was the Thing.

'Has anyone hurt you, Audrey? Is there anything you need to tell me?' His voice was very careful, his eyes deep, questioning.

'No,' I said. 'No, he didn't do that, he would never; no, no.' I repeated it over and over and the words hurt my throat and my mouth and my heart.

Mum's arms were round me all of a sudden, cradling, holding me to her chest; she was weeping over me and my stomach curdled, sickening again.

'Oh, Aud, I'm so sorry,' she wept as I vomited and the nurse hurried to clean me. 'My poor love, my poor little Audrey.'

When they'd all gone away again and I'd taken the pills the psychiatrist had prescribed, I managed to speak, dredging up words from the swamp of my mind.

'You can't say that.'

'Hmm?' She was bustling about, unpacking some things, straightening the curtains.

'Why did you say it?'

Mum didn't answer. My head was full of worry, of confusion, of fear.

'Where's Peter, Mum?'

'He's at home.'

'He shouldn't be on his own. He's five. He'll be scared.'

'I left the telly on. There's something for him to eat.'

'He needs looking after; you can't leave him. I'll tell them.'

'But I have to be here, with you.'

'I don't want you here.'

'You won't get better without me. If I don't tell them what's wrong with you, who will?'

'Get someone to look after Peter,' I told her, sitting up with my last bit of strength, determined to make this happen at least. 'And don't you dare say those things about Leo again. Don't you dare.'

Mum stood over me, shaking her head.

'I can say what I want, Audrey. I'm your mother and I'm responsible for you. There's no point trying to pretend, Aud. I can see what's happened to you. You could be hurt; you could need treatment. I want you to let the doctor examine you. And what about STDs, pregnancy? You'll need tests.'

'Mum, no.'

'It's all right,' she said. 'It's all right, Audrey. I'll sort this. You just lie back; you just concentrate on getting better. Leave everything to me.'

Leo

'You what?' Leo stared at Sue. She repeated herself, saying the words again really fast, in this weird, quiet voice. It didn't matter. Each one hit him like a fist.

'Audrey tried to commit suicide. I've just had Lorraine on the phone. She was wondering if we'd watch Peter for her, while she stays with Audrey.'

'Hang on, wait a minute. You're joking, aren't you? This must be a joke.' Leo stood stock still in the middle of the kitchen. The bright sun streaming in through the pretty picture window was an affront. The cheerful curtains, the bunch of flowers in a painted pottery vase on the table, the garland of holly and ivy around the fire, his own fresh skin, clean from the shower. None of these things were possible if Audrey was hurt, in trouble. Leo couldn't breathe. He couldn't think.

'Leo, I know this is hard to deal with. We knew she was fragile. Lorraine warned us; I tried to tell you.' Sue's voice was gentle, but the words weren't. They were accusing. His heart hammered; his eyes hurt.

'There is no way she would do that. She's not like that. She was so happy.'

Suicide. His head banged, the word hissing, curling. How? Pills? A blade? He couldn't think of it. Leo blocked out the image and replaced it with Audrey's face, tipped to the sky, her skin pale and her eyes shining with the green of fresh starts. And then he saw the dressings on her arms. She hadn't really explained and he hadn't wanted to pry. But he'd seen her smile again and again. She'd held his hand and wrapped her arms round him and whispered in his ear that she liked him. That she was so happy. Suicide. Why? No. She would have come to him, should have come to him. Called him. Run. He would have stayed up all night, holding her hand, being there, talking, helping; anything for Audrey. She knew that, didn't she? Hadn't he made it clear? He should have told her. Leo sat down, his body heavy, his heart sinking into his belly, into his shoes.

'Lorraine said something about bipolar again. That would explain it, wouldn't it? The highs, the lows.' Sue took her glasses off, rubbed them on her jumper and put them back on. She put her hand on Leo's shoulder. He looked up at her with eyes that were dropping tears.

'I don't know. What the fuck do I know? She was fine. I'm telling you. She was.' His fists curled. He couldn't swallow.

Sue held him. Leo was shaking now. It was fury and fear; he knew those feelings, and the sickness in his stomach, the dizziness, the floor spinning and dipping like he'd been thrown high in the air; no safety net to catch him. He didn't mean to cry like a baby. He couldn't help it. He wanted someone to make this better and no one could. Sue's arms, squeezing him tight, didn't help.

'Lorraine'll be here soon with Pete. I said of course we'd help. I mean, what else could I say?' she said.

'I'm going to see Audrey,' Leo told her, pulling away, wiping his face and walking to the door. Nothing Sue could say could make this any better; she didn't under-stand. Grabbing Sue's car keys, he said, 'She'll want to see me.' It was the only thing he was sure of.

'Hold on.' His aunt pulled him back. 'Maybe that's not such a good idea, not just yet. Let's check with Lorraine.'

'I don't want to check with Lorraine. I want to see Audrey.' His finger stabbed the air. He imagined Lor-raine's face. Imagined jabbing at her like that. Tried to breathe.

'Calm down.' Sue grabbed his hand and tried to hold him.

'No.' He pulled away again. Why had Audrey done this? He didn't understand. And then he did. Leo stopped. He looked at Sue, the realization sinking in.

'Leo, what is it?'

'Fuck,' he whispered. It was clear. Audrey hadn't wanted to come with him to London at all; she'd been worried and uncertain, but he'd promised it would all be OK. He'd dragged her round London and back to his parents' house and then they'd had sex and maybe she hadn't really wanted to; maybe she'd felt she had to, that he expected it, that that's why they were there. No. It was all his fault. Leo wasn't going to calm down. Not now. His heart raced; he had to get there. He had to explain. That he had expected nothing, that he loved her whatever.

A car came hurtling up the drive and pulled up outside the gates, barring them. Lorraine jumped out, opened the back door, produced Peter like a rabbit from a hat and marched through the gate towards them, taking long, purposeful strides, Peter trailing behind.

'Here's Pete,' she called out to Sue, ignoring Leo. 'I'm so thankful to you for helping us out like this. I'll be back for him as soon as I can, but I need to be with Audrey.'

'What's happened?' Leo asked. Lorraine turned to him.

'That's not a question you've got the right to ask,' she snarled.

'I'm sorry,' Leo said, 'about New Year. I didn't mean –'

She didn't let him finish.

'Too late now,' Lorraine said. 'Audrey's very sick, that's all I can say. And it's breaking my heart.' Sue stepped forward, reaching out to pull him inside, but Leo moved fast, following Lorraine back down the drive.

'I want to see her. Lorraine, I have to talk to her.'

'No chance,' Lorraine said, and Sue caught up.

'Come inside, Leo. Give Audrey some space. Come on – let's go and help Peter settle in. OK?'

He stared at Lorraine and she stared back at him, then strode away and jumped back into her car. He felt the imprint of her accusation on his skin for the entire day.

Audrey

I heard Mum talking outside the curtains, then a man's voice replying; it must have been the doctor whose name I had already forgotten. I'd forgotten a lot. My dad, my past, my life. How the Thing got me, how to escape. They kept giving me pills and were watching me swallow. But I'd already been here two days and that was long enough.

'I want her detained under section three,' Mum was saying; words I didn't understand, but guessed the meaning of. 'I can't cope at home and I'm scared she'll try again. There's no way she can come out, not without proper treatment. She needs to be looked after; we need proper help. Doctor McGuiness, I want my daughter sorted.'

'The team is still assessing Audrey, Mrs Morgan.'

'Lorraine.'

'Lorraine, but, as you may know, such a decision isn't taken lightly. Audrey still isn't talking to us. We need to take care here, make sure we make the right choices. We all want Audrey on the road to recovery and will do absolutely what we think is best. Sectioning her may not be in her best interest at this point.'

'What if I want a second opinion?'

'That is your absolute right. But you'll find we need –'

Mum broke in, interrupting, 'Yes, I know. Two separate doctors, and an AMHP. I'm a nurse. I know the procedure, doctor.'

'Right. Well, it will take us a little while to find the best plan of care for Audrey, as I'm sure you'll appreciate.' I listened for annoyance, for agitation, but the doctor was perfectly calm. It sounded like he was talking with a smile, trying to placate her.

'She still hasn't been examined,' Mum said, changing tack. My stomach twisted and I balled the sheets in my hands.

'No. She refuses to be examined. We won't force her against her will. Audrey says she hasn't been raped.'

I could almost hear Mum's eyes rolling. 'Of course she does. She's ashamed. And terrified. Don't you know anything about the psychology of rape victims?'

'As I said, we are taking absolute care to ensure Audrey gets everything she needs.'

'The longer you leave it, the less likely you'll find evidence.'

'Has Audrey told you she's been assaulted, Mrs Morgan?'

There was silence. I gripped the sheets and screwed my eyes tight again. Oh, God. No, she can't do this.

When they pulled back the curtains at last and saw me lying there, I sat up and stared the doctor in the face.

'Mr McGuiness, I haven't been raped,' I said in the kind of voice I thought a determined, sane, certain person would use, although there was very little evidence I would ever be any of those things again. I coughed, briefly. 'I

279

swear to you, I haven't been assaulted. And I don't want to be examined.'

Mum came over. 'Shhh, love, don't get upset.' She tried to hold me, tried to find a way to pull me towards her, smother me. I wriggled free, pushing her with my bandaged hands.

'Mum, I mean it. Leo did nothing to me. Nothing like that.' My face flared and I looked down at the sheets. 'He didn't hurt me,' I repeated, because that was the truth. 'We had sex, but I wanted to. I asked him to.'

Mum made a noise as if someone was strangling her. I couldn't look her way.

'OK, Audrey, thank you,' the doctor said, and he sat down beside me. 'I want to spend some time with you. Talking. This is one of the things I'd like to discuss. Is that going to be all right?'

'Yes.' Co-operating was the only way out; I saw that now. It would be hard though; I was so tired.

'I'm sixteen,' I told him. 'I don't need my mother with me, do I?'

'No. If you'd rather talk to me by yourself, that will be fine.'

I tried to look together, folding my hands neatly on the covers, sitting up nice and straight. Mum hovered, but I sent a message with my eyes. *Back off*, it said. *Leave Leo out of this*. I turned back to the doctor.

'Thank you,' I told him.

Leo

Leo wanted to visit more than anything. Remembering being in hospital, all that time spent lying down, staring at television screens, walls, ceilings. Hearing nothing, seeing nothing, lost in a grey vacuum, his thoughts like scrambled pieces of paper, ripped, shredded, churning. How the only thing he'd needed was someone who cared to sit by his bed, not to talk or tell jokes or ask questions, but just to be there. He knew Audrey would want him nearby. He remembered the loneliness, the cold horror of it, of feeling utterly abandoned, hopeless and lost. But Sue said no. That Audrey wasn't taking visitors. Just direct family.

'What about Peter, then? He should go, shouldn't he?'

They both stared out of the window at the little boy playing on the lawn with Mary. He threw the ball and the dog fetched, dropped it at his feet. He picked it up, repeated the action. No smile. No jump or run or laugh. It had taken Sue all morning to persuade him just to do this.

'Lorraine thinks it'll upset him.'

'He misses her.'

Sue sighed. Clattered the dishes into the sink.

'I don't know what else to do, Leo. I'm sorry.'

'I can't stand this.'

'It must be bringing back horrible memories for you.'

'No, it's not that; I don't care about that. It's her. I can't stand the thought of her being on her own.'

'Lorraine's there.'

Leo walked away from his aunt, slammed out of the back door, jogging over to Peter. He grabbed the football.

'Come on, Pete. Let's play.' And they spent another desperate hour pretending nothing was wrong.

Peter hadn't mentioned Audrey, not once since he'd arrived. That night Leo read him a story and tucked him up in bed. He remembered his own mum doing the same thing, smiled at the thought, then laughed quietly to himself. She'd been reading him *Robinson Crusoe* when he was five, not *Horrid Henry*. Still, he'd loved it. Even the vocab tests the next morning.

'You all right, mate?'

'Yes, thank you.' Peter had pulled the covers up to his nose. His big eyes stared at Leo, unblinking.

'You sure?'

'Yes. I'm OK.'

As Leo turned to go, Peter sat up and lunged, grabbed him round his legs, almost toppling him on to the bed in a clumsy, desperate hug. Leo crouched and held him in his arms for a long time.

The next morning he and Peter got their coats and set out for the bus. He told Sue he was taking him to the library and she gave him a pile of books to return, so it looked like they'd have to do that too. First, though, they were going to see Audrey.

Peter was quiet on the journey.

'You OK, Pete?' Leo said.

Peter nodded, his thumb in his mouth.

'Look.' Leo drew a silly face in the condensation on the window. 'You draw one.'

Peter didn't look; he stared at his stones, kicking his feet back and forth.

When they got to the hospital Leo asked at reception for the ward. They took the lift, up to the fourth floor.

'This hospital looks like the other one,' Peter said.

'What?'

'The other one Aud was in before.'

'When? Why was she in hospital before, Pete?'

'I don't know,' Peter said, running ahead.

They didn't need to press the button to gain admittance on to the ward; another visitor was coming out and they slipped through and faced yet another impersonal corridor.

'Where's Audrey?' Peter asked.

'I'm not sure. Come on – let's see if we can find her.'

The nurses' station seemed the obvious place to ask. Leo cleared his throat and in his best thoroughly well-brought-up voice asked if they might see Audrey.

The nurse, Kitty her badge said, smiled. 'Oh, I'm sorry. She's with the doctor. But you could come back later? Leo, is it? And Peter?' She came round to speak to them, crouching to say hello to Peter and giving him a big smile.

'Yes, all right – when?'

Kitty straightened up and checked her watch.

'She should be done in half an hour or so. Why don't you wait in the family room? Or tell you what, her mum's just up there, sitting with one of our other patients. I'll grab her for you; she'll be delighted to see you, I'm sure.'

'No,' Leo said, stepping back. 'No that's OK.'

'It's no bother.' And Kitty was off, striding down the ward. Leo hesitated, took a step to follow Kitty, and then a step back, grabbed Peter's hand and pulled him after her.

Lorraine's face said it all. Her smile strained like the buttons on her shirt, her skin pulled into a grimace that held no welcome. With blank eyes, she escorted them back down the ward, through the doors and into the elevator.

'She can't see you, Leo. Or, well, she doesn't want to see you. She told me to say. She'd rather you didn't see her, the state she's in. She's in a mess, you know. So, best leave it.'

'I don't mind. I just want her to know I care.'

'Oh, she knows that, she does. Don't you worry.'

'OK.'

Lorraine walked them out of the building and down the road, back to the bus stop. Leo was still carrying Sue's bag of library books. It was unutterably heavy.

Audrey

Mr McGuiness kept on coming back. He wanted to know a lot of things: what I thought about, dreamed about, ate and drank. If I was sleeping, if I was anxious, if I had suicidal thoughts. He asked me what I hated, what I loved.

'Peter,' I said straight away; it was the first easy question, 'my little brother.'

'How old is he?'

'Only five. He'll be six in the summer.' I looked up and smiled at the psychiatrist. He smiled back, like we were pals, chatting over a coffee. 'I have a little boy,' he said, 'similar age. Great fun.'

'Pete's really into wildlife; we built this den, but it collapsed. We're going to make another though, soon; Leo's going to help. We've been writing it all up in a book, all the things we've spotted. We've seen a muntjac. Hares. And we're waiting for a badger. And then there's the kestrel.' It seemed so long ago, that perfect day. Impossible it had happened now.

'I can tell you really care about Peter, Audrey.'

I nodded. He waited.

'I do. I really do.' I shut my eyes. Imagined his bright face. The innocence in his big eyes. He'd lost a tooth before Christmas and there was a gap now in his smile.

'Anything else?' The doctor waited and I knew I had to dig deeper, present more of my heart on a plate.

'Yes.'

'Will you tell me?'

'I love my boyfriend, Leo.'

'Um, hmm?'

'And . . .' There had to be more. I still hadn't said it. If I left it out, then there'd be questions asked. He'd dig and dig at me until he got the right answer.

'And?'

'I suppose I love my mum.'

'Only "suppose"?'

'No. I love my mum.' Saying it was hard, like coughing up a bone; it hurt my throat, scratched at my eyes. It wasn't a lie, not really.

'Audrey?'

'Yes.'

'Why are you crying?'

I shook my head. That was all.

Later Mum dropped in on me. I knew she was around the ward, all day, every day, but she'd found other things to do. Patients to talk to, or their parents, the nurses to laugh with. She brought them cake and coffees from the shop downstairs, she told me. They were a great bunch.

'So, love.' She settled herself. 'I was thinking, how about we do some of your blog?'

'What?'

'Yes, it's the perfect chance. I've been keeping it up and running, but, you know, you could take some of the work off me, couldn't you?'

'I don't want to. I don't know what to put.'

'Not this again. You are a lazy bugger, Aud. There's

loads happening. I'll get a couple of pics and upload them too.'

'No. Not of me like this. Please.'

'Oh, don't be daft. You look great; just lovely, like always. It's like a little holiday this, isn't it? You getting waited on hand and foot and fussed over all day long. You're a lucky old girl.'

She handed me the laptop. Plugged it in. Loaded the page.

I began to read. She wasn't lying when she said she'd been keeping it up to date. There was a picture of me I hadn't known she'd taken, lying asleep, my arms on top of the covers, so you could see the bandages nice and clear, masses of text underneath. I didn't need to read it and pushed the laptop at Mum.

'Take that picture off.'

'What? Why? It's a nice one.' She scrutinized it again, looking from different angles.

'I'm asleep. You took it while I was asleep; you didn't tell me.'

It felt weird, like she'd stolen something. A kidney, a limb. Another piece of my heart.

'Come on, Aud, get cracking. I'll leave you to it – back in ten, see how you're getting on,' Mum said.

I had to do it. I had to find that other girl, the one I'd imagined – the one who lived in this blog and made Mum happy; the sad, desperate girl who was going mad and was trying to die. How to create her out of the sticks and bones of my heart? How to build her out of the rubbish dump of my life? She felt things that girl, and we didn't share the same pain. Her pain was particular. That girl wanted to die. And I didn't. I wanted to live. I took a deep breath and started to type very slowly with one finger. I stabbed each key and made the lies come alive.

THE PAIN PLACES: ME AND MY DEPRESSION
BY AUDREY MORGAN, AGED SIXTEEN
AND FOUR MONTHS

There's not much I can do right.

That much we had in common, I thought, pulling a face and stabbing delete as hard as I could. OK. Try this.

Can't even die properly, can I? Guess I screwed up again, but I shouldn't be surprised. My whole life's a screw-up, a nasty sick mess.

That was more like it. It wasn't me talking now; it was her. Because I had Leo and Peter. I had lots to live for. OK, carry on.

The doctor says I'm very lucky Mum found me when she did. Lucky. That wasn't the first thought that entered my head when I woke up and found myself stuck in hospital again. No. I was angry, because they wouldn't even leave me in peace to do what I want with my own life. Now I've got to get better, because there's no point being in hospital, and I need to get out of here. It's swapping one prison for another. The prison of my mind and the prison of my life and this prison here. Walls and ceilings and doors hemming me in. They watch me all the time, checking I'm not up to anything, like I'm a criminal.

I paused. Thought about it. Was this right? Was this going to help? No, I needed more.

Well, there's no point being sorry for myself. The only person I should be sorry for is my mum. She's the greatest. She's helped me all these years, looked out for me, and what do I do? I get it wrong every time. I wish I could make her happy. Mental illness is terrible for families, I know that. But Mum's never complained, even when I've been a total nightmare, like now. She's one in a million, my mum, and when I say I owe her big time, I really mean it. I'm planning something for her, a massive surprise, and one day I'm going to pay her back for everything. Make her see how grateful I truly am. I swear, there's no other mother alive like mine.

I can't help thinking though, it'd be better for her, for everyone, if I'd have died.

That was better. Mum would like that. She would love it. I lay back, exhausted from the effort, my wrists aching again. The cuts had been deep, Mr McGuiness said, but I didn't remember them putting in the stitches and sewing me back together like a broken doll. He asked how I knew where to cut, how I was brave enough to cut so deep. I just shrugged and didn't mention the Thing who drifted up out of the waters and into my room. How it had known. How it was the Thing's hands who'd worked upon my own.

Leo

His mum answered the call on the first ring; she usually did.

'Leo, darling, how are you?'

It was good to hear her voice. He smiled and it felt strange.

'I'm fine, Mum.'

'So, what's happening? It's what, two in the morning UK time – why aren't you sleeping?'

'I missed you, couldn't sleep.'

'Missed me? Hmmm. Girl trouble?' Leo lay back against his pillows. His mum was in a good mood, not fretting about his insomnia at least.

'Sort of.'

'You always were hopeless. And I mean that in a good way.'

He couldn't take offence and laughed at her insult, remembering the little Valentine's cards he'd made as a kid; his mother taking him to post them every year through the letter box of the little girl with bright blonde hair who lived across the square and sometimes sat with him on the see-saw. She'd thought it sweet. She could be sentimental when she chose.

'I suppose so. Remember Suki?'

'I do. You were devoted. But seriously, Leo –' her voice

lost the smile – 'remember what Graham said. No stress. Hopeful things. Your Audrey isn't being difficult?'

'No. She's not. She's lovely, Mum. Really.' Lovely but in hospital. Lovely but in trouble. And he still didn't know how to help.

'Yes, Sue says so too. But I hope you have other friends, my darling. And lots of interests. What have you been up to?'

He told her about New Year's Eve. About the piano. Playing again; how good it had felt.

'I'll get a piano sent to you. Sue will love it.'

'No, no, you don't have to do that.' It was too much; she always went too far. Never saved his presents for his birthday, handed over everything the second she bought it; too excited to hide, wanting his smiles.

'No arguments. You said it made you feel good. Well, that's all I care about. The only thing that matters is your happiness, you know; that's all I've ever wanted.' There was no point trying to stop her now. Leo didn't want to.

'Thank you. That would be brilliant.'

'Yes.' He could hear how pleased she was. 'Yes, I agree. Now get some sleep. And call again soon.'

'Love you, Mum,' he said, and for a while he felt a little better.

Audrey

The night was another long one. I sat up, watched the clock and listened to the ward. When the nurses passed by and checked on me, I pretended to sleep. Mum was around somewhere, I guessed, and sometimes the breath I felt on my cheek was hers. I knew its bitter ripeness: chewing gum and tobacco. Unwashed teeth.

If I fell asleep, I knew the Thing would come. It was time. It was creeping closer. For a while it had been sated by the blood, pleased with all the attention. Now it craved more. I'd heard the thudding, just faintly, at the back of my brain. But the Thing wasn't going to get me again. It wouldn't take much for them to lock me up for good, so I had to watch. Given half a chance, It would pick apart the stitches in my wrists and undo me all over again and then I would be lost. No.

Better to be on my guard. *Keep watch and ward*, I thought, remembering a line of poetry from somewhere. A line from the mouth of a madman. But it was my line now. And I wasn't mad. Only I knew the truth.

Leo

He decided that he would have to send something, get a
message through; whatever it took. He remembered
Audrey suggesting pigeon post and thought now that
she'd been right. They were divided as if by an ocean or a
war, but it was only really Lorraine who kept them apart,
and he hated how powerful she'd become; he wished he
could fight through the waves that churned around
Audrey and sail her away.

He didn't have a pigeon, but he had paper. He sat in his
room tearing page after page from the copy of the com-
plete works of Shakespeare his mother had bought him
for his eleventh birthday, choosing lovers' speeches both
old and young. He folded fast, made flower after flower.
Soon he had a bouquet. He started another.

Later, after Sue had made Peter have another bath and
she'd brushed out his thick mop of hair, she sat reading to
him before the fire and Leo joined them.

'What's that?' Peter asked, staring at Leo's hands, which
were full of paper flowers, fragile and glowing like stars.
They held messages and a heart, a story torn and re-
fashioned. Love's labour, not yet lost, not yet.

'It's flowers for Audrey. They're perfect, Pete, because
they're paper. They'll never die. We can drop them at the
hospital. Do you think she'll like them?'

He crouched down and Peter nodded, solemn and frowning as he reached out to touch very gently.

'I didn't make her anything,' he said. 'Can I make some?'

Sue found an old book of maps, long out of date, and Leo crouched beside Peter and began to tear and to fold. First he showed the little boy how to make a heart.

'I want to do a bird. A bird to perch on your flowers,' Peter said. 'Audrey likes birds.'

Leo frowned. It was tricky. 'OK.' He took a breath. 'Here's how, then. Look.' He began to show Peter, his fingers working slowly, very patient.

'Wait,' Peter said, and grabbed a pen and the paper from Leo's hands, opening it out again.

'First I have to draw us. Me and Aud, I need to put us on the map.' He began to scratch out two stick figures. One tall with long hair, the other little, almost insignificant, beside it.

'That's better,' he said, smiling, handing the paper back to Leo, and they lay sprawled on the rug making a bird, which Leo hoped one day would fly.

Audrey

Mum said I shouldn't get up.

'Why? I want to.'

Truly I was tired. How lovely it would be to sleep for a hundred years or more. But that was the road to disaster: my body would give up; my brain switch off, my eyes turn dull and glassy. I would be Madison.

'You'll tire yourself out. And the doctor will be here soon on his rounds. I want you in bed for that.'

'I'm bored.'

I swung my legs over the side of the bed and stood up, a little shaky on my feet but better than I thought.

'This isn't a good idea.' Mum hovered, I waved her away. I was sixteen, old enough to go for a walk.

'It's fine.' I gritted my teeth. 'Get off.' I shrugged her hand off my arm. The Thing hadn't got me and I had to make sure it stayed that way.

'I'll get you a chair.'

'I don't need a wheelchair. Leave me alone.'

I walked the length of the ward, pushing myself to stride and stamp. The other kids stared at me. Someone shouted. Mum said I should make friends, but I was used to ignoring their calls and sped up a little. But still it took too long. I wanted to run. To fly. If I had one wish it would be for wings.

When the doctor came I was standing by the bed, Mum trying to lever me back in.

'She's worn herself out,' Mum told him, exasperated.

'Exercise is a good idea,' Mr McGuiness told us.

'The pills make me tired,' I told him. 'I don't want them any more. I don't want to be on medication. I don't need it.'

'The medication is to help you, Audrey.' I hated that patient tone and hated being spoken to as if I were stupid. I wasn't going to take it any more.

'Yes, but – it doesn't work. It doesn't stop it –'

'No buts, Aud. Listen to the doctor.'

'But, Audrey,' he continued, as if Mum hadn't spoken, 'we've decided you're ready to go home. We'll continue to see you as an outpatient, of course, but a transfer to the local inpatient unit isn't going to be in your best interests at present.'

'You mean they've got no beds,' Mum spat. 'This is a joke. Audrey's ill. Seriously ill.'

The doctor listened to Mum for a while longer, nodding, but he didn't appear to hear her and nor did I. I could only hear his words, on a loop, that in the morning I would be free. My heart began to gallop. This was definitely a chance. I had to get away from her. She'd lied about Leo and I couldn't forgive that. Mum had to know she wasn't going to get away with it and that I had my own plans. My brain worked fast: what could I do? Where could I go? The farm; to Peter and Leo and Sue.

The doctor was talking still, about my next appointment, about the medication, about how to contact him or the team. Mum seethed and I smiled, my legs jiggling and jumping, my pulse thudding in my ears.

I slept well enough and by the afternoon I was finally ready to go. Smiling and waving at the nurses, I let Mum push me out of the ward in a chair. She thought I would sit there like Madison; she thought she could pull a string in my back, make me say the words she'd decided a good girl would utter. She thought she could say Leo was a rapist. She thought lots of things and all of them were wrong.

PART TWO

Audrey

'Get in the car, Aud,' Mum said, sat in the car, poised to go.

It was getting dark. It was cold. But it was time.

'No. I'm not going with you back to the Grange. I can't trust you, Mum. You're a liar.'

Her head whipped round. 'You what?'

'I'm not going back there,' I said.

'Get in the car now. This is ridiculous. Where else do you think you're going to go?'

'Somewhere else. On my own.' I took a step back. The first step away.

'There is nowhere else. It's the only option available. So, tough luck, lady. Get in and let's get going. You've wasted enough of my time as it is.'

'No.'

I turned and walked, taking the route she couldn't follow by car, across the flower beds, through the pedestrian walkways. She yelled, her voice flying out, like a line thrown into the water, baited, hooked.

'Audrey, don't be stupid – come back.'

I put my head down and tucked in my arms, concentrating on putting my feet one in front of another, forging a straight line out of there. I knew I was strong enough. I could do this.

When Mum didn't follow, I picked up speed, my heart

clattering in my chest as I turned a corner. And another. Found the road. Saw a sign. Picked up my feet again, counted the steps as I walked along the main road, cars speeding past, headlights on full beam.

'*One, two, three, four,*' I chanted, '*five, six, seven, eight. One two three four five six seven eight.*' As long as I counted I would be free, as long as my feet moved me forward I would break away. The wind was cold, but it pushed me on. The evening was dark, but in the shadows I could hide. Mum would not catch me. Another car rushed past. Another. And then —

'Audrey!'

Mum was there, slowing to drive beside me as I walked, the window down, hanging out and yelling.

'Get in this car now,' she called.

I pretended I couldn't see her, couldn't hear her. I shifted into another gear, higher, faster, and counted. *Onetwothreefourfivesixseveneight.* I had to get the energy from somewhere; I had to find the strength. I was a machine: hard, metal, strong. Arms like pistons, I pushed on.

'Audrey, I mean it. You're digging yourself a big hole here. You think this behaviour is normal? You need help — get in the car.'

My legs scissored and my breath came in sharp bursts, but it wasn't enough. The traffic was backing up behind Mum: horns were blaring, cars dangerously overtaking, their drivers shouting. I needed another way to get away from her.

'Get in the car,' she repeated, coaxing now. 'Come on, we'll talk about this. We can sort it out together, like always. Come on, love, you'll catch your death. You need me to help you. You need me.'

I kept walking, turned off the High Street and on to the country lane that wove out of town and towards the villages. If I could keep going, if I didn't give in, then things would change. Hurting Leo, lying about Leo; that was something I wouldn't take. She couldn't have her lies and she couldn't have me, so it was time to make it happen. Time to show her I meant it. She didn't get to destroy everything. She didn't have that power.

'Audrey.' Mum leant on the horn. I put my hands over my ears and walked. Faster and faster.

A gate. A field, frozen mud. I didn't pause, didn't think, hauled myself over and began to run. If she chased me? Who would win? It had to be me. The cold bit and scored at my skin and I ran until my lungs burst, leaving her calls behind, stumbling to a walk – my legs not so strong, not yet, not pounding like they should – like they ought to. I was young, but I was old, and the thought stopped me. It wasn't right. The horizon was full of nothing; there was no point searching there. A thin line of trees, barely visible in the darkness, stood sentinel over the scene. *Move*, I thought, *just move*, and I jogged forward. That was the way. *Keep going; don't stop*.

The darkness swallowed me. I wondered if I was turning in circles. I wondered about the sinking sand. About mud and falling and drowning and dying and no one finding me ever. I stopped again and turned round. Looked back. Which way? Why weren't there signs? Why wasn't there a guide, someone to hold my hand and lead me on.

'Dad, where are you?' I whispered. 'Dad, come and get me. *Find me, please.*' But no one answered. No one came. The air was as dry as bone. I trudged on, counting my steps again, just to keep going.

I found the embankment by accident; followed the path, still looking over my shoulder, staggering and tripping over roots, guessing my way to the farm, wishing I could read the stars.

It stood there waiting, warm. Still too distant, but I saw lights burning in the windows, smoke curling from the chimney, and I moved forward, through the field, onwards, certain that once I arrived, then I'd be home.

But Mum's car was in the drive. I hadn't been fast enough; I could never outrun her.

What did I do now? Creep to the barn and hide there, like a rat skulking in the straw, or tell her straight that I'd finished with the Grange? The Thing wasn't going to stop. It wanted to win. It was so big now, fully grown, and hungry. And Mum: Mum was a liar. She wouldn't protect me.

The barn. Hide. Yes, keep safe.

Before I could move, the door swung open and a figure stood in the doorway: a silhouette, searching, staring out into the night. I stood back against the wall, out of view, holding my breath tight, my chest bursting. The figure moved. It was Leo. My heart jumped, hurt again. And then a smaller form joined him, took his hand, tilted his head, a small voice piercing the dark.

'Is it Audrey? Can you see her?'

Peter, my brother. He needed me. He was waiting for me to come home to him. To look after him. There was no choice now. I stepped forward as they turned away. I had to follow them inside.

When I pushed open the door they were gathered at the table drinking tea, chatting in low voices. I watched for a second. No one had heard me; perhaps I was shrinking, vanishing, too small to be seen. Then Leo turned.

'Audrey!' My name bounced around the room, echoing, strange and disembodied. They were laughing at me, staring, pointing. I put my hands up to my face, wanting to hide again. Wishing I'd stayed in the shadows.

'Here she is,' Mum said, and held out her arms. Her face split, divided. One mother, two. The Thing at her shoulder. Its ragged hair grey and long. Its eyes dark and grinning. *Ah, here you are*, it said, *at last*. I froze. No. Not here. Not at the farm. It couldn't have found us here.

'Aud, are you all right, love? Audrey? You must be freezing.'

And it hit me. The cold, the exhaustion. I felt sick. My legs gave way. Their faces dissolved. Someone's arms caught me before I hit the stone floor, and a voice, close.

'Audrey, you're safe, you're all right. It's me, Leo.'

Leo

She was there and not there, shaking in his arms as if she'd seen something that had frightened her out of her wits. Her body was freezing, her shoes muddy and ruined, her tracksuit bottoms thick with mud and water.

'Audrey? It's OK; are you all right?'

He picked her up and carried her to the sofa, Sue brought a blanket. Lorraine bustled around.

'I'd better call an ambulance,' she said, her mobile already in her hand.

'No, it's all right; she just fainted.' The last thing he wanted was Audrey gone again as soon as she'd arrived. If they gave it a moment, she'd open her eyes and tell them what was up.

'Leo, leave this to me. I'm a nurse.'

'Hang on,' Sue said. 'Just a moment – look, she's coming round.'

Lorraine pushed him aside, crouched beside her daughter, her voice soft and crooning.

'Audrey, my sweetheart, Audrey, love, Mum's here, you're all right now, love, all right now.'

She smoothed Audrey's brow, held her hand, reached in her bag, pulled out a foil of pills, squeezed one on to her palm.

'Take this, Aud, come on, your medication – you're late

with it tonight. All this silliness. Goodness, what a state you've got yourself in. We'll get the ambulance, get you back to the hospital; don't worry.'

Leo watched as Lorraine slipped the tablet on to Audrey's tongue. Watched Audrey roll it around her mouth. Wondered if she swallowed it. She sat up, coughed. Put her hands over her mouth, then coughed again.

'Mum. I'm OK. I'm sorry, sorry.' She let Lorraine straighten her clothes, comb out her hair, fuss over her, smoothing her cheeks, pulling at her lips as if to rearrange her features entirely. Lorraine looked up and smiled at them all.

'That's all right, love. Now, let's get you back to A and E. Right?'

Audrey stared at her mum. The fear was back in her eyes. He was sure he saw her inch away, pull towards him.

'Can I stay here?' she said fast, glancing at Sue, then him. 'I'm tired.'

His aunt's eyebrows disappeared under her fringe. Leo stood up, put his hand on Sue's shoulder.

'It's late. She can stay; she doesn't need to go back to the hospital, does she?' he repeated, insisting.

Audrey sat up. She took off her glasses and stared at her mother.

'I'm going to stay here, Mum. All right?'

Lorraine said nothing.

'It's fine by me,' Sue said. 'You stay too, you and Peter. Audrey seems OK now. It must have been the shock, the stress. There's plenty of food; we should all have something to eat.' She bustled over to the range, put a pan on the hob, filled another with water at the sink.

'Oh, no, we couldn't impose. We'll go. But I don't like to leave Audrey, not after she's been so ill. She isn't right. Running off like that. Thank God she came here as I suspected.' Leo glanced down at Audrey's wrists. Still bandaged. She saw him looking and blinked. He looked away. Shit, what did he say to her about that? He wondered if she'd got his flowers, if he'd made it clear that it didn't matter. He was on her side, whatever. Lorraine was right; she seemed spaced out. And why had she come here and run away from her mother? He wanted answers but couldn't ask.

Audrey

Go, just go, I thought. *Get out of here, Mum.* The longer she stood there, the more Sue offered tea and food and a soft warm bed, the more likely she'd hang about.

'I'll see you tomorrow. I'm going to stay here tonight, OK?' I said.

It looked like she was going to refuse, but something changed her mind. Maybe it was them all watching – Sue and Leo. Maybe she got it: that I knew she was a liar and that if Sue and Leo knew what she'd said, then that would be it. Everything would come out.

'All right. All right, have it your way. But if there's a problem, call me. And make sure you take your medication, Audrey.' Mum gathered up her things.

'Come on, Pete.' She looked directly at me when she spoke. 'Peter, I said, get your things.'

My brother looked up; he looked at me, then at her. He'd been quiet, I realized, barely saying a thing.

'Are you all right, mate?' I whispered.

'I want to stay with Aud.' Peter's hand tightened on mine. He'd been biting his nails. I caught Leo's eye and was about to try and argue for Peter too when Mum came over, kissed my cheek, grabbed his arm.

'No, come on now – let's be off. I'm tired. Sue's probably had enough of you.'

She straightened up and laughed but it wasn't funny.

'He can stay,' Sue said, mild, smiling. 'You all can.'

'No, no. God, people will think you've started up some sort of home for waifs and strays, Sue.' Mum's laugh was more false than ever, her hands clenched and unclenched. 'I'll take him back with me, get him sorted for school in the morning. You can see your sister tomorrow, Peter. We'll pick her up.'

And there was no more arguing. Peter trailed behind her, looking back over his shoulder, pleading. I screwed my eyes tight shut. Only heard the door close and Sue calling goodbye and Mum calling thanks.

Peter would be all right. He'd be OK. I'd find a way to make sure of it.

'Thanks for having me,' I said to Leo. He was sitting beside me, just waiting.

'My pleasure.' His grin was a treat. So normal. Leo moved closer. He took my hand; he whispered something in my ear. Something about him being pleased to see me. I couldn't listen properly, still thinking of my brother. Where had I been? Leo murmured. He'd been waiting, he said, demanding my attention, dragging me into the present. I turned my head and his lips were on my cheek. Close to my mouth. He was warm, real. He was alive and so was I now. Free for the moment.

'Hey, you two.' Sue sounded surprised, and we jumped apart. 'Give the girl a chance, Leo; she's just arrived. Just out of hospital.' He jumped up at her rebuke, his smile cheeky.

'Sorry. Can I get you something, Aud? Drink, another

blanket? Foot massage. I dunno. You name it, wish, command, humble servant, et cetera, et cetera, et cetera.' He made me laugh. It was good.

'No. No, just sit here,' I told him, and he nodded like he understood that was all I needed.

The next thing I did was flush the pills down the toilet, every single last one. The silver foil crumpled and tore and with each rip I felt better.

'Are you sure you should be doing that?' Leo stood in the doorway of the bathroom watching. He didn't try and stop me, but his voice had an edge, a little tension.

'Certain.' I washed my hands and turned back to Leo. Bright smile at the ready. But I'd seen myself in the mirror; I knew I looked like hell. The smile wasn't going to fool anyone.

'Right, where were we, what, ten days ago?' I said, breaking the silence. He started walking back to the living room, jogging down the stairs.

'I think we'd just had the best night of our lives? Something like that.' Leo threw the words over his shoulder. I caught them with relief. He would play along.

'Yeah, that was it. How could I forget?'

So why the hell would you try and kill yourself one night later? We sat beside one another on the sofa. Sue had disappeared, leaving us in peace, and the unspoken question hung heavy and dark between us. It laughed at me. I swallowed. Nothing would ever be the same.

'I guess I should explain,' I said.

'OK. Yeah. If you want.' He didn't sound angry, but he

did sound worried. I swallowed and shifted away from him a little, preparing myself. This was going to be hard. I'd thought about what I would tell him and had it ready, but actually saying the words was a different matter. I'd never told anyone before.

'Right, yeah, so, you know, I never really told you much before about what it's like, my illness.'

Leo was waiting, sitting very still.

'Well, right, one part of it. This is going to sound, I don't know, weird, but what happens is, there's this Thing.'

'Thing?'

'Yeah, that's what I call it. I don't know how else to describe it.'

'You mean, like a voice or something?'

'Maybe, a bit like that, yeah. A presence; it's just there.'

Leo was trying to understand, listening hard.

'Well, it was because of it,' I was whispering and talking fast. 'It wasn't anything to do with you, you know, or us, or what happened.' I felt hot, so stupid, and looked down.

'So, hang on, this Thing, it made you try and kill yourself?'

I twisted a long strand of my hair in my fingers, knotting and tugging. 'Don't say it like that.'

'Like what?'

'Like I'm mad. Like you don't believe me. I can't help it. I know it's not how other people are, Leo, but it's how I am, and I don't like it, but I have to live with it.'

'So why did you chuck your pills away?'

'Because I don't need them.' My voice was too high. It

was ridiculous. I couldn't talk about this; it wasn't something you could explain.

'Aud.' He took my hand, brought me to a halt. 'You should really think about this. I'm worried what'll happen if you don't take your medication. You saw a psychiatrist, right? And he prescribed them?'

'Yes.'

'So, chucking them away, it's risky.'

'OK.' I sighed and covered my face with my palms. 'I'll ring Caldwell. Get another prescription. All right?'

'First thing?'

'Yes, first thing.'

Leo sat back, but he wasn't satisfied. I looked at him. The frown he wore was indelible.

'And you'll be seeing someone, right?' Leo said, still watching me.

'Yeah, as an outpatient. I have to go to see the psychiatrist. That's the condition. Mum wanted me sectioned. Sent to some residential place.'

'Yeah?' Leo's voice was cautious. He looked as if he thought maybe that would have been a good idea.

'Yeah. Somehow the doctor didn't agree. I guess the gods smiled on me for once. He was nice, Mr McGuiness. He was cool.'

'OK.' Leo leant over and pulled me close; he hugged me tight and I let out a huge sigh. I'd done it and he hadn't run screaming from the building. 'I'm just glad you're all right, that you're home. I'm just glad you didn't die, Aud.'

'Yes,' I whispered into his shoulder and couldn't stop the shudder.

'But listen; you can talk to me, you know. If you need to. Seriously, about anything, because I've been sort of where you were. No voices or anything like that. But my head was a mess. I know it's scary. Just, please, don't do this again, Aud – don't turn away, don't –'

I stared out of the window for a second and then looked back at him, clenching my fists, digging my nails into my palms. I held up my wrists, showed him the bandages.

'Listen, Leo. Seriously. You think I want this? You think I want to be the girl who does things like this? Well, I don't. I don't want to die. Not now, not for a long, long time.' He stared at me and I swallowed, forcing my voice to soften. 'Firstly, there's you.' I stood up and began to pace, counting the reasons on my fingers. 'I need to know what happens with us, don't I? I can't miss that; literally, the loveliest thing in my life. I never thought I'd have a boyfriend, definitely not one like you.'

'Aud,' he said, trying to interrupt, but I shook my head.

'No. Listen. I need to know if you and me –' I glanced at Leo, he was watching, quiet now, leaning forward – 'if we get to have a future. I want to be with you again. Like before. I want to be loved like other girls are loved and to love you back, like you deserve. I want you to teach me how to play the piano, "Chopsticks", at least.' He laughed, wiping his eyes. 'Don't, don't cry. Please, not for me. I'm not going to die before I've had more of all this. Us, you.'

'OK, stop it, then, just shhh.'

'No. There's stuff I've got to say. I have so much to do, lists and lists of little things. I've never been to Spain or

anywhere abroad, or passed an exam or worn a beautiful
dress or dyed my hair black or climbed a mountain. I want
to learn to swim. Learn to drive. Maybe, I don't know,
maybe go to university, if I can. At least get an education.
I want to know the things you know, Leo. Stuff other
people know. Then there's Peter. You think I could leave
him? He's my life.' I paused, trying to get a hold of myself.
'I have to see Peter through, have to see what life brings
him, be there for the ups and downs and just the day to
day.' Shit. I'd let my brother go. How could I say this when
I'd let him go? I bit my lip and turned back to the window.
'So, don't worry. I'm not going. Not anywhere,' I finished,
in a whisper.

Leo nodded. I heard him walking towards me, didn't
turn, but he put his arms round me, his head on my shoulder and I knew he believed me.

Mum showed up early the next morning with Peter beside
her in his uniform ready for school. The start of a new
term. Yet again, I'd be absent. I grabbed Peter and hugged
him tight, then pushed him away and examined his face.
He looked OK. I wiped a bit of breakfast from round his
mouth with my thumb and he twisted, half smiling, rubbing at his chin with his sleeve. I nodded. And he smiled
wider. I was glad there was colour in his cheeks, maybe
he'd just been pale from tiredness the day before, from
the worry and things not being right. Later we'd play.
Maybe Leo could take him out on the pony for a bit after
school. Or at least we'd kick a ball around. All these prom-
ises were on my tongue, but Mum got in there first.

'Come on, Aud. Your first appointment. Let's get there on time, eh?' Mum said, waving at Sue, bending to pat Mary. The dog growled, her hackles rising. Mary never growled and Mum's laugh was high and false as she pulled Peter to the door and beckoned for me to follow. She was scared I'd told Sue and Leo, I reckoned, about her lies and her accusations. That was my ammunition for later.

I grabbed my coat and waved goodbye to Sue. There was no getting out of the appointment; I would prove to Mr McGuiness that I was fine, get discharged and forget this had ever happened at all.

Later on Mum drove back in the direction of the Grange. She seemed all right, not too wound up, so I must have done OK. It had been the usual stuff: eating, sleeping, what did I think, how was I feeling. I'd told them everything they wanted to hear and even told the doctor I needed a new prescription because I'd lost the other packet of pills

As she drove along the winding roads, wittering on about the soap she'd watched the night before and the doings of her favourite character, I interrupted, saying, all casual, 'Drop me off at Leo's, Mum. I'm going to stay there a bit longer. He says it's fine for me to stay.'

'What? No chance, Audrey. Are you trying to make a fool of me or what?' She scraped at her bottom lip with her teeth.

'No. I just don't want to live at the Grange.' With you. With It. I didn't add.

'You're not going to win this one.' A quick glance, sharp, assessing; she pinned me with her stare. I pushed it back at her.

'I am. Because if you don't do it, then I'm going to tell them what you said about Leo. I'm going to tell them you told the doctors he raped me.'

'I never said that, Aud.' She stared at me, her mouth hanging open, her eyes wide and shocked.

'You did. I heard you. I can't trust you any more.'

'When?' Mum was shaking her head. I thought back, trying to remember. I was sure I was right.

'When I was first admitted. You wanted them to examine me; you were going to get the police.'

'Examine you? What are you talking about, Aud?' She made a *pfft* noise, and put her foot on the accelerator. 'You didn't hear that, nothing like it. You must have hallucinated; you were in a bad way, you know. Out of it most of the time. That's why I can't believe they've let you out.'

'Mum, stop it.' I gripped the seat, clinging on to what I believed I knew.

'No, Audrey, you stop it. I think we all know who the person with problems is here, don't we? It's not me; it's you.' Her finger stabbed in my direction and the car veered. 'Who will they believe, eh? The girl who just slit her wrists, the girl who's mentally ill, or her long-bloody-suffering mother?'

I sat in silence. I hadn't imagined it, had I? Why would I make something like that up? I put my head back and shut my eyes, trying to fix the information. But fingers of another memory crawled up my spine. Another GP. Just after I started having trouble with seeing things, hearing things, being too scared to sleep. Mum talking. Saying things that weren't true about my dad, telling the doctor about stuff I didn't understand.

'Has anyone touched you?' the doctor had asked then. 'Has something happened that you weren't comfortable with? With an adult?'

'No.' I remembered my voice. Really clear. This was wrong. 'No. Never. No.'

Mum had started crying. I didn't know what happened next and closed down the memory. Winding down the window, I leant out, gulping in fresh air. Maybe that was why Dad had left us. Perhaps she'd threatened him too. We drew up outside the farm; Mum pulled on the handbrake and turned off the engine. She leant over me and wound up my window and stayed close. The air was hot and smelled of cigarette smoke and her rich, heady perfume.

'Get your things. We're going home.'

'I can tell them to ask Mr McGuiness.'

'As if. They'll think you're raving. Now come on.'

It was quiet in Sue's kitchen: Mum stood chatting with Sue while I went upstairs. The room I'd used was pretty and clean, with a faint smell of wood smoke from the open fire downstairs. On the dressing table was a white china vase painted with delicate blue flowers, filled with a spray of winter jasmine. The bedspread was white, its edges scalloped. I sat for a second, smoothed it flat and followed the delicate pattern with a finger. I thought. I thought about everything.

When I went back downstairs I said, 'Mum, can I talk to you for a minute?'

She looked up, smiled, and followed me into the living

room. The smile dropped the second she closed the door behind us, like a rock into a pool.

'What?'

'I'm not coming. Either make a scene or just leave me to it. Whichever way you want. I don't care. I'll fight you.'

'Audrey. I thought I told you –'

'No. You see, I'm not listening any more to your threats. I'm not playing along. You don't get to control me any more.'

'Control you?' Mum's mouth curled in disbelief

'I don't trust you. You lie. You got rid of my dad and now you're trying to get rid of Leo. So you can just leave me alone. You won't make me go back to the Grange. Never, not ever.'

'Oh, just stop with the drama, Aud. Get your bag. Or do I have to pack it for you?'

'I mean it. I'll tell Sue, I bet she'll have me a bit longer. When I'm sorted Peter can come and live with me.' I frowned. Peter was the only part of the plan that didn't work; he wouldn't understand. My dad had left me, but I wouldn't leave him. I rubbed my forehead. I'd have to go round every day, at least, just to hang out. And make sure he came over to the farm at the weekends. He could sleep over when Mum was on nights and I could still walk him to school and pick him up at the end of the day. It might work.

'You're being ridiculous,' Mum said.

I took a deep breath. Standing up to her, finding the strength to fight back – it took a lot and I was already tired. But she couldn't win this one, no matter how hard she tried to wear me down.

'I'm not. Face it, Mum. Things have got to change. We can't be like this any more. You can't wreck everything. You can't lie about people.'

She approached me and took me by the shoulders, her hard bright nails digging into my skin. Her eyes grabbed mine. They were vicious, angry. Her mouth was a slick red line drawn tight over her teeth.

'Mum, I will tell them everything unless you let me go.' The words, the threat. What did I mean? Somewhere inside me, deep in all the things I'd forgotten, the dark patches of my heart, the grey tunnels of my brain, I knew. It was finding the words and acknowledging the pain. That was the hardest, and my legs swayed and almost gave way. I ran to the bathroom, getting there just in time, before I began to throw up, heaving and retching, shivering and hot all at once. I didn't look up when the door creaked open or when Mum sat on the side of the bath, waiting for me to finish.

'What a mess you're in,' she said. 'Come home; come on, Aud.' I retched again when she touched me.

'I'm not going, Mum,' I whispered. 'Leave me alone.' Mum looked at me for a long time and then nodded.

'All right, then, Audrey. I will.'

Leo

Sue didn't like it that Lorraine was so upset. She told Leo about it when he got home from school; about her flying from the house in a mess.

'I don't know what's happened between them, but there's problems there, Leo. Poor Lorraine. She's doing her best.'

'Well, they'll sort it out. Probably best if they get a bit of space.' Leo bit into his apple and leant against the worktop, considering.

'Yes, I hope so. I hope we're not interfering.' Sue turned the page of the newspaper, scanning the articles without really seeing the words.

'We're not.'

Audrey came into the room. She was wearing his jumper; it was too long for her, the sleeves covered her bandages and her hands. She stood beside him, very straight, her chin high.

'Is it OK, Sue –' she cleared her throat – 'for me to stay for a bit?'

'Course she can, can't she, Sue?' Leo said, trying to make this seem casual. Normal.

Sue frowned and sipped her drink.

'Of course, I'm happy for you to stay for a bit, Audrey, if it'll help. But try and calm down a bit – think things over. In the long run, it would be better if you could work things out with your mum, don't you think?'

'Yeah. I guess.'

'How about we see if she wants to come over? One night this week? We can have a meal; you two can talk, sort this out. It's terrible to leave cross words out there. And I guess she hasn't got over your New Year's adventure.' She frowned. 'It wasn't exactly sensible, was it, running off without leaving her any idea of where you'd be? Or me, for that matter.'

'Yeah, yeah, we already apologized for that,' Leo said.

Sue shot him an exasperated look. 'I know. But I think Audrey should talk to her mum. She's got your best interests at heart, like all mums do, rightly or wrongly. And she loves you.'

'Please, don't make me, not yet,' Audrey said, and Sue raised her eyebrows, gestured with her hands.

'I can't make you do anything. I just think she'll be worried. I've seen how she gets, Audrey, so I can understand where you're coming from and that if you've had a row you wouldn't want to go home just yet, but she'll calm down. It's been a very stressful time for all of you.'

Leo nodded. 'It'll be OK, Aud – try not to worry.' He had no idea what their fight had been about – Audrey wasn't saying – but if it meant she stayed on a little longer, then he was cool with that.

'Yeah, I guess.'

Sue finished her tea and Leo saw how she watched them, Audrey especially, as if she were a puzzle she was trying to piece together. Audrey's smile didn't seem real though; he guessed what she was doing, trying to look sensible, in control. He'd been there. But inside everything had been coming apart. He tightened his grip on Audrey's hand.

'OK?'

'Yeah, I'm OK.' Her smile was watery, like her eyes. Today she was fathomless, inexplicable, and there was no making sense of the sadness.

Audrey

That night I overheard Sue on the phone. I should have been asleep, but I was more awake than ever and Sue's voice came straight through the wall. Blunt and firm.

'Leo's girlfriend . . . yes, she's a nice girl . . . gentle . . . but she's a funny one, there's something not quite right. She has a lot of problems.'

There was a long pause. I felt my face burn, my hands shake, and screwed my eyes tight as if then I wouldn't hear all the horrible things she was going to say about me.

'I'll let her stay a couple of days. Don't worry, I'll keep an eye on them . . . Yes, I know you do . . . Yes, all right . . . but don't worry, you know how Leo gets. He's passionate about things; he's passionate about her . . . She's nice, very innocent. I told you.'

She must have been talking to his dad, maybe his mum. What did they think of me? That I was crazy, weird, unstable. That my family wasn't nice, that I would hurt their son, drag him down. That I was bad news. No. It wasn't true; I'd prove them wrong.

In the morning I tidied away the breakfast things, washed up and tried to help. I hadn't slept much and my hands still shook, clumsy. A glass slid from my fingers, shattering on the stone floor. I jumped.

'Sorry, I'm so sorry.' I stared at Sue and she looked back at me, holding up her hands in a shrug.

'It's OK. Only a glass. Not to worry.'

'I'll clean it up, pay for another.'

'No, no. I'll do that,' said Sue. 'You rest, Audrey. Go back to bed, don't overdo things.'

'Thanks,' I whispered, not meeting her eye.

'Have you thought more about what I said?' Sue asked, her voice stopping me as I got to the door. 'About talking to your mum? The offer's still there for her and Peter to come over for supper some time.'

'No. Thanks. It wouldn't help. She's really angry with me, Sue. I don't think she'd listen.'

'OK. Well, you just think about it. And have a good day; try not to worry. These things usually work out.'

'Yeah.' I looked out of the window, then back at Sue. She was standing waiting, as if she expected me to say something else. When I didn't, she did.

'Audrey, you know, I don't want to pry. And I know you're seeing the psychiatrist. But you can talk to me, you know, about anything.'

'Thanks, Sue,' I whispered, and I wished I could talk to her somehow. She was so kind. But the knots in my head were too tight: Mum and Peter and Leo and the Thing, bundled up into a huge confusion. 'I'll be OK,' I said, and shut the door behind me.

There was no point going back to bed or sitting about at the farm. Leo had gone to school and so would I, but first I wanted to see my brother.

*

They knew me at the primary school and when I said I needed to give Peter a message they let me in, all smiles and concerned glances. Of course: Mum would have told them the story. Peter's teacher passed me in the corridor and stopped for a moment to tell me how well he'd settled now and that he was making excellent progress at last, although he was still quiet sometimes. A little reserved. Mum ought to hear that. I rubbed at my frown and waited outside Peter's classroom, but he avoided me, slipping past, and even though I called after him he just ran out into the playground, without looking back.

So I walked back to college and into the classroom and sat down at my desk like I'd never been away. When people spoke to me – teachers, Jen – I answered them and pretended to smile, but I couldn't escape the feeling that I'd lost something precious, like I was scouring the woods for a jewel: tiny, hidden under layers of rotting leaves. That unless I found it, it might disappear forever.

Leo and I found Peter at the end of school, standing outside the primary. When he caught sight of me he stepped away again, moving along the railings.

'Mum's coming to pick me up,' he said, turning his back and pulling free when I took his arm. 'She said I'm not allowed to talk to you.'

'What? Peter, you have to talk to me, please.'

'I can't, Audrey.' There were tears in his voice and I reached out again, holding on this time. 'I told you, I'm not allowed,' he said, struggling, as prickly as a hedgehog. He was hurting; he thought I'd left him and that I didn't care.

'Hey,' said Leo, 'it's OK, Pete.' Leo crouched beside my brother and tried to catch his eye, but Peter turned his head away, squirming out of my arms.

'I'm not allowed to talk to you or go round to the farm or even say your name.'

'So Mum's cross, then, is she?' I said, trying to lighten the mood, which was stupid, and my stupid smile didn't help either.

Peter nodded and turned and looked at me properly for the first time; he was pale, his cheeks were a harsh red, his eyes bright with tears and anger. 'You left me, Aud, and I don't like it on my own.'

And then he ran away from me, dodging through the cars to the other side of the street to meet Mum, who'd just pulled up and was watching us. Peter ran round the car and got into the front and, as I stepped out to follow, they pulled away.

'Shit,' I said. 'Shit.'

'That's about the only word for it,' Leo agreed as he put his arm round my shoulders and pulled me away from the kerb, away from the sight of my brother disappearing into the distance.

I needed Peter. I needed him to forgive me. It was hard to think of how to make that happen. He and I were a team. We managed things together. Who would help him with homework – check spellings and the sums he was just starting to manage, read in the evenings, watch TV when Mum was out? Stand in goal for hours, watch the world, collect the memories and store them safe?

I needed him and lots of other things. I needed my life

and my future and to feel strong again. I needed legs of steel but I was weak.

'When will she be at work?' Leo asked as we walked back home along the embankment towards the farm. I tried to work it out. But I never knew where Mum was or what she'd be doing next.

'I'll do anything I can to help, Aud. You do know that, don't you?'

'What can we do about Peter, Leo? What are we going to do about him?'

'He'll be all right, won't he? Your mum's not weird about him too, is she?'

I thought about it. She wasn't. Peter was OK. But then I remembered all the nights Mum wasn't there and saw Peter on his own, in the big, empty building full of whispering shadows; I knew how he hated being alone. He might forget to turn off the oven or be confused about the heating and sit in the cold. He would be scared. I scrunched up my eyes, wiped at my nose with my sleeve.

'Come on, Aud. Try not to worry. Let's plan something, something fun. And let's try and get Pete to come too.'

'All right, thanks.' I thought I'd be so happy. Free from the Grange, from the Thing. But the euphoria hadn't come; the Trafalgar Square feeling was lost. I felt empty, dull.

'Good, how about this weekend? We could see what's on at the cinema or something – a cartoon or something Pete might like. Sue'll give us a lift.' Leo talked on, planning where we'd go and what we'd do. But in my head all

I could see was Mum's car and Peter's face at the window, thin and sad, caught behind glass. Where I'd always been.

A bag of my things was waiting on the doorstep of the farmhouse. My stuff, almost all of it, parcelled up in a binbag as if I were rubbish Mum was ready to chuck out. Along with Madison and Winnie the Pooh.

'What's that?' asked Leo, eyeing the doll as I began to unpack, placing things in drawers, not sure, not certain, wondering if they'd be better left in the bag, ready for when I had to leave. The thought of staying longer than another day, a night, of leaving Peter that long . . . What if something happened?

Leo picked up the doll, staring at her stupid face. He waggled an arm, then made her do a stupid dance.

'Nothing. Mum gave it me for Christmas.' But even as I said it I started to cry. Mum thought I'd like her. She had only been doing her best. Leo didn't ask me why I was crying; if he had, I wouldn't have been able to say.

'It's OK,' he whispered over and over until I moved away.

'What?' he asked, but I couldn't answer, wiping my face on my sleeve, and buried my face in a jumper that still held the smell of our flat: Mum's cooking, the washing powder we used, her perfume, her fags. It smelled of home and maybe home didn't smell that good, but it was still all I had. I'd left Peter.

'Come downstairs, come on,' he said, standing by the door. But I didn't move.

'Sorry,' I whispered, 'I'm sorry.' And Leo walked away and left me on my own.

You dream of things like being free. But free is a trick. I'd been knit to Mum so long, my skin wound and bound with hers, that to pull away left edges unravelling, my body fraying. And it hurt to be torn like that, to have pieces of me missing. I crawled into the bed and tried to hold myself together. I thought about them, Mum and Peter. Wondered what they were doing, how she would explain to my brother. If she would be fair. If Peter would understand.

Leo

Sue was preparing the dinner and Leo went to join her. He picked up the peeler and started on the carrots. Usually this was easy; she'd ask him about his day, then they'd talk about something she'd heard on Radio 4, or whether or not she should take Mary to the vet again. The dog was getting old. It was a sort of shared stream of consciousness; whatever came into their heads, they blurted it out. Tonight was different; his aunt was quiet for a long time. Then it burst out of her.

'You'll have to talk to your mother.'

He hadn't thought about that and didn't see why.

'You do it, if you're bothered, Sue.'

'I already did. She wasn't pleased. You should ring her and explain things.' It occurred to Leo that maybe Sue was as scared of his mother as he was. No, not scared, that was the wrong word. Wary. That fitted better. She was hard to handle and difficult to argue down.

'She doesn't need talking to. Plus, I don't want to go there. You know what she's like.'

'Yes.' Sue drew the word out, elongating the vowel.

'Audrey's a house guest. It's none of my mother's business who stays in your house.'

'Hmm. Unless that house guest also happens to be your girlfriend, Leo.'

'Whatever. I'm almost eighteen.' He put down the last carrot and started to chop fast with the sharp knife.

'Anyway, she won't be staying long, will she?' Sue said. 'I'm sure they'll make up. They're close, those two.'

Too close. That was part of the problem. Leo wanted to keep her as long as he could, but already it felt like she was ready to go. Her mind was fixed anywhere but here, on the present, with him. Leo couldn't climb inside her head and switch off all the other buttons though; he couldn't reprogram her to be happy. She wouldn't let him help, or even understand. Still, he'd wait.

Later, the kitchen full of heat and the smell of supper, he called upstairs.

'Audrey, dinner's ready.'

She didn't answer. Leo stood waiting at the bottom of the stairs, listening, but it wasn't a surprise when she didn't come. He got the feeling that she'd already slipped away.

Audrey

Of course Mum hadn't brought the paper bird or my hearts. Not my rose or the superhero either. I wondered if she'd found them; I could see her going through my things, sniffing out all my secrets, poring over my life, trying to pull me back to the Grange.

I walked downstairs later, after Sue and Leo had had their dinner, and asked if I could use the phone.

'Sure,' Leo said, looking up and smiling. 'Go ahead.'

I dialled Mum's mobile number but it rang and rang. I'd wanted to get away. Now I wanted to hear her voice. *Aud*, she'd say, *what are you playing at, Aud? I love you, come home, everything's different now. I'm sorry, I made a mistake. You'll be safe here with me. I was just angry, upset.* Why wouldn't she pick up? I needed to hear those words and speak to my brother, just to say goodnight. Just to say I'd be back soon.

I went back to bed. It was another hour before there was a tap on the door, very soft; so quiet that it wouldn't have woken me if I'd been asleep. I couldn't think about Mum. I had to think about now, the future, and what I was running towards. I still had Leo. That was something. That was a very big something.

'Come in.' I sat in my nightie with the covers pulled up to my chin.

'Hi,' Leo said, putting his head round the door. 'Are you asleep?'

'Does it look like it?'

'Well, no. Good.'

He sat on the side of the bed. I moved forward, crawled over the duvet, reached for his hand. 'I'm really sorry.'

'What for?'

'For being weird. All kinds of weird.'

Leo started to laugh. 'I thought you knew I liked weird? I thought we'd clarified that some time ago.'

'Leo, I really like you. I mean, I like you more than I like anyone in the world.'

'Good.'

'Right, then. Come here,' I told him, jumping back under the covers. 'Get in.'

'Sue's downstairs,' he said, raising his eyebrows, but already pulling up the covers, kicking off his shoes.

He climbed in next to me and for a while we lay there, side by side, not touching, not talking.

I looked at his profile. The mess of thick dark hair. The gentle curves of his cheeks and his lips, full but not smiling. His eyes were half closed and thinking; I wondered about what.

It grew darker. And in the dark everything was easier.

'Leo,' I whispered.

'Yeah?' His fingers linked mine, tightening like a lock. It was like other times, better times.

'Nothing,' I said, because I couldn't tell him to kiss me or hold me or touch me. Too shy to speak, I touched his face and put my head on his chest, trying to mend the pieces of myself that were all undone. His breathing was slow, easy, his arms tight and strong.

'You make me better,' I whispered, and he put his hands in my hair, pulling my face to his and kissing away my fear.

'You too,' he said. 'I wish we could be like this always, never have to get out of this bed, just hide up here. Forget the rest of the world even exists. I'd keep you safe forever, Audrey.'

I kissed him back, because I loved him and he was good and I didn't want to stop. His hands touched my body. I touched his.

'It's boiling under here,' he said, kicking off the covers and moving away from me, just a fraction. The windows were steamed up. The air hot.

'So?' I whispered.

'So, maybe I should go back to my own bed.' He avoided my eye. Something had changed. Even if he didn't know it, he saw me differently now. The Thing had ruined us.

'Or not.' He lay back down, played with my hair, touched my cheek.

'OK. I don't mind if you stay.'

'I will. But we can't do anything. Not that I don't want to. Just that, I think we should wait.' Because you're not right. Because you scare me. Because I don't know what you might do to yourself and I don't want to be blamed.

I nodded and tried to smile and wondered how to show him that it wasn't my fault.

Leo

The piano arrived a week after Audrey moved in. They stood on the drive watching the guys unload it.

'Careful,' he couldn't help saying, and Audrey bumped his shoulder with her own.

'They're the experts, Leo. Don't worry – look, they're bringing it inside.'

He dragged one of Sue's kitchen chairs into the living room as soon as the piano was installed; he sat down, flexed his fingers.

'Right,' he said. 'I may be some time.' He released a flurry of notes and before long Leo had forgotten where he was or who was listening, and as the piano sang back to him the feelings he poured into its keys he felt lighter, better, at peace.

Sue and Audrey gave the standing ovation.

'I can't believe you're that good,' Sue said. 'Your dad did say, but I thought he was exaggerating.'

'Dad said?'

'Of course; he was always boasting.'

Leo grimaced and stood up, indicating Aud should take the chair.

'First lesson time,' he said. 'We'll learn "Chopsticks". Duet. Right?'

'Cool.' She was in the seat before he had time to blink

and for the next hour they made a lot of noise. Turned out Aud was tone deaf, but so what? He'd guessed as much from her singing on the Tube and if anything it made him like her even more; every time she hit a bum note she just shrugged and tried again, persevering, determined, her tongue caught between her teeth, brow set in concentration.

'Your mum's ace, Leo,' Audrey said over dinner. 'You're lucky.'

He nodded and Sue agreed.

'Call her later. Skype, introduce Audrey. It's about time, Leo.'

Sue was right. There was nothing to hide and he wanted his mother to approve. It was all he'd ever wanted, he realized, and he had a feeling she wouldn't let him down.

Audrey

Leo's Mum was gorgeous. I don't know why I was surprised. She called for his dad the second she saw me sitting there beside Leo, and for the next fifteen minutes she talked, in this beautiful voice, sweet as a song. Her smile was perfect, her skin bright and glowing, her hair shiny, black, cut into a sharp, chic bob. How was I? she asked, her eyes, even darker than Leo's, staring at me from out of the screen. Had I settled in? Was there anything I needed or anything she or her husband could do? Was Leo being good to me? I smiled and stuttered. I hadn't prepared for this. I'd imagined harder questions, about my ambitions and my IQ. I stammered my answers until Leo intervened.

'Mum, chill. Aud's fine.'

But they continued to be charming. How lovely it was to talk to me at last; how lovely I was. Could they entice me over to Hong Kong with Leo for a visit? I nodded and Leo nudged me sharply with his elbow.

When Leo finally said goodbye and turned off the computer, I stared at him.

'I am in love with your mother.'

'She has that effect on everyone.' He half laughed, pulling me closer. 'Next time it may not be quite so easy,' he warned.

'Stop it, Leo. I didn't think she'd be so nice. And your dad. I like them both. And I'll definitely come to Hong Kong.' I squeezed his hand.

'Good. Well, that's a plan, then,' he said, and I liked the sound of that.

It was the end of January and the farmhouse got surprisingly chilly in the evenings, so I used it as an excuse to go up to Leo's room and lie with him on his bed, just to keep warm. I loved his room; it was in the eaves and you had to crouch to avoid the sloping walls and ceilings. His windows were carved into the roof. The walls were plastered with posters; some looked ancient, like they'd been there forever, others were newer. Everything was tidy and perfectly in order. Apart from the books scattered by his bed, spilling off the bedside table on to the floor, and the photographs of his family pinned up all over the wall – people I'd never met and he rarely talked about – covering every surface. A gorgeous girl with long dark hair hung from his arm in one picture, wearing an evening dress and glittery jewellery. She looked so sophisticated, so glamorous. Leo looked happy too. He'd never mentioned her and I'd never asked much about that bit of his past. Part of me wanted to tear the picture in two; instead I didn't let myself look.

I spotted something I'd not seen before among the collage of posters and pictures. It was the drawing of me that Jen had started, months ago, half finished, pinned up there.

'You nicked that.' I pointed at it. He acted innocent.

'I didn't. Jen said I could have it.'

'Hmm. Well, I'll be checking with her. Otherwise, I think you'll find it's stolen property.'

'You'll have to fight me for it,' he said, pinning me to the bed so I couldn't move. He collapsed beside me and we lay listening to music turned down very low and reading. Leo was studying some old poet and sometimes he read his favourite lines aloud, putting on funny voices, and I'd laugh into the duvet. Later he explained *Hamlet* and agreed he'd been a dick to Ophelia when I pointed this out.

'Plus it's too sad,' I said. 'They all die.'

'Well, it's tragedy, isn't it? What do you expect?' There was no arguing with that. Still, I'd have a go.

'Cruel though. Shakespeare must have been a bit of a sadist, killing all his characters off like that.'

He grinned. 'That's one perspective. But don't blame him; he's just the writer. It's what the genre requires.'

And no arguing with that either.

'How did you get to be so into all this anyway?'

Leo folded his arms behind his head and stared at the ceiling.

'Well, I guess I have to give my mother credit where credit's due. When I was really little she took me to see plays, comedies mainly, in the college gardens around Cambridge in the summer. You'd have liked it. No one dies in comedy, not that I can think of. But you get a lot of love triangles, all that girly stuff.' I poked him in the ribs and he pretended to be hurt – rolling on the bed in mock agony. Using it as an excuse to grab me, hold me.

'Go on, tell me more.' My head on his chest, he

continued. I listened to his heart as he breathed. *Da-dum. Da-dum. Da-dum.*

'We'd have a picnic. Her friends would be there, and other little kids. I got caught up in it, loved the atmosphere: the thickness of the trees, fairy lights glinting in the dusk, all the magic brewing. The words. And Bottom, mostly.'

'Bottom?'

'*Midsummer Night's Dream.* It'll be on somewhere this summer. We'll go.'

'OK. OK. So, I get it. It's nostalgia, is it, that makes you love these plays? Cos of the old days, being with your mum?'

'No. No. Only a little. It's the stories. The language. Magnificent. Unforgettable. Like you.'

That really made me laugh, and Sue banged on the wall, calling that she was trying to get to sleep.

Leo carried on talking, in a whisper though. We could sit up all night, gossiping and dreaming like this, but now Leo talked about spring. The things we'd do in the spring. He had a long list.

'First I'll take you to the coast. The first bright day we have, Aud. It'll be early though, I'll warn you now. But no yawning and trying to wriggle out of it. We'll drive out there and we'll take a boat and go out to sea. And then we'll see the seals. You'll love it. I promise, cross my heart. I won't let you fall in. No need to be afraid.' He put his hand on his chest and then mine, drew the mark. I held his hand.

'Are you feeling all right? Do you think the medication is helping now?' Leo asked.

'Yeah. I am.' I felt clearer, more awake. Like the world wasn't quite so jagged, not so full of sharp edges. Leo didn't need to know I never swallowed the pills he thought he saw me taking.

'What about the therapy?'

'Yeah, in a couple of days. So don't worry, OK?'

'Sure, OK.' Leo got up and stretched and booted me back to my own bed.

The next day I stood outside the primary school at lunchtime and stared through the thick green netting at my brother playing football in the playground. That was the closest I could get. At least they were letting him play now, and he was shouting to one of his little friends to pass.

'Over here,' he yelled. The ball was kicked his way and I held my breath as he caught it clumsily and dribbled towards the goal. I smiled, narrowed my eyes, squinting into the hard winter sun as Peter was tackled but kept the ball and ran forward, taking aim. He walloped it as hard as his little leg could manage, and then as the ball swung wide, missing completely, he swore, his mouth twisted with rage, and lashed out with a fist, punching the air with a look on his face I'd never seen before. I didn't know he knew words like that. I wanted to go and help and soothe, but the fence barred my way and I couldn't comfort him like I had when he was a toddler and would fall, scraping a knee or a palm. I remembered kissing him better, flicking out grit, not sure where I'd learned how to do that.

The bell rang and the boys began streaming back inside. I waited, hoping to catch him.

'Peter,' I yelled through the fencing, following along on the outside. He pretended not to hear.

'Pete, wait, hang on. I just want to talk to you.' But he wouldn't stop, ran past me, slamming into other children, pushing his way forward as if my voice made no noise.

I caught up with Leo in the corridor before the last lesson. He was decisive.

'Well, why don't you go round? See him.'

'But what if –'

'So what if she's there? She can't stop you from seeing your brother, Aud. You want me to come?'

'No. I'll be fine. Thanks.' There were things I had to do alone. I hadn't managed to see Peter once since I'd moved into the farm. It couldn't go on. Mum had to let me see him and explain, and I had to start taking care of him again. He needed me and I needed him. And there were so many questions I needed him to answer. Like, how was he feeling? Was he all right? Had he had breakfast, lunch, dinner? Was Mum reading him stories? Helping with his homework, taking him to parties and the park? Running his bath? *Face it, Aud,* I thought. *You know the answer to those questions. You need to sort this and sort it now.*

Walking back into the Grange felt strange. The front door was open, as always, as if it had been ready and waiting all this time and the smell from the moat followed me inside, dank and dirty.

I banged on the door of the flat.

'Peter?' I called. 'Pete?' I cursed the fact I didn't have a key.

But there wasn't a sound; nothing stirred. And I walked away with a heavy sinking feeling in my stomach, like milk thickening and curdling, churning and sour.

I went back again the next day, Leo with me this time. Treading those stairs, I knew I had to be brave. And my legs were so much stronger, my wrists almost healed. I was going to Dr Caldwell in the morning to get the dressings changed. Maybe she'd leave them off altogether.

The door was locked again. I rattled the handle.

It was obvious Peter was in there. I could almost feel him, on the other side of the door, and it drove me crazy.

'Please, Peter, open up. Let us in. I want to talk to you. I want to check everything's all right. I want to hang out for a bit.' I scratched at the wood like an animal. 'Or you could come out, come back to the farm with me and play football with Leo. It'll be OK, if Mum comes, I'll deal with her. I promise.'

There was movement. A stirring. We waited, holding our breath. And then a piece of paper slid under the door, and written on it in sprawling spidery capitals were the words: GO A WAY.

'I guess that's another no, then,' Leo said, turning to go.

'We can't leave him here.' I pulled him back by his sleeve, still staring at the bit of paper.

'Why? He doesn't want to come out, Audrey, so give him a bit of time to get over it. He's still upset.'

'I know. That's the problem. I'm worried. He's five, Leo. He can't just be left alone. He shouldn't even be on his own.' I banged on the door again.

'We could call the police? Social services?'

'What? I can't do that.' Was he taking the piss? Leo shrugged and leant against the wall.

'Right, well, I'll break it down, then.'

'You can't. Stop being ridiculous.' I shot him a look to shut him up. 'Pete, Peter. Come on, this is silly. Please open the door, mate. I love you, I do. Please.'

After another long silence, I leant my head against the door frame. 'Please,' I whispered into the wood, 'Please, Peter. Don't hate me.'

'You can't do anything, Aud,' Leo said as he put his arm round my shoulders and pulled me away from the door.

'He's my brother. I can't abandon him.'

'You're not. You're there if he needs you. You've shown him that. He knows where we are, right? And I guess Lorraine'll be back soon.'

'Yeah, I s'pose, we'll wait till then.'

Mum passed us on the stairs. She didn't even look my way, like I was finally invisible. And then we walked home, treading across the boggy field, thick with January rain. I tried not to think about Peter, not to turn back, not to look again. But if it hadn't been for Leo, I would have run straight home.

Leo

Spring wasn't far away. Leo had a feeling everything would be all right in the spring, and he had made a heap of plans for things Audrey and he would do: first the trip to the coast and the seals, then maybe the theatre in London – Shakespeare, perhaps, something fun. There were concerts too, and cafes and exhibitions, gigs, and the dream of a holiday to Paris or New York – or even Hong Kong, like his mother had suggested. After school Sue picked him up and drove him to town. Audrey wasn't the only one who was still seeing someone. He told Graham about the plan with the seals, how he knew it was something Audrey would love, and Graham smiled and rubbed his hands together.

'That's what I call optimism. Good sign.'

'What do you mean, good sign?'

'That you're doing well, that you're going to do well from now on. I don't think we need to see each other any more, do you?'

'No. But I guess I'll miss you,' Leo confessed.

'Me too, pal.' Graham held out his hand and grasped Leo's. 'You've come a long way. The lad I first saw – what, two years ago? He's grown.'

Leo smiled. Graham had strong warm hands. It felt like a handshake between mates.

'Yeah. There's just one thing,' Leo said.

'Fire away.'

'You know I told you about my girlfriend, Audrey?'

'Sure. The last I heard you two were madly in love.'

'Yes, well. After New Year, you know she, well, she cut herself badly.' Graham looked thoughtful, sat back and didn't speak: his tactic when he wanted Leo to keep talking. So Leo explained how Aud was staying at the farm, how well she seemed, that she wanted to see her brother and her mum was being difficult, what he could do to help.

'Sounds to me like you're doing all the right things, Leo. She's seeing someone about her issues, yes?'

'Yes, but she doesn't tell me about it. The thing is, I don't think she'll stay. I'm scared she'll leave – go back there.'

'Where?'

'The Grange. Her mum's place.'

'And what if she did?' Graham tipped his head to one side, looked as confused as Leo felt.

'That's what I don't know. But I'm scared to find out.'

Audrey

The next morning I woke up with cramps in my belly. My first thought was that this was it. That I really was sick, that Mum had been right and there was something terribly, awfully wrong with me. With my body this time, not my brain. And then I got up and went to the bathroom and saw the faint pink stain on the toilet paper.

My period. At last.

The sign that I was like other girls. Changing, growing up. *Better late than never*, I thought as I washed my face and brushed my teeth, staring in the mirror, seeing just me. Audrey. No Thing to grimace back at me, to leer and laugh and mock.

'What are you smiling like that for?' asked Leo over breakfast, and I just smiled harder and sipped my tea. He didn't need to know. It was my secret.

'I just reckon it's a good day, that's all,' I said. 'I'm going to try again with Pete, and I think today's the day. Look, the sun's shining for a change; that's a good sign.' Leo agreed, munching on toast, spilling his coffee as he spoke about all the ways in which everything was good and was going to get even better.

'Optimism,' he said. 'We're the last of the eternal optimists, Aud.' Kissing me as we walked out of the farm, on our way to school.

It was easy to ignore Lizzy's smirks and jibes when I was in this mood. I walked over to the primary school at lunch, carrying a bar of chocolate I'd bought for Peter from the canteen. They weren't really allowed chocolate, but I thought I'd sneak him a few squares as a treat and beg him to let me walk him home.

But the receptionist said he wasn't in. Everything stopped. A thudding started in the back of my brain, slow, steady, determined.

'Why?' I managed to ask.

'Your mum called in. He's had a tumble.' She gave me a sympathetic smile. The banging in my ears grew louder.

'Did she say anything else?'

'No. Just that he'd be straight back to school as soon as he was better. Poor little sausage.'

I ran back to college, then stopped, screeching to a halt on the drive. No, I couldn't go into class. Peter was not well. This wasn't supposed to happen. I spun round, ran back out of the gates and down the streets towards my brother, the crashing stamp of the Thing building and growing, demanding I come home.

The Grange was waiting. The water moved fast in the wind, rippling and stirring, and I ran over the bridge, across the gravel, not pausing to stare. Up the stairs, two at a time, I stood on the landing and forced my heart to slow. It was rushing fast, a clock overwound.

No one answered when I knocked and banged on the door, so I went back outside and walked up and down the drive, then sat on the long concrete steps of the Grange, certain that eventually they'd return.

The car pulled up the drive. At first I couldn't see Peter; it looked as though only Mum was in the car, and my heart dived. Where had she left him? I ran forward as she parked up, and banged on her window.

'What?' She opened the car door.

'Where's Peter?'

She nodded, gesturing over her shoulder. He was asleep on the back seat, a blanket over him, most of it dangling on the floor.

'Is he OK?' His mouth hung open; he was dribbling on the seat, his hand loosely resting beside his face. Pale. He looked so little. I remembered him in his cot, blond hair curling on the white sheet, eyelashes casting delicate shadows on his perfect soft cheeks. I'd sat beside him, peeping through the bars of his cot, sat and watched him sleeping, waiting for him to wake, making sure he didn't cry. And now I'd left him. How could I?

'He's fine,' Mum insisted.

She unbuckled her seatbelt, pushing herself up to stand beside me before slamming the door, making the car shake. I jumped.

'What are you doing hanging around here?'

'I wanted to come and visit. I've been worried.'

But too scared. Too scared to see what was happening. Blindly believing that all was well, all was normal.

Mum opened the back door and shook my brother awake.

'Come on, lazy bones,' she said. 'Get in the house.'

And Peter struggled up, wincing as he climbed out of the car. I stared, stepped forward.

'What's happened to Peter? What's the matter with him?'

'Nothing. He fell over playing football. I took him to A and E. It's his ankle, twisted. Maybe a break – they weren't sure. He might need another X-ray. We'll go back tomorrow.'

I ran forward and picked up my brother. He nestled into my shoulder, still sleepy, and we followed her inside. As I carried him, I tried to be clear.

'What do you mean he fell over? How? How could he twist his ankle that badly?'

Mum didn't answer. I held him closer; Peter's skin felt hot, clammy and damp. His breath didn't smell right either, too sickly, too sour. I whispered that it would be OK, that I was here now. He whimpered a little, clung tighter, but still said nothing.

'What do you want?' Mum turned to look at me when I pushed my way into the flat, still holding my brother in my arms. He was heavy, a dead weight, but I didn't want to let him go. Mum sounded bored; she lit a cigarette. I watched the smoke rise, curling like a noose, and carried Peter to the sofa, kneeling down beside him. His ankle was strapped up with thick tight white bandages. I put my hand to his forehead, then rested my cheek, gently, against his skin, feeling it burn. Opening his eyes, Peter looked at me, bewildered, scared, and grabbed my fingers.

'Can you read me a story, Aud?' he whispered, then rubbed at his face, blinking. I nodded, swallowing back tears, and tried to smile again.

Mum was watching.

'I suppose you want money off me, don't you?' she said. 'I suppose that's why you're here.'

'No. Please, Mum, let me stay, just for a bit.' I looked at her. 'I've missed you both. And I'm worried about you. Managing everything. Work, and looking after Pete. Let me help.'

There was another pause. Her breathing was heavy as she considered. The sound of her sucking on her cigarette filled my ears, like the hiss of the water, the pull of the tide.

'We don't need help, not from anyone,' she said in the end. A smell drifted from the kitchen as she wandered away – burning hair, burning skin. Peter needed me. It wasn't safe for him here.

'Are you all right, baby?' I asked.

'Not a baby, Aud,' he said, and I smiled, touched his cheek.

Peter shut his eyes, shifted on the sofa, squirming, his face twisted up.

'Does it hurt, Pete?' I asked, and he nodded, just a tiny movement of his head. I ran to his room for his blanket and a pillow and a book.

Mum was standing in the doorway.

'He'll need his medicine soon,' she said, checking her watch.

I looked at her.

'I'll give it to him,' I said. She shook her head and looked at me as if I were mad.

'Stay, Aud – I want you,' Peter whispered, pulling at my sleeve, grabbing with both hands.

I followed Mum into the kitchen.

'When are you coming home, then?' she asked. 'You've

made your point. You got your own way. But it seems like you can't keep away, doesn't it?'

'Soon, Mum. I'll be home soon.' I tried to see what she had out on the worktop, what medicine my brother might be taking, but there was nothing out of the ordinary, just the usual rubble of stuff.

'Does that mean tomorrow? Next week? Next month? I need to know. I have my plans to make. If you don't come back, I could rent that room out. It's costing me.'

'Soon,' I said. There was no way Peter could come back to the farm with me now; no way she'd let that happen. 'Tomorrow,' I said, deciding, 'as soon as I've packed up my stuff. I'll be here in the morning. Right, Mum? And leave Peter alone. I'll be back to look after him, OK?'

'He's my son, Audrey,' Mum said. 'I'm the one who does the looking after round here. Not you.'

Much later, when I got back to the farm, Leo wanted to know where I'd been. He didn't say it, but he sat playing the piano, waiting for me to tell him.

'Peter needs me,' I said in the end.

'Why? What's happened?'

I stood up and sat beside him, touching a key: a low, deep note. He took my hand and began to examine the lines, gently tracing my future, and I did not dare ask what he found.

'Nothing much. I guess I shouldn't have left him in the first place.'

'What do you mean? He's OK, isn't he? Has something happened?' Leo didn't get it. Whatever he thought, I couldn't stay at the farm with him forever, like we were living in some fairy tale. Reality was different. This was it: I was going back. I had to choose. Me or Peter. The farm or the Grange. My brother needed me; he'd always needed me, and I'd abandoned him. I'd left him lonely and afraid. I was selfish and thoughtless and cruel. Like Mum.

'Yeah, he's OK. It's just, Mum works a lot. And that means that it's easier if I'm around to make sure Pete's OK.'

Leo stood up and began to pace, running his hands through his hair.

'Look, Aud, I know things are weird with your mum. That's stating the obvious. But you can't let her keep getting away with it.' He stared out of the window, still talking. 'Obviously because she's your mother it's hard. But sometimes you have to stand up for yourself.'

'I have. Why do you think I'm even here? I've made my point and now I have to straighten things out.' I went to join him. The Grange looked way too near tonight, black against the night sky. My head thudded, the echoing aftershocks of the afternoon.

'Yeah, I know. I know. But you shouldn't back down now,' he continued.

'I'm not backing down. Things will be different.'

Leo turned and looked at me. His expression was hard. 'I don't think you should go back.'

He knew what I was planning and I searched his face for understanding, wrapped my arms round his waist, put my head on his chest. He stood still, not returning my hug, his body tense. I let go.

'What would you suggest I do, then? Just forget about Peter? About my family?'

Leo turned away. I didn't need this. It wasn't helping.

'Can't you be nice about it? Please?' Curling my fingers into fists, I stopped myself from touching him. I didn't know how to have this argument.

'No. Sorry. I think it's the wrong decision, Audrey.' Leo looked back at me, his eyes really dark, his voice very serious. I wanted him to smile. I wanted him to nod and agree.

'But it's my decision. I'll be all right. There's nothing to worry about. Me and Mum, we had a row. I left. That kind of thing happens to people all the time. No big deal. You knew I couldn't stay here forever. You knew I'd go eventually.'

He held up his hands, warding me off, trying to calm things.

'All right, sorry I spoke. I wanted to say though, if you need help, you can talk to me. I want to help, that's all.'

I focused on the facts. It was up to me to get back to look after Peter.

'Thanks,' I muttered, 'but we're fine. There's nothing to worry about.'

Leo shrugged. I wanted to scream at him, *My brother needs me; he needs me more than you do.* But I couldn't. The words were trapped. All my words were trapped.

'Can you leave me alone, please?' I whispered. 'I need to be on my own.'

'Sure,' Leo said, and he left and shut the door very, very quietly behind him.

Audrey

I packed my things that night, then went and tapped on Leo's door.

Leo was awake. He smiled and told me to come in. We sat by the window for a while, staring out together. It was close, cramped on the little seat. There wasn't much to say. I wanted a better goodbye, I suppose.

Outside a light rain began to fall, tapping very softly on the window.

He peered outside. 'It's raining.'

I shrugged.

'What's wrong?' he said.

How could I tell him that everything had changed? There weren't the words for it. I counted the days on my fingers, just over three weeks. That's how long we'd had. Just twenty three days. If it hadn't been for Sue, shouting up that Leo had a phone call, I don't know what I might have said. There was no point though in saying anything at all, so I went down to the kitchen and sat on my own, staring at the laptop screen, trying to breathe, to slow everything down, to think straight.

I typed in a few words.

Mothers who hurt their kids
Mothers who make their kids ill

Hundreds of pages shot back at me. I could have sat

there all night reading, but I heard Sue coming and shut the page fast.

Four words stuck in my mind: *factitious disorder by proxy*. Whatever they meant.

Leo knocked later and I pretended to be sleeping. I was still thinking about the words. And then the dream began.

It started with my mother. Right beside me, I could feel her, smell her, hear her humming, filling my ears with her song. She straightened my sheets, called me, trying to rouse me from sleep. But my legs were fixed, my arms pinned. My body had been shaped and cut to fit this bed, nailed into place, and I wanted to wake, to run, to fly. But the song flattened me, like a spell, knotting like a sheet, a paralysing shroud. My mother held a feather to my lips. It did not stir. And then I saw something rise. My shadow. My reflection. The Thing. The thumping started, merged with her humming – a terrible song, thick and deep – and I was sinking and drowning and almost, almost dead. The Thing climbed from my body, drifted out of my pores, seeped into the room. It took shape. And when it turned and looked at me for a moment, its face was full of holes.

Someone was shaking me awake. For a second I was still in the dream and screaming. It was Mum. It was the Thing.

'No!' I screamed, lashing out, ready to fight. 'Get off me – get away.' Pushing, shoving with all my strength. I wasn't going to bleed again; I wasn't going to die.

'What's the matter? Audrey? Is it a nightmare?'

Sue.

Her voice stopped me and I sobbed.

'I'm sorry, Sue. Yes, just a bad dream, I think. Sorry.' The room adjusted, repairing itself in the light that came in from the doorway, where Leo stood, framed and staring. I wanted to tell him to come to me, wanted to let him care. But I didn't call and Sue held me instead. It was better that way.

Leo didn't agree. An hour later, just as first light broke, he was there, shaking me awake.

'Sorry, Aud,' he whispered, 'but you have to get up now.'

'What?' I groaned, my body aching, my head sore.

'Remember? I promised you, we'd go see the seals. It isn't spring, but we'd better go now, I think. I don't want to wait.'

He pulled open my curtains; the sun was just coming up and the sky was clearing. I stood beside him and we watched it lifting from the horizon, spreading waves of light over the dark fields. Transforming the world.

'It'll be cold,' he said. 'Bring a jumper, a coat, and hurry.'

He packed a flask of coffee, bread and jam, bananas. Sue was already up and out.

'She says we can take the car.'

I followed Leo into the cold morning, still bleary-eyed, and climbed up into the seat beside him. Not touching though.

'OK. Hang on.' Leo rumbled the engine into life, his face set in concentration.

'There, sit next to me,' he said, and I moved along the seat, scrunched up closer. A little warmer. But this was torture. I edged away again.

'It's not far; don't worry. We'll be there in an hour.' We pulled out into the back lane, then he jumped out to shut the gate.

'An hour?' I called, but he was smiling as he climbed back into his seat.

'Yup. What's an hour in the grand scheme of things? It's nothing, right? We'll be back early afternoon.'

But my brother was sitting in the Grange waiting for me, and every minute was cruel now; not knowing how he'd slept, how he was feeling, or what Mum was doing. I had to get back fast. This was a waste of a time.

'I've thought of other things, Audrey, things we can do.' Leo cast another look my way as the car ate up the miles. I tried to look like I cared.

'Yeah, what?'

'We should go to a festival, in the summer. All of us. You, me, Pete. Meet up with some of my old mates.' I wondered if he meant that shiny girl and tried not to mind.

'Yeah, that'd be good,' I said, watching the clock. I couldn't think about tents and campfires or sunshiny skin and hours outdoors. Those things were for other people. The Grange was waiting for me.

'We could camp. Stay up all night. Stare at the stars. I think I'm going to get a guitar, start playing again.'

'Yeah, OK,' I said. Leo frowned, but I stared out of the window and we didn't talk again until we arrived.

There were a few other passengers waiting for the trip. Leo bought tickets, held out his hand to help me down into the boat, and we sat apart from the others, his arms holding me close. The sea slapped the sides and I squealed as the spray hit my face. Leo wiped my glasses for me, put them back on my nose, fixing them gently round my ears.

'You warm enough?'

'I'm fine.'

'Good,' he said, and he kissed me in front of everyone and I didn't care. I couldn't feel it now. It was stupid to feel anything.

'Wait till you see the seals,' he said. 'Seriously, they're cute.'

And they came, nosing around the boat; inquisitive little faces peering at these aliens come to invade their world. There were birds too: gannets, gulls. A curlew. Leo told me their names and I sat and watched it all as if from a distance, as if another girl sat in that boat with that boy who was handsome and kind and good. My mind drifted.

'We could steal a boat,' I said, 'set out to sea. Never come back.'

'We could.' He put his cheek against mine. So soft, just a scratch of stubble. His breathing sweet and slow. Eye-lashes tickling. And the wind pulling his hair up and out of his face, mixing it with mine. I pulled away.

'Where would we go?' I said, leaning over the edge, trailing my fingers in the water.

'France, Italy, Australia, the world,' he murmured, 'any-where you like. I'll go with you; just ask.'

'Some day,' I said, and the wind caught the words, threw them wistfully into the sea, where they churned in the waves, were thrown like flotsam on the shore.

Leo

There was so much he needed to say to her. But it was like treading a path through fire. She could flare at any moment, burn him with her words. It had happened before, the heat searing her cheeks, her eyes flashing bright with tears. It was clear she didn't want to be here; he'd thought she'd love it, but she hadn't smiled once. Leo thought about his mum. If someone said something against her. That she was a pushy bitch. That she had hurt him. If Graham asked Leo who was responsible for his breakdown. Not that Graham ever had, it wasn't his job to apportion blame, he said. But what would Leo say? Would he just say, 'My mother,' and leave it at that? He didn't think that would be right or fair. What about everything she'd given him? Did he just throw that on the heap? Pretend none of it was worth anything?

'We should get going,' Audrey said. He knew what that meant. The binbag of clothes in her room at the farm was a crumpled rebuke, waiting for her return, reminding him that he hadn't done enough. As soon as they got back, she was going to leave. She nudged him again, waiting for an answer. No one else had ever fitted right next to him, like this. No one else had made him feel like she did.

They were on the beach, drinking coffee from his flask, huddled up in their coats. It wasn't warm enough to sunbathe, barely warm enough to be outside. You might say they were stupid to be here at all. Leo pushed that thought aside. *Carpe diem*, Graham said; Leo didn't give a shit about clichés, because there was a lot of truth in those words. Perhaps now was the time to tell her he loved her. It didn't come out like that.

'So, you're going back, then?'

That question, his voice so bitter and unkind. He hadn't meant it like that, and it ruined the moment. Totally. She edged away, just a little, over the rock, sliding on seaweed like a mermaid ready to slip back into the sea. The waves crashed closer, storming the beach, then hissing away.

'Yeah, I reckon.' She stared out, not meeting his eyes, as if the yearning horizon held everything she needed.

'Would it make any difference if I asked you not to?'

She didn't answer. She didn't want to talk, but it didn't matter now; he'd started and had to finish. He was going to say it. What did he have to lose?

'Audrey, if you go back, I'm scared about what'll happen.'

'What do you mean?' The fire in her was rising; he could see it on her neck, fingers of rage creeping up towards her face, obliterating the health in her cheeks and turning it to hate. He didn't want her to hate him.

'I mean. Life's a bitch, Aud, but you don't have to walk into its jaws; you don't have to let it bite you. You can stay with me. Sue doesn't mind; she likes having you.'

'She doesn't. She feels bad. She and Mum are friends; it puts her in a spot.'

'Well, sod it. What does it matter what Sue thinks?'

Audrey stood up and spoke again: 'Look, Leo. The reason I'm going back to the Grange is for Peter. You know I hate being away from him, and he's my brother, so he comes first. I've decided.'

'All right. I know that.'

'So why do you think you can try and dictate what I should do? Like coming here, wasting the morning. I have stuff I need to get on with. I need to be with my brother.'

Waste the morning? Is that what she thought? And all this: the seals, the sea, the breakfast on the beach – she threw it back at him. Her words stung, catching on his skin like tiny hooks on a line.

'I've been trying to help,' Leo said.

'But I don't need any help. Just don't get involved – keep out of it. I don't need you fucking interfering in everything I do, do I?'

'Audrey, this is mad.' She flinched. 'I mean, what the hell?'

She interrupted him again, not giving him time to finish a thought or a sentence: 'This is it, Leo.' And then, after a pause: 'I don't want to see you any more. Right?'

'What?' Where had this come from? Her eyes were a dull jade. Cruel. The wind blew and the clouds raced. Audrey kept talking, gesturing with her hands, holding them up, the words coming fast.

'I mean it. You and me; just forget it. I don't want to be with you any more. You crowd me; you get in my face. I just can't take it.' She turned her back on him, her shoulders sharp and hunched. 'So. We're finished. Don't try and see me; don't get in touch. I don't need you. Right?'

'Audrey,' Leo said, a million words bubbling up in his throat to shout back at her, but she stormed up the beach towards the car park before he could put them into order.

'Let's go,' she called, and he followed her, paces behind, the gap between them growing wide, like a hole opening up in the ground.

Audrey

When we got back to the farm Leo walked straight inside. He didn't say goodbye or help me with my bags. Sue frowned and hollered after him.

'Leo, come on, where's your manners?' But he just walked away.

I understood; I didn't blame him. It's what I'd asked for. We were over. Sue drove me instead. The bag was too heavy to drag across the fields. I still couldn't manage on my own and that made me dig my fingers into my thighs. Pathetic. I didn't dare look back: what if I gave in? What if I shouted, *'No! Turn round. I've changed my mind'*? So I focused on Peter. I thought of his hug, how we'd play cards later the two of us, Snap maybe, or I'd teach him another game, then read his bedtime story. The thought should have made me happy but I was numb.

'I'm glad you've made peace with your mum,' Sue said as she drove, glancing at me, casual, and not.

'Mmm.'

'But what about Leo? You've not fallen out? Not you two.'

'No. It's my fault, Sue. Don't blame Leo. We broke up.' I swiped at my eyes. The sea was still on my skin, salty and strong. My hair knotted with the wind. But the memory of the boat, Leo close, holding me tight. That was cold.

'I don't blame anyone. I just hope you can still be friends. He's been so happy recently.'

'We are friends. Always will be.' I swallowed, but my throat ached and everything was too close, too real, and about to explode. It wasn't the time. I couldn't do it here.

She dropped me in the driveway.

'Thanks, Sue. For everything. It was so kind of you to have me. Sorry for just landing on you like that.'

She hugged me. 'Come over often. I'll miss you too.'

She had to prise herself away; I didn't want to let go. She was all I had left of him.

'Say hi to your mother from me. I'll give her a ring in the week,' Sue said, stepping back. 'Tell her it's been a pleasure. And I'm glad you've made up.' She smiled; she really thought that was it.

'I will,' I called as she hopped back into the car and, wheels spinning on the gravel, drove away.

And then I picked up the black binbag, and my school bag and walked towards the Grange. The moat sang behind me, circling, the water drawing closer, and Mum stood on the step, the door propped open to the dark.

PART THREE

February

Leo

Leo didn't look at the Grange for days. He walked to and from the farm, his eyes on the horizon, towards the sea or school; anywhere but there. But it still loomed in his consciousness; he still felt its presence, a hard darkness in the distance that couldn't be reached. The land expanded and grew in his imagination until it was impossible to contemplate going anywhere near that place ever again.

After a couple of days – dull, dark days – Jen came up to him and stopped him in the corridor.

'Where's Aud? We're supposed to be doing our presentation in History today,' she said. 'We need to go through it.'

'She's not staying with me any more.' Leo tried to walk by, but Jen followed.

'Oh, right. So she sorted things with her mum, did she?' Her voice was curious, glad.

'I guess so.' Leo gritted his teeth.

'That's good, but why's she not coming in?'

'Who knows? Ask someone who gives a shit, Jen.' Leo walked away from her, back down to the art block, but then he didn't go in, and instead sat outside watching a group of kids arsing around with a football and tried to forget.

School broke up for the February half-term and

someone was having a Valentine's party. Leo's lip curled at the thought, but in the end it wasn't as he expected. A huge converted barn filled with kids from the sixth form, Year Elevens too, very loud music and bottles and bottles of alcohol. Somebody's parents had gone on holiday somewhere hot, and pissed-up girls and boys crawled over their property like ants. Leo spotted Jen dancing and avoided her. He found himself drinking Jack Daniel's and coke and decided he liked it and would keep drinking it until he couldn't see. There was dancing and loud music and darkness and every time the barn doors opened Leo stopped himself from looking round. Of course she wouldn't come. There was no hope of that and he was a fool for thinking she would. Even if she did, he wouldn't speak to her. It was too late for that.

Leo slumped on a sofa, still holding the coke bottle that was half full of whisky. Someone passed him a spliff and he took it and dragged in the sweet smoke. He'd wasted the last six months of his life, he thought then, hanging around like a love-sick idiot, mooning after a girl who didn't give a shit. What an idiot he'd been; people must have been laughing their asses off – Leo the fool, Leo the mug – he thought, and when a girl called Lucy, who had long red hair and sweet brown eyes, sat beside him, he didn't move away. He passed her the spliff and his drink. He put his arm round her.

'So, you're not seeing that Year Eleven any more,' she shouted above the music.

'No.'

'I get it.' She held up her hands, laughing. 'Don't go there, right?'

Leo nodded.

'Well, I'm glad. I've fancied you for two years, Leo. Two whole years. And you never even looked at me!' She was shaking her head and laughing at herself, and he thought she must be drunk too to say something like that. He swigged from the bottle again; it squashed and cracked under his fingers. Lucy's face was very close. He ground out the spliff under his boot and when she kissed him he kissed her back. It really didn't matter.

March

Leo

'So, Leo, when are you going to make it up?' Sue had avoided mentioning Audrey for weeks. 'You've not seen her since the end of January. What's the story?' For the first time ever there was territory between them that couldn't be crossed; like a minefield it stretched, dangerous and loaded with unasked questions. Now she was exasperated. He could hear it in her voice.

'Let's not talk about it.' He gave a tight smile.

'Have you spoken to your mum?'

'What about?'

She sighed and turned back to the shopping she was emptying out of the car. He grabbed a couple of bags in each hand and hefted them into the house. His phone buzzed in his pocket. It would be Lucy again.

'Well, I for one am sick of this. Poor Lorraine's run ragged. You know Audrey's not too well again. Why don't you make it up? Just be friends, at least?'

'Don't think so.'

'Suit yourself. But I'm going round. I'm going to see what we can do. Come if you like, or don't. Right?'

He watched Sue stride out across the fields in her jeans and wellingtons and fleece. Usually Leo admired his aunt, but today he thought she was being a fool. Lorraine wouldn't let her in. They'd been cut out. Audrey could have things the way she wanted them; as far as he was concerned, they were finished for good.

Leo checked his message: Lucy wanted to meet, to go out to the pictures, then for a pizza. He put the phone back in his pocket without replying and turned up the record. Mick Jagger shouting 'You Can't Always Get What You Want' broke the peace of the farm and he smashed out the chords on the piano, his teeth gritted, his jaw set.

And he was right. Three quarters of an hour later Sue was back. Red-cheeked, windswept. The kitchen door slammed behind her, the wind snatching it out of her hands. Leo stopped playing. She stood in the doorway of the living room and looked at him.

'No one home. Stupid, I should have phoned first.' Sue threw up her hands. 'This place is filthy, Leo. Spring clean. And you can help.'

They spent the afternoon scrubbing every corner, as if that would clear things up.

April

Leo

School was busier than ever. All anyone talked about was exams. Revision. The future. Well, what did he have to lose? Leo got his head down and studied. When he came home from school there was the piano. He bought a ton of sheet music from a music shop in town and worked his way through it, learning by heart, testing himself. And sometimes he imagined his audience. Audrey, usually. Always. Her head tipped to one side, her face full of concentration, deep in thought. Then he'd slam the lid of the piano and try to forget her again.

Then the call came from his mum.

'Leo.' She was sharp.

He'd been on his way out for a run and didn't need this conversation right now. Stretching his hamstrings, he answered, 'Yeah? Hello to you too.'

'I'm sorry. I'm not in the mood for small talk.'

'You don't say.'

'No. Well, I just called your school, since you've been so unforthcoming regarding your university applications.'

'Oh.'

'Indeed, you may well say, *Oh.* Your tutor informs me the forms were never even filled in.'

'Yeah –'

'Would you care to explain?'

'Look, at the time, I was thinking about other stuff and I thought about having a year out, staying on here with Sue, maybe going travelling. I don't know. But, yes, you're right – it was stupid.'

'Was it Audrey?' His mother clearly thought she already knew the answer to that question.

'No.'

It wasn't really a lie. He'd decided long ago that he needed more time. His mum's voice softened.

'All right, well, never mind. I just wish you'd spoken to me, or to your father – you can talk to us, you know. We could have helped you; we want to help you, but, well, you'll soon be eighteen. You have to make your own mistakes some time, I suppose. I've been trying not to interfere.'

Leo had been pacing; wearing out her carpet, Sue would say. Now he sat down.

'Thanks, Mum.' He stared out of the window.

'All right. But you will apply next year?'

'Yes.' Next year. But what about now? He sighed.

'And how's the piano?' she said, trying to lift him, he knew.

'Fine. No, it's wonderful. Thank you.'

'Will you play for me now?' He laughed and stood up again, carried the phone to the living room and propped it on the window sill. Opened the lid and flexed his fingers. Mozart, he decided; everyone loved Mozart.

Jen Blake approached him at lunchtime a few weeks before Easter. She was one of the few who'd bothered to be welcoming or remotely friendly to Audrey. Did it really take that much effort just to be nice?

'So, what's going on with Audrey?' she said. An answer didn't come fast and Jen stared at him, her face confused.

'They said she's not well. Miss Jones, did, I mean.'

'Did she?' Leo replied in the end.

'So, I guess it's bad?'

'I wouldn't know.'

Jen pursed her lips and folded her arms.

'Is she coming back, or what?'

'Not sure.'

'But she's missed loads,' Jen insisted, her eyes following his when he tried to look away.

'Sorry, Jen. I don't know what Audrey's plans are.' Leo picked up his sandwich, really wanting the conversation to end. It was pointless, ridiculous. And he was angry now, struggling to swallow.

'Look, you should ask her yourself,' Leo said when it looked like Jen wasn't going away. 'It's nothing to do with me.'

'Oh, right. You're with Lucy.' Her voice was accusing. 'I remember now – you don't give a shit. You split up.'

'Correct. We split up.' The words were mean, but true. It was how he felt, spliced and sharp. Like a piece of wood smashed with an axe. And this feeling that he'd never see Audrey again, that maybe she didn't even exist any more – it was horrible. *I am half sick of shadows*, he thought, and remembered reading her that poem, and how she'd sat up, leant forward for the words, rapt. Were there other girls

like that? Would he find someone else who would understand him like Audrey did? He thought of the times he'd
held her and wanted to say something, something so she'd
understand. *I love you.* That was it; that was all. He never
had and now it was too late. Leo screwed the sandwich up
in its wrappings and lobbed it into the bin.

'Right, well, if you do see her, could you give her this?'
Jen said, handing over an envelope. 'It's an invitation to
my party. Sweet sixteen. Not.' She pulled a sarcastic face
and Leo managed to laugh and took the paper. He almost
said no. And then he reconsidered; he could drop it at the
Grange on his way home that evening; that would be OK.
He wouldn't have to see Audrey. But if she was there,
maybe. Maybe he would.

'OK. Sure.'

'Thanks, and say hi from me. Tell her I miss her. And
get well soon, all right?'

'All right.'

Lorraine's car wasn't in the driveway so Leo pressed the
buzzer for the flat. No answer. The front door hung
open like always, so Leo stepped inside, cautious, slow. It
was weird being back here; he should just post the envelope and go. But he lingered in the lobby and kicked at the
pile of junk mail on the floor, wondering what he could
make fast and leave in the letter box. A quick message, a
surprise, just so Audrey would know he'd been there and
that he was thinking of her. He picked up a pizza menu.
Folded it in half and in half again. It was no good; he let
it fall to the floor. She'd said no contact. For a moment he

had an urge to take his pen out of his pocket and scrawl on the high white walls of the hall. He would write in the biggest letters, so she wouldn't miss it, couldn't ignore it; her name, so maybe she'd see how he couldn't forget her, no matter what she said, and read his apology written there – indelible.

AUDREY AUDREY AUDREY AUDREY AUDREY AUDREY

What did he want to say sorry for? For giving up? He didn't know. He didn't even know if he should be sorry for anything. His dad had always called him sissy, baby, little mummy's boy, and he was right. His shoulders slumping, Leo wandered round the outside of the building to the fire escape and thought of all the times she'd been up there, watching, like a bird high in her eyrie or a sailor in a crow's nest. The image worked. Leo smiled. Audrey, he thought again, and his heart picked up speed, kicked and punched at his ribs, just as it always had at the thought of seeing her. What if she was there? Waiting, like always? She would be, surely. It was that feeling, that before-an-exam sort of panic and rush. He felt a little dizzy and took deep breaths before he climbed to the top, the metal clanging beneath his feet. But he was alone and sat down, where she used to sit, and watched the world and tried to imagine what it was like to be her.

May

Leo

By the time Mr Bruce finally saw *Macbeth* for what it was –
a piece of political propaganda designed to flatter James I
and entertain the masses – he and Leo had come to a
truce. Leo answered his questions and participated in the
lessons and Mr Bruce accepted that his Marxist rereading
of the play was wrong. On many levels. For a treat, Brucie
said, they could do a bit of acting.

'I want to see the tragedy in sixty seconds. Key quota-
tions, freeze frames, whatever. I leave it to your ingenuity.'
Brucie smiled. Sadist.

Leo teamed up with a couple of other guys, Jon and
Billy – nice enough; they'd always got on. They messed
about, improvised, got it together. When the bell rang,
Jon followed Leo out into the corridor.

'So, I hear you play keyboard.'

'What? How'd you hear that?'

'Dunno. Grapevine. We need someone for our band.'

'What band?'

'It's a new project: me and Billy. He's on drums, I'm
vocals, guitar. You interested?'

'Maybe; what sort of stuff do you play?'

'Oh, we write our own music. Bit of folk, Americana,
country.'

LIES LIKE LOVE

'All right.' What the hell. He didn't have much else to do. It might be fun; take his mind off all the things Sue said he needed to stop thinking about.

'So, tonight, seven o'clock, here.' Jon scribbled down an address. 'See you later, mate.'

Leo was shocked. They were good, really good. Lyrics dark and seeping with menace as Jon sang in a deep throaty voice about black waters rising, biblical fear, girls with eels in their hair. Leo listened for the chords. He could do something with this definitely. Touching the keyboard, working it out, he felt right, good. Wished Audrey was here. She'd loved to hear him play. Don't think about that, not now. Just make noise.

They worked on the songs for a couple of hours. Went down the pub after. Apparently the landlord didn't mind they were underage so long as no one got rat-arsed. The local police turned a blind eye too.

Jon was the talkative one; Billy didn't say much, communicated mostly in grunts, but he was the lyricist. *Still waters*, thought Leo, smiling.

'That was fucking great, Leo,' Jon said. 'So, you're in? We could get a couple of gigs this summer.'

'Yeah, I'm in. Why not? But I tell you what – you should maybe try a RAT distortion pedal. I had one. I'll see if I can find it, let you have it.'

'You play guitar too, then?'

'Sort of. I can play a bit of most things.'

'Renaissance man,' said Jon, laughing, draining his pint. Real ale. Leo liked it.

When Billy got up to put something on the juke box, a girl sidled into his seat. Swishy hair, sickly perfume. Sat too close. Lizzy. Leo stifled a groan and, for the millionth time, regretted the manners instilled in him from birth.

'Hey. So, how's it going?'

'Fine.' He looked at her, wondered what she wanted this time.

'I haven't seen you out much.'

'Oh.'

'Mum says your girlfriend's proper sick. Sorry, I mean your ex.' She put emphasis on the word, grinding in the reminder.

He stared at Lizzy. There were no sea-coloured clouds in her eyes or flowers in her hair; there was no poetry in her head. She didn't wear glasses, wasn't humming some silly song that she sang with Peter. It was simple: no one else shone. No one else made his skin prickle, his belly lurch. His heart ache.

'Yeah, I told you she was mental. Psycho. You should have listened.'

Jon and Billy were listening. Leo would not ask her what she meant. He would never give her the satisfaction. He sipped his drink, not sure how rude he could be and still get away with it. Lizzy smiled round the table, her little white teeth glistening and sharp, but no one smiled back. She nudged him, giggled and sipped her drink, some radioactive-looking alcopop.

'She's proper schizo, Leo. I knew it. She always freaked me out. My mum reckons they'll have to put her away soon; she was in the surgery the other day, all monged out, Mum said.'

Leo tightened his grasp on the glass in his hand, knuckles hard and white. Jon asked him something, if he wanted to meet up again next weekend, and he nodded as Lizzy interrupted again.

'So, you've joined the band, have you? Is that what this little gathering's all about?'

This time Leo answered her. He could speak about this without losing the plot.

'Yeah. They're really good. Play really well – I love their stuff. I'm a bit rusty though –'

Jon interrupted. 'He's not. He's like some genius. And he's going to be our chick magnet.' Jon swigged the end of his pint and nodded at Leo, making him laugh.

Lizzy nodded, not getting it. 'You're right.' He reckoned she actually batted her eyelashes at him. He felt a little queasy.

'We're all going on to Amy's. You coming?' she said, moving closer, wriggling her skirt a little further up her thighs, adjusting her hair so it swished too close to him.

'No.' Leo stood up. 'I ought to get going.'

'See you, then,' she said, following him. 'At school on Monday?'

'Sure. Take it easy.'

And he walked away from them, out of the pub on to the black roads towards the embankment, finding his way in the dark by the moon glowing silver bright in the night sky.

Leo stopped, halfway home. Put his hand in his pocket.

Took out his phone. It had been so long since he'd spoken to her. It was no use pretending he didn't care.

The phone rang and rang. Clicked on to answer machine.

'Sorry,' he said. 'Sorry.' Over and over and over.

Audrey

When Mum wheeled me in to see Mr McGuiness he stared, although I'm sure he wasn't meant to. He must have had training not to gawp like that; surely I wasn't the worst he'd seen. My body had bent and adjusted to the chair, adopting its shape, so it was harder to walk now, harder to stand. Sometimes at night I lay in bed and tried to cycle my legs in the air, but it was hard; I got out of breath fast.

'Audrey won't get up. She says she can't walk,' Mum explained. 'Of course, we both know that's not true. But it's part of her illness; it's the way it's affecting her, doctor.'

'And the hair?' he asked. I'd forgotten about that and grown used to the look. Mostly people thought I was having chemotherapy; Mum never contradicted them and I was too tired to mind now. In a way they were right – there was a cancer, but it grew outside my body, operating in disguise.

'She shaved it off. The lot. I couldn't believe it when I found her – all that beautiful hair all over the floor. I cried.' Mum sniffed and Mr McGuinness nodded and didn't stop Mum's explanations, her stories. It was amazing how sure she sounded, as if she believed every word she was saying. 'Like I said, it's the illness. It's like she's trying to destroy herself, any way she can. Like she wants to be ugly and awful. Heartbreaking.'

Mum's eyes goggled and popped at me, then at the doctor. She sat down, pulling her chair closer to mine, then took my hand and I let it rest in her palm, trying not to feel – the touch of her skin made me want to gag, to turn myself inside out and worm free. Mr McGuiness cleared his throat. My head swam with the stories and the words, questioned the facts and the fiction, the truth and the lies. What was memory? What was dream? I'd looked up those words. *Factitious disorder*. I knew what they meant now. I knew it meant we were pretending. I was her proxy. Last night I'd lain awake thinking it through, wondering – how long had I been a lie? How long had I been a puppet? What was real about me? I didn't know. My mouth worked the words, *factitious disorder*, twisting and chewing them like gristly meat. The psychiatrist stared.

'Right, of course I remember you, Audrey, from when – way back in January? What's been happening?'

'Nothing much,' I said. Acting nasty, mean, like Mum said I should.

And then I shut my mouth and left it to Mum; she was better at this than me. But, like Dr Caldwell, he didn't want to know and got me on my own. Mum left the Thing though, nestled beside me. It prodded and poked as I explained, reminding me to tell him, tell him all.

Leo

Leo decided it wasn't good enough just to be sorry. He waited for Peter after school and fell into step beside him. Peter marched on his little legs, his backpack too big, hanging from his shoulders. Leo tried to take it but Peter dodged away.

'Your mum picking you up?'

'No.' He scurried faster, his hair flying. It was long, past his collar, like Leo's. His little chin jutted up to look at Leo, who recognized the expression on his face. Defiance. Pain. Bewilderment.

'How about Audrey?'

'She can't.'

Leo didn't ask why not. It wasn't fair.

'Anyway, I'm big enough to walk on my own now, Mum says.'

'Can I walk back with you, then?' Peter nodded and they walked on together and it was almost like the old days, almost.

'I saw a heron the other day,' Leo said. 'Are you still watching the birds, Pete?'

'No.' He hesitated. 'We don't really go in the woods now. Aud can't go. I'm going to watch TV when I get home.'

'How about a game of football first?'

Peter's eyes shone. He looked his old self for a moment. 'Really?'

'Yes, let's go. Come on.'

As they passed the ball, Leo tried to get Peter to talk. At first it was hard work; the answers were short, simple, vague.

'Do you remember your last house, Pete? Was Audrey not well then too?'

'I don't know,' Peter said.

'Did she go to school?'

Peter shrugged.

'She always looked after me,' he said eventually. 'She's my best friend.'

'I know. Me too.'

'But you don't like her any more,' Peter accused.

'What? Who said that?'

Peter ran, dribbling the ball away from Leo. 'No one ever likes us,' he shouted over his shoulder, 'not really.'

Audrey

There were so many pills now. I swallowed each one, the procedure long and slow. Afterwards my words slowed and slurred and I sat beside Mum, staring at the floor or her hands as they knitted and scratched and pressed the keys on her phone. Time was rubber and though I tried to poke my nose through into each day, stretching and testing, pushing against its thickness, it never gave; it never let me in. And there were places in my brain I didn't visit any more, high places, where I might find a bird on a branch, its head turned to the sky. Instead I stayed below, down in the darkness, the pain places, locked inside.

One evening, somewhere at the end of May, I looked up. I'd been lost in that blackness, and Peter was staring, looking at me like I was a stranger. I sat up straighter and tried to smile, to seem normal, and glanced around for a pack of cards, a book, to distract him.

'What's happened to Audrey, Mum?' Peter said.

Mum looked up from her magazine. She flicked the ash off her cigarette and looked back down, her eyes scanning for her place.

'Your sister's a very poorly girl, Pete. You can tell your friends at school, if you like, and your teachers. Tell them that Audrey's not well. That she's seeing the doctors, up at the big hospital.'

I reached out and held Peter's hand. Gripped as tight as I could. This wasn't supposed to have happened. It wasn't the plan. Peter stared at me again. His eyes watery.

'Are you going to die, Aud? I don't want you to die,' he whispered.

I managed a smile, managed to mouth a *no*. But we'd had the conversation, of course, so many times. I remembered now. Suddenly realized why.

When I was five I said I'd probably wear my Snow White costume. Mum liked that idea, made a note and set it aside with the matching satin shoes, bag and headband. Dad bought me a Jessie outfit to replace it and I marched around in sparkly red boots, swinging imaginary lassos for some time after. Aged ten, I opted for yellow – my favourite colour – yellow dress, flowers, and the song 'Yellow Submarine' instead of a hymn. That was the start of my Beatles phase, when I'd listen to Dad's LPs at night, playing them turned down really low, when Mum and Peter were asleep. She hadn't been quite so keen on that, said it was a bit too fun, but that she'd bear my thoughts in mind. Age thirteen, I said I'd think about it and felt a bit sick when I did so later, alone in my room, staring at a ceiling I'd painted black, where I'd stuck constellations I didn't know the names of, that the city sky had never shown me. And now I had no idea. But the whole family knew what Mum's send-off involved. A lot of Elton John. Her name picked out in pink roses on top of her coffin. Plumed horses, undertakers in long black coats. A procession, if possible, like in the videos she watched of Princess Di's funeral; Peter centre-stage, stoic, pale (I, of course, would be long gone by then). And the headstone: 'Devoted mother. Who lived for others, not herself.' She made up the wording and I said nothing. Now I knew it wasn't true.

Later that evening I finished washing up, walked slowly, excruciatingly, up to Peter's room, ignoring Mum's voice calling me back. I was reading him *The Lion, the Witch and The Wardrobe* and it felt very heavy in my hands.

'Go on, read it, then, Aud.' Peter sat up, excited, ready. I put the book down; I didn't have the breath. There were special voices required for the witch and Aslan, for Lucy and Edmund. Energy was needed to bring the words to life, and when I looked at the page the sentences seemed too long, like snakes twisting out of the book and fading to nothing. Peter picked it up, opened it and began to read aloud to me instead. But he couldn't manage, stuttering and tripping over the long words and the difficult punctuation. If I wasn't around to read him this story, then who ever would? He'd never know the end. I must have groaned.

'What is it?' Peter said. 'Why do you sound like that?'

'I'm fine, don't worry.' I coughed, trying to clear my throat.

'Sorry, Aud,' he said, patting my head.

'What are you sorry for, mate?' I took his hand.

He snuggled up to me. 'Do you wish you hadn't come back?'

'No.' It was a struggle to get that out. It was only half a lie. I wished there was another way to do this. But it was too late to run away now; I couldn't make it. The thought banged in my brain and I ground my nails into my palms.

Leo's face flickered on my eyelids, his face when he'd tried to ask if something was wrong: anxious, biting his lip, how he'd flushed when I'd said no and pushed him away. And he hadn't been to see me. Not for months. There had been no letters, no secret messages twisted out of ancient paper.

'Do you ever see Leo these days, Pete? Up at the school or anything?' I whispered. Mum might be listening. She was always listening. There was a long pause. Peter rubbed his head on the pillow. His hair would be ratty with knots in the morning.

'Yeah,' he whispered back, blinking. He put his mouth to my ear. 'Mum says I'm not allowed to tell you though.'

'What?'

'If I tell you, you won't get well.' He frowned.

'Just tell me. It's OK.'

'He meets me after school and he asks about you every day, Aud.'

I sat up, leant forward. 'What do you say?'

'I say that you're OK. I didn't tell him about your hair falling out.' He reached forward and touched my head again, running his palm over the smooth shell. Mum shaved it almost every day. He shrugged. 'Shall I tell him that you're ill? Do you think he'll come and see you then?'

'No.' I grabbed his hands and squeezed. 'No. Don't tell him that. Thanks, Pete.' I dropped a kiss on his head, pushed myself up and walked slowly out of the room.

'Night, little brother.'

'Night. I love you, Audrey.'

'I know.'

Audrey

Everything took a long time. Getting my shoes on, finding a jacket, keys. Slow was no good, and I slammed doors, vicious, angry. *What happened to you, Audrey?* But I couldn't answer the question and pressed it down, stamping it underfoot like a crawling spider.

There was no one around. Too early for Peter to be home. Too early for Mum. What I needed was someone to talk to. But not someone I knew. No one who would ask questions. I couldn't take horror. Sympathy. Blame.

The garden was budding into life. It was early summer out here, the grass neon bright, the sky sun blue and the clouds building a candy-floss staircase too delicate to tread. Willows reached with long graceful arms, dandling long-forgotten children, their whispers a story of the past. I couldn't stay in the Grange forever, shut up in the attic like the woman in the book I used to read. But the sky loomed too large; it spread and swung. There was too much of it all, too much air and space and sky, and underneath my feet the ground was screaming and the sky was hurting and the bones of the world were about to break. I stumbled. Leo had promised adventures and the thought of that made me turn from the green because nettles grew among it all, long and cruel. Like my mother. If you touched them, they'd leave a stain, a sting, but it was their long hard yellow roots that were the problem, like a live wire running under the earth, under my skin. Connecting, tying a trap.

Peter is well, I reminded myself, *your brother is alive, healthy, growing.* That was all I'd wanted when I'd returned. But I hadn't seen the future – that I'd lose myself like this. That hadn't been part of the plan. I thought it'd be like before: bad, but not so bad that I couldn't see better times ahead and plot a way out, a path upwards. And now the future was so dark, as if all the blinds had been pulled down, shutting me up, closing down my life.

I couldn't go far or fast. My legs hurt. Ankles, knees, thigh bones like twigs, muscles like sponge. And a brain like a nest of maggots, rotten and wrong. I walked. Where to? Dr Caldwell had wanted to know what was wrong. Dr Caldwell had asked me to tell her. She would understand. I could go there now. I could. She would listen. I had the words. I knew what to say.

Tell Doctor Caldwell.

Now and then a car roared past. I flattened myself into the hedge each time. And then one slowed, driving close. The Thing was at the wheel.

'Get in, Audrey,' it said, leering from the window. 'Get in this car.'

I kept my eyes down, on the road, and tried to squeeze past. If I wasn't careful, the wheel would run over my foot. I could feel it happen somewhere in the future, a blinding pain, a crushing agony. Flesh breaking, bones snapping.

'Get in,' it said. 'We're going home.'

June

Audrey

Mum and I went everywhere together after that. Another day, another week, another month. The sun was out but we were on our way to the clinic when Mum pulled over at the newsagents in town to get another pack of cigarettes. She was smoking a lot, coughing at night, and I kept my window wound down and rested my head on my hand, staring out, waiting for her to come back. Across the road people walked in and out of the supermarket, trolleys rattled on wonky wheels. The sounds of that and the traffic jangled and blurred.

'Hey.'

I must have been half asleep because the voice made me jump. Leo's voice.

No time to fix the window, no time to hide. I'd been spotted and it was a shock. In my imagination, Leo had drifted and changed: a ghost, insubstantial – like me. He belonged to another existence, a different girl. Not this strange being I had become. And now Leo was here, right in front of me, it was strange to see how solid he was. How tall. Alive. I took off my glasses. Rubbed my eyes. Nothing was clear. The lives other people, my friends, were leading without me. I was used to pills, my psychiatrist. The antiseptic white of hospital waiting rooms. The bright pretend fun of the clinic. The rotting walls of the Grange. Not this.

I realized Leo was staring at me. He was waiting for something. Time opened, stretching in shock.

'Audrey. What happened?' Leo, my Leo – because that is what he always was and would be in my heart – leant forward, resting his hands on the door, his head close. So close, I could smell him. I shut my eyes and breathed him in, and I know I smiled for a second. Sun, fresh grass, paper. He'd been reading somewhere; under a tree, I guessed. The imprint of blades of grass on his arm. Nature's tattoo. Ink on his fingers, I smelled that too, the rich, thick scent – a better sort of blood. I could touch him easily; his arms were near my face and the warm afternoon rose from his skin, curling towards me. I could have buried my face in his T-shirt; I could have held his strong, warm hand. Once upon a time.

'You look – I mean, you look bad.' His voice was low. *Disgust*, I thought, wishing I could cover my head, my face. But it was too late to put anything pretty there. Moving back, trying to hide where there was nowhere to hide. The day revealed everything.

'Thanks.' I tried to make it a joke. Laugh it off.

Leo bent closer. I breathed him in, as if I could steal some of what he had. Youth. Courage. Beauty. He looked as if he were going to say something, his mouth forming shapes, words on the tip of his tongue. And then Sue appeared beside him, the grin on her face falling, like the sun crashing out of the sky.

'Audrey?'

'Hi,' I managed. They should just go away, stop staring.

'I didn't realize –' she began, and then I interrupted.

'Please. Please don't. I'm all right.' My smile was plastic, a mask, but Sue smiled back, reaching forward into the car, as if to hug me. But here was Mum and there wasn't time. Sue straightened up and looked at her. Leo too.

'Mrs Morgan.' A curt nod of Leo's head, his eyes darting poison.

'Hello, Sue,' Mum said, as if she'd not heard or even seen Leo. 'All right, are you?' She rooted in her bag for her keys. I leant over and opened the door for her, my fingers fumbling with the catch.

'I'm fine, Lorraine, but how about you? You didn't say it was, I mean, we didn't realize . . .'

Sue's words rose, then trailed off as Mum bowled into the car, turning her key and making the ignition scream. She muttered under her breath, jammed the car into gear and stamped on the accelerator. As we drove away I looked in the wing mirror at Leo and his aunt. They watched the car until we turned a corner and I couldn't see him any more; then where did they go? It wasn't my business.

Leo

'What the fuck was that?' Leo said, as Sue hurried away, turning to walk back to the car.

'I don't know, Leo. We always knew she was unwell, unstable . . .' His aunt's voice trailed into nothing and they rode the rest of the way home in silence. It was worse now; worse than ever before, Leo could see that. He'd almost not recognized Audrey; she seemed to have shrunk, her bones protruding through her skin, her veins a stark blue against the white of her neck, her forehead. And her hair? Where had her hair gone?

'Sue,' he said, as they pulled into the drive, 'I can't stand this.' He thought he might choke on the words; he wanted to hit something and slammed his fist on the door. 'It's my fault, Sue. I shouldn't have let her go back. We should have done something.' Jen's words, Lizzy's. He hadn't listened. Not hard enough.

'What?' Sue looked at him, uncomprehending; reached out and held his arm. 'You can't blame yourself, Leo. This was something we all saw coming, I suppose. Audrey was never right, was she?'

Leo was furious. That his aunt could be so blind convinced him that no one would ever understand Audrey or bother to try to help. He should try to help. He was the only one who could.

'She was – she *was* right; she was fine. Lovely, you said so yourself.'

'Well, I mean, not right mentally.' Sue was struggling to find the right words but he didn't care.

'Bullshit. There was nothing wrong with her. Just this thing with Lorraine. I never liked her. I never did. And now – look what's happened! I have to do something.'

'You can't blame Lorraine,' Sue repeated. 'Come on, I know the woman's a bit odd, but seriously, Leo, I know it's very sad, but she's done her best by Audrey. And I don't see what you can do about it. I'm sure Lorraine's getting her help. And that's what Audrey needs. Professional help. We were in no position to offer her that.'

'No. I don't agree.' Leo jumped out of the car and ran inside the farmhouse. It was time to try and make some sense of this, but he had no idea how. He could go and see Dr Caldwell, he supposed, or maybe try and find out something about Lorraine, because that was where the problem lay; he knew it.

Google brought up few results. He scanned the references to Lorraine Morgan, then typed in Audrey's name too. Clicked on a link, a blog.

THE PAIN PLACES: ME AND MY DEPRESSION
BY AUDREY MORGAN, AGED SIXTEEN
AND NINE MONTHS

Where would I be without Mum? I ask myself that question one hundred times a day when I'm lying, so tired, and she's sitting beside me, reading aloud, or just knitting, just being there.

I want to tell her here how sorry I am for being this way. Mum, I love you, and thank you for everything.

She's fought every battle for me. She's the one who's got me treatment, found me my amazing doctors and never given up. Without her I think I'd be dead. I know I would be. Remember New Year? Remember that? What I did and how sick I got?

Leo stared at photographs, read posts, rubbed his eyes, read again; Audrey couldn't have written this stuff, about cutting, about depression, about suicidal thoughts. About Lorraine. It wasn't his Audrey.

He stood up and picked up the phone; he could call her and ask her to tell him exactly what this meant. He held the phone and sat down and read again, scrolling back to the most recent post.

I'm so afraid now of what I might do, of who I might hurt, including myself. Because I'm angry and afraid and trapped in my head with the fear and the voice that tells me I'm no good.

And my depression lies on me. It's a heavy blanket, piles of heavy blankets, suffocating, so thick that I can't breathe some-times, I can't move. Mum says I'll get better, that lots of people feel this way. She tells me the sun's shining outside, but know-ing that doesn't make it go away. Living with an illness like this makes you different and most people just don't want to know, they don't want to understand. When Mum takes me out I see the way the people in this town look at me. They step back, as if I stink, as if I'm nasty. They think I might hurt them, do something disgusting, maybe piss myself like a baby or swear

and shout and say all the things they can't admit. Like life is
shit. Like living hurts. It does. Just look at my scars.

Embedded into the text was a photograph of her wrists
taken in black and white – almost artistic, the arms naked
and thin, far too thin. Her hands held out in what to Leo
looked like supplication, empty palms upturned, and the
flesh ridged and patterned, criss-crossed with the proof
of her pain. He slammed the laptop shut and lay on his
bed and cried.

Audrey

Mum stopped at the supermarket on the way home; I was in the wheelchair. It was cold near the chiller cabinets and I started to shiver and when I started I couldn't stop.

'What's up?' Mum was filling the basket with treats. I blanked Leo from the day; it hadn't happened. I hadn't seen him.

'Let's get Pete from school,' she said, 'and go home and have a picnic in the garden. The weather's perfect for it, but you'd better put a sun hat on.' She examined a bottle of sparkling wine, then put it down, picked up another.

'Can we go to the sea?' I asked, the idea striking like a little bit of blue sky. Peter would love it. It would be warm enough for him to swim and I could take a blanket, wrap up if I got cold. It was one of the things I'd promised him, one of the things we'd planned to do. This way I could at least pretend. It didn't look as if we'd get to Spain. Not this year.

'Well, I don't see why not. I fancy getting a bit of a sun. Good idea.' She made her decision, shoved a couple more things into the basket and wheeled me to the checkout, her shoes squeaking across the tiled floor.

The lady on the till kept looking at me, but I dropped my head and closed my eyes.

'She's tired,' I heard Mum say, 'been a big day. We just

heard –' she lowered her voice – 'it's terminal. Cancer.' I didn't even flinch.

'Oh. Oh, my God,' the girl said, sounding as if someone had just told her that she herself was dying, 'you poor thing.'

'I know. It's all right. We're managing. She's so brave; she wants to take her brother on a picnic to the seaside after school. It's amazing really. She's my inspiration. My miracle.'

I thought Mum was going to cry. The girl on the till too. The whole fucking queue waiting behind us. Once I could have stood up and walked away. Not now. Too late. I wouldn't get away. Mum wasn't lying any more. It had all come true. I looked up.

'Please,' I said, 'can we go?' And Mum gathered her bags, hung them on the handles of the chair and pushed me out into the bright, which hurt, burned my brain like radioactive poison.

'Here we go, love,' she said, lifting me into the car. 'You're a star, Aud, you know that?'

'Thanks, Mum,' I told her, muffling my voice in my hands, wiping at my face, my eyes. She didn't notice I was crying, or if she did she didn't care. I tried to remember the last time she'd asked me how I was and realized it was never.

She was still talking. I hadn't been paying attention.

'But, Audrey, sweetheart, I thought you wanted to plan – I mean, we've been here before, a thousand times, and there's got to come a point where you face up to it. I mean, I've got mine all sorted, have done for years.'

The funeral. Again.

'*Rhubarbrhubarbrhubarblalalalala*,' I sang, my hands over my ears.

She darted me a cross look, swatted at my hands, carried on talking over the sound of the radio and the gobbledygook I was spilling like it was Shakespeare.

'I don't mean to be harsh, love, but it's the same for all of us. You never know when your time's up, and for you, Aud, that day's closer than for most. I mean, you're lucky, we all know that, like a cat with nine lives or something.' She gave a little laugh. 'But still, you're a very poorly teen. I mean, who knows what'll happen now? Mental illness is a serious condition. And you're not doing well.' Her eyes were fixed on the road ahead and she ignored the traffic queuing at the junction, spinning out to overtake them all, wheeling us on to the road that ran out of town and towards the school.

We stopped at home for things we needed, then collected Peter from outside the school gates. He punched the air with excitement when I told him our plan. But once we hit the route towards the coast, the roads were jammed with traffic: camper vans and caravans slowed everyone down, queuing for the weekend and blocking the twisty country lanes.

'For fuck's sake,' Mum muttered, shifting in her seat, adjusting her seatbelt for the millionth time. There were damp patches under her arms, staining her top, sweat on her upper lip. I knew she was hot. She didn't see I was cold.

'Mum!' Peter held out his hand. She was supposed to give him a quid every time she used the F word, but she batted his outstretched palm away.

'We're turning round.' She flicked on the indicator.

'No!' he wailed. 'We'll be there soon. Please, Mum! Look, the traffic's moving again. Please.'

She sighed and faced forward again. 'I'll give it five more minutes. Get a CD on would you, Aud?' She lit a cigarette, her arm resting on the window.

I rummaged in the glove box, trying to find something different, but the selection was the same. We knew the words to these songs too well. I wanted a better song to sing.

'Here –' Pete leant forward again – 'this.'

'What is it?'

'A friend gave it me.' He nudged my arm. 'So put it on, Aud. Go on.'

I took the plastic case and opened the box. There was nothing written on the disc. I turned to look at Peter, but his face was the usual picture of innocence. A glimmer of mischief in his eye gave him away, and if I'd still had eyebrows I'd have raised them. What was he up to?

The cars began to move and I slotted the disc into the player, dreading what was going to come out. 'Crazy Frog' or whatever it was called. Something daft, anyway.

Mum shifted into second, and the first chord sounded. The breath left my body and it didn't matter any more about the hot car, the stink of the cigarette smoke, the flies dead and black on the windscreen; my breath caught somewhere in my chest. Just the sound of excitement, of dancing, of John Lennon screaming at me to twist and shout, as he had long ago, when Leo had held me and we'd competed to see who could raise the roof.

Ignoring the look on Mum's face, I turned up the music, filling the car with the rising chorus, blasting it out into the countryside, singing along in my head, my lips mouthing words that meant more than anyone knew. And it came over me that I was still alive and Leo was right there with me, sharing a pillow in Sue's spare room – a room that had been mine for a while – an earbud apiece, his fingers drumming the rhythm on my skin.

The song faded, I sat back, happy, waiting for what would come next. It was classical. Mum reached out to switch it off but I batted her hand away. Mozart. I saw him at his piano, in his jeans and bare feet, utterly engrossed in the music until he turned to me and smiled. *Classical music's the new rock and roll*, he'd said, teasing. And I'd got up and sat beside him and put my head on his shoulder, not really caring about rock and roll or anything, just Leo, who made me feel peaceful and good. I wanted to get out of the car. Run all those miles back to the farm. Because Leo still cared, he still thought about me, and this was the proof.

'Where'd you get this, Peter?' I heard Mum saying, somewhere distant, as the violins swooped and soothed. But she must have liked it too, because she shut up and we sat there, all of us, suspended in the music, silly smiles on our faces.

I turned and looked at Peter; reached back and put my hand up to his cheek, touched his soft skin and he grabbed my fingers, squeezed tight.

'Thanks, mate,' I said.

'Love you, Aud,' he whispered, so only I could hear.

*

The sun sank like we'd switched time to slow motion and Peter ran in and out of the water, dipping his toes into the waves. I borrowed Mum's phone and snapped him splashing in the shallows, his skinny white body forging a path forward before he half dived, disappearing for a second, then coming up, spluttering for air, already blue with cold. The camera clicked and buzzed. I turned and caught Mum in my sights, staring out over the sea.

'Hey,' she called, 'come here, Aud. Get one of the two of us.' I couldn't resist her smile. The invitation. Like we were normal, like she loved me, as if this was something we'd do any day. As if we'd print this picture and put it in an album to look at years later, remembering good times. Happiness.

I sat by her on the blanket we'd brought from home, positioned the camera, posed and snapped away.

'That's it – let's see.' We looked back through the pictures together. We were nothing alike, not really, but there was something in our eyes, magnified by the lens. I zoomed in, looking harder. And then I saw it. The fear. The Thing. Not just in Mum, but in me too: I was killing me too. But I didn't have to go on with this. I didn't have to die.

'Gorgeous,' Mum said, kissing my cheek, her arm tight round me, holding me close to her. 'Fancy an ice cream?'

When I nodded she got up and wandered back up the beach to the row of cafes across the way. Peter came running up from the sea, shaking water from himself as if he were a little puppy, his skin prickling with goosebumps. I passed him the towel.

'Quick, get dry – you'll freeze.'

'I know, it really is freezing in there, Aud.' His teeth were chattering. I pulled him close in a hug.

'What d'you expect; this is England, isn't it? Fun though.' The waves hurled and splashed. I shuddered but kept my smile fixed, for Peter's sake.

'Yeah, look.' He pointed out to sea and I made out the surfers, riding waves. 'I want to do that.'

'When you're a bit bigger you can.'

'You too, Aud?'

'Sure.'

Peter looked at me as if I had all the answers. But there was so much I couldn't help with, so many things I wouldn't be there for. Unless. I searched the sky for the staircase again, the route out and away. Too late. I'd missed the ride.

'Are you getting better?' he asked, and I nodded.

'Yeah, Pete. I'm fine. Don't worry.'

Peter didn't answer, just huddled beside me, dripping on to the blanket. I breathed in the smell of the sea on his hair, towelled it dry and smiled at the roses that were returning to his cheeks.

'Are you sure? How do you know?' Peter asked, and I didn't want to lie again; for too long lies had been safer than the truth – like caves to hide in when there was a storm coming or a mist crouching over the fens. The lie had always been that we were safe. That we would grow up like other kids, grow straight and tall and live good lives. And we'd stayed inside that lie long enough for us to forget that when it put out its arms and held us we stayed forever cold. The lie for my brother was on the tip of my tongue – another pebble of betrayal I was ready to drop at his feet. I tried to stop it but it spilled of its own accord.

'You know, Pete, you don't need to worry. I'm here. I always will be.'

'Don't leave, will you, Aud? Don't leave me again?'

I swallowed; I hadn't wanted to know that he worried about it, was still afraid.

'No way, dude,' I said, talking over the pain in my throat.

'Why isn't our mum like other people's mums?' His big brown eyes gazed up at me, lashes still sparkling with water. I smudged away the dried salt from his cheek.

'What d'you mean?'

'You know.' He pushed my hand away, wanting answers.

'Yeah, I do.' He'd never voiced this before and I realized all the things he'd been hiding, wondered what else was bottled up, and searched for the right words. The ones that would make him feel loved and important and secure. Dad had taught them to me, so long ago that I'd almost forgotten, so I made up my own and hoped for the best. It came from the heart and that had to be right.

'I don't know why she is why she is. But she loves us, Pete. And we love her, don't we?'

He shrugged.

'We do. She's our mum. And no one's life is easy or simple all the time. The main thing you have to know is that, whatever Mum says or does, you're a special person, Peter. In fact you're more than special – you're incredible.

Seriously, the best brother in the whole wide world. When you were born it was the happiest day of my life.' He pulled an embarrassed face; he was growing up, I realized, and beginning to understand the things I'd thought I could hide. But at least his smile was real. 'I mean it. And I always want you to remember that, all right? You are precious and perfect. Don't ever let anyone hurt you. Don't ever be afraid to shout for help if you need it.'

He stared at me, eyes wide, and I hugged him again.

'Don't worry. No one will hurt you. But just in case. If it happens, then you run. You run and you shout and you don't stop shouting until someone helps.'

'OK,' he whispered. There was a long pause, with just the crash and rush of the waves to disturb us; that and the cries of gulls, the odd rumble of passing traffic back on the road.

'Is that what you were doing, when you went to Leo's?' he asked, and it was a while before I could answer.

'Sort of, mate.'

'Mum said you didn't love me any more.'

'That wasn't true.'

'You did love me, because you came back.'

'Right.'

'But why did you come back?' He frowned. 'Didn't it work? Running away?'

'It did. It did. But I had to come back, didn't I? I missed you too much to stay away.' It was impossible to explain, to make this make sense, but I had to try. 'But you, you're different. Everything will be different for you. I did get away – you saw that – it can be done. If you need to go, just go. Right? Swear? To a teacher, to Leo or Sue. People you trust, OK?'

'But I trust you, Aud.'

'I know. But you've got to promise me.'

'I swear,' Peter whispered, and we caught each other's little fingers, making a pact. I breathed out and then we couldn't talk any more because Mum came sliding down the sand with three cones, dripping vanilla and strawberry sauce, flakes like little leaning towers.

'Here we are – quick, lick before it's all down my arms.' She laughed and Peter jumped up and grabbed our cones, devouring his, passing me mine, as if we'd only been talking about the weather.

After they'd eaten the ice cream and finished off mine, Mum pushed me along the pier for a while in my chair. The last of the sun felt like a hug and I shut my eyes and let it seep into my skin. Under the blanket it was warm. I felt like sleeping. The day had worn me out.

'Aud, let me push you,' said Peter, jerking me awake, and he grabbed the handles from Mum. At first he walked, veering from side to side, getting the feel of it, but soon he began to pick up speed, moving faster and faster. I held on, laughing, as he weaved the chair through the other pedestrians, shouting, 'Beep beep, beep beep!' We rampaged down the pier, and we didn't listen to Mum calling, 'Stop, wait, hang on.' She'd never catch us – she ran like a geriatric hippo – and I let him push me as fast as he could, facing forward into a breeze that caught my clothes and filled them like sails. We were almost flying. 'Faster,' I shouted. 'Go on!' And with one last spurt I'm sure we took off for a second; just for a moment we were airborne, my brother and I, finding our wings, treading the clouds, climbing high towards heaven.

'Wheee!' I cried, putting my hands above my head, flying into the sunset, up, up and away.

But my brother's strength began to wane; after all he was only a child, small and human and scared, and he slowed, rolling me gently forward to the end of the pier. He paused by the railings, panting and laughing.

'You should have let me go,' I said, 'let me keep flying.' I craned my neck to look at him; he was still catching his breath.

'No way, Aud,' he panted. 'I wouldn't do that. Not ever.'

And then we waited for Mum to catch up with us, red-faced, shouting about the danger and the stupidity and how I was lucky I hadn't fallen out or in. She couldn't steal our smiles though, and Peter held my hand all the way back to the car, just like when he was little and I knew he still needed me. And I needed him too.

Audrey

'We think we'd like Audrey to come in,' Mr McGuiness said, steepling his fingers, staring at me with his bright, clear eyes. 'We'd like to admit her to the adolescent mental-health unit, as soon as possible.'

I looked at Mum. She nodded, opened her mouth to speak, but the doctor ignored her. 'I think you need twenty-four-hour care now, Audrey. I don't think these sessions are enough; we're not making progress.'

'It's not your fault, doctor,' Mum said. 'You've tried your best, but, yes, I agree, we need more help; I've been saying so all along.'

McGuiness didn't answer her. He kept his eyes on me.

'Audrey, why won't you get up? Out of that chair?'

'I can't,' I said, like Mum had told me. Only it was almost true now. I didn't have the energy. There was no point.

'Why can't you?' he repeated. I screwed my eyes shut.

'The Thing won't let me. It told me not to,' I said, low, angry.

'The Thing. You say it lives in the Grange.' He tapped his pen on his desk. 'You know it won't be there when you're on the unit? You'll be able to walk then, won't you? And to eat properly? And talk to us?'

I opened my eyes and looked at Mum. I wasn't sure.

Mum took my hand, but I didn't squeeze back. I didn't like the sound of this unit. Other girls, blank-eyed, pale-faced, their voices like grated metal. Looking at me, shouting things, following me around.

'I'm not going,' I said. I wasn't leaving Peter. No way.

The doctor looked down and shuffled paper for a while. He wouldn't find his answers there. He should look at us. Look hard. *Please, look at me, look at her*, I thought. *Please understand.*

The doctor proceeded to list a range of new treatments, how much good this unit could do for me, how I was lucky they had a space, that I could go there this afternoon.

'We need to intervene before this progresses any further. Don't worry, Audrey,' he said, 'you'll find it's comfortable. The staff are very well qualified; you'll get everything you need to get you up and running, out of that chair. I want to see you on your feet. Eating healthily. Getting some fresh air and exercise. And of course there'll be the daily therapy; that'll be of huge benefit.'

Mum sat further forward on her chair and I let her do the talking.

'You know, doctor, it's such a relief to hear this. After all this time, the things we've been through. I knew if we kept trying, we'd get to the bottom of Audrey's illness, but I need to thank you, personally, for everything you've done. Your persistence and professionalism.' She paused for a second, considering. 'And, of course, I guess, if the worst comes to the worst you could try ECT, couldn't you?'

I didn't know what that was. Mum was looking at

Mr McGuiness, her hands braced on her knees, and I saw the strain in her jaw, knew she'd be chewing the inside of her cheek and that her mouth would be filling with blood. He frowned.

'That treatment is usually a last resort. I'm confident we can make a big difference for Audrey without it.'

'Yes, but,' Mum began, 'electroconvulsive therapy could be the answer; I know of many cases –'

'We'll have to see how things go,' Mr McGuiness interrupted. Very decisive, trying to take control.

'Of course, well, I presume I'll be with her,' Mum said. 'I'll need to stay with Aud, won't I?'

'No,' the doctor said. My head jolted up. I looked at Mr McGuiness through the scratched lenses of my glasses. He'd said Mum wouldn't come. That I would be without her, alone. That was different. I could get well fast. Get home fast. I would tell a doctor or a nurse when I got there, straight away. And Mr McGuiness would rescue Peter; he'd have to.

Mum cleared her throat. 'Audrey won't be able to cope in hospital without me. I'm her carer.'

'As I said, I think she'll find the team are very supportive,' he said, explaining that there'd be nurses and doctors designated to care for me.

Mum coughed again, twisting the strap of her handbag, heat rising under her skin.

'I don't think you understand. I have to come too. She needs me.'

'But what about your son, Mrs Morgan?' Mr McGuiness asked.

'Yes, Peter, he'll be all right, I'll leave him with neighbours like always.'

'Like always?' He raised one eyebrow.

'When Aud's sick, when she needs me.'

'I see. On this occasion that won't be necessary. Of course you'll be able to visit Audrey, you and Peter both. She'll be able to come home too, to visit. But the residential place is only for Audrey herself. Right now it's the best place for her.'

Mr McGuiness was clever. I crossed my fingers. Tried to send him messages with my eyes. Blinking fast. Then slow. SOS.

'We'll see you soon, Audrey,' he said, looking at me, the interview over.

'I'll make sure she's there, doctor.' Mum gave him her best smile before she looked at me, sighing, rubbing her hand on the fuzz of my hair, but underneath I could see she wasn't happy; this wasn't what she'd planned. 'We'll be all right until later, won't we, Aud?'

I nodded and closed my eyes and sat back in the chair. She wouldn't let me go. There was no way.

'I want to come now,' I said.

'I'm sorry. It'll be later today.' Mr McGuiness's voice was surprised. 'But I'm pleased to hear you're so positive about this, Audrey.'

I leant forward, dug my fingers into my thighs, pressed as hard as I could. Why wasn't he listening? I could scream. Shout. Maybe that would change something.

'Please, Mr McGuiness, let me come now,' I said again, tears near, my voice high and panicky.

He stared at me for a long time.

'You'll be admitted today, Audrey. The unit will telephone your mum when the bed is ready. I know this all sounds very daunting, scary even. But try not to worry.'

I looked at him again. Tapped on the side of the chair with my fingernails. The same rhythm. Dot dot dot. Dash dash dash. Dot dot dot. Mr McGuiness held my eyes; I saw the question in them, like he was waiting for me to speak. Mum covered my hand with her own.

'I'll see you later, Mrs Morgan. I'll be at the unit when you bring Audrey; we'll talk more then.' He held out his hand and Mum took it and then pushed me away. I felt his eyes on us as we left and I knew we'd never see Mr McGuiness again.

'Right, well, we've reached the end of the line here, Aud. If that doctor thinks I'm letting you go into some God-awful mental-health unit without any idea what he's playing at and without me there to keep an eye on you, he's got another think coming. They want to take you away from me, but they can't.' Mum started the car, reversed out of the car park, barely checking her mirrors.

I didn't answer her. She was chewing her lips, gnawing at her flesh.

'It's time we got a second opinion,' she said.

Here we go again. Here it comes.

'Tomorrow. We'll get up early, get off. I'm sick of this place, all these snobs round here. We'll pack tonight and hit the road at first light; find a decent doctor, one who knows what they're talking about. Like I said. I think you

need the ECT. I read up on it, Aud. It's the best treatment. I've been thinking about Scotland,' she said. 'What
do you reckon?'

There was no point arguing.

Mum wanted us to pack and she sent me upstairs to get
the bags. I crouched by her bed and fished around for her
luggage, but my fingers met with hard edges and I pulled
a heavy cardboard box towards me, stuffed to almost
overflowing with papers. Her secret stash. I hadn't known
it was here.

I began to search, fast. What was I looking for? A piece
of paper, maybe, with instructions on it: *How to be happy.*
How to change, grow, begin. Instead there were scrawled notes
in my mum's writing that covered pages in jagged scrib-
bles, a jumble of phrases. I tried to decipher the words
but they made no sense, scrabbling and running like terrified children among ink-spitting bombs. And then, as I
dug deeper, I found a stack of envelopes addressed to me.
The dates on the postmarks were old, and I was surprised
I'd never found this hoard before; Mum must have
brought them from our old place and forgotten to hide
them. I screwed my fists tight. All those lies about a fire.
What had been the point? Who really cared? No one. I
prised open the first, carefully, but it fell apart; the tacky
sides had long lost their stick, and out slid a card: *10 today!*
There was a picture of a girl wearing roller skates, holding
a bunch of balloons. Inside there was a ten-pound note
and a scrawl: *Happy Birthday, Aud! Love, Dad.*

I opened the next envelope, and the next. They all read

the same, marked birthdays for the last ten years. He hadn't forgotten, not once. I looked for the most recent, from my birthday in September. That was the only one I couldn't find, but, still, the rest were mine and Mum had stolen them. Dad thought about me. Dad cared.

I shut my eyes and tried to remember something, more than just this. I held the cards up to my nose and breathed in hard, trying to sniff out the past and the memories I deserved. 'Dad? What happened? Where are you? I need you now,' I whispered into the paper. There was no answer, but a memory began, like a twist of thread unravelling fast, spooling away out of my fingers, almost too quick for me to catch. The scene spun: Dad's face, soft eyes, the strength of his back. I'm riding high on his shoulders, way above the world, the sun tickling my face as I scream, *Faster, go faster!* and we gallop down the hill towards the sea somewhere, in an early-morning flash of green and blue light. My dad and me. He holds me tight. He won't let go. I will not fall. We are alive and he loves me. For a few seconds, that much I know.

I wanted more: letters, a number, an address. Here were the old articles about me, from way back, printed in the local news. I glanced over them and grabbed at another pile. Peter's birth certificate: father unknown. Mum's passport, out of date. In the picture she had long hair hanging in corkscrew curls, and she gazed into the camera with accusing eyes. I swung round, scared all of a sudden that she was standing there, watching me ransack her private stuff.

No, I was still alone. My heart slowed and I dived again

into the box. There was a fat wallet of papers, wedged at the bottom. I eased it free and began to read. The bundle contained old medical records, I realized: not mine but Mum's, dating back to the 1990s. My fingers trembled as I flicked through the pages and tried to piece together the information. There were notes about her morning sickness, her trips to the doctor, the hospitalization for high blood pressure, an early emergency Caesarean. There were so many pages, so much to understand, and I didn't have time. I flicked through, searching for something, and then towards the end of the folder I saw the words *'factitious disorder'* followed by a question mark, a follow-up recommended. The file ended there and I knew Mum had stolen it. And I knew why.

'Aud?' she shouted. 'What are you doing up there, Aud?'

'Nothing,' I called, and with fumbling, terrified fingers I jammed everything back into the box, shoving it into place.

That afternoon, as we stuffed bags full of clothes and things Mum said she needed to keep, I tried to think. Peter kept looking at me, casting nervous, wary glances.

'I like my school, Aud,' he said, 'and Jake said he'd be my best friend and I could play with him at lunchtime.'

'I know, Pete. I'm sorry.' I packed his little bag of toys and clothes, and couldn't find any other words. He began to throw his stones against the wall and I didn't tell him to stop.

The phone rang. It'd be the ward. I scrambled up but Mum got there before I could, and I strained to hear, leaning over the rickety banister.

'Wonderful, yes; we'll be along soon, thank you,' she lied, before slamming down the receiver and striding back up the stairs.

'Come on – get a move on, Aud. You've got enough stuff there, haven't you?' She grabbed my bag out of my hands and an armful of Peter's things. 'Let's get this lot in the car.'

As we packed the bags into the boot it started to rain. Big fat drops fell from the heavy, bursting sky.

'Typical,' Mum muttered, slamming the door shut, nearly catching Peter's arm. 'Get to bed now, you two. We've got an early start.'

The phone rang on and off throughout the evening. There was no way to answer without Mum knowing. Even if I did, what would I say?

When the flat was quiet, I got out of bed and pulled on a jumper and tracksuit bottoms, breathing heavily, hard.

We needed to do something and do it now. Mr McGuiness couldn't help me, Leo couldn't help me, no one could. I had to do it for myself and for Peter. I had to stop this.

The floorboards creaked under my feet, just a little, and I edged to the wall and inched along. I stopped in the hall-way and listened at the Thing's door. Her breathing was slow and deep, a snore rattled in her throat now and then. I pushed the door open, just a touch. She looked different asleep. Tired. But not peaceful; her mouth slack, twisting on silent words every now and then, chewing them over, preparing her lies. I leant over her. What did she think? What happened in her mind to make her believe that she could hurt me forever? A sob rose in my throat, and I covered my mouth, tried to stifle the noise. Too late. She turned, moaned, and I inched back away from her.

I crept out of the room. Downstairs I opened the cupboard in the kitchen, Mum's medicine store, and removed the tubs of pills, lining them up on the table. I sat at the computer, assembling my proof.

Confronted with the glare of the screen, my eyes ached. I squinted, typed with one finger:

Lithium
Fluoxetine
Diazepam
Olanzapine
Risperidone

Some had been prescribed. Others were Mum's gift to me: her love, her care. *Take this, Aud, you'll feel better. If you don't take your pills, you'll never be well. Come on, love, just one more.* I'd swallowed and choked and swallowed again, thinking one day, one day, it would stop.

And my body's revolt, its anxious twist into silence and suffering, it had all been a trick and a lie.

More words, names on half-empty tubs. Bottle after bottle. I scattered the contents over the table. I'd taken these sometimes too. But I didn't have diabetes, epilepsy, a heart condition; I didn't need statins or steroids or sleeping pills. It was a miracle I was still alive. My mouth filled with bile. This toxic cocktail I'd swallowed like sweets; I couldn't ignore it now. It had to stop.

I loaded the blog. It was hard to focus on the screen,

hard to make my fingers do the work, my brain clear enough to write. But it was my only hope.

There was no other way to put it. HELP ME, I typed.

Hurry now, I thought. *Hurry up or the Thing will come. She'll wake and chase and scratch and bite and hurt and put you in hospital, trap you again. Be fast, Audrey*, I thought. *Come on – save yourself, save Peter. Stop this now.*

SOMEONE PLEASE HELP ME. IF YOU DON'T HELP ME,
THEN MY MOTHER WILL KILL ME, I KNOW SHE WILL.

No one would believe; they'd think these the words of some crazy, psychotic teenager.

I AM NOT ILL. MY MUM IS THE ONE WHO NEEDS HELP.
SEND SOMEONE, HERE TO THE GRANGE. MY MUM IS
GOING TO KILL ME. MY MOTHER ONLY LOVES ME
WHEN I AM SICK, BUT I THINK I'M GOING TO DIE.

I typed the address of the Grange, loaded the post, then shoved back the chair, walking faster back upstairs. People read that blog; they did. They would help. They would rescue us. *Come on, Aud*, I told myself again, pulling myself up the little flight of stairs. *Come on – you have to do it. Don't lie down, don't give in, get away, get away, get away.* I wasn't dead yet, I could still live. Rain lashed the windows; the wind threw itself against the Grange. It was too late to care what would happen to Mum. She'd left long ago; standing in her place, sleeping in her bed, was the Thing. I didn't care about the Thing. She meant nothing to me. She deserved everything she got.

There was only one truth, I thought, crouching beside my brother's bed, there was only one thing I knew for sure: I had to save us. I ran my hand over my head, the hair soft, bristling with a centimetre's growth. I had not done this to myself. I was not mad and we might still have a chance.

'Pete,' I whispered, 'Pete.' Still he slept as if drugged. Drugged. As I had been.

Right now someone could be reading that message. Leo? Jen? Sue? They'd read it and come; read it and run. Or maybe they'd think I was lying, deranged. *Mothers don't make their children ill*, the Thing laughed inside my head. Or if they did believe, what then? Would Mum go to prison? Would I? All the lies I'd told the doctors. Would there be trouble about that? After all, I'd colluded. That was the word they used. *Yes*, nodded the Thing again. *You're ill, Audrey, mentally ill. You lied too. And that's because you're mad. You like all the fuss, the attention, the care. You love to be poorly; that's why you've lied. You're my little girl.*

Would they believe the words of a girl who'd tried to kill herself, who'd sat in a wheelchair for weeks, refusing to move? And what would happen to us if they believed me? What would happened if they didn't? The questions ricocheted through my brain, making me dizzy. I gripped the bed.

I stood and walked over to the window, staring towards the farm. The lights winked, died. I thought about it again and knew I had to find the strength.

And then. Noise. From Mum's room. Her bed creaked. She coughed, hacked up phlegm. I heard footsteps, a door open and close, steps treading towards me.

No. She couldn't hurt me, not on purpose. It wasn't her fault. I would tell her I understood, that I knew it was the Thing, not her, not really. Not my mum. It would be all right. We would sort this out. I could help her.

'Audrey?' She stood in the doorway.

'Mum.' *Thing*, my mind screamed. *No*, my heart cried.

'What are you up to?' She clicked on the light. Blinked. Looked at me, dressed and ready to go. She smiled slowly and spoke, clear and calm as if I were a mere child.

'This again, Aud.' She sighed. 'Running away, are we? Don't you remember what happened last time, love? You couldn't cope. You couldn't manage without me and you had to come back. You know you're too sick, love; you need your mum. Now, come on. Let's get you to bed; we've got a big day tomorrow. We're going to get this sorted once and for all. I know a good doctor, up in Scotland. He's the expert; he's the one we need.' She walked towards me, her arms outstretched.

A mother's arms should be strong and safe. Gentle. Kind. For a second I believed, once more, like I'd always believed. My mother couldn't hurt me. She wouldn't do that.

And then a flash of lightning lit the room. A hard silver streak flared through the darkness. I jumped, afraid, and the doors inside my head began to open, creaking and then banging, as if blown by the wind.

I stared inside the first room, into its cavernous space.

It took shape: I saw a bath, the toilet, my own fluffy pink dressing gown in a puddle on the floor. And there was Mum holding my wrists over the sink, the bare bulb in the bathroom illuminating the scene. I saw myself, standing, immobile. And my mother lifting her hand, something flashing, metal and sharp, and then the blood as she cut, fast and deep and sure. My breath stopped in shock. I felt the pain as if for the first time and doubled over, screwing my eyes against the horror. No.

The Thing had held me then, just as she did now. Its ragged smile, Medusa hair, her fingers sharp and clawed.

A drumroll of thunder. I heard Peter call, but he sounded far away, his voice small.

'You did it; you cut me, you hurt me, Mum,' I yelled the truth aloud, as if someone would hear and help. 'You told them I was sick. That I'm ill; that I'm mad. But I'm not and I'll tell, I will, I'll tell,' I screamed, but she grabbed my hands and stopped my mouth. Strong hands, binding, twisting, dragging.

'Audrey!' She said my name through gritted teeth as I tried to pull away.

Another door, opened, swinging wide. I stared within. Too many memories fighting to surface, all at once. I watched, as the flashes of horror appeared like stills from a film.

Here is my hand. Here the car door, and Mum slamming it hard, trapping and snapping.

Here are her fingers scraping down my throat, making me gag, making me vomit.

Here is the lotion she rubs on my arm, burning my skin.

Here she is pushing me fast into the canal: a shove to the small of my back. I am four. She knows I can't swim.

Here are the icy steps; she's behind me again. I fall. I see bone.

Here are the pills and the blades and the scars on my skin.

No. I turned away, struggling with the truth and the fear and the pain. The overwhelming tide of pain; all the years of it powering over me, crushing like a tsunami, as the storm raged outside the Grange. The water was rising, coming to take me; I heard it churn and roar.

'You lied. You told them I'm ill. You cut me up, my arms, my hair. You did it, Mum. You're sick. You need help.'

She looked at me as if I were a stranger, then threw me from her, turning her back and running out of the room and down the stairs. I followed, pulled along by the cord that tied us, that was only yet frayed.

'Wait,' I cried. 'Where are you going?'

She slammed the kitchen door, I heard the squeal of a chair dragged across the floor, locking me out.

'Mum, open up.'

'Leave me alone,' Mum screamed. 'Get away from me, Audrey, you ungrateful little bitch. Run off if you like, like you want to,' she ranted, her voice high and fast. 'You've never thanked me, not once, never cared about me, when all I've done is look out for you; my whole life I've been trying to help you, keep you safe, get you better, and this is what you do. You cheat me and betray me, Audrey. You bitch, that's what you are, just like my sister, just like my parents; no one ever gave a shit about me.'

'Mum, please; what are you doing?' Doors opened and slammed. The clatter and crash of glasses and plates, something smashing on the floor. I pushed against the door. It gave a little – she'd only barred it with a chair.

'Let me in. Please.'

I pushed again and the chair toppled and fell. Mum was at the table; she had the pills I'd spilled and scattered, scooping them up in handfuls,.

'This is what you want, isn't it? This. You hate me, Audrey? You should just say so. I'll die, I'll leave you forever – you can get on with it; go your own way. See what happens then. See how long you last.'

'Stop it,' I screamed, pulling her arms, but she'd always been too strong.

'Mum,' I shouted as she swallowed and grabbed a bottle from the fridge, swigging the drink. It ran down her chin, soaking her nightie.

Peter appeared at the door, rubbing sleep from his eyes.

'What is it?' he said. 'What's the matter?'

'Nothing, Pete – go back to bed.' I tried to shield him, put my body between them, but Mum was shouting.

'Your sister thinks I'm a liar, that I hurt her, Peter. Have I ever hurt you? Have I ever laid a finger?'

His face dissolved as she swore at me, pointed her finger, screamed how I'd ruined her life. She wouldn't stop. I needed help, but no one was coming, where were they? Why weren't they here? I swung round, searching for something, a way to make this stop, and Mum barged me, grabbing my brother, clutching him to her.

Leo

The storm set in. Sue and Leo shut and locked windows and doors, fighting against the wind. Leo stared at the thrashing trees as they wrestled and danced, the sky gyrating with clouds.

He hoped Audrey and Peter were safe inside and tried to see across the fields for lights in the distance, but it was already too dark.

Leo sat down at the piano to play – he was working out a part for one of Billy's songs, thinking he might write a song of his own, something for Audrey maybe, when the phone went. He picked it up. There was no one there. Just breathing. Shallow and faint.

'Hello?'

Nothing.

'Audrey?'

Still no reply.

'Peter?'

No one answered.

Leo hung up and walked to the computer. He'd become obsessed with the blog and knew each post almost off by heart. There'd been nothing new for a few days; now the capitals, taking up the page, jumped out at him:

HELP ME. SOMEONE PLEASE HELP ME. IF YOU DON'T
HELP ME, THEN MY MOTHER WILL KILL ME.

He jumped up from the keyboard, bellowing out a long
shout of rage.

'Where are you going?' Sue asked, discovering Leo
pulling on his outdoor things, pocketing her keys.

'The Grange.' He turned and looked at her briefly, taking in nothing.

'What? Why?'

'Something's happened. Fuck. Sue, hurry up. We have
to go.'

'Leo, you can't go over there now. Look at it outside.'
She gestured at the storm. Mary cowered at her feet.

'It's a bit of wind and rain. Come on.'

'It's a storm, and it's going to get worse.' As Sue spoke
thunder cracked like a whip above the farmhouse. It
spurred him on. He opened the door.

'Wait, then – I'll come,' his aunt said, and she pulled on
her coat and boots and they hurried out into the night.

When they got to the Grange, Leo jumped out of the
car, running across the gravel and over the moat. Something caught his gaze and he stared at the water and the
glowing white shapes floating on the dark filth of its surface. Rain pelting his face, his stomach churning, he
stepped forward. It looked like arms, legs, tiny pieces – a
baby's body? No, it couldn't be. He got a stick, and pulled
what looked like the torso closer, dragging it up out of the
mud. The cold, frozen thing slithered in his hands and he

dropped it in disgust. That doll. Madison, Aud had called it. For a second he'd thought, irrationally, that it was Peter. He swallowed back vomit and ran again, fighting with the wind, to get to the front door. Sue caught up with him.

'What?'

Leo didn't answer. He pushed the main door – it wasn't locked, accepting him like it had been waiting, always waiting – and he fell inside.

Taking the stairs two at a time, Sue shouting for him to hang on, Leo ran. There was no time to think any more. No time to dawdle and chat and do nothing.

The door to the flat stood open. Leo stepped inside, ran towards the light, and saw Audrey, then Lorraine holding Peter against her. Peter's face was white, his mouth open in a silent scream.

Aud was pleading, very quiet, holding out her arms: 'Mum, let go of him, let go.'

Sue barged in behind Leo.

'Lorraine? What's going on?' she yelled.

Leo locked eyes with Sue. Hers were wide and panicked. He thought fast: what should he do? He reached out and touched Aud's arm, but she didn't seem to realize he was there. He looked around the room; everything had been turned upside down as if there'd been a fight or a break-in, some terrible trouble. The kitchen was covered in debris. Broken pots, glasses, pills scattered, empty tubs on the floor. A chair overturned. The window shattered.

Sue spoke again: 'Lorraine, it's all right. Let Peter go.'

She wasn't going to. Her arms tightened round Peter's body. Leo took a step. Sue moved at the same time and together they darted forward. Leo grabbed one of Lorraine's arms, Sue the other, but she was terribly strong; it was hard to pull Peter free, to wrestle Lorraine to the ground and pin her. She thrashed and writhed, shouting and spitting.

'Get your hands off me; get off me.' She swore and she spat, her legs kicking out, wild.

'Aud, ring the police,' Leo shouted. 'Hurry, come on.'

Audrey was holding Peter. She had her arms round him, then she turned from the room and ran.

Suddenly Lorraine gave up, all the fight draining away. She lay exhausted on the floor and turned her face to Sue, tears trickling down her cheeks, muttering something Leo couldn't make out. Then she began to heave, her body twisting as she vomited.

He took out his phone and dialled 999.

'I need to find Aud,' Leo told Sue. She nodded. His aunt's face was a strange mixture of shock and determination.

'It's all right. I'll stay here with Lorraine until the police come. I can handle this. Find them, Leo,' she said, sounding calm.

Leo pelted up the little flight of stairs to the bedrooms.

'Aud, where are you? Audrey?'

Audrey's room was dark. He'd never been in here before, and for the first time saw the paper on the windows, the walls patched with pictures. Pictures of birds and clouds and the Milky Way. It was all sky, as if that were her element, as if she longed to fly.

445

Peter's room was also dark and cold, the window open, the wind filling it with a strange whistling noise. Leo slammed the window shut, pulled the duvet off the bed, looked in the wardrobe. He charged to the next room – it had to be Lorraine's – stepped over piles of trash, bags, clothes, and opened every cupboard, every door.

'Audrey? Pete, Peter,' Leo hollered. 'Where are you? Audrey, it's me, Leo, come out, it's OK. You're safe. Everything's all right now. I'm here, it's safe to come out.'

He ran back to Peter's room. Knelt, stared into the black space under the bed. He wasn't there.

OK, so, where else? Downstairs, the basement. Leo left the flat and ran down to the cellars, repeating his call: 'Audrey, it's me. Come on. Please.'

In and out of the rooms he crashed, banging doors, flicking on switches, lighting up the place so it burned bright in the dark, his voice disappearing into the hard concrete walls. No one appeared, no one came, so he ran up to the top of the building along the corridors, still shouting for Audrey and Peter, so loud his throat was sore. Maybe they'd run away out into the night, in fear. The rain still fell, pounding and heavy. Audrey would be soaked through if she were out there; cold and lost, perhaps, and bitterly afraid.

Then he realized where they'd be, of course.

At the top of the building, Leo found the door to the fire escape and pushed it open.

Audrey

High above everything, high above the world. Peter held my hand and I held on to him, keeping him close, safe. We'd always been safe up here; we would be safe still. No one could take us, and if they tried I knew what we'd do. I stared at the night through the rain. No moon, no stars, but there were lights down on the drive, cars coming and going. The noise of a siren. Whoever it was, I didn't care.

Voices in the Grange. They bounced and spun. All the dead girls, rising up at last, come to take us, to drag us, into the water. The moat glinted and smiled, shivery sharp. I pulled Peter closer.

Time passed. Minutes or hours, I didn't know. Shutting down, switching off. Who was I? What had happened? Peter whimpered; I began to sing. A song about going home, home sweet home. My brother tight against me, the only life raft in the storm.

'Audrey?' This wasn't Peter. Who was it? I turned my head to see. Blinked away rain, scrubbed at my glasses. A boy. No, a man. I'd known him once, I thought. But his name was lost. I clutched my brother. He couldn't take him. The man tried to make me stand, to pull me inside, but I would not go in there. Not ever. I pulled away, moving closer to the edge, holding Peter. Peter was with me

447

and that was all that mattered. I would never let him go; never again.

'Aud.' The voice was soft and gentle. 'Come on, Aud. It's all right.' The man sounded kind, but it could be a trick. Rain ran off his hair, down his face. A woman was with him. She reached out her arms. Who were they? I didn't want them; no one could take my brother from me.

'Audrey,' Peter whimpered. We were very close to the edge. Of course he was scared.

'It's OK, mate,' I said, hauling him into my arms. He clung to me, shivering. 'Shh,' I said, pulling him closer. The wind blew against us, making me stumble.

'Come on, come downstairs; come with me,' the man coaxed. The woman spoke again and I looked at them and then at the sky. The rain wouldn't stop, not ever. We would always be drowning.

'It's all right – it's us, Sue and Leo. We're not going to hurt you, Audrey. We're here to help. Please, let us help you.'

Peter whispered in my ear.

'It's OK, Aud,' he said. 'It's OK – it's Leo.' He squirmed a little, wriggling, crawling out of my arms. And I was tired now; I let him go.

I felt a hand on my arm. The man. Leo. He was smiling at me, very gently.

'Come on, Aud. Come away from the edge,' he said. Peter slithered down and I let the man hold my hand and I made the rattling journey back down to earth.

July

Leo

It was weeks before Audrey was out of hospital and then they put her in foster care. Leo had begged Sue to take them in, but she said it didn't work like that, and he knew she was right; he was being ridiculous. At least the family who'd taken Peter opened their doors to Audrey too; she wouldn't want to be apart from her brother.

'I still think we could have asked them to stay here,' Leo complained to Sue, tidying away a pile of revision notes now his exams were over.

'Well, I'm sure you can still meet up, Leo, in good time. When she's feeling better. But it's going to be very hard for her and you have to accept that. There's a lot to sort out; it's an awful mess.' Sue sighed and sipped her tea. 'I'm just sorry we didn't do something earlier. I can't believe I was so blind.' She looked at Leo. 'What on earth was going on in Lorraine's head? I mean, it beggars belief. I can't understand it.'

'Don't blame yourself,' Leo said in a dull voice, like he didn't really mean it. Although he didn't blame Sue; of course he didn't.

His aunt adjusted her specs and sucked in a breath. 'No, I should have seen it. It makes sense, I suppose, but she had me fooled. I really believed she was a nurse. Clearly I'm an idiot. Poor Audrey and Peter. I believed her. I believed everything.' She looked confused again and Leo was sorry that he couldn't explain it for her.

'Let's face it,' he said. 'We all sucked it up. Not just you. I don't think even Aud knew about her job, that she was a cleaner, I mean. How could we have guessed? It's the other stuff that's worse.'

'Well, at least her dad's stepped up,' Sue went on. 'I've spoken to the woman at social services; she says he's a decent man. They'll be all right with him, I think, although I have to say I'd like to meet him myself, just to get peace of mind. And Lorraine won't be allowed near them. I wonder what'll happen when she's out of hospital. She'll go to prison. Maybe a psychiatric unit?'

Leo couldn't muster more than a grunt in response to that.

He'd sat his exams, not knowing what he wrote. He had a feeling he had failed the lot. He played with the band once or twice at end-of-year parties. But his mind was still fixed on the night of the storm, on Audrey's face in the rain. Her eyes dark and uncomprehending. It should be over, but he couldn't forget, even though Lorraine was locked up now – for good, Leo hoped. It had been all over the papers, all over the news, and people round here had talked of nothing else. Jen Blake had sent him a letter for Audrey, but he hadn't seen Aud to pass it on, even though he'd tried to get in touch.

Every day Sue asked Leo if he wanted to talk, but there was nothing to say. His stomach turned at night as his mind churned over the truth.

When his mum called Leo had nothing to say to her either.

'It's dreadful,' his mother said. 'Disgusting, that a mother could do those things to her own children. And your lovely Audrey! Oh, Leo, I'm sorry.' Leo rested his head on his hands; it was pointless answering. You could say those words in a thousand different ways but it didn't change the facts: it was too late.

'Leo, come out here – come for a holiday. I can buy your ticket right now. Just say the word,' she said.

Leo wasn't going anywhere. So his mother booked her ticket instead. She would arrive mid August and take him to Europe. Four weeks without her BlackBerry, she promised, and that thought was the first in a long time to make him laugh.

One morning in early August when Leo was getting ready to go out – shovelling in breakfast, feeding Mary, hunting for his trainers – there was a knock at the front door. Sue had already gone out to the farmers' market in town. Leo opened it, not sure who to expect, and saw Audrey. He almost dropped his glass and had to hold the door frame to keep steady.

'Hello,' she said; same voice, different smile. Of course she would have changed. The night of the storm he'd known that; she'd looked at him as if they were strangers. She still looked frail, wearing a baggy white T-shirt with long sleeves, a faded picture of the Stones on the front, leggings, sandals. He'd never seen any of these clothes before. Her hair had grown a little, but the angles of her face were still sharp, and he had to stop himself putting his hand out and touching her.

'I've come to say goodbye,' Audrey said very softly, in the voice that still made his heart jump. Leo nodded, opening the door wider, inviting her inside, although if this was all there was he didn't know if he could bear it.

They sat at the table with cups of tea. Mary snored on the warm kitchen tiles. The sun streamed in through the window and Audrey squinted and moved out of its path.

'Where are you going?' Leo asked, coughing over the words, rubbing his hands in his hair. She smiled, almost.

'Didn't you know? They found my dad. He said he'd have us, both of us. He's not Peter's dad, you know. But he doesn't mind. So we're going back up north to live with him.' Her voice was flat, factual. The glowing spark he'd always seen inside her had gone.

'He still likes the Rolling Stones,' she said, as if that was what was important, 'and he has a dog.' She patted Mary, absent-mindedly. The dog thumped her tail.

'Are you going to be OK, Aud?' he said, and she nodded slowly, sipping her tea.

'So long as I'm with Pete, I'll be all right.'

Leo looked away. He didn't like to ask if he could write or call; he didn't want to make demands. It had to be enough that she was here, for the last time, he supposed.

'When do you leave?'

'A few weeks – I dunno; maybe longer. There's stuff to sort out. But Dad's here to visit. We might go to the sea-side tomorrow if the weather stays like this. Peter likes the seaside.' She stared out of the window, then turned back and met his eyes for the first time. 'Thanks for everything, Leo. Thanks. You helped me, you know.'

'Not enough,' he told her, leaning forward across the table, grabbing her hand. 'I should have done something else sooner, I'm sorry –'

'No,' she interrupted, pulling away gently, standing up and walking into a patch of light. 'Don't think that. It's not true.' Her smile was sweet and pure. Her hair shone, a fuzzy halo round her head in the brightness. He wished he could touch her. He put out his hand, but she was out of his reach.

'I'm going to be OK,' she said. 'I'm stronger than I look, Leo. Remember what you said? Being strong comes from being loved and I still have Peter. And I've got help now. I think my dad's going to help me.'

So she didn't need him any more? Was that it? After everything? Leo tried not to feel angry or cheated. She saw it in his eyes though, and took another step away.

'I have to move on,' she whispered. 'Try, at least.'

'I'd like to stay in touch. Maybe visit?' Leo couldn't help asking.

Audrey shrugged. 'Maybe,' she said, but he knew she was just saying it to be kind, and he wished she wouldn't, because it was far too cruel, and once upon a time she'd have said straight out, *Don't be daft, Leo. Don't be so flipping daft.*

Audrey walked away back down the lane towards a car and he watched until he couldn't see her any more.

Audrey

I wanted to get back to Peter; leaving him for too long made me nervous. Him too. He'd be sitting at the window, waiting. I hoped he wouldn't ask about Mum again today.

Leaving Leo like that, after everything, it might have made me cry once, before I knew what real pain felt like. We hadn't touched; I'd pretended not to see when he'd stepped forward and opened his arms. Just the fifteen minutes I'd spent in the farm had been hard enough.

The air was warm but I was wearing long sleeves, not ready to see the scars again. Therapy would help; it was already helping, but after that night I'd put all the bad things back behind closed doors and was taking them out one by one to examine, when I could, to try and understand. It might take the rest of my life, but that would have to be OK. I didn't know when I'd see my mother again. I didn't really know how things would be with my dad. That was strange; that we were strangers. It hadn't been like I'd dreamed, but at least he wanted us for now. Sometimes I worried he'd change his mind; sometimes I dreamed the Thing wasn't really gone. I needed to get away from here, because the Grange still loomed in the distance over the fields and the moat still glittered darkly in my dreams.

I put my hand in my bag, rooting for gum, and my

fingers curled round something right at the bottom, crushed into a corner and wedged there, trapped. I excavated the paper and pulled it free. My superhero, lost long ago, flattened and twisted out of shape. I fumbled, trying to reassemble the tiny person that Leo had once made for me, reading for the first time its message as I smoothed out the creases. 'Hope' the first word of the poem read, and I traced the open strength of that capital letter, the two elegant vertical lines, straight and proud, the horizontal linking and connecting. It was strong, but gentle too. Like Leo had always been. I read the rest of the poem, then shut my eyes and saw the bird, Hope, come to life; I felt it stir for the first time inside me, just a flutter. Staring up at the sky, I saw more birds – swallows – and then, yes, it had to be, Peter's kestrel, circling, wild and free overhead. The farm wasn't far and Dad wasn't in a hurry. 'No worries, Aud,' he'd said, 'be happy.' And I ran back and stopped outside the gates, staring at the pretty house beyond. I ripped a page from my notebook, scrawling on it my dad's number. And I pushed it through the letter box, a message for Leo that was more than just a goodbye.

Acknowledgements

To Amanda Preston, my excellent and lovely agent, I send lots of love and a million thanks. Likewise, the wonderful Penguin and Puffin teams, especially my brilliant editor Anthea Townsend for her input, ideas and enthusiasm and Amanda Punter for her continued support. A giant thank you to Bella Pearson too, who worked last-minute wonders. To Wendy for being incredibly kind and helpful.

Many thanks to my family who continue to put up with me. To Eve and Scarlett for being the best daughters ever and for occasionally letting me go on the computer. Thanks to my sisters Emily and Margaret for your unwavering support and reading on demand, and to my brother Christopher and sister Felicity for being ace. Thanks also to Janet, Guy and Oliver for everything you've done to help. You're all amazing.

Thank you to my brilliant friends for your ongoing support, especially: Juliette (for speed-reading and confidence-boosting, and being always ace), Corrin (especial thanks for giving lots of feedback quite a long time ago), Adrian, Kathryn, Tunc, Sarah, Diana, Helen, Sorrel, Marie-Louise, Keira, Dave, Anna, Jo, Jean, Amina and Joe. Thanks to Sam for the beautiful website and to Pete Salt for answering questions. Thanks to all the lovely St Mary's Cambridge staff and girls for their enthusiasm. Thank you to the bloggers and readers who've been so kind, especially: Jim, Amanda and Faye. Thank you to the immensely talented Peter Phythian for the music. Huge thanks to Teri for being so generous with her time and with her praise.

Thanks to Mabel the dog for taking me for walks. It's been a big help.

Massive thanks and love to my parents. I am very lucky to have you.

And thank you to my dearest Alistair, for everything. Don't go changing.

Support for teens dealing with physical or emotional abuse, mental illness, depression and/or self-harm

If you've been affected by any of the issues in this book, or would like to find out more, you may find these links helpful.

- Childline: www.childline.org.uk
- The Samaritans: www.samaritans.org
- NSPCC: www.nspcc.org.uk
- Mind – a mental-health charity: www.mind.org.uk information-support/types-of-mental-health-problems/self-harm
- NHS support: http://www.nhs.uk/conditions/stress-anxiety-depression/Pages/low-mood-stress-anxiety.aspx
- YoungMinds – information on child and adolescent mental health and services for parents and professionals: www.youngminds.org.uk

Reading Group Questions

1. What were your first impressions of Audrey and Leo? How did these opinions change as the novel progressed?
2. Discuss how important Audrey and Leo's relationship is to the novel. For what reasons are they drawn to one another? Why does Leo fail to act earlier to 'save' Audrey? Could their relationship have a future?
3. How does Audrey's relationship with her mother differ from Leo's relationship with his? How does it differ from Leo's relationship with Sue? Is the absence of father figures significant?
4. Which scene had the biggest impact on you?
5. Do you agree with Audrey's decision to return home in Part Three?
6. The Thing features prominently in the novel. How did this affect you as a reader? What did you think the Thing was?
7. Audrey and Peter share a special connection as brother and sister, and a lot of Audrey's decisions are made with Peter in mind. How would Audrey's story have been different if Peter hadn't been born?

8. The author holds back a lot of information from the reader, making gradual revelations as the narrative develops. What devices does she employ to do this? How did this affect your enjoyment of the story? Were the revelations surprising?

9. The relationship between Audrey and her mother is incredibly complex. Imagine yourself in Audrey's mother's shoes. Why do you think she acts in the way she does towards Audrey? What drives her and what does she gain from it?

10. Did you find it possible to have any sympathy for Audrey's mother?

11. Leo comments that: 'A paradox is a strange contradiction ... Something that's true and false.' What do you think is the significance of his remark? How does this relate to the title, *Lies Like Love*?

12. How did you feel about the ending of the book? How did it change the way you looked at the rest of the story? What would you have done differently?

Read on for an extract from

Black Heart Blue
by Louisa Reid

AVAILABLE NOW

Rebecca

After

They tried to make me go to my sister's funeral today. In the end I had to give in. The black dress Hephzibah had worn last year when Granny died hung heavy from my bones and I wore it like armour. She'd always been bigger. Born first, stronger, prettier, the popular twin. I'd been walking in her shadow for sixteen years and I liked its cool darkness; it was a safe place to hide. Now I shivered in the stark January air. It was the first day of the New Year and my sister had been dead for one whole week.

Granny had been kind and we'd looked forward to staying with her like other kids look forward to Christmas. It was a chance to eat chocolate and watch television. A chance to read books until well past bedtime. At Granny's we were allowed to laugh out loud and play dress up, she even let us try her make-up. Hephzi loved make-up, the more sparkly the better. Granny made sure my sister got a bra when she was twelve and started to show. Sometimes she'd take us to the cinema and we would watch unsuitable films: Disney princesses, cartoons, Harry Potter. She was The Mother's mother and she loved us. She used to kiss me and tell me I was lovely. Her little love. No one else ever said that. As we got older we visited her less and less. No need, said The Parents, we could make ourselves useful at their church events instead of lounging about at Granny's. Years yawned wide with her absence. I know Granny missed us. When she rang up and one of us managed to answer, her voice sounded thin and far away like a paper aeroplane spiralling out of sight. And then she died.

I've recorded today as another black day and it's there, a story inscribed hard on my heart. The tales I keep hidden within are many; if you ever open me up then you'll read the truth. Look inside, peel back skin and flesh, excavate bone, and there you'll find a library of pain. Perhaps you will ask me to explain. I am, after all, the curator of this past. But some things are too terrible to tell and those words are buried deep. Those are the words I never even whispered to my sister, those are the words that I daren't say aloud. I wish they wouldn't cry in the walls of my room and hunt me down in my dreams.

There's a scar on my heart for when Granny died and one for the day Hephzi first didn't want to walk home with me from school. I had to lie to explain away her absence when I arrived back at the vicarage alone; I said she was doing extra maths. This was when we started college in September, four months ago. At college everyone noticed how pretty and sweet and funny my twin was and soon she was being invited to parties and talking to boys. Because I was her sister I didn't get picked on all that much but I think the other kids laughed at me behind my back. Maybe Hephzibah did too. No one would meet my eyes. Even the teachers found it hard.

But now she's dead. And it was her funeral today.

The coffin was white. The Mother cried. The Father presided over the ceremony. When the good God-bothering folk of the village asked him how he could bear it, he said he had to, that it was his duty to his daughter. And I stood at the front in Hephzi's black dress and wondered if she could hear what was going on from inside that wooden box and whether she was lonely and cold too. She would know now, for the first time, what it meant to be really left out. Her school friends clustered at the back of the church crying. He couldn't forbid them from coming but his frozen gaze made it clear that they weren't welcome. I stared at the floor and loathed them all. Hypocrites. They didn't help us while she was alive, why were they here now when it was far too late? When the service was over no one spoke to me and I was left standing on my own, waiting for The Parents to finish being consoled.

Alone felt wrong; anyone could see me now that Hephzi was gone. There is usually a pair of eyes somewhere, flicking over me in fascination and dread. I feel those looks like they're ants, crawling under my skin. Eventually Auntie Melissa, The Mother's sister, came over and asked me how I was. They'd come all the way from Scotland and I barely recognized her at first, but she ventured an arm around my shoulders and tried to hold me. When I didn't answer her concerned murmurs and shrank away from her touch she backed off. I didn't talk to my aunt because I knew he had his eye on me and I was busy telling Hephzi what they were all doing and listening carefully, hoping that she might answer back.

A week without her has been too long.

But now it's dark and the day is almost over. I'm supposed to sleep in this room still, with the other empty bed just a few feet away. Hephzi's bed. Sometimes I wake up in the middle of the night, disturbed by my own screams and the racket coming from the wall, and for a moment I can see the slight hump of her body there, turned away from me, like always, breathing softly.

He just wanted a decent book to read ...

Not too much to ask, is it? It was in 1935 when Allen Lane, Managing Director of Bodley Head Publishers, stood on a platform at Exeter railway station looking for something good to read on his journey back to London. His choice was limited to popular magazines and poor-quality paperbacks – the same choice faced every day by the vast majority of readers, few of whom could afford hardbacks. Lane's disappointment and subsequent anger at the range of books generally available led him to found a company – and change the world.

'We believed in the existence in this country of a vast reading public for intelligent books at a low price, and staked everything on it'
Sir Allen Lane, 1902–1970, founder of Penguin Books

The quality paperback had arrived – and not just in bookshops. Lane was adamant that his Penguins should appear in chain stores and tobacconists, and should cost no more than a packet of cigarettes.

Reading habits (and cigarette prices) have changed since 1935, but Penguin still believes in publishing the best books for everybody to enjoy. We still believe that good design costs no more than bad design, and we still believe that quality books published passionately and responsibly make the world a better place.

So wherever you see the little bird – whether it's on a piece of prize-winning literary fiction or a celebrity autobiography, political tour de force or historical masterpiece, a serial-killer thriller, reference book, world classic or a piece of pure escapism – you can bet that it represents the very best that the genre has to offer.

Whatever you like to read – trust Penguin.